Tom Holt was born in 1961, a sullen, podgy child, much given to brooding on the Infinite. He studied at Westminster School, Wadham College, Oxford and the College of Law. He produced his first book, *Poems by Tom Holt*, at the age of thirteen, and was immediately hailed as an infant prodigy, to his horror. At Oxford, Holt discovered bar billiards and at once changed from poetry to comic fiction, beginning with two sequels to E. F. Benson's *Lucia* series, and continuing with his own distinctive brand of comic fantasy in *Expecting Someone Taller*, *Who's Afraid of Beowulf?*, *Flying Dutch*, *Ye Gods!*, *Overtime*, *Here Comes the Sun*, *Grailblazers*, *Faust Among Equals*, *Odds and Gods*, and *Djinn Rummy*. He has also written two historical novels set in the fifth century BC, the well-received *Goatsong* and *The Walled Orchard*, and has collaborated with Steve Nallon on *I, Margaret*, the (unauthorised) autobiography of Margaret Thatcher. Thinner and more cheerful than in his youth, Tom Holt is now married, and lives in Somerset.

Praise for Tom Holt:

'Literate, light fiction, an under-appreciated genre of which Holt has made himself a master'
Washington Post

'A rival to the comic throne'
Starburst

ODDS
AND
GODS

Tom   Holt

ORBIT

An *Orbit* Book

First published in Great Britain by Orbit in 1995
This paperback edition published by Orbit in 1995

A CIP catalogue record for this book
is available from the British Library.

ISBN 1 85723 299 2

Printed in England by Clays Ltd, St Ives plc

Orbit
A Division of
Little, Brown and Company (UK)
Brettenham House
Lancaster Place
London WC2E 7EN

Dedications are traditionally used for currying favour.
Accordingly:

To Chris Bell and David Barrett, for the favour
And to Michelle Hodgson and Menzies Khan, for the curry

1

On the cloudy heights dwell the gods. They are spirits of light, deathless and ever young. They feast continually in palaces wonderful beyond description, and theirs is a happiness which mortals could never possibly attain.

Indeed. Pull the other one for a veritable feast of campanology. The true facts of the matter are as follows.

In the Sunnyvoyde Residential Home dwell the gods, the whole miserable lot of them. They are cantankerous old buggers, deathless but decidedly no longer young. They witter and bicker continuously in day rooms painted that unique shade of pale green used only in buildings set aside for the long-term storage of the sick and elderly, and they hate it like poison.

All except for Ohinohawoniponama, a vegetation spirit formerly revered by a small tribe of Trobriand Islanders. Since the entire tribe died of influenza a century ago, taking their language with them, nobody can understand a word he says; but it doesn't seem to matter. He smiles a lot, is no trouble at all to anyone, and spends most of his time in the television room watching Australian soap operas.

'Of course he's happy,' commented Marduk, over lunch in the dining room. 'Poor bloody savage, he's never had it so good. Probably thinks he's died and gone to Heaven.'

Marduk had been the warrior god of the ancient Sumerians, which made him one of the oldest gods in Sunnyvoyde. He was, by his own reckoning, six thousand years old, crippled with arthritis, and (in the words of Mrs Henderson, the matron) a bit of an old crosspatch. Which is like defining death as feeling a bit under the weather, or describing the Second World War as a free and frank exchange of views.

'Let me just stop you there, Mardie,' interrupted Lug, shadowy and enigmatic god of the pre-Christian Celts, as he walloped the bottom of an inverted ketchup bottle. '*Died and gone to Heaven*. I mean, we are talking about an immortal god here, and I just wondered if you'd care to clarify . . .'

'You know perfectly well what I mean.'

'Ignore him, Mardie,' said Freya, the Germanic Queen of Heaven, surreptitiously polishing her fork. 'He's just being insufferable.'

'I thought I was being enigmatic and shadowy, Fre.'

'Your tie is in the gravy.'

There had been a, let us say an *understanding*, between Freya and Lug ever since the World had been created out of the bones of Ymir the Sky-Father (or, in Lug's case, scooped out of the churn of the stars into the butter-pat of Time; the Creation is a highly personal thing to all gods and they get very embarrassed if you ask them to talk about it). Obviously, since Freya's people spent most of their time massacring Lug's people and driving them into the sea, nothing could ever come of it; until now, when it was really rather too late.

'I don't know why they let his sort in here,' Marduk carried on. 'Lowers the tone, I say.'

'His sort?' Lug asked, ignoring the kick on his shin from the other side of the table. 'Footnotes, please.'

'Wogs,' Marduk replied. 'In my day, we'd have had his lot up the top of the ziggurat and tied to the altar in three minutes flat. Now, of course, we've got to have them in here with us, which I say is wrong. And they get special food.'

'Live and let live, I say,' mumbled Adonis, Greek god of spring and beauty, through his few remaining teeth and a mouthful of soup. As usual, nobody paid him any attention, and he continued his noisy struggle with the Spring Vegetable.

'Special food, Mardie?' Lug smiled at Marduk over a forkful of lemon sole.

'It's only the Hindu lot,' Freya said. 'And that's just because they're vegetarians.'

'Vegetarians!' In his prime, Marduk had feasted on the hearts and entrails of prisoners of war. Nowadays virtually everything except plain bread and butter gave him wind. 'Stuff and nonsense. What do they want to be vegetarians for? It's just attention-seeking, that's all.'

'I think it's something to do with their religion, Mardie.'

Marduk scowled. 'What the devil do you mean, religion? They're supposed to be *gods*, for crying out loud. Gods can't have religion. Makes you go blind.'

'Would you pass the salt, please?' said Freya briskly.

Gods do not possess eternal youth; they grow old, just like everybody else. Only rather more slowly.

It is also a fallacy that gods are better than anybody else; quite the reverse. Since there's absolutely nobody who dare criticise them, for fear of being blasted with thunder, they are free to behave exactly as they see fit, which is usually very badly.

It therefore follows that Sunnyvoyde is even trickier to run than the average, run-of-the-mill old folks' home. The fact that Mrs Henderson manages it at all is little short of a miracle. That she runs it with a rod of iron only goes to show the quite devastating force of personality she has at her disposal.

For example, when Quetzalcoatl, the Feathered Serpent of the Aztecs, finally and reluctantly agreed to let his godsons book him in, he was implacably determined to have his own bathroom with hot and cold running blood, all his meals served up in jewel-encrusted skulls and his own retinue of seven thousand dog-headed fiends to devour the souls of anybody foolish enough to give him any lip. After five minutes of negotiations with Mrs Henderson, however, his demands were rapidly revised to staying in bed an extra half-hour and being allowed to substitute a fresco of souls in torment for the framed print of happy kittens above his bed. The happy kittens have, by the way, now crept back to their rightful place, and Quetzalcoatl is usually in his seat in the dining room for breakfast by 7.15.

Only one resident of Sunnyvoyde, therefore, is allowed to have his meals in his room. When asked, Mrs Henderson explains that he's not as young as he was and it wouldn't be fair to expect him to make the effort to come down to the dining room three times a day. Which is, indeed, part of the truth.

'Just put it down on the table, Sandra love,' said Osiris, 'and pass me the remote control thing while you're there.'

'Huh.' The nurse feigned irritation. 'And what did your last servant die of?'

'Atheism.'

'Ah.'

'And the one before that was eaten by crocodiles.'

'Right.'

'Sacred crocodiles, naturally.'

'It's apple crumble again today,' said Sandra cheerfully. 'You like apple crumble.'

Osiris sighed. 'Sandra pet,' he said, 'I'm an omniscient god. Lying to me is the proverbial hiding to nothing. I can't abide apple bloody crumble.'

'Then turn it into something else, Mr Clever,' Sandra replied, arranging the napkin tastefully in the shape of a pyramid. 'Go on, say Whoosh! and turn it into chocolate mousse.'

'I'm not allowed chocolate mousse, and well you know it.'

'There you are, then,' said Sandra. 'Go on, you know you like it really.'

'Get out,' Osiris said, 'before I turn *you* into a hedgehog.'

Sandra grinned at him and shut the door. A nice girl, that. Pretty too, if you like them a little bit on the plump side. Ah, thought the erstwhile Egyptian god of plenty, if only I was two thousand years younger.

The reason why Osiris got his meals in his room instead of having to come down and be sociable wasn't because he was more powerful than the other gods, or more sublime, or even particularly older. It was just that he owned the place and could, if he so chose, give Mrs Henderson the sack.

Several millennia of being ritually murdered each sunset by his brother Set, torn into small pieces and reassembled in a hurry and pitch darkness by his slightly-less-than-nimble-fingered wife Lady Isis in time for his daily resurrection at dawn had left the old boy a physical wreck. Several of his component parts were palpably in the wrong place; and even now he still had nightmares about the many times Isis had finished the reassembly job, sewn him back up again and then turned to him and said, 'Ooh, I wonder where this bit was supposed to have gone.'

His mind, however, was as sharp as ever, or so he kept telling himself; and he attributed this to the fact that it had spent so much time out of his body, while the good lady wife had been rewinding the intestines and poring over the wiring chart. Osiris was firmly of the opinion that a mind in a body is like a racehorse pulling a brewer's dray, or a girl with three Ph.D.s becoming a housewife and dissipating her talents on ironing shirts and buying groceries. All that time and mental energy burnt up in operating limbs and keeping the senses ticking over took its toll, and eventually you were left with something barely capable of working the heart and keeping the bladder under some semblance of control.

He contemplated his lunch.

Apple crumble. You knock your pipes out for thousands of years re-enacting the primal struggle of light and darkness, and at the end of it, some chit of a girl tells you that you like apple crumble and expects you to believe it. And hot custard! If he had a shilling for every time he'd told them he couldn't be doing with hot custard . . . well, he'd still be the richest being in the cosmos, only more so. Hot custard!

He paused, slamming the door on his train of thought.

I'm going soft in the head, he said to himself. Here I am, the embodiment of sublime wisdom, having a paddy over a bit of hot custard. This is worrying. I've been here too long.

Instinctively, he stretched his back and tested his legs against the floor. There was no strength left there at all, only pain. Damn.

Osiris had never been a solar deity. If there was one thing that irritated him more than hot custard, it was being confused with a glorified tram-driver who had nothing to do all day but lean on a dead man's handle and try to bump into too many clouds. His eldest boy, Horus, did that job (hence the name of the family firm, Osiris and Sun) and it suited him perfectly. Horus had, of course, retired long since and lived in the opposite wing of Sunnyvoyde where (as Osiris liked to think) they put the *old* people. They rarely met these days, although whenever they did Osiris never missed the opportunity to get up his offspring's aquiline nose by shouting out, 'Hello there, young 'un,' across a room full of people. Isis too lived a separate life in a small room in the annexe, which she had decorated with an extensive collection of photographs of the British royal family. Good riddance to them both, Osiris felt. If he hadn't had to drag out his life surrounded by idiots, he could really have *been* somebody.

There was a knock at the door; which meant it was Sandra back again. None of the other nurses bothered to knock.

'A visitor for you, Ozzie,' Sandra said.

Osiris blinked. 'Are you sure?' he said. 'I don't have many visitors. I was inoculated against them years ago.'

'Well, you've got one now, isn't that nice? It's your god-son.'

'Oh bugger.'

The meek shall inherit the Earth.

Eventually. When everyone else has quite finished with it, and the meek have stopped saying, 'No, please, after you.' Until then, the cocky little bastards shall inherit the Earth; which means that by the time the meek get their hands on it, they'll wish the old fool had left them some money or a clock or something instead.

Hence the institution of the godchildren. Everybody knows that when it comes to affairs of the heart, gods come second only to the characters in a long-running soap opera for spreading it around. At the height of the Heroic Age, the average god scarcely dared set foot outside his own temple for fear of process-servers with paternity suits.

And the mortal children of the gods had children, and so on, and so forth; and eventually the divine spark became sufficiently dilute to allow the ultimate descendents to pack in minotaur-slaying and damsel-rescuing and become chartered accountants instead.

But in each generation there are throwbacks, particularly where the bloodlines of two or more gods happen to coincide; and from this genetic sump Humanity has always tended to draw its statesmen, its generals, its social reformers, its idealists, its princes of commerce and all the other unmitigated pests who have contrived to make a ball of wet rock spinning in an infinite void into the camel's armpit it is today.

These are the godchildren. And, sooner or later, they find out who they are; and, more to the point, what they stand to inherit, if only . . .

*

'It's not supposed to do that.'

Predictably enough, there was a moment of complete silence.

'Yes, George, we know that,' said Sir Michael Arlington, breaker of awkward silences to Her Majesty's Nuclear Inspectorate. 'That's why we sent for you, all the way from bloody Iowa. Do you feel up to hazarding a guess as to why?'

'You could do really good baked potatoes in it,' said a white-haired scientist at the back of the gathering. 'I mean, a quarter of a nanosecond in there, add a knob of butter and there you go.'

'You could indeed,' replied Sir Michael. 'And when it was ready it'd probably be able to walk out on its own. Any *sensible* suggestions would be very welcome.'

'It's gone wrong.' Professor George Eisenkopf, resident nuclear genius at the University of Chicopee Falls, Iowa, and the State Department's leading authority on civilian atomic power, scratched his nose with the plastic coffee-stirrer he'd been given on the plane. 'It isn't working properly,' he added, in case there were any laymen present.

Sir Michael winced. 'Please, George,' he muttered, 'don't worry too much about blinding us with science. In what way has it gone wrong?'

'I don't know.'

'Great. Is it about to blow up?'

'Too early to say.' Professor Eisenkopf leaned forward and tapped a couple of keys on the computer keyboard in front of him. The screen flickered, flashed a few columns of figures and announced itself ready to play Monster Nintendo.

'Sorry,' mumbled the baked potato enthusiast, nudging past and pressing some other keys. 'Only my wife's nephew came to see the place the other day, and I haven't had time to . . .'

'Don't worry about it.' Professor Eisenkopf studied the data he'd called up, and pursed his lips. 'You're going to find this a bit hard to relate to, guys, but there's something alive in there.'

'In where, George?'

'In the core,' the professor replied. 'As far as I can tell from this box of tricks, sitting on top of the goddamn pile.'

Sir Michael nodded. 'Probably grilling a few sausages,' he said.

'Pardon me?'

'To go with the potatoes.'

Not all the gods retired. Some of them still soldier on, mainly because they're horribly overworked and never had time to train a successor.

Just such a one was having a well-earned sit-down and a cold beef sandwich in the infernal heart of Bosworth Pike power station. His name was Pan, and if you add -ic to his name, you get his portfolio in the sublime Cabinet.

'Knit *one*,' he said to himself, squinting at the diagram, 'and pearl *two*.'

He was knitting a matinée jacket for Truth (who, as is tolerably well known, is the daughter of Time) and he had an uneasy feeling that he'd gone wrong somewhere. He had a further unpleasant suspicion that the faint brown check which had crept into the pattern about twelve rows back was in fact his beard.

'Nuts,' he said, and let go of the needles. The knitting flopped, suspended from his chin. He reached for the scissors.

The fact remained that his analyst had recommended knitting as tremendous therapy for hypertension and stress, and over the last few millennia he'd tried just about everything else, several times.

Under him, the ground started to glow green. He licked a fingertip, pressed it ever so gently against the side of the pile, and was rewarded with a loud sizzle. Just nicely ready, in fact. He stood up.

Pan is, of course, a nice god; or at least it's wise to believe so, because our beliefs have a profound effect on the divine self-image. This isn't a comfortable thing for the gods themselves – the Egyptian deity Serapis, for example, never tries to eat a piece of toast without cursing the Faithful for believing in the existence of a crocodile-headed god – and it's by no means unknown for a god to wake up one morning to find himself a totally different shape or species simply because of some thoughtlessly imaginative revival meeting held on the previous evening. Mortals believe that Pan, although an incurable practical joker with a sense of humour that would have appalled Josef Goebbels, is fundamentally one of the good guys and incapable of doing anything that would actually result in lasting harm.

He was going to have his work cut out this time, though.

On the other hand, he was a god; and to the gods, all things are possible, at least in theory. Thus it was that when the emergency repair squad broke into the reactor cell three days later, wearing their lead suits and clinging like covetous limpets to their lucky rabbits' feet, their Geiger counters showed up a radiation level several points below the normal ambient reading.

What they did find was a toasting fork, an unopened pat of butter and five stone cold baked potatoes.

There are some people who like lawyers.

For example, Ashtoreth, the antediluvian moon goddess of southern Palestine, was thrilled to bits when her great-great-great-great-great-great-great-great-great-great-great-great-godson Hyman was made a partner in the leading New York firm of Kaplan and Hart, and drove the other occupants of Sunflower Annexe to the brink of violence by talking loudly and incessantly about Her Godson Hymie, The Lawyer.

Other deities with whom lawyers are popular include: Ahriman, the Father of Darkness; Hermes, patron god of thieves; the Scandinavian Loki, god of lies and deceit; and Belenos, in whose honour the Druids burnt men alive in wicker cages. You can't beat a lawyer, according to Belenos, for the generation of plenty of hot air.

Osiris, for his part, had always reckoned that he could take them or leave them alone, with a marked preference for the latter option. Visits from his current godson were therefore as welcome as a rat in a morgue.

And that, he felt, remembering where he was, is no bad analogy. I really shouldn't be in this place. Hellfire, if only the dozy old bat hadn't had the exploded diagram the wrong way up the last night we did the reassembly, I wouldn't be. I'd be out there, bombarding snotty little tykes like Julian with meteorites.

'How do, Julian,' he said, as his godson entered the room. 'Brought me some grapes, then.'

'Yup.'

'Can't stand grapes.'

'No matter.' There was a gonglike sound as the bag of grapes hit the bottom of the tin wastepaper basket. 'Look, I've got to be quick, I'm due in a meeting in forty minutes. How's life treating you, anyway?'

Osiris paused, stroking his chin. 'Life,' he pronounced, 'is a bit like mashed swede. A little bit's nice for a change now and then, but you wouldn't want to live on it.'

'Yup.' Julian stared at him for a few seconds and blinked twice. 'The leg still playing you up, then?'

'Aren't you going to write it down?'

'Write what down?'

'What I just said,' replied Osiris testily. 'That was a Teaching, that was. You're supposed to write down Teachings.'

'Um.'

'And don't give me that boiled cod look, because there's been dafter things than that said out of burning bushes, take it from me. How's Phyllida?'

'Sorry?'

'Your wife.'

'Oh.' Julian glanced at his watch. 'Fine. I'd have heard if she wasn't. Look, I hate to rush off like this but it really is a very important meeting . . .'

'And Ben? And little Julia?'

'They're fine too. Ask after you all the time. Anyway, it's been great seeing you.'

'Your children,' said Osiris icily, 'are in fact called Emma and Clinton. Keeping busy, are you?'

'Yup, thanks. It's been an uphill job, holistically speaking, with the recession bottoming out, but the medium- to long-term overview of our bedrock client base is definitely more positive than negative, and . . .'

'Just remind me,' said Osiris, 'what it is you do.'

Julian sighed. 'I'm a lawyer, Oz,' he replied.

'Oh,' said Osiris. 'Oh well, never mind. You've just got to try not to give up hope, that's all. I heard a good joke about lawyers the other day.'

'I know them all, thanks, Oz. Look, I'll call you. You look after yourself. Don't do anything I wouldn't do, okay?'

'Son,' replied Osiris with conviction, 'I wouldn't do anything you would. Shut the door on your way out.'

Julian looked at him. 'You feeling okay, Oz?' he asked.

Osiris looked up, startled by his tone of voice. 'I believe so,' he replied. 'As well as can be expected for someone whose small intestine now runs slap bang through the middle of his bile duct. Why?'

'Oh, nothing,' Julian replied absently, as he picked at the handle of his briefcase. 'You just seem kind of odd today, that's all.'

'Odd. Right.'

'Not quite, you know, a hundred and ten per cent.'

'Julian, my boy, if I was a hundred and ten per cent, there'd be a seven-and-a-quarter-inch-high replica of me standing beside me on the hearthrug. Go on, now, sling your hook.'

'You haven't been, for example, hearing strange voices or anything?'

'Yes,' Osiris snapped, 'yours. Now piss off.'

'Okay, okay. Same time next week, right?'

'Right.' Osiris sighed. 'Unless, of course, I'm in a meeting. The doorknob is the round brass thing about three feet up from the floor. A half-turn to the right usually does the trick.'

As Julian retreated down the corridor, he played back his mental tape of the interview, ignoring the crackles. Yes, the old fool had sounded strange; but on reflection, no stranger than usual.

Hey!

Julian stopped, standing on one foot, and suddenly grinned.

He'd just had an idea.

2

Once, long ago and far away, a bard sang in the mead-hall of King Hrolf Kraki.

There was dead silence from the King's warriors, his carls and servants as the poet traced the intricate pathways of kenning and metaphor, trope and simile, in the still, tense circle of the tawny glow of the hearth. Nobody moved, and the dark yellow mead glistened untasted in the drinkhorns, as the words of the lay sparkled in the air like frozen dewdrops on a spider's web. This moment, this splinter of time, caught like a fly in amber, mounted in a ring of golden firelight.

It was an old song, so old that nobody knew where it had come from or when it had first been sung. It began at the beginning, when Ymir the Sky-Father had first opened his eyes and seen nothing, nothing but the cold and the wind and the loneliness of the first day. On it swept, gathering pace as the singer peopled the shadowy corners with ghosts: Sigurd the Dragon-Slayer; Arvarodd, who once strayed into the land of the Giants; Weyland the craftsman without equal, whose skill brought him only sorrow; Brynhild, who slept for a thousand years on the fire-girt mountain. And now it crawled on to its terrible end, this song without pity, under the control of no singer; the last days, the rising of the Frost-Trolls, the swallowing of the sun and moon by the Wolf, the last battle on the Glittering Plains, the going-down of the gods themselves. As the poet sang, the world seemed to grow tight and brittle, and King Hrolf nervously motioned for more logs to be heaped on the fire.

And then the poet told of the new dawn of the gods; how they rise again from the ashes of the burnt Valhalla and build a new castle that will never be thrown down, a shimmering, sublime fortress of golden stone where Odin and Thor and Tyr the One-Handed and Frey, who is the friend of wretched mortals, will reign for ever, feasting and delighting in the song and restoring vintage traction engines. And there will be no more winters in this . . .

'Doing what?'

The poet shut his eyes. For one blessed moment he thought he'd actually got away with it.

'Um,' he said, 'restoring vintage traction engines. And no more shall hoar-frost fasten on hawthorn . . .'

'Vintage what?'

Sod, fuck and bugger this stupid, lousy song, muttered the poet to himself. Because some bastard always stops me and asks *What's a traction engine?* and I don't sodding well *know*. And neither did my father nor his father before him, and does it really bloody well *matter* anyway?

'Traction engines. I think they're, um, things that gods sort of, well, restore.'

King Hrolf leaned forward, gathering the cowl of the poet's hood in his frying-pan-broad fist. 'Are you,' he growled, 'taking the piss?'

'No, honestly, that's what it says in the song, and . . .'

'The last one of you clowns,' the King went on, knitting his brows into something like a long, scraggy thorn windbrake, 'who thought he could come here taking the piss . . .' The King's face melted into a savage grin. 'Thorfinn, tell this ponce what happened to that other ponce, will you?'

Thorfinn, whose eyebrows were slightly less bushy than his lord's but would nevertheless have made ideal starter-homes for discerning partridges, obliged. Usually a man of few words, he seemed to strike a vein of eloquence that would have allowed the poet to jack in minstrelsy and open a nice little newsagent's shop somewhere quiet.

'. . . Right up his jacksy, and then set fire to it. Talk about a pong, we had to have the roof off in the end, and you still get a taste of it when the wind blows in from the fjord. Was that the one you meant, chief?'

'That's the one.'

The poet twitched. 'Honest,' he said, 'it really and truly says traction engines. Do I look like the sort of bloke who could make up a thing like that?'

There was a long, horrible silence; and then King Hrolf smiled.

'Oh,' he said, 'right. *Traction* engines. That's where you get two bits of rope and a winch and you tie one rope to the bloke's ankles and the other round his neck, and you – yes, got you, fine. Just the sort of thing you'd want in Valhalla, for when it's raining out. Sorry, you were saying?'

Twelve hundred years later, it's safe to point out that Hrolf had got it all wrong. By traction engines, the primeval bard had meant big steam-powered locomotives with lots of shiny brass handles and valves and tappets and bright green paint. Or rather, to be precise, one such machine.

She was called *Pride of Midgarth*, and right now she had just emerged from under a layer of old dustbin liners and potato sacks in the big coalshed round the back of Sunnyvoyde. It had taken a millennium of painstaking effort to get her looking the way she did now; which was a right mess.

'I told you,' said Thor, taking a step backwards. 'Wait till the first coat's completely dry before you bung on the second, otherwise it's going to smear. But no, someone had to know best.'

Odin scratched his head. 'The paint must have been no good,' he said. 'I told you, just because it's cheap . . .'

'Nothing wrong with army surplus paint,' Thor replied. 'Provided,' he added irritably, 'it's allowed to dry properly. Provided some great jessie doesn't go slapping a second coat on while the first's still tacky.'

'I think it looks rather nice,' said Frey, absently chewing a peppermint. 'Sort of dappled.'

Thor ignored him. 'It'll have to come off,' he said. 'Strip it right down all over again, then go over it top to bottom with wire wool and Trike, and then back to square one. God, what a waste of bloody time!'

'Not necessarily,' replied Odin mildly. 'We could always—'

'Look, pillock,' Thor interrupted, 'it's my bloody engine, we'll do what I say just for once. Before you ruin it completely.'

Odin shrugged. It was indeed Thor's engine, and always had been. Two thousand years ago it had been the chariot of the thunder, on which the Lord of Tempests rode across the sky on his way to do battle with the Frost-Trolls. One thousand nine hundred and fifty years ago this Wednesday fortnight, however, it had popped a gasket in the upper inlet manifold, flooded the outer compression chamber and seized the main driveshaft bearing solid on the integral cam. After belting it around with his hammer and using a certain amount of intemperate language, Thor had dumped it in an outhouse and bought himself a replacement; a sort of twenty-thousand ton fire-spitting phosphorescent milk float with scythed wheels and a built-in rev inhibitor that limited the maximum speed to six miles an hour. It was pathetically slow but very cheap to insure, and it didn't keep breaking down in the middle of the Glittering Plains, slap bang in the epicentre of enemy territory and miles from the nearest call box.

Thirteen hundred and twenty years ago come Lammas Eve, Odin had idly remarked that they could have fun doing it up again once they retired. It would be a nice little hobby for them, he'd said. They could get it running and hire it out for flower shows and village fetes and gymkhanas.

Nine hundred and ninety-six years ago, the gods of the Great Aesir had clocked off for the last time, received their signed testimonials and gold watches from the Scandinavian nations, and retired to New Valhall, a purpose-built specially-designed complex in the upmarket suburbs of Musspellheim. It was replete with every conceivable feature required by the discerning ex-god – ceaseless feasting, piped eddas, twenty-four-hour-duty Valkyrie service and so on – and the Aesir valiantly put up with it for three very long weeks before sloping off in the early hours of the morning, leaving a note propped up against the Test-Your-Wrath machine and no forwarding address. And taking with them the vintage traction engine.

'Maybe,' Odin suggested, 'we could just rub it down with wet-and-dry and paint over it.'

'Don't be such a pillock,' Thor replied.

Four hundred and seventy-five years ago, Mrs Henderson had put her foot down. She had no objection, she had said, to her residents having little hobbies. Jigsaw puzzles, yes; also ships in bottles, even one-seventy-second scale models of the Temple of the Gods of Death and Destruction in Tlaxopetclan built out of matchsticks, provided always that the person concerned tidied away afterwards and didn't get glue on the carpets. Great big oily traction engines in her newly decorated television suite, no. Either it went, or they did.

So it went; as far as the coalshed, and for four hundred and seventy-five years (ever since Pizarro conquered Peru, and long before Sir James Watt was even thought of) Odin, Thor and Frey had snuck out after lunch on the pretext of taking a walk, and snuck back in several hours later to wash up and leave oily handprints all over the towels in the downstairs cloakroom.

'Quick,' Thor hissed, 'someone's coming.' There was a frantic scrabble and a heaving of potato sacks, just before the door opened. But it was only Freya, come to ask her brother Frey if he wanted to make up four for bridge.

'Not now, sis,' Frey replied. He glanced downwards, subconsciously aware that something seemed to be wrong, and observed that he was standing in one of the tins of green paint. He sighed.

'You're not playing with that thing again, are you?'

'What thing do you mean, sis?'

'You know perfectly well.' Freya tutted. 'Like silly children, the lot of you. I think you'd better get cleaned up and come back inside before Mrs Henderson catches you.'

'But sis . . .'

'Come on.'

Frey sighed. He'd had a sister ever since the earth was without form and void, but even now he sometimes caught himself thinking, Why me? What harm did I ever do anyone? 'All right,' he muttered. 'But I'm not going to play bridge with a lot of old—'

'Yes you are. And you two . . .' She looked round. The other two gods had somehow managed to disappear. 'Children,' she repeated.

As soon as the shed door had closed, Odin and Thor crawled out from under the sacking and dusted themselves off. They looked at each other.

'Women,' said Thor.

'Quite.'

Legend has it that the massive glass and chromium offices of Haifisch & Dieb, the greatest law firm in the world, have never been totally empty since the firm was established, on the second day of Creation, to cope with the anticipated flood of product liability claims.

On this night, the lights were still bright on the top floor, home (to all intents and purposes) of Julian Magus, the firm's managing partner. He was sitting at his desk, talking through an idea with a colleague from the Probate and Trusts Department.

'Basically,' said the colleague, rubbing his lead-heavy eyelids, 'your options are somewhat restricted.'

'Go on,' replied Julian.

'Well,' the colleague continued, 'on the inheritance front, expectations-wise, I feel I have to advise that we're into a pretty narrow band in relation to the justifiable aspirations position. Like, prima facie and on the facts as presented to me, before there can be an inheritance, there has, strictly speaking, to be a death.'

'Yes.'

'This is going to be a problem, isn't it?'

'There's no such thing as a problem, Leon,' Julian replied slowly, 'only an opportunity in fancy dress. You'd do well to remember that if you ever want to get on in this profession.'

'Well, yes,' said the colleague, his palate suddenly dry, 'absolutely. I think we're one hundred per cent *ad idem* on that viewpoint. Sounding a slight note of caution, however . . .'

'Yes?'

'I mean,' said the colleague, 'obviously we've got to get the terminology up together before we can progress this. I mean, if we start with the actual definition of death, maybe we could do something there. Like, where in the book of words does it actually say you can't be dead till you stop moving? There's judicial authority to support a view that—'

'No,' said Julian, 'you were right the first time, the death side is a complete washout. Hiding to nothing time. I was thinking,' he went on, leaning back in his chair and steepling his fingers, 'of approaching this from another angle entirely.'

'Laudable,' said the colleague quickly. 'And the precise vector you had in mind?'

'How about,' said Julian, 'a power of attorney?'

The colleague winced. It was bad enough having to be here, on his own, with Julian Magus, the Great White Shark of the legal profession, knowing that a misplaced comma, let alone an inopportune word, could torpedo an entire career that had been thirty years in the carving out. The golden rule is, never disagree with The Man. Any lawyer worth his clove of garlic and silver bullet will tell you that.

'Highly lucid thinking there, Jule,' he therefore said. 'Certainly an avenue we must explore with the last breath in our bodies. But just very briefly turning it upside down and looking at it in the mirror, I've got this little niggle somewhere that says that all the gods gave the godchildren powers of attorney hundreds of years ago. Like, when they retired? I must have lost you somewhere.'

'Powers of attorney, yes,' Julian replied, staring at the corner of the ceiling. 'But not permanent ones. They could be revoked like *that*, any minute. What we want is something a bit more lasting.'

'But.' The colleague could feel the hot breath of Mr Cock-Up on the back of his collar, but somehow he couldn't help himself. 'I mean, I'm clearly being really *dumb* here, but all powers of attorney can be revoked. Can't they?'

Julian smiled. It was a long, slow smile. Generations back in its evolutionary matrix, wolves and bears and sabre-toothed tigers had played their part in its development. That smile alone was worth hundreds of thousands of dollars every year to the firm of Haifisch & Dieb.

'Not if the person giving the power is certified insane, Leon,' he said. 'I'd have expected you to have thought of that one for yourself.'

3

'Oh come on. Not again.'

Mr Kortright, supernatural agent, the only man in history ever to tell the goddess Kali that she probably had something there but it needed a lot of working on, shrugged. 'It's the best I can do for you,' he said. 'Good solid work. You should be grateful.'

'But it's so *demoralising*. I'd rather do voice-overs.'

At his end of the telephone connection, Mr Kortright smiled wryly. 'Pan, good buddy, if I could find some way for you to break into voice-overs, I'd be a very happy man. You've just got to face facts, buster. Your stuff – well, these days the kids don't want it, okay? They got video games, they got consciousness-expanding drugs, they got all kinds of stuff they never dreamed of in your day. Jumping out from behind bushes and shouting "Boo!", you're lucky to be working at all.'

'I can do other things,' Pan replied nastily. 'I can turn you into a tree, for starters.'

'Go ahead,' Kortright sighed, 'faites ma jour. As a tree I wouldn't have to try and find something positive to say about Herne the Hunter and his Amazing Performing Roedeer. And it wouldn't change the fact that passé is passé. Look, you want the job, or do I give it to Huitzilpotchli?'

Pan blinked. 'Who?'

'Little Pre-Columbian guy, square ears. He also does ritual

chants and juggles with the skulls of enemies slain in battle.'
Mr Kortright cringed involuntarily. 'Usually he drops them.
Go on, the choice is yours.'

'All right,' Pan said, 'I'll do it. But it's the last time, all
right?'

'That's the spirit, kid. You can't beat an old trouper.'

Pan replaced the receiver, and allowed his shoulders to
slump. It hadn't always been like this.

'Taxi!' he shouted.

Back in the old days, before all the rest of them packed it in,
he'd really been somebody. Back then, of course, they didn't
have all this psychology.

A yellow cab drew up to the kerb, and a bald head appeared
through the driver's window. 'Where to, mac?' it said.

Back then, if you wanted to have an emotion, you had to
have a god. If you wanted to feel jealous, you were visited by
Eris, Lady of Strife. Anybody who fancied a spot of overween-
ing pride had to wait until Hybris, the spirit of Arrogance,
worked through her backlog sufficiently to fit you in next
Thursday morning. Sexual desire was impossible without the
presence of Eros, the blind, flying archer; a deity so overworked that it was a miracle humanity reproduced itself into
the third century BC. And if you wanted a spot of blind terror,
Pan was your man.

'Wall Street,' Pan replied, opening the passenger door. His
hooves clunked on the sill of the door. For all that he kept them
discreetly hidden in Helena Rubinstein designer chinos and
top of the range Reeboks, Pan had the legs and feet of a goat.
Worse; a goat with rheumatism.

'And get a move on, please,' he added. 'It's absolutely
essential I get there by ten.'

The cab driver turned round in his seat and scowled at him.
'Hey,' he said, 'I'll get there as fast as I can, don't panic.'

'Sorry. Force of habit.'

Nowadays, they had emotions. Like all manifestations of the

Do-It-Yourself tendency, emotions were quicker, cheaper and somehow, to Pan's way of thinking at least, infinitely tawdry. And there was no romance any more, no glamour. You couldn't bribe Paranoia with a sacrifice of firstling lambs, or appease Claustrophobia with a hymn and a prayer. All right, Lyssa and Hecate wouldn't have taken a whole lot of notice either, but at least you'd have had the feeling of getting a personal service, provided by trained professionals. And say what you liked about the gods, they'd had style.

Once.

'Thanks,' Pan said, leaning forward and putting his hand on the doorhandle. 'Anywhere here will do.'

'Okay.' The cabbie drew up, looked at the meter and asked for his fare. Pan stared at him. It wasn't the best he'd ever done, but it was still good enough.

'Hey, mac, no offence. So maybe it's a bit on the high side. Let's just talk it over, and . . .'

Stare.

'The ride's on me, okay?'

Stare.

'Look.' The taxi driver was sweating. 'How'd it be if I gave you fifty bucks and we forgot the whole thing?'

'Done.'

Perks, Pan thought, folding the money into his pocket and cloppity-clopping his way up Wall Street; one of the few fringe benefits. And am I prostituting my Art, putting the wind up tradesmen? Yes. Good.

Wall Street. Again. It was as bad, he felt, as appearing on chat-shows. He pushed open a pair of huge smoked glass doors and trudged in.

His mind wasn't on the job and he overdid the stare he gave the security guard. He felt a bit guilty as he walked on, leaving the poor man cowering under the front desk with a paper bag over his head.

He overdid the elevator, too. As soon as he got out of it, the wretched thing bolted straight up to the thirty-second floor and stayed there. It was gone midnight before the maintenance men were able to talk it down.

It was, he realised, because he was feeling depressed and bad-tempered after talking to Kortright. And the reason it had got to him so badly was that what Kortright had said was true. He was indeed over the hill. Over Everest, even. Maybe it was time he retired, like all the others.

By now he had won through to the dealing room itself, and he stood in the doorway, looking for a suitable victim. His eye lit on a small, round young man with glasses and just enough hair remaining to thatch a toolshed in Lilliput. He walked over and leaned on the computer terminal.

'Hi,' he said.

'Yes?'

'In twenty minutes,' said Pan, staring, 'the dollar is going to fall so far it'll probably burn up on re-entry.'

The market maker gazed at him out of round, glazed eyes. 'Why?' he said.

'It's the British,' Pan replied. 'The War of Independence was fixed. Results of tests show that George Washington was on steroids.' He paused, turned up the stare by about three degrees, and bent it into a grin. 'If I were you, I'd start selling now.'

'Thank you. Thank you very much.'

'Don't mention it.'

By the time he reached the ground floor, walking down fire stairs that seemed to want to edge away from him, the dollar was so far down you couldn't have traced it with a metal detector, and switchboards were jamming and systems going down right across the world as the financial rats scrambled to leave the floating ship. As he pushed through the doors and set hoof to pavement, Pan was acutely conscious of the buzz, the high feeling of having scared the recycled food out of tens of thousands of people who'd never done him any harm in their entire lives. It was a good feeling. It was what being a god is all about.

But, he reflected as he clattered down into the subway, it's still only a cheap commercial job, and I'm lucky to get that. Dammit, it *is* time to retire.

Definitely.

First thing tomorrow.

'The rear crankshaft cotter pin, thirty-six,' Odin repeated, 'is connected to the offside flywheel, seventy-two, by a split pin, nine.' He peered through his bifocals at the diagram.

'Give it here,' demanded Thor impatiently. 'You've probably got it upside down again.'

Odin tightened his grip on the instruction manual, which was twenty centuries old and held together with brittle yellowed Sellotape. 'It's perfectly simple,' he said, for the seventh time. 'We must just have overlooked some perfectly obvious . . .'

'Where does this bit go?'

Odin and Thor looked round, and saw Frey, patron god of all those who stand about with their hands in their pockets while other people do all the work, held up a small oily widget. 'I found it on the floor,' he explained.

'Bloody hell,' Thor exclaimed, 'that's the manifold release pawl. Why the hell didn't you mention it before?'

'You were standing on it.'

'Give it here.'

Twenty minutes with a screwdriver later, Thor straightened his back, wiped his forehead with the dirtiest handkerchief in the universe, and picked up the widget; which sprang salmon-like from his fingers and was at once lost to sight in the deep carpet of wood-shavings, empty crisp packets and bits of paper that covered the floor of the shed.

'I think,' said Frey, 'it landed somewhere over there.'

Odin sighed. 'Now then,' he said, 'let's all stay calm.

Everything is always somewhere.'

'Not necessarily,' Thor replied, burrowing his way head-first into a pile of empty sacks. 'What about Excalibur? What about the lost kingdom of Atlantis? What about . . .?'

'You know what I mean.'

'Only because I'm a bloody good guesser.'

'Excuse me.'

Thor looked up. His hair was full of coal-dust and a dead mouse had entangled itself in his beard. 'Now what?' he demanded.

'This time you're kneeling on it.'

'Am I?' Thor said. 'Ouch!' he added. 'Yes, you're quite right, well spotted. Right then, let the dog see the rabbit. Now, where did I put my screwdriver?'

'The rear crankshaft cotter pin, thirty-six,' said Odin, 'is connected to the offside flywheel, seventy-two . . .'

'I've just done that.'

'You can't have.'

'Why not?'

'Because,' Odin replied, 'here's the split pin in my hand.'

Yes, thought Thor, so it is. If I was to kill you now, there's no way it would be murder. Pesticide maybe, but not murder. 'Fine,' he said. 'Frey, pass me the mole wrench.'

Atheists would have you believe that there are no gods, but this is patently absurd; because if there were no gods, who made the world? Look at the world, consider the quality of design and workmanship. Consider who is supposed to have made it. Convinced? Of course you are. The San Andreas fault wasn't San Andreas' fault at all.

'Now then,' Thor said. He'd skinned his knuckles, banged his head on the rocker arm and caught his nose in the overhead cam. He was also a thunder and lightning god, and thunder gods, like doctors, never really retire. It would be as well for the world's sake if the engine started first time.

'Ready?'

'Ready.'

Thor turned the crank, and there was a loud groaning noise. It could have been the gears waking from nearly two thousand years of sleep; or it could have been the laws of physics saying that there was no way the engine was going to work because all the bits had been put back in the wrong places, and being told by the other forces of nature to put a sock in it. Whatever it was, it was followed by a splutter and a roar and then a peculiar sound like a hippopotamus pulling its foot out of very deep mud . . .

'It's working,' Thor shouted. 'Sod me, it's bloody well working! Will you just look at—'

. . . Followed by a loud bang, and then silence. Small bits of sharp metal dropped down through the air. There was a very peculiar smell.

'I don't think it was meant to do that,' said Frey.

'Are you a doctor?'

'No,' replied the postman, 'actually I'm a postman. Did you want to see a doctor?'

'Are you sure you're not a doctor?'

'Yes. Now if I could just get past . . .'

Minerva, former goddess of Wisdom, stood her ground. She was still in her dressing gown, worn inside out, and her slippers were on the wrong feet. 'I told them,' she said, 'I want to see a doctor. I keep telling them, you know, but they don't listen. Will you have a look at my knee?'

'If you like,' said the postman, taking two unobtrusive steps backwards. 'But I am in fact a postman, and—'

'They're still trying to poison me, of course,' Minerva confided. 'You tell them, they'll believe you if you're a doctor.'

The side door opened, and Thor put his head round. Having taken in the scene at a glance, he winked at the postman, tiptoed up behind Minerva and shouted very loudly indeed in her ear.

'Right,' he said, a few moments later, 'shouldn't have any more nonsense out of her for a day or two. Last time she didn't come down for a week. Have you got a parcel for me? Registered?'

'Um,' replied the postman. Of all the places he delivered to, Sunnyvoyde was the one he dreaded most. Since his round also included the Grand Central Abattoir, the explosives factory and the Paradise Hill Home for Stray Killer Dogs, this was probably significant.

'Name of Thor?' he asked.

'That's me.'

'Sign here, please.'

Back in the seclusion of his room, Thor ripped the package open and ploughed his way through the obligatory balls of rolled-up newspaper and grifzote shapes until he found what he was looking for. He examined it.

For once they hadn't sent the wrong bit. He was impressed. Maybe his luck was about to change.

He stuffed the small metal object into the pocket of his cardigan and stumped off to find Odin. On his way he bumped into Frey, who was trying without much success to hide a bunch of bananas down the front of his jacket.

'Has it come?' Frey asked.

Thor nodded, and produced the object. 'Probably not quite to size,' he said, 'but we can soon have a few thou. off it with the file, and then with luck we should be in business. Why are you trying to hide those bananas up your jumper?'

'Sssh,' Frey hissed. 'I'm not supposed to eat bananas, the old bag thinks they give me wind.'

'And do they?'

'Whose side are you on, exactly?'

Half an hour later, the vital component was in place, and the three gods stood nervously beside their pride and joy. Somehow the thought that when the crank turned, this time the engine might fire and run and the beast would be back in action once again was extremely unnerving, and the emotions registering on the gods' unconscious minds must have been akin to those of a doctor who, having managed to eliminate all known illnesses and cure death itself, suddenly remembers that he has a wife, three children and a mortgage to think of.

'Ready?'

'Suppose so.'

Odin rolled up his sleeve, gripped the handle firmly, and turned it. There was a clatter, a dull thump and—

'Gosh,' Frey said, 'it works. Well I never.'

'There's no need to sound quite so surprised,' Odin replied. 'I mean, it was really pretty straightforward when you think about it.'

'Was it?'

'Oh yes.'

'Where did I get the idea that it was horrendously difficult from, then, I wonder.'

They stood for a while, staring. Ten seconds later, it was still working. And ten seconds after that. And ten seconds after that . . .

'Okay,' Thor said briskly. 'Now we've got it going again, what are we actually going to do with it?'

To the gods all things are possible, all things are known.

'Um,' said Odin.

'I mean,' Thor went on after a longish pause, 'there's all sorts of things we *could* do with it.'

'Oh yes.'

'All sorts of things.'

'The possibilities are endless.'

'Only . . .' Thor bit his lip. 'Just now, like on the spur of the moment, I can't quite remember, you know, offhand . . .'

Small, muffled bells rang in Frey's memory. 'Something to do with fun-fairs, I think,' he said. 'And church fetes and that sort of thing.'

'Really?'

'I think so,' Frey replied. 'Of course, it's been a long time.'

Odin came to a decision. 'Why don't we take it for a ride?' he said. 'You know, a test drive. Just to make sure it actually is working all right. Before we actually do, um, whatever it was we were going to . . .'

'Good idea.'

'Fine.'

In retrospect it was a pity that, in the excitement of the moment, they drove out through the shed door without remembering to open it first; but at least it proved that the old jalopy was still as robust as ever. The gods, however, didn't let it worry them, once they'd brushed the bits of doorframe and hinge out of their eyes. Almost as soon as the engine started to move, a strange exhilaration seemed to sweep over them; a longing, almost, for some long-forgotten sensation that had something to do with speed, the open sky, the wind in one's hair . . .

They were airborne.

'Thor.'

'Yes, Frey?'

'Is it meant to be doing this?'

'Doing what, precisely?'

Odin was poring over the map. In his left hand he had a magnifying glass, and in the right a compass.

'Estimating our windspeed at thirty knots,' he said, in a loud, clear voice, 'that down there must be Budleigh Salterton.'

Frey turned and looked at him, vertigo temporarily pigeonholed. 'What did you say must be Budleigh Salterton?'

'There,' said Odin, pointing, 'just below us now. I always was pretty clever at this dead reckoning stuff.'

'You mean that there?'

'Yes. Which means that, if we continue this course for another—'

'That's a cloud, Odin.'

'No it's not, don't muck about. We've got a schedule to work to, remember?'

Thor and Frey suddenly remembered Odin's thing about maps. It had slipped their memories until now precisely because, a very long time ago, they had induced Odin on pain of being gutted on his own altar never to so much as look at another map for as long as the world existed. For his part Odin knew for a certainty that he was an excellent map reader, but the landscapes mucked him about by moving around when he wasn't looking. Other things that mucked Odin around included doors, piles of cans in supermarkets and all known electrical appliances.

'If it's not a cloud,' Frey persisted, 'how come it's grey and wispy and you can see the ground straight through it?'

Odin sat still for a moment, staring at the map and chewing the end of a pencil. The pencil in question had once been part of a pen-and-pencil set presented by God the Father to God the Son on the occasion of his passing his Religious Education O-level. 'All right,' he said, 'Budleigh Salterton is somewhere over there.' He waved an arm in a circle round his head. 'So I make it that if we carry on the way we're going, we should be in Papua by nightfall.'

'Since when,' Thor interrupted over the clatter of the turbo-props, 'did we want to go to Papua? Come to that, where is it exactly?'

'Now you're the one doing the kidding around.'

'Straight up,' said Thor. 'I had this mate, you see, who was really into hang-gliding. He could read a course off a map sooner than you could say Jack Robinson.'

'Who's Jack Robinson?'

'He's a figure of speech.'

'Oh,' said Frey. 'One of them.'

'It's in the middle of the Indian Ocean,' said Odin, holding the map about an inch from the tip of his nose. 'Principal exports include—'

'Yes, but why do you want to go there?'

Odin looked up. 'I don't,' he said. 'All I said was, if we carry on this line till nightfall, that's where we'll fetch up.'

'Oh I see,' Frey said, 'it wasn't an announcement, it was a warning.'

'Would you mind shutting up for a moment, please,' Odin said. 'Only I am trying to navigate here, and it's never easy at the best of times.'

'So don't fly at the best of times,' Frey replied. 'In fact, not flying at all would be all right with me. Have either of you two noticed how far we are off the ground?'

'For pity's sake, Frey,' Odin said, not looking up, 'don't be such a baby. Are you chicken or something?'

Frey scowled. 'I am a god, remember. I can be anything I jolly well like. Only I'd prefer to do it down there, if it's all the same to you.'

Thor sighed. 'You know,' he said, gazing out over the kingdoms of the earth, spread out before him like items of kit at an army inspection, 'I used to be really good at this. Flying around and stuff. Only somehow,' he went on, biting his lip, 'somehow I'm not sure I can still—'

'Don't be so feeble,' Odin replied. 'It's not something you forget; it's like riding a bicycle.'

'Sure,' Frey muttered. 'You wobble about for a while and then you hit the ground.'

'That's not what I meant at all.'

'And anyway, when was the last time you ever rode a bicycle?'

'Don't change the—'

'Come to that, have you ever ridden a bicycle at all? Ever?'

'Loads of times.'

'Name one.'

'Look,' Odin said, struggling to pull together the various strands of his thought processes, 'this isn't about riding bicycles, this is about flying. And here we are doing it. And we know *exactly* where we . . .'

For ever afterwards, the locals of that part of Cornwall referred to the rocky outcrop into which the Aesir now flew as Shooting Star Hill. The giant crater formed by the crash became a popular venue for outings and picnics, and attractive colour postcards are available at several local newsagents.

'What,' said Frey, struggling to his knees and spitting out earth, 'happened?'

'Easy mistake to make,' replied a voice, conceivably Odin's, emanating from the upper branches of a fir tree. 'Could have happened to anybody.'

'Will somebody please get this traction engine off me?'

'Low cloud,' Odin went on, 'and a damn great pointy hill; you're bound to have accidents sooner or later. Whoever created this region had absolutely no consideration whatsoever for the safety of air traffic. In fact I've a good mind—'

'But you keep it for special occasions,' interrupted Thor, from under the engine. 'Look, stop fartarsing about, you two, and get me out of here.'

'Yes,' grumbled Frey, grabbing hold of the front fender and heaving, 'but what happened?' To the gods all things are possible, and their strength has nothing to do with muscle and sinew; rather, they draw power from the earth, the sky, the sea. 'Don't just stand there, you prune,' he shouted at Odin, who had made it down from his tree and was scrabbling about for his map, 'grab the other end of this before I drop it on my toe.'

'Coming.'

'Too late.'

'When you've quite finished larking about,' said Thor's voice, from some way down, 'perhaps you'd get on with the job in hand.'

'All right, just give me a minute, will you?'

'The sooner I get out, you see, the sooner I can kick Odin's arse from here to Christmas.'

Between them, Odin and Frey manhandled the hundred-ton machine out of the way, rested it gently on the ground and rescued Thor, who had made a man-shaped hole of the kind usually only seen in Tom and Jerry cartoons.

'Are you saying,' Frey enquired, 'that he managed to fly us straight into the side of this mountain?'

'Actually,' Odin said, 'she's not that badly damaged. Not badly damaged at all. Front wing's a bit the worse for wear, but a few minutes with the lump hammer and you'd never know it was there.'

The reason why gods never fight among themselves is quite simply the futility of the exercise, combined with the prodigious danger to the environment. Two all-powerful, immortal, invulnerable beings going at it hammer and tongs are guaranteed to damage absolutely everything within a fifty-mile radius, with the sole exception of each other.

'Lump hammer, did you say?'

'That's the ticket, Thor. Just pass it over, would you?'

'On its way.'

Five minutes or so later, Frey (who had found the packed lunch and eaten the honey and raisin sandwiches and two of the chocolate mini-rolls) got up, wandered across the now considerably enlarged crater and stirred one of the two recumbent forms with his toe.

'All right, chaps,' he said. 'Now you've got that out of your systems, shall we be cutting along?'

'Good idea.'

'Where to, exactly?'

4

'Yes,' said the thug. 'As a matter of fact, I am a doctor. What's it to you, prune-face?'

'Oh.' Minerva, former Roman goddess of Wisdom, blinked. Vague thought-shapes swirled in her brain, struggling to fight their way through the fog and the mist. 'You don't,' she quavered, 'look much like a doctor to me.'

'Shows how much you know, you daft old bag,' the doctor replied. 'Now sod off, will you, there's a love, because we've got things to do.'

Minerva hesitated. The next line was welling up in her mouth, the words that she always said to everybody; but somehow, for once, they didn't seem appropriate, and she wasn't even sure why she wanted to say them. Nevertheless, she did.

'I shouldn't be here, you know,' she said. 'I shouldn't be here at all.'

The second thug, who was also a doctor, grinned. 'Too bloody right,' he said. 'In a pine box ten feet under's where you should be. Now sling your hook.'

'I'm terribly ill, you know,' Minerva said, or at least her lips shaped the words. Prompted by a massive sense of danger, her mind, what was left of it, was doing something it hadn't done since Machiavelli was an adolescent. It was thinking. Little flashes of electricity were crawling along the overgrown, corroded synapses of her brain. 'By rights,' she went on saying in the meanwhile, 'I should be in a hospital.'

'Let go of my sleeve or you will be.'

Two intrepid electrical discharges met in a jungle of decaying silicone somewhere in Minerva's cortex. It was like Livingstone and Stanley; and the one who might have been Livingstone might have said *Another fine mess you've gotten me into*, because the next words Minerva uttered were comparatively rational but factually incorrect.

'You're not a doctor,' she said.

'Get stuffed.'

The first thug, who really was a doctor, gave her a shove and she sat down heavily on an aged sofa, twisting her knee. Thirty centuries of outraged divinity suddenly woke up and screamed at her to turn this arrogant little mortal into a beetle. She tried it. She missed.

'Come on, Vern,' said the second doctor. 'Let's get it over with and get out of this dump.' He strode forward, not aware that in doing so he'd stepped on Inanna, the great goddess of Uruk, who went *splat!*

In the corridor that led from the day room to Lilac Wing, a nurse blocked their path.

'Excuse me,' she said, 'but who are you and what are you doing?'

'We're doctors.'

'Nobody told me anything about any doctors.'

'So bloody what?'

The nurse, who was the same Sandra who had managed to make Osiris eat hot custard, moved her feet slightly, making it impossible for the two men to brush past her without actually knocking her over. 'May I ask what you're here for?'

The two doctors looked at each other. Because they really were doctors, and had therefore served their time as the lowest form of life in a busy hospital, they still had buried deep in their psyches the basic fear of nurses that all doctors carry with them to the grave. This fear springs from the subconscious belief that the nurse knows a damn sight more about what's going on than they do, and for two pins will show them up in front of the patient.

'We're here to see someone.'

'Oh yes? And who might that be?'

The first doctor glanced at the back of his hand, where he'd written the name in biro. 'It's a Mr O'Syres,' he said. 'We're here to—'

'To give him a medical,' the second doctor interrupted.

'That's right, a medical.' The first doctor started to feel better; this was convincing stuff. He decided to expand it. 'He's thinking of taking out some life insurance,' he went on, 'and so we were asked—'

'You're sure about that?'

'Course we're sure.'

'*Life insurance?*'

'That's right, love, so if you'll just show us the way.'

'Yes, of course,' said Sandra. 'Just follow me.'

She led them to the big broom cupboard and opened the door a crack.

'This is Mr Osiris' room,' she said. 'I won't put the light on because he's asleep at the moment. If you just go in quietly and wait for him to wake up.'

As soon as they were inside, she turned the key and ran for it.

By the time she'd reached Osiris' room, the penny had dropped. Two doctors. What is it that needs two doctors? Easy. She pushed open the door.

'Oh,' she said. 'Sorry.'

She hadn't actually seen Mr Osiris without any clothes on before. True, she'd heard things about him; how he'd undergone a lot of surgery in the past, had all sorts of bits removed and so on. She wouldn't have been worried by scars. Zip fasteners, though, were another matter.

'For pity's sake,' Osiris said, reaching for a towel. 'You could have given me a heart attack.'

'Sorry.'

Osiris looked down at the middle of his chest, and grinned. 'Weren't expecting to see that, were you?'

'No,' Sandra admitted. 'Doesn't it get rusty when you have a bath?'

Osiris shook his head. 'Stainless steel,' he replied. 'I had them put in to make it easier for my wife.'

'Ah.'

'Was there something you wanted?'

Sandra's brain dropped back into gear. 'Get dressed, quick, and I'll help you into your wheelchair,' she said. 'There's two doctors come to certify you.'

'I beg your pardon?'

'Certify you,' Sandra hissed, grabbing a dressing gown and shoving it on to his lap. 'Say you're mad. I've locked them in a broom cupboard.'

Despite the ravages of time, Osiris still retained a fair proportion of the vast mental capacity required of a supreme being. He scowled.

'It's that little bugger Julian,' he growled. 'You wait till I get my hands on him, I'll make him wish—'

'Quickly!'

She helped bundle Osiris into some clothes and got him into the chair. The corridor was empty.

'Typical bloody lawyer's trick,' Osiris was muttering under his breath. 'Have me certified and then take over all my powers with one of those damned attorney things. I knew I should never have signed it.'

'That's awful,' Sandra replied absently. 'If we can just make it to the service elevator, we'll have a clear run out the back to the car park.'

'Mind you,' Osiris went on, 'you've got to hand it to him for brains. Chip off the old block in that respect. Mind out, you nearly had me into the wall there.'

'Stop complaining.'

As they passed the door of the broom cupboard, they could hear the sound of strong fists on woodwork and, alas, intemperate language. It looked to be a pretty solid door, but that wasn't something you could rely on. Never trust something that was once a tree, Osiris reflected. He'd met a lot of trees in his career as a nature god, and had learned a thing or two about them in the process. One: don't sit under them in thunderstorms. Two: never lend them money.

'All clear.'

'Hold on a moment,' Osiris said. 'Where exactly is it we're going?'

Sandra glowered at him impatiently. 'Somewhere you'll be safe, of course,' she said. 'Look, they'll be out of there in no time at all, so do you mind if—'

'*Where?*'

'My mum's, of course.'

'Ah,' said Osiris. 'Right.'

'Is there somebody in there?'

The first thug, who was of course a doctor and therefore well aware of which of the small bones in his hand he'd broken while banging furiously on the door, stopped hammering and yelled, 'Yes! Let us out!'

There was a pause.

'Are you a doctor?' said the voice.

'What do you mean,' said Julian, 'escaped?'

The first thug pressed a coin into the slot, taking advantage of the hiatus in the conversation to choose his words with care. 'He got away,' he said. 'One of the nurses locked us in a cupboard. When we got out . . .' He shuddered. It had taken a long time, and he was still getting nightmare flashbacks from the conversation he'd had with Minerva through the door. 'When we got out, he wasn't in his room. We searched the whole place from top to bottom. He's legged it.'

'Wheeled it,' suggested his colleague, shortly before collapsing against the side of the phone booth with severe abdominal pains. Since he was of course a doctor, he could have told you the technical name for them.

'You buggered it up, you mean?'

'Yes,' admitted the first doctor; then, recalling who he was talking to, added, 'without prejudice, of course.'

'Fine,' said Julian, after a while. 'I do hope for your sakes that you're heavily insured, because I happen to specialise in medical negligence claims.'

'Hey,' said the second thug, grabbing the receiver, 'that's not fair, we were only . . . Why are you laughing?'

'I'm sorry,' Julian replied, 'it's that word you just said, fair. Always has that effect on me. Now listen, you find him and get him committed like immediately, or the two of you'll find yourselves having trouble getting work as snake oil salesmen, let alone doctors, kapisch?'

'Now hang about,' shouted the second doctor, and the pips went.

'Damn,' said his colleague. 'Now what do we do?'

'What the man says would be favourite. Any idea how we go about it?'

'No.'

'And you call yourself a doctor.'

'Shut up.'

Situated in its own extensive grounds among acres of rolling cloudland, Sunnyvoyde commands extensive views over three galaxies, but is a bit of a cow to get to if you have to rely on public transport. Add a wheelchair into the equation, and x suddenly equals extreme difficulty.

'You're sure there's a bus?' Osiris demanded. He was starting to feel the cold.

'Of course there's a bus. How do you think I get to work every day?'

'And what is a bus exactly?' Osiris wrinkled his omniscient brow. 'I mean, I've heard of them, of course, but I don't think I've ever actually seen one. After my time, really.'

Sandra blew on her hands and jumped up and down until the sensation of a cloud wobbling under her feet got too much for her. 'It's a sort of square box,' she replied, 'with a wheel at each corner and seats inside.'

'It's a box you go inside?'

'That's it.'

'Ah. You mean a coffin.'

'No. Coffins don't have wheels.'

'Bet?'

'It's bigger than a coffin.'

'Bigger than a large coffin?'

'You can judge for yourself.'

Exactly on time, the bus drew up and stood for a moment, its engine running and doors closed, as if it was catching its breath. 'Have you,' Sandra asked, 'got any money for the fare?'

'Money?'

'Round flat metal discs with someone's head on one side and—'

'I mean,' replied Osiris irritably, 'I didn't know you had to pay to go on these things. Yes, thank you. Would two gold pieces cover it, do you think?'

'I would imagine so.'

'Hold on, then.'

'What are you doing?'

'It's a bit,' Osiris grunted, 'like I imagine putting contact lenses in must be. Come on, you little – oh blast, I've dropped one.'

'No,' Sandra explained patiently, 'you don't have to put them on your eyes. The man just takes them from your hand and gives you a ticket.'

'What's a ticket?'

'Just leave all the talking to me, all right?'

'Ruddy funny way to go about things, if you ask me.'

Osiris' bad temper soon evaporated when he found that he was only charged half price, and after a few minutes it was obvious he was enjoying himself immensely. The way he kept yelling 'Whee!' and pretending to steer told its own story.

'Will you stop that. People are staring.'

'I'm used to that.'

'Yes,' Sandra whispered back, 'but we want to be inconspicuous, remember. We're escaping. Running away. Or had you forgotten?'

Osiris had the good grace to look embarrassed. 'Sorry,' he said. 'Hasn't really sunk in yet. I've been a lot of things in my time, but Most Wanted wasn't one of them. Usually,' he added, 'quite the reverse.'

'Really?' Sandra searched in her bag for a peppermint. 'I thought you gods were loved and worshipped. You know, revered and stuff.'

'Revered, yes,' Osiris replied. 'Loved, no. All right, people say a lot of nice things to you when you're a god, but it's either because they want something or they're frightened of getting a thunderbolt up the jacksie, not because they think you're fun to be with. Masses of prayers and sacrifices, but nobody ever remembers your birthday.'

'Gosh,' said Sandra through her peppermint. 'I didn't even know gods had birthdays.'

'Proves my point, doesn't it? Should I be sitting here, do you think? Only it does say, *Please give up this seat if an elderly or disabled person needs it.*'

'I think you qualify on both counts.'

'Do I? Well I never. It must be very complicated, being a mortal.'

It was one of those slow buses. From Sunnyvoyde, it meandered at the pace of an elderly glacier with corns past the Islands of the Blessed, across the Elysian fields, round the back of Valhalla – long since sold for development and converted into possibly the most nerve-jangling theme park and paintball game centre in the cosmos – along the Nirvana Bypass to the Happy Hunting Grounds Park and Ride, where the bus suddenly filled up with dead Red Indians carrying shopping bags. Shortly after a brief stop at the Jade Emperor's palace, Osiris fell asleep, and only woke up when Sandra tugged at his sleeve. He looked out of the window.

'Come on,' Sandra was saying, 'the next stop is ours. I'll get your wheelchair out of the rack.'

'Hey,' said the god. 'Where *is* this?'

'Wolverhampton.'

'But it's so ruddy *small*.'

'You should have thought of that before. Like on the sixth day, for instance.'

'That wasn't me,' replied Osiris, defensively. 'That was the other bloke. Thing, name begins with a J.'

'Up we get.'

Although he never dared mention it to his priests for fear of causing immortal offence, Osiris had never been a great one for ceremony and fuss; but there are certain ways of going about things that are bred in the bone, and when a god visits Earth, he expects more of a welcoming party than a small child on a bicycle and a stray cat. Osiris sighed.

'And people actually live here?' he said.

'Yes.'

'How do they fit in those titchy little houses?'

'We manage.'

'Which way now?'

'Actually,' Sandra said, opening the gate and pushing the wheelchair through, 'we're here.'

'Surely not.'

'Look. If you're going to be difficult we can turn straight round and go back. Just because you're a god doesn't mean you own the place.'

'Well, actually . . .'

'You know what I mean.'

Sandra opened the front door, parked Osiris' wheelchair in the small front parlour, and went through into the kitchen. From behind the kitchen door, Osiris could hear a buzz of voices. The door opened.

'Mum,' said Sandra, 'meet Mr Osiris; he's a god. Mr Osiris, this is my mother.'

Sandra's mother was a small, potato-shaped woman, who looked as if she'd been repeatedly washed in bleach but not ironed. She stared at the god suspiciously.

'Is he staying for his tea?' she asked. 'Because I was going to do liver.'

'Actually, Mum,' Sandra replied, 'Mr Osiris'll be staying with us for a week or so. You see, he's escaping from his godson, who wants to take over the world by having him certified.'

'He'll have to have our Damian's room, then.'

'That'll be fine.'

Sandra's mother sniffed. 'He's not one of those vegetarians, is he? Only I thought we could have steak and kidney tomorrow. There's vegetable soup if he'd rather, but it's only packet.'

'Steak and kidney will be fine, Mrs . . .' Osiris said. 'I really don't want you to go to any trouble on my—'

'And what about clean towels,' Sandra's mother went on, 'what with him being in a wheelchair and everything, because it's Thursday tomorrow and the man's coming to fix the aerial in the morning.'

'Mum . . .'

'And you haven't forgotten I have my feet done Mondays now instead of Wednesdays, have you?' Sandra's mother sighed. 'Though I suppose he could have the small chair from the lounge and I'll move the nest of tables into the kitchen. For now,' she added. 'Can he use the, you know, on his own?'

'Mr Osiris is a *god*, Mum. I'm sure he'll be no trouble at all. Will you?'

'You'll hardly know I'm here, Mrs ...' Osiris sucked his lower lip. Either he was missing something or else Julian's doctor friends were well within their rights wanting to have him certified. Two weeks in this place, he added to himself, and I might even give myself up.

'Does he want a scone?'

'Yes.'

'Right.'

Sandra sat down and took her shoes off. 'I'm sure you two'll get on like a house on fire,' she said, looking at the ceiling. 'She likes visitors really.'

Well quite, Osiris muttered to himself. After a day or two she probably puts vases of flowers on them. 'It's very kind of you,' he said aloud, 'doing all this for me. You're sure it's no trouble?'

'No trouble at all.'

'Oh.'

'We are *not* lost.'

Thor glanced up at the sky. 'Anyone else saying that,' he said, 'would have grounds to be worried about sudden bolts of lightning.'

'What?'

'Perjury,' Thor explained. 'If it's any help, that down there looks very much like Bury St Edmunds.'

'What do you know about Bury St Edmunds?'

On the chariot flew, whirling like a fast black cloud over the sleeping landscape of (for the record) northern Italy. Where its shadow fell, thin and ghostly in the pale moonlight, dogs whined and sleepers turned in their beds, crossing themselves and dreaming strange dreams.

'A damn sight more than you do, probably,' Thor replied. 'Look, there's the High Street directly below us, and that bright light there must be Sainsbury's.'

'Sainsbury's?'

'Since your time,' Thor replied, not without slight embarrassment. Odin and Frey looked at each other.

'All right,' Thor snarled, 'so I've got this, um, acquaintance in Bury St Edmunds, and from time to time she sends me the odd postcard . . .'

'*She.*'

'She's seventy-five years old, for crying out loud,' Thor snapped.

'Well, you're no spring chicken yourself.'

'Shut up and navigate.'

There had been a time – not so long ago in divine chronology, but for the gods all things are different – when the passing of Thor's chariot made the skies boil and the earth shake; but no longer. There were many reasons – the decay of faith, the decomposition of the ionosphere, the fact that when Odin put the main crankcase assembly back together he somehow managed to connect up the swinging arm direct to the connecting rod without linking it up to the reciprocating toggle – and all probably just as well. Mankind cannot bear too much unreality, and there are rather too many military airfields and guided missile bases on the north-east Italian border to make overflying in an environmentally disruptive UFO a sensible course of action.

'What's she called, then?' asked Frey.

'What's who called?'

'Your bit of stuff in Bury St—'

'She is not,' Thor growled, 'my bit of stuff, okay? Mrs O'Malley is a highly respectable—'

'Carrying on with married women now, are we?'

'. . . widow who happens to have a sincere and scholarly interest in Scandinavian folklore, and who happens to have consulted me on a few points of reference concerning the—'

'What's her first name, then?'

'None of your business.'

'Ethel. I bet you it's Ethel.'

'Look, can we please talk about something else, because I find this whole conversation extremely childish and pretty damn offensive.'

'So it is Ethel.'

'No it's *not*.'

Beneath them, a flash of silver, a few silhouettes against the sky, the glitter of the moon on a broad expanse of still water. The early fishermen of the Venetian lagoon looked up from their nets and wondered what they had just seen; a black cloud flitting across the moon, a cold, sharp breeze ruffling the lagoon into a myriad feathery waves, a distant sound as of far, unearthly voices bickering.

'And *that*,' said Odin triumphantly, 'must be Scarborough.'

5

Mrs Henderson frowned.

It hadn't been a good day, so far. She'd completely lost one resident, another was out loose somewhere on the transparent pretext of buying socks, she'd had intruders on the premises claiming to be doctors (which unsettled some of the more ethnic gods, to whom doctors were people in leopard skins with short tempers and impaling sticks) and now one of the nurses had called in sick. Her intuition told her that Chaos was back in town looking for a rematch.

About three quarters of the residents of Sunnyvoyde would have you believe that they had been solely responsible for putting Chaos in her place and giving Order the confidence to come out of her shell and form meaningful relationships; but Mrs Henderson knew better. Chaos, as far as she was concerned, was a Greek word for what happened when you let people try and run their own lives, and it wasn't something that she permitted in her establishment, thank you very much. Had Mrs Henderson been in charge of the Garden of Eden, stewed apple would have been on the menu every second Wednesday, and anyone who didn't eat it all up would have had it put in front of them at every meal until they did.

'Melanie,' she said into the intercom, 'just come in here for a moment, will you?'

It was time, she decided, to stop getting in a fluster and start sorting things out. The doctors had gone, and any further reference to them would be firmly discouraged. Mr Lug would be back eventually, and she would have a few well-chosen words with him when he did, and that would be all right. Sandra, the nurse who had had the misfortune to contract some unspecified illness, would be given the opportunity to select a career more conducive to her obviously delicate health. Mr Osiris, though, was a different matter entirely. Although the precise situation wasn't totally clear, Mr Osiris would appear to have booked out for good; his toothbrush was gone, as were his gold watch (presented to him by the people of Egypt in recognition of four thousand years of loyal service; he was ever so proud of that) and the little jar he kept all his leftover organs in. And Mr Osiris owned the place. She wasn't quite sure what to do about him.

By way of explanation: an unresolved uncertainty in Mrs Henderson's life would be a bit like a Tyrannosaurus in Central Park; out of place, extremely rare and, after a fairly short interval, extinct.

'Yes?'

'Melanie, I want you to put a call through for me. It's a Los Angeles number. Fairly urgent, if you don't mind.'

She wrote the number, and a name, on a yellow sticky and handed it to her secretary, who glanced at it, looked up sharply, caught her employer's eye and left the room quickly.

There, said Mrs Henderson to herself, problem solved.

There was no reply to Melanie's call, except for the inevitable answering machine.

Thank you for calling Kurt Lundqvist Associates. There's no-one in right now to take your call, but if you leave your name, your number and details of the supernatural entity you want killed after the tone, we'll get back to you as soon as we can. Bleep.

On the credit side, Osiris was blissfully unaware of the second front that was just opening up against him. On the debit side, he was sitting in front of a big plateful of Sandra's mother's rhubarb crumble.

'Gosh,' he croaked. 'How delicious. And is all that for me?'

It was a prospect, he felt sure, that would have intimidated anyone. To someone whose stomach currently lay sideways alongside his left lung, the result of a fairly basic misunderstanding on the part of Lady Isis of pages 34 to 56 inclusive of the instruction manual, it was enough to cool the blood.

'Tell him,' said Sandra's mother, 'he needn't finish it if he doesn't want it all.'

'Yes, Mum.'

'Mind you, there's starving children in the Third World who'd be really glad of a nice bit of rhubarb crumble.'

It'd certainly make them count their blessings, Osiris reckoned. He picked up his spoon and picked tentatively at the southerly aspect. Care was needed in making the first breach in that impressive structure; one false move and the whole lot might come crashing down on him.

'Yes, Mum.' From behind the cover of the big vase of plastic flowers, Sandra winked at him, setting off an alarming sequence of memories which he thought he'd cauterised years ago. Dear God, yes, the first time he ever went to tea with Isis's parents. Isis's father was the Word and her mother was the Great Void; and they weeded out their daughter's ineligible suitors by means of the diabolical practice of Trial By Massed Vegetables.

With a start, Osiris realised that all these goings-on were causing him to revisit his lost youth; which was a nuisance, to say the least. He hadn't enjoyed his youth one little bit. In fact, far from losing it, he'd left it behind, so to speak, by means of an open window and a rope of knotted sheets.

'Tell him,' said Sandra's mother, 'there's some nice hot custard if he wants it.'

'Oooh yes,' Sandra replied. 'Mr Osiris *loves* hot custard, don't you, Mr Osiris?'

Gods don't make particularly good liars; they don't get the practice, because they don't feel the need. Nobody asks a god why he's late for work this morning, or was it him who broke the window, for fear of getting a response along the lines of, Yes, and you want to make something of it? Several thousand years of married life had, nevertheless, left Osiris with a reasonable grasp of the basics of the craft.

'Yes,' he said. 'How delightful.'

While Sandra's mother was out of the room, doing whatever it is you do to bring about hot custard, Osiris leaned across the table and grabbed Sandra by the wrist.

'No offence,' he hissed, 'but you've got to get me out of here. Much more of this *Does he like cold custard?* stuff, and somebody not a million miles from here is going to go to bed a different shape.'

'Don't be horrid. That's my mum you're talking about.'

Osiris sighed, letting go of Sandra's wrist. 'I know,' he said, 'and I'm being very ungrateful. Old god's privilege, that is. But she treats me like I don't exist. You shouldn't do that to a god, you know. We're insecure enough as it is without people not believing in us all over the place.'

Sandra bit her lip. 'I don't think she can see you very well,' she said.

'Ah.' Osiris nodded. 'I might be able to help you there. What is it, cataracts? Glaucoma?'

Sandra shook her head. 'No,' she said, 'her eyes are fine. I think it's her, um, imagination that's a bit wanting in places. I don't think her disbelief suspends very well. After all, this *is* Wolverhampton. There haven't been any gods in these parts for, oh, I don't know how long. There's certainly never been any gods on the Orchard Mead Housing Estate.'

'That's terrible,' Osiris said, shaken. 'I mean to say, surely everybody is capable of believing in gods. We built you that way, for pity's sake.'

'I'm afraid you're a bit out of touch, Mr Osiris.'

'Strewth.' Osiris leaned back in his chair and thought about it. It wasn't a concept he found easy to get hold of. People could dislike gods, sure enough. Despise them, certainly; hate them, even. But not believe in them at all – that was like people not believing in rain just because they didn't like getting wet.

'I'm sorry.'

'Not your fault.' Osiris sighed. 'You're quite right, I am out of touch. No wonder I've felt all weak since I got here. There's much of it about, is there, this not believing?'

'Lots and lots.'

'What do people believe in, then, if they don't believe in gods?'

'Hard to say.' Sandra rubbed her nose pensively. 'The telly, of course. And family life. And Wolverhampton Wanderers Football Club, which only goes to show what you can do if you really set your mind to it.'

Osiris shook his head slowly. Belief is to gods what atmosphere is to other, rather more temporary life-forms; they live in it, and it shapes them, in the way that millions of tons of water overhead shape the curiously designed fish that live at the very bottom of the sea. This can, of course, have its unfortunate side. When, for example, the Quizquacs of central Peru had finally had enough of their god Tlatelolco's obsession with human sacrifice *à la nouvelle cuisine* (one small human heart, garnished with fine herbs and served with the blood *under* the meat) they exacted a terrible revenge, not by ceasing to believe in him, but by believing in him with a fervour never before encountered even in such a pathologically devout race as the Quizquacs. They also chose to believe in him in his aspect as an excessively timid field vole inhabiting an enclosed kitchen full of hungry cats.

'I've definitely got to get out of here,' Osiris said. 'Look, don't let me put you to any more trouble. Just call me a taxi and I'll go and find a hotel somewhere.'

'A hotel?' Sandra laughed. 'You wouldn't last five minutes.'

'Wouldn't I?'

'No chance.'

'What makes you say that?'

By way of reply, Sandra reached for her handbag and produced a mirror. Osiris took it from her, automatically smoothed his hair, and had a look . . .

'Oh,' he said. 'Oh I see.'

'Exactly. Now perhaps you understand why Mum doesn't choose to be able to see you very well. It's just as well she's got such a limited imagination, or she'd be halfway up the wall yelling for the Social Services by now.'

The face Osiris had seen in the mirror was, beyond question, his own. That was, of course, the problem. The plain fact of the matter is, gods are radiant. They shine; and no amount of face powder and foundation was ever going to have any effect on the dazzling glow that was pouring out of him. You could have got a healthy tan just by briefly catching his eye.

'It hasn't done that for ages,' he said weakly. 'Why's it doing it now?'

'They've got some sort of infra-red thing back at the Home,' Sandra replied. 'Suppresses it, or filters it out, something like that. Out here, of course . . .'

'Gosh.'

'I'm used to it,' Sandra went on, 'and besides, all of us nurses are given these special contact lenses, otherwise we'd spend all day wandering about bumping into things. It's a dead giveaway, I'm afraid.'

Osiris handed back the mirror, noticing as he did so that the plastic frame was just starting to melt. 'Any suggestions?' he muttered.

'Well.' Sandra helped herself to a planklike slice of bread and butter. 'At first I thought of seeing if we could get you a job as a lighthouse keeper . . .'

'Good thinking.'

'Only that would take some time to fix up, and we've got to keep you out of sight until I've had a chance to find out exactly what's going on. Really, your best bet is to stay here and sweat it out.'

'Sandra . . .'

'What choice do you have?'

'Yes, but that mother of yours. I mean, please don't get me wrong, salt of the earth . . .'

'If by that you mean she makes you feel like having a very big drink, yes, I find that myself, too.'

'It wouldn't be so bad,' Osiris said mournfully, 'if only she'd admit I was here. Actually talk to me, things like that.'

Sandra nodded. 'Actually,' she said, 'I reckon it might be possible to get her to do that.'

'Oh yes? How?'

'You could try offering her a very substantial sum of money.'

Even with Sandra's mother talking to him, Osiris found it hard to settle. True, he now had his own room, with a view out over the shunting yards and a small black-and-white portable television capable of receiving two channels; but the waves of disbelief were definitely getting to him, and he didn't like the effect it was having. Twice he'd dropped things because his hands suddenly became translucent and feeble, and he was getting pins and needles all over his body. He scarcely had the strength to wheel himself over to the telly to change programmes.

Never mind. He looked up at the clock, which told him it was almost time for *The Young Doctors*. Soap operas were something of a lifeline to him, on the grounds that if the inhabitants of this peculiar country could watch this sort of thing without serious credibility disorders, they were capable of believing in anything. He switched on the set and settled back in his chair.

Adverts. Was there time to plug in the kettle and make himself a nice cup of . . .?

He knew that voice.

. . . *Absolutely free when you buy two or more packets of new Zazz with the unique biological fragrance* . . .

Surely not. He must have retired years ago. Only, Osiris reflected, if he had then surely I'd have seen him about the place, and I haven't. And nobody could call him inconspicuous.

But hurry, hurry, hurry, because this special offer must end soon, so don't miss out on this unique chance to save, save, save . . .

It was him, for sure. Osiris could tell by the way that, in spite of everything, he was gripped with this insane desire to buy fabric conditioner. Not because he wanted it, but because he was afraid of missing out on the unique special offer. Very afraid. Panic-stricken, even.

'The old bugger,' Osiris chuckled. 'Well, fancy that.'

'Guess what?'

'I've brought you some tea,' said Sandra, putting the tray down on the bed. 'It's boiled chicken with cabbage and mashed potatoes, with stewed plums and custard to follow.'

Osiris looked away. 'I've just seen someone I know, well, more heard than seen, and you'll never guess—'

'Come on,' Sandra said, 'eat up. Don't want the custard getting—'

'And,' Osiris went on, 'I've made up my mind what I'm going to do next.'

Sandra narrowed her eyes. 'I don't like the sound of this,' she said. 'I thought we'd agreed that you were going to be sensible and stay here until we'd got things straightened out.'

'Ah yes,' Osiris said, 'but that was before I found out my old friend Pan's still on the loose.' He produced a theatrical chuckle. 'Talk about a complete lunatic, the times we've had together, it'll be a holiday just—'

'Pan?'

Osiris took a deep breath. 'He's a god,' he said. 'And he's doing voice-overs on the commercial breaks. Obviously he hasn't retired yet. And we go back a long way, Pan and me. He wouldn't begrudge a bit of house room for an old chum. So, first thing in the morning, I'm going to phone that TV station and leave a message for him.'

'I see,' said Sandra stiffly. 'And you think—'

'Yes.' Osiris scowled. 'Please don't take this the wrong way, but I feel that at my time of life I'd be better off with my own kind. I've made my mind up, and—'

'It'll all end in tears, you mark my words.'

'I'm a god,' Osiris said grimly, 'and I'll do what I damn well please. I invented free will, dammit, so why shouldn't I have some for a change?'

Sandra shrugged, and put the tray on his lap. 'All right,' she said, 'that's fine. Only what makes you so sure this Pan person will want you descending on him out of the blue and getting under his feet?'

'Don't worry about that,' Osiris said, and a grin the size of Oklahoma spread slowly across his face. 'That's not going to be a problem, you mark my words.'

'Eat your nice tea.'

'And that's another thing . . .'

'Or,' Sandra said meaningfully, 'there'll be second helpings of everything.'

'Oh. Right. Yes.'

'Don't worry,' Thor said, wiping his forehead with his sleeve and scrabbling in the toolbox. 'I can fix it. No problem. Just get out of my light and let the dog see the . . .'

To the gods, all things are known. 'I still think it's the main bearing,' Odin said. 'Else why was it making that tapping noise?'

'What tapping noise?'

'I distinctly heard a tapping noise five minutes or so before she seized,' Odin replied. 'I'd have mentioned it only you'd have bitten my head off.'

'I'm hungry,' Frey observed, from under the shade of his golf umbrella. 'We've missed dinner and breakfast and I'm damned if we're going to miss lunch too.'

'Belt up, Frey,' Thor replied, rubbing his beard with his oily left hand. 'Odin, can you remember which way round the cotter pin's supposed to go on this axle?'

Frey stood up and shaded his eyes with his hand. In front of him, the Alps rose in dizzying white majesty, blinding in the cold, clear sunshine. 'Are you sure that's Matlock over there?' he asked.

'Nowhere else it could be,' Odin replied. 'But look at the map if you don't believe me.'

'I think I'll just go for a stroll.'

'Don't get lost.'

Frey grinned. 'I'm only going as far as the nearest place they sell food,' he said. 'I don't suppose I'll be very long.'

He walked away down the slope, picking his way with care through the rocks. Hm, he thought, gazing out over the surrounding landscape, so that's why they call this the Peak District.

He hadn't gone far when he came across a man and a woman walking slowly up the hill. The man was about sixty, the woman perhaps a year younger; they were plainly but neatly dressed, and the man was leading a laden donkey. Frey smiled; here was a source of inside information.

Now there is a well-established tradition that when the gods walk abroad among men, they do so in some form of disguise; gods manifest themselves as beggars or weary travellers, goddesses as washerwomen or old crones gathering firewood. Men say that this is typical underhand management behaviour, sneaking about and spying, like unmarked police patrol cars on motorways. Gods know that the real reason is to spare gods the embarrassment of not being recognised by their adoring worshippers. Frey shrugged his shoulders and became in a fraction of a second a weary traveller *à la mode*; aertex shirt damp with perspiration, heavy flight bag over one shoulder, suitcase in hand, crumpled sun-hat perched on head. He cleared his throat.

'Excuse me,' he said. The couple turned and looked at him.

'Excuse me,' he repeated, his memory trying to recollect the local cuisine of north Derbyshire, as reported by popular television drama. 'Could you possibly tell me where I might be able to get cod, mushy peas, pickled gherkins and a really tasty chip butty, please? And jam roly-poly and a nice strong cup of tea,' he added.

The man and the woman looked at each other and conferred in a foreign language, which Frey (to the gods all things are known) thought was probably Portuguese.

'Sorry,' said the man haltingly. 'No understan Inglis. Sorry.'

Between gods and men there are differences, and there are similarities; as between, say, the very rich and the very poor. Divine public relations have in the past tended to play down the similarities, understandably enough; but in more recent years this approach has been revised. Hey guys, the gods now say, we aren't really all that different. We're just guys and gals, same as you. If you prick us, they say, do we not bleed? Well, no, actually, they admit, we don't; and anyway that's not a particularly apt example to choose, because anyone trying to prick us is likely to find himself on the bad end of many millions of volts of static electricity. But you know what we mean.

Accordingly, it's not too remarkable that as Frey continued his journey down the hill, and the man and his wife plodded on up the hill, exactly the same phrase should have leapt spontaneously into their minds.

'Bloody tourists,' they all thought.

*

'Of course,' said Mrs Henderson, 'we're all extremely concerned. Extremely. Taking off like that, a god of his age.' She paused, and Julian's extra-perceptive senses caught a whiff of a point being surreptitiously made. 'I'm very much afraid,' she said, 'that Something might Happen to him.'

'Really? Such as what?'

Mrs Henderson shrugged, as if to say that in a curved universe, anything is by definition possible.

'I'm sure he'll be all right,' she said. 'After all, he is a god and fundamentally quite sensible, for his age. But with this terrible cold weather we've been having ... And he hasn't taken his blue pills with him.'

'You don't say.' The two looked at each other, and electricity crackled in the air. It was as if the two thieves crucified on either side of Our Lord on that first Good Friday had put their heads together and decided to cut out the middle man. 'His *blue* pills,' said Julian slowly. 'That could be serious.'

'Very.'

'I dread to think what might happen to him without his blue pills.'

'Not that anything will, of course ...'

'No, of course not.'

'It's just that it's always advisable to consider the *very worst* that might happen. Just in case.'

'Quite so.'

'Which is why,' said Mrs Henderson, taking a deep breath and hoping very much that she hadn't completely misinterpreted the messages emanating from under Julian's eyebrows, 'I've taken the liberty of engaging a, um, private enquiry agent to see if he can, um, find your godfather for us.'

'Splendid. Splendid.'

'A Mr Lundqvist.'

'*Ah.*'

'He came very highly recommended.'

'Top rate man. Exactly what I'd have done, in your position.'

'Oh I *am* glad.'

Julian allowed himself the luxury of a smile. It would cost a paying client about a year's salary to be smiled at by Julian, but he treated himself to a smile a month at cost. 'If Kurt Lundqvist can't sort this business out,' he said, 'nobody can.'

The same Kurt Lundqvist was, at that precise moment, locked in hand-to-hand combat with a tall gentleman with projecting teeth and a conservative taste in evening dress at the bottom of an open grave somewhere in what used to be called Bohemia.

It should have been a perfectly straightforward job – go in, garlic under nose, whack the hickory smartly through the aorta and home in time to catch the closing prices on Wall Street – but he'd recently taken on a new assistant, and she wasn't yet a hundred per cent *au fait* with the technical jargon of the supernatural contract killing profession.

'Look,' he gasped through clenched teeth as the Count's icy fingers closed around his throat, 'can we cut this a bit short, because I'm due in Haiti for a rogue zombie at six-thirty. I don't like to rush you, but . . .'

A right pillock he'd looked, reaching into his inside pocket and fetching out a five-pound lump hammer and a prime cut of best rump steak. He would have various things to say to Ms Parfimowicz when he got back.

'Nothing personal,' grunted the Count, 'but I'd rather we went through the motions. Aaaaagh!'

'Okay, that's fine,' Lundqvist replied, as his right hand finally connected with the butt of his .40 Glock automatic. 'I'm about through here anyway.'

The bullet wasn't, strictly speaking, silver; but it was a Speer 170-grain jacketed hollow point, backed by six grains of Unique and a Federal 150 primer. By the time the echoes of the shot had died away, the Count didn't seem in any fit state to discuss the finer points of metallurgy. You would have to be abnormally thin-skinned to take 'Gluuuurgh!' as any sort of valid criticism.

Nevertheless, Lundqvist felt peeved. It wasn't the way these things ought to be done. You had to preserve the mystique. Once people cottoned on to the fact that any Tom, Dick or Harry could blow away the Undead with a factory-standard out-of-the-box compact automatic, they wouldn't be quite so eager to pay through the nose for the services of a top flight professional.

A quick glance at his watch told him he was badly behind schedule. A quick scout round produced a three-foot length of broken fence post, and a few strokes of his Spyderco Ultramax lock-knife put enough of a point on it to do the job. He was just dusting himself off and searching the pockets for any small items of value when his bleeper went.

'Lundqvist here.'

'Oh Mr Lundqvist, I'm sorry to disturb you like this, I hope I haven't called at an inconvenient moment.'

'No, it's okay. While I think of it, what I had in mind when I gave you the equipment list this morning was stake S-T-A-K-E, not—'

'Oh gosh, Mr Lundqvist, I'm most terribly sorry, really I am, I never thought—'

'That's fine,' Lundqvist broke in – in order to have the time to wait for a natural break in the flow of Ms Parfimowicz's apologies you had to be a giant redwood at the very least – 'it wasn't a problem as it turned out. Just remember for next time, okay?'

'I will, I promise. I'll just quickly write it down and then I'll be sure to remember. That's stake spelt S-T-A . . .'

'Ms Parfimowicz,' Lundqvist said firmly, 'quiet. Now, what was so goddam important?'

'Oh yes, I'm sorry I got sidetracked, I must stop doing that, it must be so *irritating* for you. A Mrs Henderson called – she's not in the card index but she knew the private number so she must be genuine, don't you think – and she wants you to kill a god.'

There was a brief pause while Lundqvist grabbed for the receiver which he had somehow contrived to drop. 'I don't think I heard you right,' he said. '*Kill a god?*'

'That's what she said, Mr Lundqvist. Of course I could have got it down wrong, I know I'm still having trouble with taking the messages off the machine, but I'm pretty sure—'

'Mrs Henderson, you said?'

'That's right, Mr Lundqvist. Do you want me to spell that back for you?'

'I'll be straight back. Call Haiti, cancel the zombie, make up some excuse. This is more important.'

'Oh.' The voice at the end of the line quavered slightly. 'What excuse can I make, Mr Lundqvist?'

'Tell them . . .' Lundqvist grinned. 'Tell them I had to go to a funeral.'

6

Love, according to the songwriters, is the sweetest thing; but tea as made by the great god Pan must come a pretty close second. It's just as well that Pan is immortal, because if he were ever to die, several third world countries whose economies depend in whole or in part on the cultivation of sugar cane are likely to fall on hard times.

'Have another biscuit,' said Pan with his mouth full. Osiris shook his head.

'Two full of cake,' he explained. 'Couldn't eat another thing.'

'To the gods,' Pan replied, helping himself, 'all things are possible.'

'All right, then. I like these little ones with the coconut on top.'

All living things yearn for their own kind; and it had been a long time since Pan had spent any time with a fellow god. As far as Osiris was concerned, he had several thousand years' unhealthy eating to catch up on. So many doughnuts, so little time.

'Well, then.' Pan leaned back in his chair and nibbled the chocolate off a mini swiss roll. 'So what have you been up to all this time?'

'Nothing.'

'Nothing at all?'

Osiris nodded. 'The first six hundred years after I retired, I just had a bloody good rest. After that, I found I'd got out of the habit of doing things. My own fault, really.'

'Institutionalised.'

Osiris let his eye wander around the room. His reactions were mixed. On the one hand, he thought, the very idea of an immortal god, one of *us*, being afforded so little respect by mortals that he could only afford a bed-sitting room over a chemist's shop in a suburban high street was so infamous that it made his palms itch for a thunderbolt. On the other hand, it was a damn sight bigger than his gloomy little kennel at Sunnyvoyde (and he *owned* the horrible place, remember), and it was quite plain from the most cursory inspection that Pan didn't have little chits of teenage girls in white pinnies barging in whenever they felt like it, moving his possessions about and confiscating his digestive biscuits. True, there was about a thousand years' arrears of washing up in the sink, but the price of liberty is eternal housekeeping. He wrenched his mind back to the subject under discussion.

'I suppose so, yes,' he said wistfully. 'To begin with you think, Hey, this is the life, five meals a day brought to your room by beautiful young girls. Then you realise that for the last thousand years you've noticed the food but not the girls. Then you start to wonder what's happening to you.'

'Yeah.' Pan nodded, but in his mind's eye he could picture his compact, thoroughly modern, utterly squalid kitchen. He had a perfectly good dishwasher, but it was a while since he'd actually seen it, because of all the dirty plates piled up on every available surface. 'Mind you, five meals you haven't had to cook for yourself. It's definitely got something going for it.'

'Not much, though.' Osiris shifted slightly in his wheelchair, which seemed to have shrunk. 'How come you never retired?'

'Couldn't afford to,' Pan replied. 'Purely and simply a question of money.'

'Really?'

'Really. I look back now and I say to myself, If only I'd had the good sense to take out a personal pension plan back in the third century BC, I wouldn't still be having to get out of bed at six-thirty every morning to go to work. Mind you, it's always the way. When you're that age, you think you're going to live forever. Or, more to the point, you think you *aren't* going to live forever, so why bother? Were you, um, planning to stay long?'

Osiris nodded. 'Depends on how long it takes.'

'How long what takes?'

'For me to outlive my godson,' Osiris replied. 'The way I see it, all I've got to do is stay out of the way of him and his precious doctors until they kick the bucket. And in our timescale, that just gives us time for a quick game of poker before I've got to be getting back.'

'Poker?'

'It was only a suggestion. If you'd rather play snakes and ladders or . . .'

Inside his soul, Pan grinned. The ability to cause sudden panic isn't the world's most useful skill; it's not like plumbing or carpet-laying, the sort of thing that'll always keep the wolf strictly confined to the downstairs rooms. But it surely gives you the edge when playing poker.

'You're not proposing,' he said coyly, 'that we play for money, are you?'

'Money?' Osiris looked at him. 'I didn't know you could.'

'I've heard that it's possible.'

'Gosh. I suppose you sort of bet on who's going to win each hand.'

'I suppose so. Want to give it a try?'

'Why not? Do you know how we go about it?'

'I expect we'll pick it up as we go along.'

Three hours later, Pan came to the conclusion that maybe he'd been a trifle injudicious. Given that he was immortal, and assuming that he managed to continue doing these lucrative voice-overs he'd just broken into right up till the scheduled destruction of the Earth, he'd probably be able to pay Osiris back eventually, provided he didn't get charged interest and went easy on the food and electricity.

'You've played this before,' he said.

'I learned recently,' Osiris replied. 'About six months ago. One of the nurses at the Home has a boyfriend who's a lorry driver. Apparently they spend a lot of time in transport cafés playing cards. We usually have a game or two every Friday evening while he's waiting for her shift to end.'

'I see. Do you think your godson's likely to be dead yet?'

Osiris glanced at his watch. 'I doubt it,' he said. 'There's this other game he's taught me if you'd like to try something else. I'm not *quite* sure of the rules, but—'

'No thanks.'

'Oh.' Osiris shrugged. 'Well, in that case we'd better settle up. I'd rather have cash, if it's all the same to you.'

Pan winced. 'To be absolutely frank with you,' he said, 'I'm just the teeniest bit strapped for cash at the moment. Would you mind if I, er, owed it to you. Just for a week or so, you understand . . .'

Osiris smiled pleasantly. 'I can do better than that,' he said. 'You do me a small favour and we'll call it quits. How does that sound?'

There was a deafening crash, and the air was suddenly full of broken glass.

All over the building, alarms should have gone off. Haifisch & Dieb had security systems that projected into several as yet undiscovered dimensions; so sophisticated were they that bells rang and lights flashed on monitor screens if a hostile philosopher started postulating that lawyers might not exist in a perfect universe. But even the most elaborate setup won't work if someone has been round snipping vital wires and stuffing socks in the mechanism at strategic places.

'Hi,' said Julian, not looking up. 'Take a seat, with you directly.'

Kurt Lundqvist let go of the rope on which he'd just abseiled in, and with an easy movement drew an enormous handgun from a huge shoulder holster. He levelled it at Julian's heart, and cleared his throat discreetly.

'Fifty-calibre Desert Eagle,' said Julian, apparently to the seventy-page lease open on his desk. 'What's wrong with the trusty old Glock, then?'

Lundqvist winced slightly. 'My new assistant,' he said. 'Goddamn woman will insist on tidying the place up. It'll turn up eventually.'

'Tsk.' Julian clicked his tongue sympathetically, drew a few squiggles on the page with a red felt-tip, and closed the lease. 'Good of you,' he said inevitably, 'to drop in.'

'I was just passing.'

'Sure. Now then.' Julian leaned back in his chair – it was the sort of chair that was designed to define its occupant, and it told you better than any words could that you were sitting on the wrong side of the desk – and steepled his fingers. 'I got a job for you,' he said.

'So I'd heard.'

'I think you're the right man for this job.'

'Thanks.'

'You come recommended.'

'Glad to hear it.'

Julian reached across the desktop and drew a file towards him. 'Highly recommended.' He opened the file, flicked through a couple of pages and nodded. 'You've been around a fair while, I see. Like, it was you who finally killed Dracula in 1876.'

'Yup.'

'And 1879. And 1902. And 1913.'

'You can't keep a good man down.'

'And 1927. But not since.'

Lundqvist shrugged. 'Actually, you can keep a good man down, just so long as you use a big enough stake. In this case, a telegraph pole.'

'Cool.'

'It worked.' He smiled faintly. 'First time, anyhow. Though

I hear they get some really bizarre wrong numbers in those parts even now. What is it you want done?'

Julian shrugged and turned a few more pages. 'Hey,' he said, 'this one you did a year or so back, that really was a bit out of the ordinary.' He tossed over a polaroid of a stunted green shape, vaguely humanoid but with a weird head and strange, long fingers. 'I thought he made it back to his own planet eventually. There was a film about it. Lots of kids with bicycles.'

Lundqvist said nothing, but shook his head. Julian suddenly felt ever so slightly unnerved.

'But he was kinda sweet, wasn't he?' he said.

'So what?'

'How did you find him, exactly? I thought he was well hidden, after the story broke.'

'I tapped his phone.'

'Figures.' Julian closed the file. 'Well, I want you to think of this job as the culmination of your extremely impressive career. Afterwards, of course, you'll have to retire. You'll never be able to work again.' He paused and smiled. 'Mind you, you'll never need to work again. The package I have in mind is extremely favourable.'

'Look.' Lundqvist leaned forward and stared at him across the desk. 'The only packages I know about go tick tick. Cut to the chase, okay?'

'Okay.' Julian folded his arms. 'I've got a god needs taking for a ride.'

'A god. I see. Any particular one?'

'Osiris. You know him?'

'By repute.' Lundqvist's eyes glowed. 'Any reason, or just general resentment about the Fall of Man?'

'My business,' said Julian quietly. He picked up the pen and fiddled with the cap. 'Let's say he's taking up space required for other purposes. And time, too.'

'Yeah?'

'Yeah.'

Lundqvist stood up. 'I ought to blow your fucking head off right now,' he said.

In a curved and infinite universe, everything has to happen eventually, somewhere. Julian stared. For the very first time he was at a loss for words.

'Now listen to me,' Lundqvist hissed. He reached out a hand and gathered a palmful of Julian's tie. 'Two points. One, gods are immortal. This makes them pretty damn difficult to kill. Not,' he added with a hint of pride, 'impossible. But difficult, certainly.'

'Not for you, surely.'

'That's beside the point.' Lundqvist tightened his grip on the tie. 'The second thing is, I don't kill gods. I'm the good guy, dammit. I'm on their side. I sort out the bad guys, that's what I do. Talking of which, the only thing standing between you and reincarnation under a flat stone is professional ethics.' Lundqvist grinned suddenly. 'And I wouldn't rely on that too much.'

'You'll be sorry.'

Lundqvist's face was white with rage. 'Hey, man,' he growled, 'I'd have thought you'd have known, threatening me is not wise. The last guy who threatened me is now an integral part of the Manhattan skyline.'

'No threat intended. All I meant was, you don't take the job, you don't get paid a very large sum of money. I'd be really sorry if I missed out on a chance like that.'

'Stuff your money,' Lundqvist replied. 'I got principles, okay?'

'Principles?' Julian raised an eyebrow. 'Kurt, for god's sake, you're a multiple murderer. Isn't it just a bit late . . .?'

Julian found himself hovering in the air about six inches away from his seat, with a square foot of his shirtfront twisted in Lundqvist's hand. 'I got principles,' he repeated. 'You touch a single hair on that god's head and you'll wish you'd never been born. Or rather,' he added, with a disconcerting grin, 'you'll wish you had been born. In vain, it goes without saying. You copy?'

'Save it for the customers, Kurt,' replied Julian, although he could have done with the air he used in doing so for other, more urgent purposes. 'How much? Name your own—'

'Fuck you.'

'Actually, I was thinking that money would be more appropriate. Still . . .'

Julian hit the back of his chair like a squash ball, and his head slumped forwards on to the desk. A splash of blood from the cut on his forehead fell on the lease, fortuitously blotting out an unfavourable rent review clause he'd previously overlooked.

'Am I to take that as a definite maybe?' he asked.

For a moment, Julian was convinced Lundqvist was going to kill him. The gun reappeared from under his arm – God, Julian thought, as he stared down the endless black tunnel of the muzzle, after a hard day's work that thing must smell *awful* – and there was a click as the hammer came back. But there was no bang; because Lundqvist was a professional, a high-class operator, and the golden rule of top specialists is: no free samples. A moment later, there was only a space where Lundqvist had been, and the wind blowing intrusively through the smashed window.

'Shit,' Julian mused aloud. 'Ah well, never mind.' He swivelled his chair round to the computer terminal on his desk, tapped a couple of keys and waited while the machine bleeped at him.

Ready.

Julian frowned. 'Ready what?' he said.

Sorry. Ready, sir.

'That's more like it. Right, do me a scan on the following wordgroup.'

He tapped again. The machine flickered, told him a lot of things he knew already about all rights being protected, and finally produced a column of names. The heading was:

International A-Z Compendium of Atheists

7

The visitor looked startled.

'Yes,' he replied. 'Of philosophy. What seems to be the problem?'

Lug elbowed the visitor tactfully in the ribs. 'Ignore her,' he whispered. 'She says that to everyone.' He started to tap his head meaningfully, caught Minerva's eye and tried to make it look as if he was scratching his head. The visitor ignored him.

'Will you take a look at my leg?' Minerva said. 'I keep asking to see the doctor but they never listen.'

'We really ought to be getting on, because we've got a lot to—'

'Certainly,' said the visitor. 'I shall be delighted to look at your leg, although it's a pity you didn't ask me six thousand years ago, before it got all wrinkled and yuk. Still, better late than never.'

'Really, you shouldn't encourage her, she can be a real—'

'Yes,' said the visitor, 'that's definitely a leg. I'd know one anywhere. It's the foot at the end I always look for. Mind you, who is to say that I'm not in fact an ostrich dreaming that I'm a doctor of philosophy looking at a leg? A very charming leg, it goes without saying, even now.'

A hand in the small of the back propelled the visitor out of the television room and into a small enclosure used for the storage of cleaning equipment. Lug closed the door.

'Since when have you been a doctor of philosophy?' he demanded.

'Not long,' Pan admitted. 'I saw one of these adverts in a magazine. You send them fifty dollars and they give you a degree. I could have been an emeritus professor, only they don't take credit cards.'

'Right. Look . . .'

'Chicopee Falls.'

Lug blinked. 'I'm sorry?'

'Chicopee Falls, Iowa. University of. If you're interested I can let you have the details.'

'No thank you,' said Lug firmly. It was, he decided, a bit like having a conversation with someone positioned twenty minutes in the future, with frequent interruptions from someone else five minutes ago in the past. 'Look, will you stop changing the subject? You're getting me all muddled up.'

'Sorry,' replied the god of Confusion. 'Force of habit. What can I do for you?'

Lug moved a dustpan and brush and sat down on the electrical floor-polisher. 'I don't know,' he replied. 'You came to see me, remember?'

'So I did.' Pan leaned on a vacuum cleaner and grinned. 'Got a message for you.'

'Oh yes?'

'From Osiris.'

Lug looked at him blankly. 'His room's just down the corridor from mine,' he said. 'Why can't he tell me himself?'

'Because,' Pan replied, idly unwinding the flex and tying knots in it, 'he's done a runner. Gone into hiding. Didn't you notice all the kerfuffle a few days ago, when those two doctors came to declare him insane?'

'Declare *him* insane?' Lug thought about it. 'It's a good point, though,' he added. 'I mean, if she asked them if they were doctors, they wouldn't find it odd at all. Sorry, I'm doing it now. Why were they trying to do that?'

'So that his loathsome godson could take over his powers and get at his money, he reckons.' Pan leaned down and buffed his nails on the polishing mop. 'Apparently, the godson's managed to get him to sign a power of attorney.'

'Sneaky.'

'Very.' Pan yawned. 'Anyhow, I'm here just to tell you so you won't be worried about him. That's about it, really.'

'Why me, though?'

Pan shrugged. 'No idea,' he said. 'But he was absolutely clear about it, you were the one I had to tell, so if you wouldn't mind just signing this receipt, I can be on my way.'

'Oh. Sure. Have you got a pen handy, by the way, because I think I've—'

Just then the door opened, and a small head the colour and shape of an acorn appeared round it.

'You doctor?' it asked. 'Doctor of phirosophy?'

Pan raised an eyebrow. 'Sorry?'

'Minerva say you doctor of phirosophy. Please, you take rook at soul for me? Soul not very good, maybe sick. You maybe give prescliption or something.'

'That's Confucius,' Lug whispered. 'He doesn't speak very good Eng—'

'I'd be delighted,' Pan replied. 'Now then, where does it hurt?'

The rest of Confucius followed his head into the room. 'Not hurt at all,' he replied, bowing from the hips. 'Maybe not exist at all. Plato he say—'

'Ah,' Pan replied. 'I think what you really need is a doctor of theology. Sounds more a theological job to me.'

'So. You know where I find doctor of theology?'

'It just so happens that I'm a doctor of theology. University of Chicopee Falls, Iowa, class of '87. Just go next door and take your id off and I'll be with you in a jiffy.'

As the door closed behind him, Lug frowned. 'Do you have to do that?' he asked. 'It's going to be a complete bloody shambles here for weeks now, you realise.'

'Sorry,' Pan replied. 'But I've got my Hypocritic Oath to think of.'

'You mean Hippocratic.'

'I know what I mean,' replied the Father of Misunderstandings. 'Now then, I've given you the message. Be sure not to tell *anyone*. You got that? Anyone at all.'

Lug blinked. 'If I'm not to tell anybody, why tell me?'

Pan got up, brushed himself off and winked. 'Don't ask me,' he replied, 'I'm only the messenger. Moving in a mysterious way just sort of goes with the territory, don't you find? Thank you for your time.'

Force of habit can be a tremendously powerful influence. Between the broom cupboard and the front door. Pan diagnosed three prolapsed souls, five ingrowing personalities (doctor of psychiatry, University of Chicopee Falls, Iowa; buy two, get one free) and a nasty case of entropy of the mind's eye. He got out of the building about thirty seconds ahead of the security guards and their ten-stone Rottweiler.

He was strolling back towards the bus stop when he realised that someone was following him. A mortal, female, young and, if you were in the habit of confusing quantity with quality, reasonably attractive. She was wearing a white overall thing and had a watch pinned to her front. He stopped until she'd caught up with him.

'Excuse me,' she said. 'Are you Pan?'

'Who wants to know?'

'I do.'

'That's all right, then. Only you can't be too careful these days.'

The girl frowned at him. 'I'm looking for Mr Osiris,' she said. 'Is he staying with you?'

'How did you find out?'

'He heard your voice on a telly commercial just before he left my house without saying where he was going,' replied the girl. 'When the commercial came on in the television room back at the Home, I asked around the residents to see if they knew whose the voice was, and they told me it was you. Then when somebody said Pan had just been in the place causing trouble—'

'Bloody cheek!'

'. . . I rushed out after you and here I am. Will you take me to see him?'

Pan considered for a moment. 'How do I know you're on his side?' he asked.

'If I wasn't, would I be asking you?'

'But you work at Sunnyvoyde, don't you? I don't think he's particularly keen to go back, you see.'

The girl smiled ruefully. 'Not any more I don't,' she said. 'I got sacked for helping him get away.'

'You must be Sandra.'

The girl nodded. 'He needs looking after,' she said. 'Don't get me wrong, I think he's awfully nice, but . . .'

'You think so?' Pan scowled. 'Let me give you a word of advice. If you're holding two pairs, kings and jacks, and he's sitting there with that befuddled look on his face as if he's trying to remember which century he's in, fold immediately. Better still, just play for matchsticks. Provided,' he added, 'you have the title deeds to a couple of rainforests tucked away somewhere. I can think of a lot of ways of describing your friend, and awfully nice is definitely on the B team reserve list.'

Sandra giggled. 'He's good at card games, isn't he? My boyfriend owes him ninety-seven million pounds, at the last count. And he only learned to play recently.'

'Beginner's luck, huh?'

'He's told you,' Sandra went on, 'what that nasty godson of his is trying to do to him?'

Pan nodded. 'Ingenious little sod,' he said. 'I forget now who it was thought up the idea of mortals in the first place, but they've got a lot to answer for. Present company excepted, of course.'

'You should try doing my job,' Sandra replied, nettled. 'Have you ever tried getting lightning stains off formica?'

'Oh, gods aren't perfect, I know,' Pan said hastily. 'But at least we don't—'

'Or clearing up after they've been playing Sardines? I hate to think what it must've been like when you lot were running things.'

Pan sighed. 'Pretty much like it is now,' he said, 'except your lot had someone definite to blame. Sometimes,' he added, 'I think that was all we were there for. It worked, too. The race that despises together rises together, I always say.'

'Here's the bus, look.'

'Oh good,' said Pan, patron deity of all those who couldn't organise piss-ups in breweries. 'Somehow I always feel at home on public transport.'

'We have to plan our next move,' said Osiris, 'very carefully.'

To the gods all things are possible, all things are known. Ask a god what's the quickest way to the post office and he'll be absolutely sure to know, even if he's never set eyes on the town in question. And Pan was a god (he had certificates to prove it; seventy-five dollars each or ninety-nine dollars fifty if you opt for the deluxe parchment-look display version). But how he came to be in a beat-up yellow van with a plump girl, a monolithic driver with spiky hair and an earring and the Son of Nuth, Opener of Ways, remained a mystery to him for ever.

'You can drop me off at the next traffic lights,' Pan said hopefully. 'Thanks for the lift.'

'Sorry, I need you to help me with a few things,' Osiris replied. 'You don't mind, do you?'

'I'd really have loved to help out, but . . .'

'I'll pay you.'

There was complete silence except for the sound of an old

van with a dicky exhaust going over a pothole.

'Actual money?'

'The currency of your choice.'

'How much?'

'How much did you have in mind?'

And Pan thought, Gosh. I could retire. I could pack it all in and buy a little place somewhere and stay in bed till gone eight o'clock in the morning. No more horrible poxy jobs just to pay the rent. No more Panicograms. No more promotional videos for fallout shelter manufacturers. No more jumping out of cakes at rich depressives' birthday parties.

'Count me in,' he said.

'Fine.' Osiris nodded. 'As I was saying, we have to plan our next move very carefully. Use our heads, that sort of thing.'

As he said the word, he looked at his companions. There was Carl, Sandra's boyfriend; six foot nine of mortal muscle, a man only too delighted to use his head if it involved breaking down doors or stunning opponents. There was Sandra herself; female, it had to be admitted, but her heart was in the right place, which was more than he could say for himself. And there was Pan. As for him; well, there are many legends concerning the genesis of the gods, but the version that Osiris gave the most credence to was the one where, on the eighth day, the Creator found Pan at the bottom of his packet of breakfast cereal. Put another way, Pan was the sort of god Mankind probably found it necessary to invent, if only by way of getting its own back. Still . . .

And there was him. Which made it all sort of all right. In a way.

'Our objective,' he went on, 'is to stop my godson Julian getting control of the Universe by having me certified and taking my place by virtue of a power of attorney. Agreed?'

'Can we stop at the next service station?' Sandra contributed. 'I knew I shouldn't have had that last cup of tea before we—'

'In other words,' Osiris said, 'we're up against a lawyer. A really clever, unscrupulous, dishonest, conniving lawyer. Now, who do you think we ought to go to for help?'

Silence again.

'Anybody got any ideas?'

Pan shifted in his seat. 'Let's get this straight,' he said. 'You're asking us who we think is likely to prove a match for this ultimate legal vulture godson of yours, somebody who can play him at his own game and win?'

'That's right.'

'If you want my initial reaction,' Pan replied, 'might I ask if the expression "a hiding to nothing" is at all familiar to you?'

'Excuse me.'

For a moment Osiris was bewildered, and looked round the van to see who was the amateur ventriloquist. Then he realised. Carl had said something.

'Go on,' he said.

'How about we get a better lawyer?'

'Don't be so ...' Osiris stopped himself from finishing the sentence. To the gods all things are known; except, apparently, the bleeding obvious.

'Good idea,' he said feebly. 'Yes, I was wondering who was going to be the first to—'

'Cos a better lawyer, right, he'd be able to run rings round this other lawyer. Stands to reason.'

'Is there a better lawyer?' Sandra interrupted. 'I thought your Julian was the best there is.'

'Rubbish.' Pan blew on the window and started to draw a smily face in the condensation. 'He's just another mortal, right? You get an immortal lawyer, and Julian won't know what hit him. Well, not what hit him first, anyway. I expect the second, third and fourth time he'll be saying, Hello, godpapa.'

'An immortal lawyer,' Osiris mused. 'You know of one, do you?'

Pan laughed. 'Sure,' he replied. 'Of course, he doesn't *call* himself a lawyer, too much self-respect, but to all intents and purposes that's what he is.'

'Oh.' Osiris came from a culture whose written language consisted of hieroglyphic picture writing, and so the thought that crossed his mind at this point was little-sketch-of-a-light-bulb-being-switched-on. 'Oh, *him*. Yes, that's very good. I think we're actually getting somewhere at last.'

'Who are you talking about?' Sandra asked.

Pan grinned. 'He has many names,' he said.

'What, you mean like Sanderson, Linklater, Foot and Edwards? Lawyers are funny like that, aren't they?'

'No,' Pan replied wearily. 'I mean, different people know him by a lot of different names, but in fact he's the same person.'

'The same as who?'

'Himself, of course.'

'He's the same as himself. I see.'

Pan gave Sandra a long look, assessing her as a potential apprentice. There was definitely raw natural talent there.

'He's one bloke,' he said slowly, 'but he's known by different names to different people. Got that?'

'I really would like it if we stopped somewhere soon, because—'

'All *right*.'

The van changed lanes and took the next exit, signposted to the Pinfold Gap Service Area. The occupants got out and Sandra sprinted off, leaving Osiris in his wheelchair between Pan and Carl. A few seconds later, a big Japanese four-wheel-drive with tinted windows purred in and parked just behind the van.

'Where are we?' Osiris asked.

'I dunno,' Pan replied. 'Godforsaken place, wherever it is.' He looked down at the wheelchair. 'In a manner of speaking, that is. I thought you knew where we were going.'

Osiris shrugged. 'Away was the general idea when we

started off. Now we know where we're going, it might be a good idea to get the map out and plan a route.'

Pan shook his head. 'I wouldn't worry about it,' he said. 'Where we're going is dead easy to get to, wherever you start from.'

'But you know a short cut, I suppose.'

'Only in my professional capacity,' Pan replied. 'I know short cuts to everywhere for business purposes, goes without saying.'

Osiris nodded. 'We'll take a look at the map,' he said.

The door of the four-wheel-drive opened slowly, and its driver climbed down and came up behind the three of them, walking with practised stealth. He was holding something dark and shiny down by his side.

'Osiris,' said Pan quietly. 'Don't look round, but I've got a feeling . . .'

'Freeze!'

'Thought so.'

Behind them, Kurt Lundqvist levelled his gun. 'You in the chair,' he said, 'roll forward five paces. You other two, turn slowly round.'

Pan swallowed. He was, of course, immortal and invulnerable. He also wanted to stay that way, and a good working definition of immortal is someone who hasn't died *yet*. He raised his hands.

'Has he got a gun?'

'How should I know?' Osiris replied in a loud whisper. 'I haven't got eyes in the back of my head, you know. I did once, mind,' he added. 'That was the day she forgot to put her lenses in.'

'Shut it,' Lundqvist snapped. 'You two, hands on your heads. Quickly.'

They did as they were told.

'Okay.' Lundqvist took a good look at them over the sights of the Desert Eagle. 'Now then. Are you two guys doctors?'

*

Many years ago, when the world was so young that parts of its rocky skeleton were still soft and flexible, Pan had been to the first of a series of evening classes on Coping With Stress. By the end of the evening he was so tense with frustration and rage that he had to see a physiotherapist, but elements of the recommended procedures still lingered down in the back of the sofa of his mind.

Relax, he told himself. Make a conscious effort to loosen the muscles of the back, neck and chest. Take a long, slow, deep breath. Smile.

'A doctor of what?' he asked.

'Medicine,' Lundqvist replied. 'And keep your goddamn hands where I can see them, okay?'

Hang on, Pan said to himself, I know that voice. He turned his head slightly, just enough to get a splendid view down the barrel of the gun.

'Kurt,' he ventured, 'is that you?'

'Yes,' Lundqvist admitted. 'Now answer the question.'

'Not,' Pan replied, 'of medicine. Look, Kurt, it's me, Pan. Stop waving that bloody thing about, will you, because you're giving me bad vibes, and I can get all of them I want at trade discount.'

'How about him?' Lundqvist said. 'He looks like a doctor to me.'

'Well he isn't,' Pan snarled. 'And what would you know, anyway? The only doctors you come across tend to be arriving as you leave.'

'All right,' Lundqvist said, lowering the hammer and putting the gun reluctantly away. 'You can put your hands down now, but no . . .'

Osiris turned round and scowled, giving Lundqvist the impression that he'd just arrived in the next life only to find he'd spent the last sixty years devoutly worshipping the wrong god. 'Who is this idiot?' Osiris asked.

Pan grinned. 'Meet Kurt Lundqvist,' he said. 'He kills people. Well, people is pushing it a bit, I suppose. Things would be nearer the mark.'

'Does he really,' Osiris said. 'How interesting. We have a name for that where I come from.'

'Yeah?' Lundqvist tried a sneer, but his reserves of bravado were down to barrel-bottom level. 'And where's that, exactly?'

Osiris grinned, and pointed.

'Kurt,' said Pan quickly, 'I'd like you to meet Osiris. He's a god. I think it'd be a really good idea if you two could somehow start again from scratch, because—'

'I was hired to kill you,' Lundqvist said.

'Were you, now? What an interesting life you've led so far. Which,' he added, 'is probably just as well.'

'Yes.' Lundqvist nodded. 'I refused. First time I ever turned down a commission.'

'How extremely sensible of you.'

'And,' Lundqvist continued, scrabbling about for a few vestigial threads of the initiative, 'I came to warn you.'

Osiris raised an eyebrow and looked at Pan, who was staring fixedly at the petrol pumps in an effort to convey the impression that he was somewhere else. 'Warn me of what?' Osiris asked.

'There's two doctors looking for you, to certify you as insane. So, when I saw you with two suspicious-looking characters . . .'

'Wasn't that thoughtful,' Pan said quickly, realising as he did so that he was well up in the running for Asinine Remark of the Aeon, burning off 'peace in our time' and close on the heels of 'when I grow up, I want to be a lawyer'. 'Don't you think that was a thoughtful thing to do?'

'Very,' Osiris said. 'You seem to know this idiot from somewhere.'

'Sure,' Pan said. 'We go way back, Kurt and me. Why don't we all go and have a . . .?'

There was a chunky, solid sort of a noise, and Lundqvist slowly toppled forward and fell on his nose. Behind where he had been standing was Sandra, holding a brick.

'Oh marvellous,' Pan said. 'Look, grab his legs and let's go and have a coffee. We'll all feel much better with a nice hot drink inside us.'

Mrs Henderson narrowed her eyes, until it was hard to imagine any but the most anorexic of photons scriggling its way through to her retina.

'Won't do it?' she said. 'How very strange. You did offer him money?'

Julian nodded impatiently and would have said something sarcastic had he not foolishly got in the way of Mrs Henderson's eye. She made him feel uncomfortable. Sure, he still knew deep down that he was the only possible candidate for Senior Partner of the World, but something at the back of his mind was telling him that, nevertheless, his hair was uncombed and his socks smelled.

'A great deal of money?'

'A very great deal of money,' said Julian, with feeling. 'More than I earn in a month.'

'How very odd.'

Julian got up and walked to the window. From Mrs Henderson's office, you could see all the kingdoms of the earth on a clear day. 'Not that it matters,' he said. 'There are more ways of killing a cat.'

Although he had his back to Mrs Henderson, he could feel death rays on the back of his collar, and realised that he'd said the wrong thing. Of course, Mrs Henderson kept cats. Probably three of them, with matching names. Meeny, Miny and Mo would be a fair bet. And they'd have their own little baskets and their own little saucers with their names on, and birthdays and favourite chairs with smelly old blankets on them; and anybody crazy enough to kick one of Mrs

Henderson's cats was definitely not long for this world, and very likely on dubious ground for the next.

'More ways,' he said, 'of sorting out our problem than the obvious one,' he therefore said. 'How come,' he added, without looking round, 'my godfather owns this place, anyway?'

Mrs Henderson shrugged. 'I needed some capital,' she said, 'he wanted somewhere to retire to. At the time it seemed a perfectly sensible arrangement. And it has been, too, until lately.'

Julian sat down on the window-seat and gazed out over the cloud-meadows, marking them off in his mind's eye into a grid plan of building plots. 'So what happened to change your mind?' he asked.

'Well.' Mrs Henderson paused for a moment, marshalling her thoughts. 'I suppose you could say there's been a lot of latent friction between us for some time. Your godfather has, well, ideas about how this establishment should be run. I have my own ideas. They are the correct ones. I have devoted a lot of time, energy and money to this project, and I have no intention of seeing it come to nothing.'

A twinkle of light appeared in Julian's mind. 'You want to raise the fees,' he said.

'Among other things, yes.'

'And he wasn't happy with that?'

'Correct.'

Wow, Julian thought. For that, she's prepared to murder a god. He turned slowly round and looked at her, dispassionately. Yes, she would have made one hell of a lawyer.

'Of course,' she went on, 'this wilfulness on his part suggests most strongly to me that your poor godfather is, let's say, a wee bit confused in his mind these days, perhaps not quite up to looking after his business affairs. It's for that reason I really would welcome his being examined by a doctor. For his own good, of course. But if he won't co-operate, then really, perhaps the euthanasia approach might well be the kindest thing.'

'For his own good.'

'The welfare of the residents is, naturally, my one and only consideration.' She smiled. 'All the residents, naturally.'

'Naturally.'

When I am master of the universe, Julian memorandised to himself, Mrs Henderson's permanent welfare will be one of my first considerations. It would be a positive pleasure devising something that would be in her best interests, ideally with nine dozen six-inch nails playing a prominent role.

'Anyway,' he said, wrenching his mind back from this agreeable digression. 'If he's disappeared, so much the better. All we need is for him to stay disappeared for the prescribed period of time and we can legally presume that he's dead. That ought to be—'

'But he's a god,' Mrs Henderson interrupted. 'Surely—'

'So?' Julian grinned. 'Everybody is equal in the eyes of the law, remember. And the law says that someone who can't be traced after a certain period of time is legally dead. End of problem.'

'And if he does turn up within the time?'

'Easy. We get him certified. It's what we in the legal profession call Catch-44.'

'I see.' Mrs Henderson rubbed her nose with the knuckle of her left forefinger. 'And meanwhile?'

'Meanwhile,' Julian said, 'I hold his power of attorney.' He sat down opposite her and crossed his legs. 'Exactly what level of fee increase had you in mind?'

'Let me get you some tea,' said Mrs Henderson.

8

To get from the Pinfold Gap Service Area to the Garden of the Hesperides, you can follow one of two routes: the easy, long way, or the quick, difficult one.

'Turn off here,' Osiris said. 'We haven't got all day.'

The easy, long way is overland to Folkestone, ferry to Ostend, through Germany and Austria to what used to be called Pomerania, then turn right and on down through Armenia to the Caucasus, follow your nose and you're there. When you find yourself falling over backwards trying to see the tops of the mountains, you know you've arrived. There's even a chair-lift to the top, although it's not a hundred per cent reliable; it was installed in 1906 and the only maintenance they've got around to doing is one coat of paint on the railings at the bottom and a dab of grease on the ratchet once every change of General Secretary.

'Are you sure you—?'

''Course I'm sure,' Osiris replied. 'I've got the map, haven't I?'

The other way is overland to Greater Pinfold, leave the van in the car park opposite the church, scramble three quarters of the way up Pinfold Fell to the small cave that very few people know about, and summon a demon, using the handy implements provided. The demon then does the rest. In theory.

'Wouldn't it have been simpler,' Sandra interrupted, 'just to phone his office and make an appointment?'

The two gods and Kurt Lundqvist looked at her.

'Well?' she said.

'No,' Pan replied.

'Why not?'

'For one thing,' Pan said, 'he hasn't got an office. For another, he's not on the phone. For a third, he doesn't keep appointments. Satisfied?'

Sandra frowned. 'Funny sort of a lawyer,' she said. Pan shook his head.

'Not in context,' he replied. 'You wait and see.'

'Oh.' Sandra thought for a moment. 'So what exactly do you have to do if you want to see him, then?'

Osiris and Pan looked at each other. 'It's a long story.' Pan said.

'I expect we've got time.'

There was a rumbling from the driver's seat. It could have been thunder in a tin-panelled canyon, or Sandra's boyfriend talking.

'Signpost,' he said. 'Greater Pinfold, half.'

It took two divine brains a comparatively long time to work out that he meant half a mile. 'That's fine,' Osiris said. 'Once we're in the village, go along the main street and then just keep heading uphill. You can't miss it.'

'Why hasn't he got an office?'

The two gods exchanged glances and then turned to Lundqvist, who was occupying the time in honing the edge on his Sykes-Fairbairn combat knife on the sole of his boot.

'You explain it,' they said.

'Me?'

'Yes.'

'All right, then.'

The gods, Lundqvist explained, created the first man and the first woman.

Their motives for doing so are lost in the mists of comparative religion, and speculation is now probably futile. The most convincing explanation is that at the time they were destruct-testing the maxim 'everybody makes mistakes'.

The first man was called Epimetheus, and the first woman was called Pandora. Contrary to what the scientists would have you believe, neither of them was four feet tall, hairy, stooped and equipped with a jaw like a snowplough; although Epimetheus did have a mole on his nose and Pandora's black hair had a grey wave running across it from the moment she came to life, the result of Athene neglecting to wait till the paint was completely dry.

And there they were, just the two of them; and it occurred to the gods that, apart from comprising a complete set of first editions, they weren't much use for anything.

'They're not *supposed* to be any use for anything,' Athene replied, when this point was drawn to her attention. 'They're just supposed to *be*. They're,' she added, 'the meaning of the universe.'

The other eleven gods looked at her.

'Man,' she said, looking away, 'is the measure of all things.'

'Come again?'

'Man,' said Athene, 'defines the cosmos. Man is the independent life force, entirely separate from the Creator and possessed of free will, who by the very act of observing causes all things to exist, simply by virtue of being susceptible of objective observation.'

There was a short pause.

'Fair enough,' said Vulcan, god of fire, metal and (in due course) cordless screwdrivers. 'So what's the other one for?'

Venus, goddess of love, frowned, wrinkling her lovely nose. 'Which one do you mean?' she said, and sneezed. She had just been created herself from the sea-spray crashing against the rocks of Paphos, and towelling robes and electric hair-dryers were still several giant conceptual leaps away in the future.

'The shorter one with the round bits sticking out,' Vulcan

replied. 'By the way, is it meant to look like that, or did you take it out of the oven too early?'

'Easy,' Athene replied. 'She tells Man what to do.'

There was another silence, marred only by the distant groaning of tectonic plates and the grating sound of Time running in.

'I thought you said he's got free will,' said Mars, god of war.

'Sure.' Athene turned round slowly and gave him a long, cool stare. 'And he freely decides to do what he's told. If he knows what's good for him, that is.'

'Ah. Right. Yes, that sounds pretty logical to me,' said Mars, briefly usurping Athene's prerogative as goddess of wisdom. 'So, do we cut a tape or break a bottle of wine or something, or is that it?'

'That's it for now,' Athene said. 'We just let them get on with it.'

'With what, Thene?'

Athene gave her new sister a glance of disapproval. 'Venus,' she said, 'I think you and I need to have a little talk.'

To begin with, there were the inevitable minor glitches. For one thing, Venus completely misunderstood Athene's whispered explanation of her new duties, with the result that Mars spent the first few days of human history dragging the first humans off each other before they gouged each other's eyes out; while Vulcan rather shamefacedly admitted that while installing the digestive system and associated plumbing he'd had the blueprints upside down and read the scale as inches rather than centimetres. It was, however, too late to do anything about that now, and fortuitously the system as installed did actually work, just about.

It wasn't until much later that the real design faults began to show up.

Apollo, god of the sun, was the first to notice; and for a day or so he was inclined to ignore his misgivings. It was too improbable for words. Surely not . . .

But no. He was right. He was going to have to tell the others.

'Cheerful little sods, aren't they?' he therefore observed casually over dinner. 'I mean, to look at them, you wouldn't think they had a care in the world.'

He reached for the salt, and in doing so became aware of eleven pairs of eyes fixed on him.

'Cheerful?' Mars said.

'That's the way it looked to me,' Apollo replied, a slightly defensive tone creeping into his voice. 'Of course I could be wrong. Probably am. But . . .'

'Of course they aren't cheerful,' Athene replied quickly. 'They can't be, they're mortals. Creatures of a day. Out, out, brief candle. Don't say silly things like that, Pol, or you'll upset people.'

Nevertheless, first thing the next day, Athene crept out of Heaven by the back door and hurried down to Earth. Disguising herself as a clothes moth (an inept disguise, since there were as yet no clothes, but she was flustered) she buzzed through the lazy summer air and hovered for a while outside the mouth of the cave where the mortals had taken to cowering during the hours of darkness.

Inside, she could hear giggling.

Not, she had to admit, an auspicious start; but it was probably just a freak occurrence. Any minute now they'd start snivelling and bemoaning their lot, like they were supposed to do. She spread her wings and, since she was missing breakfast, spent a thoughtful quarter of an hour in a mimosa bush.

When she returned, the first thing she noticed was a smell. A delicious smell. So enchanting was it that before she knew what she was doing she'd flown straight into the bole of a tree and knocked herself silly.

It was the smell of cooking; to be precise, mushrooms and fried tomatoes.

The gods, it should be explained, ate their food raw and drank rainwater. After all, when you're immortal the risk of catching some fatal disease from raw food is minimal; and since there's no way a god can die of starvation, meals were in any case little more than a ritual observance designed to while away half an hour of endless, all-the-shops-are-shut-and-it's-raining Eternity.

Nothing but salad for the rest of Time. Small wonder that the gods were all as miserable as sin; small wonder, too, that they regarded this as the proper state of affairs. Happiness wasn't a concept they could easily get their heads around.

Athene uncrumpled her wings, adjusted a bent antenna and took off. Something would have to be done about this.

About a week later, Epimetheus and Pandora were just waking up from a nice lie-in and wondering whether to breakfast on plantain fried in honey or glazed eggplant with cinnamon when there was a knock at the cavemouth. They looked at each other.

'Visitors,' said Epimetheus.

'Oh *goody*,' replied his wife. 'Just think, Ep, our first guests! Isn't this wonderful?'

'Rather,' said our common ancestor, jumping up and running to the cavemouth. 'Gosh, life's fun.'

Outside the cave stood a tall figure in a blue uniform, with a peaked cap. There was, Epimetheus subconsciously noticed, a strange, almost unfinished look about him; almost as if he'd been called into being by someone who had a vague idea of what he should look like, but insufficient detailed knowledge to complete the job. Epimetheus couldn't help feeling that, viewed from the back, he wouldn't be visible.

'Sign here,' said the man.

'Certainly. How do I do that, exactly?'

The man showed him, and Epimetheus followed suit enthusiastically, until the man took the pen and clipboard away from him. Then he handed him a parcel.

It was big, and chunky, and it rattled excitingly when you shook it. It also said *Do Not Open This Parcel* on the label in big red letters, and if Epimetheus hadn't been so completely carried away with the delirious excitement of it all, he might have wondered how the hell he could read the writing, bearing in mind the fact that he was only sixteen days old and writing hadn't been invented yet.

'Hey, what are we supposed to do with this?' he asked the man, except that the man wasn't there any more. He shrugged, grinned with pleasure and took the parcel back into the cave.

Seven minutes later, of course, they'd opened the parcel.

'What is it?' Pandora asked.

Epimetheus shrugged again. 'Hang on,' he said, 'there's writing on the side here.'

'What's writing?'

'This is.'

'How absolutely wonderful.'

The writing said:

Congratulations! You have been chosen as a lucky winner in our special grand gala free-to-enter Prize Draw!!

   Please accept this wonderful alarm clock radio (batteries not included) as your special introductory gift, absolutely free!

   All you have to do to be allowed to keep your wonderful new free gift is to select six items of your choice from the enclosed catalogue, crammed with exciting special offers chosen with you in mind, and let us have your order plus your cheque within seven working days. So hurry!

'Gosh,' said Pandora, after a long pause. 'What's a catalogue?'

'This is, I suppose,' Epimetheus replied, lifting a thick glossy book out of the carton. He flicked a couple of pages and whistled. 'Hey,' he whispered, 'you wait till you see what's in here!'

The very next day, the order arrived: an electric blender

(plug not supplied), a video recorder, a washing machine, a power drill, a microwave oven and an exercise bicycle. And, tucked in with the packaging, an invoice for three thousand, six hundred and thirty dollars, ninety-five cents (including delivery and packaging).

By the afternoon of that day, there was a certain coolness in the atmosphere at the cave. Epimetheus, if asked to account for it, would have explained by saying that Pandora had cracked the jug on the blender, jammed the washing machine and broken the exercise bicycle by over-vigorous use. Pandora's version would have been that Epimetheus had made a complete mess of wiring up the plugs and plumbing in the washing machine, with the result that all the appliances had blown themselves up and the floor of the cave was an inch deep in suds and soapy water. In addition, there had been a degree of asperity in the discussion as to who was going to pay the bill.

It occurred to neither of them to ask where the electricity supply and the mains water had come from; partly because they were innocents living in the first dawn of the Golden Age, but mostly because they were too busy arguing over whose fault it was that Epimetheus had used the electric drill to drill slap bang through the middle of a power cable; after which, anything to do with the electricity supply was pretty well academic.

The next morning they overslept (the alarm clock radio didn't work, because (a) Epimetheus had put the batteries in the wrong way, or (b) because Pandora had set it up all wrong, despite Epimetheus' totally lucid explanation of how to do it). What finally woke them was the sound of the bailiffs breaking in to repossess the blender, the video recorder, the washing machine, the microwave, the power drill and the exercise bicycle.

This led, inevitably, to a free and frank exchange of views on the subject of budget management, impulse buying and some people who were so mean that other people couldn't be expected to live with them one minute longer; which was in turn interrupted by the arrival of the men from the electricity company to disconnect the supply for non-payment of the bill.

By nightfall, the cave was empty. Pandora and Epimetheus had moved to smaller, damper caves at opposite ends of the mountain and were corresponding bitterly by carrier pigeon over who was to get the alarm clock radio.

As the argument raged, and the air vibrated with the clatter of hurrying wings, something moved at the bottom of the original box, out of which the free gift had come. It stirred. It blinked. Feebly, it spread stunted wings and lifted itself into the air.

In their excitement, Pandora and Epimetheus had over-looked the little creature; that slow, patient, long-suffering stowaway in the box of troubles. It didn't mind. It suffered long. Painfully stiff after its long confinement, it fluttered away towards Pandora's cave with its message of hope.

As you will have guessed, the little creature's name was Litigation, friend to all wretched mortals who have suffered wrongs and been oppressed. Next morning, when it perched on the rock outside Epimetheus' hovel and handed him a writ, it had somehow grown slightly larger and maybe even a touch fatter; but it had deep, grey eyes that seemed to say, Trust me.

By the time it arrived back at Pandora's cave, bearing a counter-writ, it was the size of an ostrich and virtually spherical, and its soft velvety paws had been replaced by whacking great talons. By then, of course, it was ever so slightly too late.

Lundqvist didn't put it quite like that, of course; his account was rather more pithy. But that, more or less, was the basic outline.

9

'Italy?' Odin asked, smiling. 'What on earth makes you think that?'

Below them, the traction engine ran smoothly, purring across the sky like an enormous flying cat. It had been Thor who'd fixed it eventually, and in doing so proved yet again the validity of his theory of simple mechanics; namely that, just because something's inanimate and incapable of perception doesn't mean to say it can't be scared shitless by being threatened with a whacking big hammer.

'Well, for a start,' Frey replied, 'the place is full of Italians.'

Odin shook his head in gentle scorn. 'It's a well known fact,' he said, 'that there's a substantial emigré Italian population in the north of England. More a Yorkshire phenomenon than Derbyshire, I'd always understood, but obviously you came across an enclave . . .'

'A whole townful?'

'They like to stick together.'

'Escorting a statue of the Madonna through the streets to a Romanesque cathedral?'

'Probably nineteenth-century Gothic.'

'Past a town sign saying *Bienvenuto in Bolzano*?'

'Twin town scheme. Very popular idea these days, twinning. Never had it in our day, of course. Nearest we ever got was, we burn your crops, you throw decaying corpses in our water supply.'

Thor, propped on one elbow on the roof of the cabin, snarled irritably. 'You'd better be right, sunshine,' he said. 'Because if this is Italy, then we're a long way from home, and the further we are, the later it'll be before we get back, and the likelier it is that She'll have noticed we've gone. And you know what that means.'

'Are you suggesting that I'm frightened of Mrs Henderson?'

'Yes.'

'Rubbish.'

Frey shifted uneasily in his seat. 'If it helps at all,' he murmured, 'I'm absolutely terrified of Mrs Henderson.'

'Huh.' Odin sniffed. 'I always reckoned you had a yellow streak in you.'

Frey stiffened. True, he wasn't the most warlike of the Norse gods; he was, after all, a god of peace and fruitfulness, of nature and the quickening earth; or, as his devotees had put it back in the good old days, a wimp. True, in the Last Days, when the Aesir had ridden forth for the last battle with the Frost-Trolls, it had been Frey who'd volunteered to stay inside Valhalla and man the switchboard and co-ordinate supply chains and monitor intelligence reports and all the other things one can find to do indoors in time of war. But these things are relative; and even a wimpish Norse god is on average rather more quick-tempered and volatile than a barful of marines at closing time on pay day. 'What was that,' he enquired, 'you just said?'

'I don't know about you two,' Thor interrupted, 'but I'm scared of her. And so are both of you, if you get right down to it.'

Odin shrugged. 'All right,' he said, 'and so am I, but that's beside the point. We're on our way home, and she'll never even know we've been gone, and that's a promise.'

'Is it?'

'Yes.'

'I was afraid you'd say that.'

'We're exactly on course,' Odin continued icily. 'Another three minutes and we'll be directly over Warrington.'

A look of recollected pain crossed Frey's face. 'It's the way she draws her eyebrows together just before she tells you off that gets me,' he said. 'As soon as you see those eyebrows move you say to yourself, Right, here it comes, but there's like this sort of twenty-second gap, and it's the waiting that gets you down. I'll swear she practises in front of the mirror or something.'

'And the tone of voice,' Thor replied. 'Don't forget the tone of voice. The way she says, "What *do* you think you're doing, exactly?" It makes you feel so . . .'

'I know.'

'Will you two stop going on about Mrs blasted Henderson?'

Thor shook his head, and looked down over the side at the ground below. It was at times like this, when he found himself gazing down from the heights upon the kingdoms of men, spread out beneath him like some enormous chessboard, that he felt an overpowering urge to drop something heavy over the side. He resisted it.

'So what's that lot down there, then?' he asked.

'Which lot where?'

'The major city with all the suburbs and arterial roads and things.'

So high up was the chariot that all a mortal would have seen was a splash of grey, flickering intermittently through the veil of thin cloud. But the gods can see things which we cannot; not with their eyes but with their minds, which thrill to the subtlest harmonies of the planet. With their minds they can see Time, smell light, hear the grinding of the Earth on its axis, feel the vibrations of the changing seasons. Thus, from this height, a god would have no trouble at all making out the Coliseum, the Forum, the Baths of Caracalla, Trajan's Column, St Peter's Square, all the crazy cross-hatched jumble of junk and jewels that make up the Eternal City.

'Easy,' said Odin, throttling back and gently feathering the airbrake. 'That's Droitwich.'

Ever since the world began, there has been a windswept hillside under an iron-grey sky where three grey women sit beneath a bent tree and spin.

What name you give them depends on who you are; but you can never be wrong, whatever name you choose, simply because what mortals call them is completely and utterly unimportant. Whether you refer to them as Parcae, Norns or Weird Sisters, nothing you can say or do will affect them in the slightest degree, because they were here first. More to the point, they will still be here long after you, and everyone else, have been entirely forgotten.

They sit, and they spin. Some people will have you believe that they are asleep, and in their sleep they dream, and their dreams are thoughts and their thoughts supply the world with wisdom. Others claim that what they spin is the web of life; its warp, its weft and the final little dismissive click of the scissors. The truth, insofar as such a concept has any validity in this context, is that they sit, and they spin, and occasionally speak softly to one another, just as they have always done, and what you may care to believe is your own affair entirely.

'I spy with my little eye' – they have no names, but let them be labelled One, Two and Three – 'something beginning with O.'

For a time they were called Graeae, and it was held that between the three of them they had one eye, one ear and one tooth, which they passed from hand to hand. This is almost certainly untrue.

'Outcrop.'

'Correct. Your go.'

'I spy with my, sorry *our* little eye something beginning with . . .'

'Hang on, I've still got the ear,' said Two. 'Here, Elsie, catch.'

'She's dropped it.'

'She couldn't see, because you've got the eye.'

'That's right, it's all my fault, as usual.'

'Where is it?' asked Three, scrabbling in the short, wiry grass with her gnarled fingers.

'Left hand down a bit, steady as you go, getting warmer.'

'She can't hear you.'

'Oh for crying out loud.'

Their sleep is dreaming, their dreaming is contemplation, their contemplation is eternal bitter resentment about who forgot to pack the spare organs. 'Got it,' said Three, 'no thanks to you two.' It is perhaps unfortunate that the only organ they have in triplicate is tongues.

'Ready?'

'Ready.'

'I spy with our little eye something beginning with R.'

'Ravine.'

'Correct. Give Betty the ear, Elsie, and do please try not to drop it.'

'I like that coming from you.'

One of the drawbacks that comes with playing I Spy for at least five hours each day in the same place ever since the beginning of Time is that you reach a point where you know all the answers.

'Mountainside,' said Two.

Three scowled. 'You might wait till I actually ask the question.'

'It's the right answer, isn't it?'

'That's beside the point.'

'Oh for pity's sake,' said One, 'let's play something else.'

'All right.'

What is undoubtedly true is that they are wise. All the wisdom in the Universe has at one time or another made the circuit of that little ring before drifting out into other, more prosaic dimensions. This means that the Three are very powerful, very wise and . . .

'Name me three rivers whose names begin with Y.'

'Yangtze-kiang, Yarra and Yellow.'

. . . Very, very bored.

'Let's play something else instead,' sighed Two. 'What about consequences?'

'No.'

'Why not?'

'Because,' replied Three, 'you cheat.'

The ear flashed from hand to hand, until it became a blur. The eye, meanwhile, lipread.

'I do not.'

'You do.'

'It's impossible to cheat at Consequences.'

'You seem to manage.'

'You two,' growled One. 'Just shut up and spin, all right?'

They sat, and they span, and Time ran round the circle. Time running in an enclosed circuit generates Truth. Truth sparking across the points of Knowledge becomes Wisdom.

'We could,' suggested Two, 'play Twenty Questions.'

'Are you out of your mind? After last time?'

'What?'

'I said, are you out of your mind, after last time.'

'What?'

'She's gone and dropped the ear again.'

'We ought,' opined One, 'to tie a bit of string to it, and then we wouldn't have any of this—'

'What?'

'Oh forget it.'

On the skyline, about seven hundred yards away, a tatty yellow van materialised and crawled painfully over the rocky ground. There was the occasional scrunge as some component or other hit a stone.

'There they are,' said Osiris, pointing. 'You see them, Carl? Just under that funny-shaped tree.'

'I got that, Mr Osiris. I think we just lost the exhaust.'

Pan closed his eyes. 'Look,' he said, 'are you absolutely sure about this, because those three old boilers really get up my nose.'

'Absolutely essential,' Osiris replied. 'Here, Carl, watch out for that—'

'Sorry, Mr Osiris.'

'It doesn't matter.'

Pan winced. 'You sure,' he said, 'we couldn't just look him up in the phone book or something? I mean, we haven't actually tried that, have we?'

'Shut up, Pan, there's a good lad. Right, park here and we'll walk the rest of the way.'

Under the tree, the three sisters stiffened, the web suddenly still in their hands.

'Visitors,' observed Two with disgust.

'Not again,' One sighed. 'That makes three times this century. What does it take to get a little peace and quiet around here?'

'What's she saying?'

'I said—'

'She's dropped it *again*.'

'One of these days,' remarked Two, after a short scrabble, 'it's going to go in the cauldron and get cooked, and then where'll we be, I should like to know.'

Folklore abounds with different versions of how to approach the sisters and implore their assistance. All known versions are completely incompatible with each other, except that all agree that the sisters must be treated with the very greatest respect. Failure to observe this simple precaution will inevitably mean that any request for information will fall on deaf ear (even if the ear hasn't rolled away under a stone or taken refuge in the lid of the sewing box), and there are rumoured to be even worse consequences as well.

'Wotcher,' Osiris called out. 'Hands up which of you's got the ear.'

'Who wants to know, shortarse?'

Osiris cleared his throat. The next bit always made him feel terribly self-conscious.

'Look,' he said, I conjure you by the dread waters of Styx, you who know all that is, all that was and all that will be. Tell me now—'

'I can't hear you,' said One, putting on her irascible crone voice. 'You'll have to speak up.'

Pan leaned forward, grabbed the ear from One's withered hand and held it to his lips like a microphone.

'He said,' he shouted, 'he conjures you, lots of stuff about how clever you are, and he wants to ask you something. Got that?'

The three sisters sat for a while, waiting for the ringing inside their skulls to stop.

'There is no need,' said One frostily, 'to shout.'

'Sorry?'

'I said, there's no need to—'

'Sorry?'

'What did she say?'

Pan grinned. 'SHE SAID THERE'S NO NEED TO SHOUT,' he said, and tossed the ear towards Three, who fumbled the catch. There was a plop as the ear went in the big black pot that stood in the middle of the circle. The sisters shrieked in chorus.

'Butterfingers,' said Pan. 'Now then . . .'

Sandra darted forward, plucked the ear out of the soup, picked a few lentils and split peas out of the funnel-shaped bit and handed it carefully to One.

'Thank you,' she said. 'All right, fire away.'

Somewhere near the French-Belgian border, a giant Mercedes

lorry thundered south-westwards through the night. Swiftly it went on its sixteen wheels, and its iron belly safeguarded a consignment of two thousand cases of tinned prunes.

The driver, a Breton, stared with weary eyes into the cone of white light his headlamps projected and whistled a tune to keep himself awake. It had been a long day and he had many miles to go, but the magnitude of his enterprise stirred in him a sense of adventure he hadn't felt since he was a lad. For there was a serious shortage of prunes in France, so the rumours said, and it was mildly flattering to be chosen to be the man who brought the canned fruit from Ghent to Aix.

As he approached the border, he braced himself for a potentially tiresome passage through customs. You didn't need too exceptional an imagination to forecast the reaction of a bored excise official to the information that the cargo aboard the truck consisted of half a million prunes. There would be funny remarks, and witticisms, doubtless at his expense; and at three in the morning after a long drive, he could do without that sort of thing, thank you very much.

So preoccupied was he with these and other similar thoughts that he didn't notice the fact that he seemed to have acquired a shadow, in the form of a big, black, four-wheel drive with tinted windows.

The first he knew about this vehicle, in fact, was when he came round a sharp bend to find the road blocked by a tractor. He slammed on his brakes and slithered to a halt; whereupon three shadowy figures jumped out of the four-wheel drive, ran up to the driver's door and pulled it open. Something metallic sparkled in the pale light of the stars.

'Just climb out slowly,' said a shadowy figure in abysmally accented French, 'and you won't get hurt. Okay?'

The driver nodded quickly. 'Fine,' he said. 'You do know what I'm carrying, don't you?'

'Shut up.'

'Okay.'

(By pure coincidence, another identical lorry owned by the same road freight company was carrying a load of twelve million cigarettes along the same route, only about three quarters of an hour behind. Because of the prune famine, the schedules had been rearranged somewhat.)

Shortly afterwards, the lorry continued its journey, with a different driver, and headed for a different destination; namely a deserted hockey field on the outskirts of Cambrai. On arrival, it was driven into a big shed, and the doors closed behind it. Lights came on, and men hurried to the tailgate to start unloading.

The gate opened.

'Hang on,' said a voice from inside the container body. 'This isn't right, surely.'

The speaker, when fixed in a spotlight, turned out to be a white-haired old gentleman in a wheelchair. He was flanked by a plump girl, a large, stocky man with an expression like bad amateur taxidermy, a tall, thin man in camouflage gear holding a very large handgun and an even taller, thinner character with goat's feet.

Slowly, the hijackers backed away. Even those of them who could stomach the sight of Lundqvist's Desert Eagle felt distinct bad vibes from the expression in the old man's eyes and the curious terminals of Pan's legs. In the version they'd heard, it had been an old lady with an axe in her shopping-basket, but this was clearly an updated rescension of the same basic urban folkmyth.

'Sorry about this,' Pan called out. 'Only, we needed a lift, you see, and there was your lorry, and we thought . . .'

There was a shot. Maybe it was fear, or perhaps just a nervous finger tightening reflexively on a trigger. The bullet hit Pan in the forehead, passed out the back of his head as if through thin air and buried itself in the mountain of boxes behind. Brown juice started to seep through the cardboard.

Then there were more shots – Lundqvist giving area fire

with the .50 calibre, which made a noise like a portable indoor volcano and took out most of the lights. The hijackers responded in kind. There were suddenly prunes everywhere.

'Stop it,' said Osiris briskly, 'at once.'

Simultaneously, every firing pin in the building jammed solid, and the lights came back on. This time, however, they were supported by unpleasantly-shaped figures with the heads of jackals; and for all their brilliance they seemed to produce more shadows than light. The hijackers came forward.

'Now then,' Osiris said. 'Someone tell me where we are.'

The gang leader, nudged forward by his colleagues, unravelled six inches of tongue from round his Adam's apple and explained. He also apologised profusely, expressed extreme regret for having inconvenienced such obviously distinguished supernatural persons, and asked if they would very kindly care to turn the prunes back into Marlboro Hundreds, as he had a customer waiting.

'Oh no you don't,' Osiris replied. 'We've got to get to Aix by morning, and you're going to take us there. Otherwise,' he added with a pleasant smile, 'something around here's going to get turned into cigarettes, but it sure ain't going to be the prunes. Kapisch?'

The journey was resumed. This time, however, the chief hijacker travelled inside the container, with the muzzle of Lundqvist's gun nestling in his ear and Carl standing behind him with a tyre iron.

'Going far?' the hijacker asked.

Osiris grinned. 'You could say that,' he replied. 'I don't think you'd want to know where we're headed, really I don't.'

'That's fine,' the hijacker replied quickly. 'Only making conversation.'

'But I'm going to tell you anyway,' Osiris replied maliciously. 'That way, either you'll tell someone else, and they'll lock you up in a loony bin for the rest of your life, or else you'll keep it to yourself and probably go stark staring mad anyway. Serve you right. We're gods.'

'You don't say.'

'And,' Osiris went on, 'we're headed for the Kingdom of Death, if it's still there. Last time I heard, they were trying to turn it into some sort of ghastly drive-in theme park, but I don't suppose they ever got the planning permission. I mean, imagine the problems you'd have with off-street parking.'

'Indeed.' To those whom the gods wish to destroy, they first give pins and needles in the left foot. The hijacker rubbed his leg against the side of the van, but it didn't help much.

'We need to go there,' Osiris went on, 'because the Three Wise Women told us that in order to locate the last hiding place of the Golden Teeth of El Dorado (which, as you know, lie at the world's end and are guarded by an enormous fire-breathing, hundred-headed answering machine) we have to find and read the Runes of Power chalked on the wall in the little boy's room immediately adjacent. That's what they said, anyway,' Osiris concluded. 'It's not April the First today, by any chance?'

'You certainly have an unusual job,' said the hijacker. 'Did you always want to be a god or did you just sort of drift into it?'

'We need the Golden Teeth,' Osiris went on, 'in order to pay our lawyer. That's just something on account, by the way, to cover initial expenses, setting up the file on the computer, routine administrative work, that sort of thing. He's very expensive, even for a lawyer.'

'He must be very good, though.'

'Oh he is. Very.'

10

'If this is Droitwich,' muttered Thor, 'they've definitely been fiddling about with it since I was last here.'

'And when was that, then?'

'1036.'

'Well, there you are, then.' Odin stood on the extreme edge of the kerb, wavering. Being omniscient, he knew all about cars; and besides, he'd seen them often enough on the telly. It was just that, en masse, thundering past like some stampeding herd of square steel cattle, they seemed a trifle, well, unnerving. Or would do, if he was a mere mortal. And there is, of course, this wretched convention that when gods walk abroad among mortals, they have to blend in. If it wasn't for that, of course . . .

'Get a move on, will you?' Thor grumbled at his elbow. 'We haven't got all day, you know.'

'Shut up,' Odin replied. 'We can't just go charging through the traffic and have all the cars bouncing off us, it'd be too conspicuous. We've got to wait for those little coloured lights to come on.'

'What, those ones up there on that stick?'

'That's the ones.'

'And that's what mortals do, is it?'

'Yes.'

'It's a funny old world,' Thor said. 'And so we've got to do like they do?'

Odin nodded. 'When in Rome,' he said.

At his other elbow, Frey made a face. 'Odd you should say that,' he said.

It hadn't been Odin's fault. Admittedly, it was the inner valve ring seal gasket that had blown, and it had been Odin who'd fitted it, and because you just couldn't get the parts for these older models nowadays it had been Odin who'd gamshacked up a substitute out of brown paper and treacle. But the brown paper and treacle gaskets of the immortal gods are by definition more lasting than diamonds, and in Odin's opinion there was no way it should have blown if the inlet manifold had been properly set up in the first place. They were now looking for a car parts store, Odin having a hunch that the gaskets off a 1991 Leyland Roadrunner would probably do the trick at a pinch.

'How do you mean, Frey?'

'I think we are.'

Odin scowled. 'What's he on about now, Thor?' he demanded. 'Because if this is some sort of wind-up you two are making up between you, I'm really not in the mood.'

Thor, who had been conferring with his colleague, shrugged. 'Sorry,' he said. 'Our mistake. Of course this is Droitwich.'

'Thank you.'

'And that ...' Thor pointed to their left. 'That must have been the Droitwich Coliseum we went past just now, and those must be the Baths of Alderman Wilkinson, and that big square building over there is probably the world famous Temple of the Engineering, Municipal and Allied Trades.'

'And what about that over there?'

'Where?'

Frey pointed towards the forbidding gateway in front of them, with its curiously garbed attendants.

'Oh that,' Thor said. 'I think that's the Catholic church.'

Enormous lorry thundering its way through the Provencal night. Exhausted driver blinking hazily through a fly-splattered windscreen. One step out of line would guarantee that he spent the rest of his life on a lily-pad.

Round a hairpin bend, to find a tractor standing right across the road. Marvellous new fifth-generation air brakes pull the rig up short before the two vehicles combine together in a Jackson Pollock of twisted metal.

If he'd been looking in his rear-view mirror, instead of sprawling over the dashboard with a gearlever up his right sleeve, he'd have seen a dark green four-wheel drive with tinted windows purr up behind the tailgate.

His door is jerked open. He looks down into the muzzle of a big black handgun.

'Okay,' hissed the masked man behind it. 'Do as I say and you won't get—'

The driver blinked twice. 'You what?' he said.

'Do as I say,' replied the hijacker, irritably, in abysmal French, 'and you won't get hurt.' He scowled. 'Trust me,' he added, 'I'm a doctor. Really.'

'I don't believe this.'

'Straight up. That's a nasty cut you've got on your forehead, by the way.'

'Must be where my head hit the wheel.'

'You should get that seen to. Any dizziness, nausea, double vision?'

'I don't think so. I've got this migraine coming, I think.'

'No spots in front of the eyes?'

'No.'

'Take two aspirin,' said the hijacker, 'get a good night's sleep and we'll see how you are in the morning. Meanwhile,' he added, 'get out of the cab before I blow your fucking brains out.'

'Yes, doctor.'

Shortly afterwards, the lorry continued on its journey, with a new driver. If it was supposed to be going to Aix-en-Provence, it was going the wrong way.

*

'All right,' said the customs official sleepily, 'what've you got in there?'

The driver leant out of the window. 'You're going to laugh when I tell you,' he said.

Out of wind-scoured, sleepless eyes the customs official glowered at him. 'I don't think so,' he said. 'Come on, where's your bill of lading?'

The man in the passenger seat rummaged about in the glove box, and handed down a packet of papers. The customs official sighed.

'Fine,' he said. 'Prunes. Okay, you two out and let's see inside.'

There was a brief flurry of conversation inside the cab.

'Hang on,' said the driver. 'Diplomatic thingummy.'

'I beg your pardon?'

'Immunity,' the driver said. 'Just a tick, here we are, passports. And this lot here's a diplomatic bag, okay?'

'Get real, will you? It's a bloody juggernaut.'

'Ah.' The driver nodded. 'Diplomatic juggernaut, though, innit? You want an international incident, be my guest.'

There was a moment's silence.

'You're absolutely sure,' said the customs official, 'that it's prunes you got in there?'

'Absolutely,' replied the passenger. 'Look at it this way. Would we say it was prunes if it wasn't?'

The customs official thought about it. The argument had a certain specious attraction. Tractor spares, yes. Engine parts, certainly. Any time a customs official sees Engine parts on a manifest, he ducks for cover and calls up the bomb disposal guys on the radio. But prunes . . .

'No armaments, then? Drugs, illicit diamonds, rare species?'

'Not as far as I know, officer.'

'Pirate radio equipment? Dutiable goods such as alcohol,

perfume or tobacco? Works of art requiring an export licence?'

'Don't think so. Are you feeling all right, by the way?'

The customs official raised an eyebrow. ''Course,' he said; and then, catching the driver's eye, added, 'Or at least I think . . .'

'You look a bit under the weather to me,' said the driver, putting his head on one side and pursing his lips, 'if you don't mind me saying so.'

'Oddly enough,' said the customs official, 'just lately I've been getting these sharp stabbing pains round about here . . .'

'Been eating regularly?'

'Not very regularly, no . . .' the customs official looked up. 'Why?' he demanded.

'We're doctors,' the passenger explained. 'Any heartburn or related symptoms?'

'Not that I'd noticed.'

'Headache?'

'Can't say I have.'

'Sure?'

'Positive.'

The driver looked up and down the road. At this time of night, they had the place to themselves. There was nobody else to be seen in the customs post. Accordingly, he swung open the door of the lorry, dealing the customs official a sharp blow just above the ear. The customs official, predictably, fell over.

'Laymen,' the driver called out, putting in the clutch and pulling away. 'What do they know? And when you wake up, take two aspirins.'

The Swiss guard hesitated, his mind scrolling back through recent memories. He'd seen something, just subliminally, for a fraction of a second; but there had been an anomaly – an abomination, even. Something had been where there should be nothing. He stood for a moment, like a statue representing

Contemplation on some baroque triumphal arch; then he remembered, and sprang into action. Just as he'd thought.

Down by the side of the sentry box, four-fifths hidden in the shadows, was an empty crisp packet. He snatched it up, marched over to the receptacle provided, and binned it. Another blow struck, he congratulated himself, against the forces of entropy.

Prompted by this thought, he reviewed his position in the cosmos, and saw that it was good. Only three months since he'd left his Alpine canton and joined the standing army of the Papal State, and already he was standing guard at the gates of the Vatican. All right, yes, the goods entrance of the Vatican, which was pretty much like goods entrances anywhere, but only if viewed superficially. I had rather be a goods entrance keeper in the house of the Lord than dwell in the tents of the ungodly.

Then the ground started to shake. Instinctively, his hands tightened on the shaft of his halberd; but a glare of white light and the low roar of massive engines reassured him. Just a lorry.

A lorry. At three o'clock in the morning. What could it be, he asked himself. And, in due course, the driver.

'Prunes.'

'Prunes?'

'That's right. Now if you'd just open the damn gates, we can unload this lot and I can go to bed, all right?'

The guard narrowed his eyes. 'Prunes?' he said.

The driver leant out of the window and manoeuvred his head until the tip of his nose was but a few microns from the guard's forehead. 'Look,' he said, 'prunes it is, and if you want to go and get the Big Fella out of his pit and ask him what he wants six million dried plums for, then jolly good luck to you and send me a postcard from Hell. Otherwise, open this flaming gate before we all die of old age.'

'Yes, but *prunes.*'

A few seconds before the driver would otherwise have put his foot down on the throttle and crashed the gate, the passenger leant across, smiled placidly, and said, 'Perhaps I can explain, my son,' he added.

'Gosh,' said the guard, stepping backwards and standing stiffly to attention. 'I didn't see you there, Your Reverence.'

'No matter.' The passenger removed the cardinal's hat and put it on the seat beside him. 'The Holy Father's compliments,' he said, 'and may we please proceed?'

'Of course, Your Reverence. Only . . .'

'Yes?'

'Prunes, Father. It just seems . . .'

'Yes?'

'Just a moment and I'll do the gates for you.'

Monsignor Donatus O'Rourke did up the last buckle on his crimson flak jacket, muttered a final Hail Mary, and drew back the plunger of the syringe, flooding the chamber with holy water. His bell jingled faintly in its shoulder holster.

'Okay, lads,' he growled into his walkie-talkie, 'this is it. Don't screw up, and let's go for it.'

Mgr O'Rourke was no back-street exorcist; he was a pro, from the tips of his asbestos gloves and ring with built-in geiger-counter to the toes of his rubber boots. People called him a mercenary, a theologian of fortune, have bell, will travel; he laughed in their faces. Whenever he did a job, he knew he was doing it for the Big Guy, in the way that he knew was right, even if the redhats round the Curule Chair had declared his methods anathema. The substantial sums of money that found their way to his Swiss account he regarded simply as contributions to the war chest. Fighting the old gods with the new technology wasn't cheap, and he'd long since learnt not to expect any funding from Holy Mother church (or, as he preferred to think of it, the Organisation). As a result, he had to do business with some pretty dubious characters, who he suspected were motivated by concerns not one hundred per cent connected with the struggle against the forces of darkness. So what? As he'd said in his evidence to the Walinski Commission, he knew that what he was doing was right, and if he had to raise his own funds in order to do it, that's the way the eucharist crumbles. Not, of course, that he'd ever even considered selling holy water to the Shi'ites as the yellow press had alleged; but even if he had, his conscience would still be clear.

His men – all hand-picked, the flower of the priesthood – should all be in position by now. He turned to the man crouched beside him, and said, 'Well?'

The man, who was a doctor by profession, nodded. 'What are we waiting for?' he said.

'Okay,' replied Mgr O'Rourke. 'Let's nuke some spooks. Go, men!'

On his command, three priests in black balaclavas abseiled down from the balcony above, landing with pinpoint precision beside the tailgate of the lorry. From their backpacks they unslung heavy black chainsaws. A second or so later, the night was torn by the sound of steel on iron.

'Second wave into position,' Mgr O'Rourke barked into the walkie-talkie. 'This is it, guys. Remember Joppa!'

Twelve priests with reeking censers scuttled out from the shadows and hit the deck, pineal glands pumping, brains clamouring, What on earth does he mean, remember Joppa? As soon as they were in place, the second section scrambled forward, dragging behind them an enormous sled-mounted bell.

'Nice work,' snapped the Monsignor. 'Red Section stand by, and – *candles*.'

On all four sides of the courtyard, enormous spotlights snapped on, drenching the ancient stones with photons. At precisely the same moment, the chainsaws screamed through the last few millimetres of the tailgate, which fell out into the courtyard with a tinny clang. The censers, launched with unerring aim, sailed through the air into the back of the lorry, filling the confined space with thick billows of scented smoke. The bell boomed.

'Doing good, guys,' O'Rourke muttered. 'Now, in there with the book, and . . .'

His lips froze. Damn. Damn. There's always something, isn't there?

'Listen up, guys,' he said, as casually as he could. 'Anybody out there got a spare bible?'

Inside the body of the lorry, the situation wasn't good. By the time Osiris had recovered from the effects of an unexpected lungful of incense and had tumbled to what was going on, it had almost been too late. Absolute chaos, he reflected, absolutely typical. Still, what the hell do you expect from a generation that believes that the Earth revolves around the sun?

He rallied his forces, which had been reduced to a manageable size by a snatch squad of PVC-cassocked priests who had knocked out Kurt Lundqvist with a weighted crucifix and whisked him away. Admittedly, the man had been trying to help; but elbow room inside the lorry had been limited at the best of times, and Lundqvist rolling around firing his gun and lobbing stun grenades had taken up rather more of it than his net usefulness warranted. Someone would no doubt get him back in due course. When the time was right.

'Carl,' he shouted. 'Fetch a tyre iron.'

'This,' Pan coughed, fanning incense out of his eyes, 'is ludicrous. Why don't we just turn them all into woodlice and be done with it?'

Osiris shook his head. 'A bit out of touch, aren't we?' he said. 'No can do, ever since we all signed the Ravenna Convention.'

Pan blinked. 'The what?'

'The Ravenna Convention.' Osiris ducked to avoid a hand-thrown rosary. 'Part of the handover deal when we packed it all in. Basically it says that the Christian mob can push us about all they like and we can do bugger all about it.'

'You're kidding!'

'Wasn't my idea,' Osiris replied. He reached up, caught a censer in mid-flight and threw it back. 'It was the Roman lot, I seem to remember, always quarrelling among themselves, reckoned they needed some sort of peace-keeping force once they retired, to stop them cutting each other's throats in the TV room and shoving laxatives in the Sanatogen.' He gave Pan a meaningful look.

'Nothing to do with me,' Pan replied. 'Never heard of it, in fact. Certainly never signed anything.' His face brightened. 'Which means, surely, I can change them into anything I like and nobody can touch me for it.'

'You,' Osiris replied, 'no. Me, yes. If you so much as transform a hair of their heads, then I'm mythology. But not,' he added grimly, 'before I turn you into a sewer god. Understood?'

'You wouldn't?'

'It's a dirty, rotten job,' Osiris replied, 'but someone's got to do it.'

'Fine.' Pan sighed. 'So what are we going to do now?'

'That's what I need the tyre iron for. Thanks, Carl. Break open those crates, will you?'

'Can I help?' Sandra, who had spent the last ten minutes sleeping peacefully after a direct hit on the side of the head from a hassock, crawled to the wheel-arch and crouched down behind a crate. It was at times like this, she felt, when the battle is raging all around and the menfolk are battling desperately for mere survival, that you wish you'd brought your knitting.

'I expect so,' Osiris replied. 'When did you last eat anything?'

Sandra considered. 'I had a packet of crisps on the ferry,' she replied, 'and a Mars bar and an apple a couple of hours after that. I'm famished,' she added.

'Fine,' said Osiris, as Carl reduced the nearest packing case to matchwood with a well-aimed blow of the tyre iron. 'Have a prune.'

'Bless me, Father, for I have sinned.'

From behind the curtain there was a faint snap, as the priest lit a Lucky Strike. 'Yeah, sure,' he said wearily. 'Okay, let's hear it. And what trivial misdemeanour is bothering us today?'

'Um.' The penitent hesitated. 'Well, I missed confession yesterday.'

'Big deal.' The priest yawned. 'You didn't have anything to confess, right? C'mon, you must be able to do better than that.'

'Well ...' There was a pause, during which the priest drew down a lungful of smoke and coughed savagely. 'I also harboured uncharitable thoughts about Brother Justinian.'

'You harboured uncharitable thoughts against Brother Justinian.'

'Yes.'

'That's it?'

'Well, yes. I suppose so.'

'You guys, you make me want to puke, you know that? Sins? You don't know sins from *nothing*. Where I come from, now, we could teach you wimps a thing or two about sinning.'

'Er ...'

'Where I come from ...' the priest paused, hawked mightily and spat, ringing a spittoon somewhere on his side of the curtain like a gigantic gong. 'Where I come from,' he continued, 'we wouldn't give you the snot from our noses for anything less than a double aggravated rape. And you come hassling me with goddamn uncharitable thoughts. Get outa here, will you?'

There was a long, puzzled silence; then the penitent said, 'Shall I say three Hail Marys?'

'Hey.' The priest clicked his tongue. 'I get this feeling,' he said, 'that you're gonna say them no matter what I tell you, so basically yeah, go for it, do your karma. Now get ... Jesus H. Christ, man, what was *that*?'

As the shock waves of the tremor died away, the priest ripped aside the curtains of the confessional and sprinted away down the cloister towards the presumed source of the noise, scattering popcorn as he went.

About thirty seconds later he turned a corner into the small courtyard by the goods entrance and stopped dead in his tracks, as if he'd just run straight into a transparent breeze-block wall.

'Holy shit!' he whispered. Not entirely without justification.

He saw, in the eerie glow of blue flares and bright white floods, a lorry in the middle of the yard, ringed by monks crouched down behind such cover as they could find. From the back of the van emanated a succession of scintillating and extremely colourful sparks and forks of lightning, which arced and buzzed their way round the yard before earthing themselves back into the van. By way of return fire, the monks were lobbing in smoking censers, lighted candles and handbells. Two rather more worldly figures on an adjoining balcony were blazing away with automatic pistols, although to no perceptible effect. There was a stifling odour of sanctity and sulphur; and, from inside the lorry, audible even above the sundry bangs and crashes, the sound of steadily chomping jaws, punctuated by the occasional rending belch.

'Hey,' breathed the priest, as the penitent scurried up and ducked down beside him, 'this is *real*, you know? Sure, back home you don't go out the vestry door without your can of Mace and your shiv, but this is something else, you know?' He laughed for sheer joy. 'Man,' he breathed, 'this is better than *Ghostbusters*.'

Two monks wheeled in a supermarket trolley laden with the biggest bible the penitent had ever seen, under cover of three Augustinian canons with perspex riot shields. A particularly flamboyant sparkle whizzed through the air, splattered against a shield, and dissolved into a floral tribute of green and orange cinders. Two monks ran up and doused the flames.

'Support group,' crackled a bullhorn, 'deploy the holy water cannon. Come on, guys, move it.'

A platform of monks darted off into the shadows and returned with one of the Papal fork-lifts from the goods entrance (painted bright yellow and emblazoned with *In hic signo vinces* stencilled on the wings). On the forks was an enormous contraption like an outsize fire extinguisher, out of which led a hundred yards of black rubber hose. Two of the monks contrived to tangle their feet in it and fall over. A pale lilac sparkle soared through the air in a graceful parabola and lit on the roof of the forklift, which promptly vanished from sight in a retina-engraving flurry of colours.

'C'mon, guys, this is sloppy,' snorted the bullhorn. 'Blue section, give cover. Purple section, deploy the book.'

With cries of 'Geronimo!', 'Yee-haaah!' and 'Blessed be the name of St Teresa of Avila, whose day this is', parties of monks wheeled the trolley forward under the cover of huge asbestos screens. All around, handbells clanged, candles flared. It was, the priest remarked to the penitent, like Bloody Septuagesima all over again.

Inside the lorry, the atmosphere was tense; and, of course, thick as cream cheese with incense from the censers. Pan, with a handkerchief over his face and a barricade of smashed crates affording some slight cover, was shooting coloured lightning from his fingertips and doing his best to dodge flying handbells at the same time. Behind him, Osiris, Sandra and Carl huddled round a heap of empty tins and chewed grimly.

'That's it,' Sandra groaned through a full mouth, 'I can't eat another one, I'm sorry. You'll just have to leave me.'

Osiris said nothing – his mouth was stuffed so full his lips could scarcely meet – but instead grabbed a can, slit the top off with his thumbnail and thrust it at her. She winced and took it.

They were eating prunes.

And, of course, spitting out the stones into an upended crate, which by now was three-quarters full. The floor of the lorry was six inches deep in empty tins, and there was syrup everywhere.

'Are you jokers nearly done?' Pan yelled over his shoulder. 'There's no way I can keep this up for much longer.'

'Tinker, tailor, soldier . . .'

'Stay with it,' Osiris mumbled back. 'Just a few more dozen should do it, if only you can . . .'

'. . . Sailor, rich man, poor man . . .'

Osiris turned his head and stared. 'Carl,' he said. 'Just what do you think you're doing?'

'Beggarman,' replied Carl, looking up. 'Eating prunes, like you said. Thief.'

'Yes, fine, but what's all this soldier sailor stuff? Have you gone completely—?'

'It's what you say when you eat prunes.'

'Is it? Why?'

'Dunno.' Carl considered for a moment, his jaws moving. 'Brings you luck, I s'pose.'

'Does it?'

'It's s'posed to, I s'pose.'

Osiris thought about it. 'Oh well,' he said, 'can't do any harm, I guess. Chartered surveyor, inspector of taxes, research physicist . . .' He paused, ejected a mouthful of stones into the crate, and wiped a torrent of juice off his chin. 'Management consultant, systems co-ordinator . . .'

'It's a shame,' Sandra observed, 'there isn't any custard. My mum always does lots of hot custard with prunes.'

'Computer software designer, trainee account executive, there, that'll have to do.' Osiris spat out the last few stones, took a deep breath and drew the crate towards him. 'Right,' he said. 'This is what—'

'Builder, milkman, postman, bookie's runner . . .'

'This is what we have to do.'

*

The monks had finally succeeded in manhandling the trolley with the book in it right up to the tailgate of the lorry. Not without heavy losses: seven of their number were ambling aimlessly round the courtyard clothed from head to foot in bright blue fire, bumping into corners and singing quietly to themselves. Another dozen lay on their backs on the flagstones, glowing alarmingly and giggling at the moon.

'Okay, you're doing great, guys,' rasped the bullhorn. 'On my command, open the book.'

And then there was a horrible moment as the whole courtyard seemed to fill with a bright green flare, as handfuls of prunestones flew out of the lorry into the air. A split second later they came down, rattling on the flags, bouncing and skittering. And there they lay.

A monk, who was on fatigues for a week for dropping a loaded chalice on the sergeant-major's foot, stared at the stones and whimpered. Bloody tourists, he thought, who exactly do they think is going to have to sweep that lot up?

Crack.

One prunestone, which had chanced to fall into a shallow pool of fizzing blue light, twitched sharply. Out of one side a tiny green shoot nuzzled its way out, groped with a tendril and touched down on the courtyard floor. A second later, it wasn't alone.

'Come *on*,' Osiris muttered under his breath. 'What the hell's keeping you?'

It all happened in a fraction of a second. There was a fusillade of tiny cracks, a scurrying of prunestone shells, a filthy smell . . .

. . . And then there was a forest. All the prunestones were suddenly sprouting. Like the fingers of a martyr to rheumatism their roots clawed a couple of times at the flags, scratched a few times at the surface, and thrust a taproot down through the stones and into the bowels of the earth. The trees grew.

When they were all twenty feet high, Osiris tapped Carl on the shoulder . . .

('Farmer, painter and decorator, handyman. Um . . .')

. . . pulled him to his feet and shouted in his ear. Carl nodded, grabbed Sandra by the hand and hauled her after him out of the lorry into . . .

Indeed. Into the forest.

Forest was, by now, the only apposite word for it. True, it was made up of nothing but plum trees (Victorias) and it didn't actually cover very much ground, but it was quite definitely a forest. What it lacked in the horizontal axis was more than adequately compensated for by the sky-scraping height of the vertical.

'It seems to be working,' Osiris said. His face was green, and he kept swallowing hard. 'That's splendid. Now then, somebody give me a push and we'll get out of here.'

The wood – to be precise, the sacred grove – was still going strong. A snatch squad of monks who had been trying to sneak into the lorry through the front passenger door were suddenly smothered in long, leathery twigs, shaken violently, and hurled backwards into the middle of the yard. No prizes for guessing whose side the timber was on.

'That's the trouble with this business sometimes,' observed one of the two doctors to his companion, as they watched the plum forest below them explode into blossom. 'Sometimes, you just can't see the wood for the . . .'

The rest of the sentence was drowned out by the crash of falling masonry. A handful of prunestones had chanced to fly through an open window, and now there were large holes in the walls, with plum-laden branches sticking out through them. A task force of monks with strimmers and electric hedge-trimmers were fighting a desperate rearguard action to save the auxiliary paraffin store.

There was a crash, as of a sash being thrown up. Mgr O'Rourke froze in the act of lobbing a chasuble and glanced up, to see an open window and an all too familiar form silhouetted in the frame. It was wearing purple silk pyjamas.

'You there,' boomed a voice from the window, 'keep the noise down. There's people up here trying to sleep.'

'Yes,' muttered Osiris, 'point taken. All I can say is, it seemed like a good idea at the time.'

'Did it?' Pan frowned at him. 'There was a time, then, when you thought it'd be a really spiffing wheeze to hem us in with an impenetrable grove of supernatural plum trees. Fine. Any similar ideas about how we're going to get out of here?'

'Look, I said—'

'And,' Pan continued, making the most of what was for him a unique opportunity to tell someone so instead of being told so by somebody else, 'any further brainwaves about how we're going to slip past all those loony monks and priests and so on once we've managed to get out of here? Or didn't you want to spoil the spontaneous excitement of it all?'

Osiris scowled at him. 'That'll do,' he said. 'There's no need to get all amusing about it. We'll just have to apply our minds a bit, that's all.'

'Maybe,' Sandra suggested, 'they'll get bored and go away.'

'That's what you reckon, is it?' Pan demanded. 'They'll eventually wander off to watch the flying pigs, or something. Well, you never know, do you. Or perhaps the sky will fall on their heads. Perhaps,' he went on, making the most of it while it lasted, 'the gods will come and rescue us. You know, *deus ex machina*, all that sort of caper.'

'Now calm down,' Osiris interrupted sharply. 'We're in enough of a hole already without you indulging in flights of fancy.'

'Flights of fancy what?'

Osiris was about to answer this with a homily on the childishness of low-grade irony when the sky darkened, the earth began to shake, and a loud crack of thunder made his teeth vibrate in his head. He looked up.

'No, we are *not* going to crash,' retorted Odin testily. 'I fixed the locknuts myself, everything is entirely under . . .'

The engine crashed.

There was silence, apart from the death-rattle of the engine as it feebly spun a flywheel or so. A few of the riper plums fell from the tree and splatted on the rear mudguard.

'. . . Control.'

'We seem,' Frey remarked, hauling himself out from under a fallen branch, 'to have landed in some sort of a forest. Odd, that.'

'Quite.'

'A forest in the middle of Droitwich.'

Odin's head popped up from inside the cab. He was covered in oil, and his spectacles lay at a crazy slant across the bridge of his nose. 'Probably a park or a picnic area,' he said. 'Look, shin up that tree there and see if you can spot something like goalposts or a bandstand, something we can navigate by.'

'Must I?' Frey gave him a troubled look. 'Come on, Odin, you know about me and heights, I get vertigo standing on tiptoe. Can't someone else do it?'

'Leave it to me,' Thor grumbled. He knelt down, tucked his socks inside his boots and laid a hand on the nearest treetrunk. 'I'm going up now,' he said. 'I may be gone for some time. If I'm not back in half an hour, bloody well come and find me, okay?'

'Okay. Oh, Thor . . .'

'Yes?'

'Before you go . . .'

'Yes?'

'Have one of these plums, they're not at all bad.'

With a bad grace, Thor started to climb the tree. Odin, meanwhile, was studying the AA book of town centre plans. Frey had found a rather squashed, almost two-dimensional banana and was eating it.

After a less than flawless climb – the tree was designed more for aesthetic and horticultural purposes than ease of ascent – Thor reached the top. He rested for a moment, then shaded his eyes with his hand and looked out. And saw . . .

'Hey, you two!'

'Well?'

'You'll never guess what I can see.'

'What?'

'I said, you'll never guess.'

'I wasn't,' said Frey, through a mouthful of banana, 'proposing to try. Are you going to tell us, or are we going to have to wait for your collected letters and diaries?'

'I think,' said Thor, 'we're actually inside the Vatican.'

Frey glanced up. 'Nah,' he said. 'I read a book about it once, the decor's all wrong. For a start, it's not the right ceiling.'

'Yes, but . . .'

'The ceiling in the Vatican,' Frey continued obliviously, 'is sort of wide and covered in these paintings. I never heard anything about plain navy blue ceilings with tiny white dots.'

'Listen . . .'

'Very famous, the Vatican ceiling,' Frey went on. 'There's this really famous picture of the two electricians wiring something up, only they've obviously not earthed it properly, because where one geezer is handing something to the other one – probably a screwdriver or a pair of tinsnips – there's this big flash and sparks running up and down the guys' arms. I think it's one of those public information posters, something like Increasing Safety in the Home.'

'I meant to say,' said Thor patiently, 'inside the Vatican grounds.'

'What makes you think that?'

'Divine intuition.'

'Oh.' Frey folded the banana skin neatly and threw it over his shoulder. 'Any people about?'

'Odd you should mention that,' Thor replied. 'Yes, there's

quite a few milling about down here. You know something? This place is crawling with priests.'

At the bottom of the tree there was a hurried conference.

'Ask them,' Frey called out, 'if we can borrow a set of welding gear.'

One of the few remaining advantages of being a god, Pan said to himself, as he raced along behind Osiris' wheelchair through the darkened streets of Rome, is that you don't have any hang-ups about believing in miracles. For instance, there we all were, trapped, no way out. Next minute, something like an enormous traction engine materialises in the sky, swoops down, smashes a gap in the outer wall, ploughs through the plum trees and lands slap bang on top of the lorry, allowing us to make a smart getaway while the priests and monks are having severe hysterics and crises of faith. Not many mortals could handle something likᴖ that, but for a god it's all in a day's work.

'Any idea where we are?'

'No,' Pan replied. 'Years since I was in Rome. Last time I was here, in fact, I remember watching the Christians being thrown to the hamsters.'

'You mean lions.'

'No,' said Pan, 'hamsters. It was a Wednesday matinée. Are they following us, do you know?'

Osiris glanced back over his shoulder. 'I don't think so,' he replied, 'but let's not take any chances. Go easy a minute, let the mortals catch up.'

'Any idea what that big engine thing was?'

'I reckon it must have been a *deus ex machina*.'

'Fancy.' said Pan. 'I always wondered how those things worked. Bloody handy, the way it just turned up like that.'

'Maybe it was fate. or something.'

'I didn't think we were supposed to get any of that,' Pan said, 'being gods.'

'Maybe it wasn't for us. Maybe it was for the mortals.

Anyway, who cares? Let's just accept it and be grateful, eh?'

'Sort of a *fate accompli*, you mean?'

Osiris sighed. He was tired, frustrated, disorientated and very, very full of prunes. It was probably just as well that the Lady Isis had at some stage mislaid most of his pancreas, because otherwise he would probably be feeling a bit under the weather by now.

'We lost Lundqvist, then,' he observed.

Pan shrugged. 'You can't make omelettes,' he said. 'I expect he'll be all right. After all, he is a professional assassin, and they're a load of monks and things. Supposed to turn the other cheek and all that. Knowing Kurt Lundqvist, he'll have no difficulty knowing what to do with a turned cheek.'

'You know him from somewhere, I gather.'

Pan nodded. 'A long time ago,' he said. 'I was up around Thessaly someplace, on a job. He was there doing his thing. Not a very nice person to be around when he's working, unless you know exactly who it is he's there to see to. I was very relieved to find out it wasn't me.'

'It wasn't, then?'

Pan shook his head. 'Nah,' he replied, 'just some local fertility spirit they needed knocking off. You know, one of those matinée idol types who has to die each winter so that the crops may germinate and the corn ripen.'

'And Lundqvist was there to assassinate him?'

Pan nodded. 'At the time he specialised in that sort of thing,' he said. 'I believe he's what they call a cereal killer.'

'If I never see another prune as long as I live,' Osiris remarked, 'that'll be absolutely fine by me. Ah, here they are. Come on, you two, we may be immortal but we haven't got all day.'

Sandra and Carl came round the corner, red-faced and panting; the result, Pan presumed, of violent exertion on a full stomach.

'Are you being followed?' Osiris demanded.

'I don't,' Sandra gasped, took a deep breath, and went on,

'think so. Haven't looked for a while. Haven't heard anything.'

'Prunes getting to you?' asked Pan, sympathetically. Sandra nodded.

'No custard,' she explained.

For some reason the mention of custard made Osiris restless. 'Right then,' he said, 'time we weren't here. Lead on.'

Pan frowned. 'Where?' he asked.

'I don't know, do I?' Osiris replied. 'You're supposed to be a god, use your flaming initiative.'

He had hardly finished speaking when they all heard an ominous sound in the distance: the blowing of whistles, and the faint sussuration of many men singing the 23rd Psalm under their breath while running. 'This way,' said Pan, decisively, and he put his weight behind Osiris' wheelchair and started to push strenuously. The two mortals found themselves struggling to keep up.

As observed previously, the art of leading the way down narrow alleys on the pretext of knowing a neat little short-cut is an essential part of the craft of spreading confusion, and accordingly Pan set a brisk pace through a maze of back-streets. By the time the mortals gave up the struggle and sagged in a shop doorway, announcing that they were incapable of one more step, it was nearly light, and several tradesmen were rolling up their shutters to catch the early customers on their way to work. Into one such shop Pan led the way.

It turned out to be a typical old-fashioned small backstreet barber's shop, with four well-worn chairs, a foxed mirror and a small bald man with a brown liver-spotted head and enormous eyebrows standing ready to greet them. On seeing him, Pan did an immediate double-take.

'Buon giorno, signori, signorina,' trilled the barber, indicating his chairs with a fine, practised flourish. 'Per favore, si sedrai qui. Che bella giornata oh my gawd it's you!'

Pan grinned sheepishly. 'Hiya, Miffy,' he said. 'Nice place you've got here.'

The barber drew his substantial eyebrows together like curtains. 'Gitonoutavityabastard,' he snarled. 'How you've got the bloody cheek to come waltzing in here after all you—'

'Excuse me.'

The barber turned on Osiris with an angry gesture, registered the wheelchair and moderated his tone with a visible effort. 'Look here, chum,' he said, 'you tell your mate here to sling his hook, otherwise I'm bleedin' well gonna sling it for him, okay? If he's not out of here by the time I count to . . .'

Osiris raised an eyebrow. 'You two know each other, then?'

The barber laughed savagely. Pan, who had stepped behind the wheelchair at the start of the exchange, nodded.

'We go way back,' he said. 'This is Miffy – sorry, Mithras, God of the Morning. He's a sun god.'

'Was,' said Miffy emphatically. 'Was a sun god. Packed it in fifteen hundred years ago. And keep your bloody voice down, will you?'

In the street outside, Osiris could hear the tramp of sandalled feet, the ominous clinking of censers. 'Look,' he said, 'we're gods. I'm Osiris, in fact, used to do the sun lark, just like you. Egypt and Upper Nubia. We're in a bit of a jam, and we'd really appreciate it if you'd just let us hide out the back there for a while. All right?'

Mithras narrowed his eyes and peered. 'You're Osiris?' he said.

'That's right.'

'Cor,' said the barber, with a faint chuckle, 'stone me! I had you down as this big tall geezer with a broad chest and a sort of Kirk Douglas chin.'

'That was me two thousand years ago,' Osiris replied. 'Rather let myself go a bit since then.'

'I used to know your lad once. Horace.'

'Horus.'

'That's it, Horus. Great lanky ponce with the head of a sparrowhawk or something.'

'That's him.'

The barber considered the position for a minute. 'All right, then,' he said, 'straight through there, you can hide in the stockroom. But as soon as you've got rid of who's chasing you, I'm gonna pull his lungs out!'

'Fair enough,' Osiris said. 'This way?'

Time was when the dungeons of the Vatican were the most fashionable in Europe, attracting a cosmopolitan elite; and the post of Chief Jailer was regarded as the *ne plus ultra* of the turnkey's profession. Nowadays, most of the cells have been turned into offices for the lesser officials or closed file stores, and the Chief Jailership has been amalgamated with the office of Assistant Downstairs Caretaker and Deputy Inspector of Drains.

The Vatican is, however, a proudly conservative and traditionalist institution; and therefore there is always one proper, old-fashioned, honest-to-goodness dungeon ready and waiting, just in case a really important heretic turns up out of the blue, with its own specialist jailer and genuine fitted rats. True, the Health and Safety insist that the rats be kept in a cage and fed and watered regularly by a fully certified and trained rat care operative, in accordance with the EC Statement of Practice; but it's the thought that counts.

'Definitely over-reacted, if you ask me,' Odin said, for the fifth time. 'Granted we were trespassing, and maybe we did inadvertently damage some masonry and a few trees, but even so.' He scowled with indignation. 'This would never have happened,' he added darkly, 'in Accrington.'

'Whosa woosa itty bitty ratty, then?' said Frey in the corner. 'Who's got the dearest little ratty paw-paws in the whole wide world?'

'You still haven't explained,' said Thor, 'why we can't just beat the shit out of them and push off. I mean, for crying out loud, Odin, we're *gods*.'

'Exactly.'

'What do you mean, exactly?' Thor snapped, standing up in the escape tunnel he'd already started digging. It was already shoulder high; they'd only been there twenty minutes and the equipment available to him was a half broken china mug and a toothbrush. 'One of these days, Odin, you're going to wake up and find the bailiffs have repossessed your brain.'

'Exactly because we're gods,' Odin replied. 'This is a Christian jurisdiction; we shouldn't be here. If we cause trouble, it could lead to a serious theological incident.'

'Not if we only pulped them a bit. Just enough so's we could escape, plus a few kicks up the jacksie for luck. I don't suppose anyone'd even notice.'

'Little rattikins want nice piece of coconut ice? Very nice, yum yum? No? Not want nice bit of—?'

'Frey, will you stop talking to that sodding rodent!'

'Oh, yeah?' Frey replied. 'And where else am I going to get an intelligent conversation in here?'

'Serious,' Odin went on, 'theological incident. Which in turn means the Pope or whatever he calls himself writing a stiff letter to the Henderson. Which means . . .'

'All right,' said Thor, 'point taken. If only I hadn't listened to you in the first place.'

'I like that, coming from you. You knew we were in Rome all along. Why the devil didn't you say anything?'

Thor made a rude noise and returned to his digging. Being a god (and to the gods all things are known) he had already worked out that his tunnel, if continued on its existing course for seven hundred and fifty yards, would bring him out slap bang in the middle of the main laundry room. They could dress up in sheets and pretend to be ghosts.

'By the way,' said Frey, in between enquiring of his new friend who exactly had the sweetest little iskery whiskery woos in the whole world ever, 'anybody got any idea who he is?' He jerked his head towards the slumped figure by the door. 'Whoever he is, looks like they gave him a right old seeing-to.'

'Dunno,' said Thor. 'He was in here when we arrived, I think. You could wake him up if you wanted.'

'All right,' said Frey. He leant across, took a firm hold of the figure's ear, and twisted smartly.

'Ow!' said Kurt Lundqvist, waking up. 'Gug. Where . . .?'

Frey smiled reassuringly. 'We don't actually know that ourselves,' he said, 'But we think it's the Vatican. I'm Frey, by the way, that's Thor and he's Odin.'

'Kurt Lundqvist. Hey, what am I doing here?'

'How should I know?' Frey replied. 'Actually,' he admitted, 'I should, because in theory I know everything, but there it is. We were supposed to go on refresher courses, but we never bothered.'

Lundqvist looked them over. 'You're gods, aren't you?' he said.

'Give the man a big cigar,' Frey replied. 'Of course, we're retired now. How about you?'

Lundqvist considered. As noted above he was basically a very religious man – you had to be in his line of work. Atheism to a supernatural hit-man would be as unthinkable as freeze-dried rain – but he was painfully aware that from time to time he'd been called upon to commit some fairly sacrilegious acts in the course of his duties, up to and including the destruct-testing of some deities' eternal lives; and for the life of him he couldn't remember whether this particular pantheon had crossed his path before. Best, he decided, to be a little bit discreet.

'I'm a journalist,' he therefore said. 'War correspondent with the Chicopee Falls Evening Intelligencer. Hey, what are you guys doing in here? And why don't you just—?'

'Because,' Thor said, 'that great jessie over there won't let us. Don't thump the guards, he says. Don't smash down the walls, he says. Wait for someone from the High Commission to come and bail us out. Fat chance.'

'Thor, you know perfectly well there are proper proce-dures . . .'

'Bearing in mind,' Thor went on, 'that the High Commission was closed down in AD 332 on the orders of Constantine the Great. Yes, I know Nkulunkulu the Great Sky Spirit of Zululand has a chargé d'affaires still, but I gather he consists of a few small clouds and a build-up of latent static electricity, which really isn't going to be much use to us in here.'

'Oh I don't know,' Frey yawned. 'Sounds like he could cause dry rot in the joists or something, and then they'd have to move us out to a hotel. Take time, though.'

Kurt Lundqvist levered himself up on to his hands and knees and looked around. As always with him, ever since he popped out of the womb and immediately grabbed the forceps and dived for strategic cover under the incubator, his first thought was to locate a usable weapon and a defensible position to fall back on. Limited scope in the conditions prevailing, and he had to content himself with seizing Frey's left shoe and crouching in the corner of the cell.

'Let's get this straight, shall we?' he said. 'You guys are gods, right?'

Thor nodded.

'And you want to bust out, but you can't.'

'Yup.'

'Not,' Lundqvist went on, 'because you haven't the capability, but because it'd be a serious breach of protocol, right?'

'Exactly.'

Lundqvist nodded. 'So,' he said, 'if you could secure the services of, say, a highly trained soldier of fortune who could bash in the guards without any nasty theological comebacks, you could do all the rest of the escaping, like, you know, the rope ladders and waiting helicopters bit, standing on your heads.'

'I guess so,' Thor replied.

'Fine.' Lundqvist smiled and felt in his pocket. 'Allow me,' he said, 'to give you my card.'

11

'It's all right,' said Mithras, 'they've gone.'

(From the same team that brought you *How many angels can dance on the head of a pin?* we proudly present the very latest in abstruse theological conundra; namely, what do retired sun gods now running small hairdressing businesses in the backstreets of Rome keep in their back rooms? Answers on a postcard, please.)

'You might have warned us,' Osiris protested.

'There wasn't time,' Mithras replied, defensively. 'Besides, I forgot it was there. Only came last evening. Bloke with a horse and cart came in for a haircut, and when I'd done he said he'd come out without his wallet, would I be interested in doing a bit of barter? And since I've got the allotment—'

'Yes,' Pan said, 'all right. We get the message.'

Mithras turned on Pan, snarling. 'Besides,' he snapped, 'I only did to you what you did to me all those years back, you bastard.'

'Did I?' Pan frowned in thought. 'Oh, I see,' he said, 'it's a sort of play on words. Yes, very good.'

Osiris raised a hand for silence. 'Excuse me,' he asked Mithras. 'I'm sure it's none of my business, but what exactly did he do to you?'

'Hah!'

'It was all perfectly innocent,' Pan muttered, as he put the width of a barber's chair between Mithras and himself. 'Just bad luck, that's—'

'There I was,' Mithras said, 'at my retirement party. Super do it was, champers, horse doofers, bits of minced-up fish in pastry cases with thin slices of egg, the works. Three thousand years in the public service, and a nice comfortable retirement and a decent pension to look forward to.' He paused to give Pan a look you could have freeze-dried coffee with, and went on. 'And just when the party's going well and I've had a few jars, up comes this creep here, all innocent like, with his, Excuse me, but have you given any thought to the long-term benefits of a personal pension scheme specially tailored to your individual requirements? Gordon Bennett, did he see me coming, or what?'

'It was a perfectly legitimate investment proposal,' Pan replied, his face covered with synthetic anger, as if he'd just been eating a doughnut filled with wrath. 'You were at perfect liberty to take independent financial advice.'

'Oh yeah,' Mithras sneered. '*Trust me, I'm a god*. Went and stuck the while lot into Mount Olympus 12½ per cent unsecured loan stock, he did, just six weeks before the battle of the Milvian Bridge.'

'Final defeat of the pagans by Constantine the Great,' Osiris asided to Sandra, who hadn't been listening anyway. 'Christianity becomes the state religion and worship of the old gods forbidden.' He nodded a few times. 'I can see your point,' he said to Mithras. 'In the circumstances, I think ripping his lungs out would be perfectly reasonable behaviour.'

Pan smiled fiercely. 'All water under the bridge, now, though,' he said, 'and anyway—'

'Is it hell as like,' Mithras growled. 'I make it you owe me ninety billion gold dinars, plus interest. I'd prefer cash, if you've got it.'

'So you couldn't retire after all?'

'Been working in this dump ever since,' Mithras replied

sullenly. 'Only thing that's kept me going was the thought of what I was going to do to chummy here just as soon as I got my hands on him.'

'I think that's very sad,' Sandra said.

'*You* think . . .'

Pan folded his arms. 'It was an honest mistake,' he said firmly. 'And besides, think of all the tax you've saved just by virtue of being grindingly poor.'

A spasm of doubt flitted across Mithras' face. 'Cor,' he said. 'I never looked at it like that before.'

'You see?' Pan replied, simultaneously crushing Sandra's foot beneath his own on the off chance that she might have been about to point out that gods don't pay tax anyway. 'That's the trouble with laymen, of course, they're incapable of adopting the holistic viewpoint. Strictly speaking, of course,' he added, 'I should be entitled to my ten per cent commission on everything you've saved, but as a gesture of goodwill . . .'

'Gosh. Thanks.'

'That's all right.'

'That's really kind of you.'

'Don't mention it.' Pan unfolded his arms and extended a hand to Mithras, who shook it warmly. 'And by way of a thank you, maybe you could help us with this little job we're doing.'

'There's a door,' said Carl slowly, 'in this wall.'

Everyone else in the room turned and looked at him. 'Straight up,' he added. 'Look, you can see for yourselves. Here, under the wallpaper.'

Careful examination did indeed reveal the edges of a door, together with a slight bulge for the lockplate. 'Well, bugger me,' said Mithras. 'I've been here one thousand, six hundred and eighty-three years, and would you believe I never even noticed it there.'

Pan knitted his brows. 'That suggests,' he observed, 'that it's a pretty old door. Does it lead anywhere, do you suppose?'

Mithras nodded. 'Must do,' he said. 'That's what doors are all about, stands to reason.'

'Any idea where?'

To the gods all things are ... Yes, well, in theory. Let's instead say, To the gods all things are known, but most of them have memories like car boot sale colanders.

Osiris smiled. For some reason he had good vibes about this. Not that that was quite so significant as it seemed; among other things he'd had good vibes about the South Sea Bubble, Neville Chamberlain's 1938 peace initiative, the groundnut scheme and Polly Peck. Nevertheless, he was prepared to ride his hunch. Being a god means never having to say you're sorry.

'Only one way to find out, then,' he said.

Twenty minutes later, it looked very much like he was going to have to get off his hunch and walk. To the casual visitor, one catacomb is very much like another, and they all smell distressingly of distant sewage and bonemeal.

'Don't mind me,' Pan said smugly. 'What with my line of work and everything, the only time I really know where I am is when I'm hopelessly lost.' He looked around ostentatiously and added, 'Home sweet home.'

'Don't worry,' said Osiris, artificially calm. 'Everything always leads somewhere. We'll soon be—'

'Sure. Has it occurred to you that this tunnel might have been undisturbed for two thousand years for a very good reason?'

Suddenly Osiris jammed on the brakes of his chair, licked one finger and held it up. 'It's a draught,' he said. 'I think we're in business.'

'Are there any of those prunes left, I wonder,' said Sandra. 'I'm hungry.'

The draught, it transpired, came from a low, unfinished-looking tunnel running off to their right. There was something about it which didn't inspire confidence.

'Right,' said Mithras, 'that'll do me. You're on your own from now on. I've got a shop to run.'

Osiris glowered at him. 'You mean you're scared. Admit it.'

Mithras shrugged. 'All right, I'm scared. It's spooky.'

'*Spooky?* You're a god, dammit.'

'Retired. And anyway, I'm well off my own turf here. Sun gods aren't meant to fool around in dark tunnels hundreds of feet underground. Well known fact, that.'

Osiris shrugged. 'Please yourself,' he said. 'Right, on we—'

'Hold on a moment, will you?' Pan interrupted. 'You're not seriously suggesting we go down there, are you?'

'Yes.'

'Why?'

Osiris considered; and while he did so, Pan reminded him that their objectives were (a) short term, to escape from the two doctors and all those lunatic monks, and (b) long term, somehow to get their hands on enough loot to pay their incredibly, monumentally expensive lawyer. Neither purpose, he ventured to suggest, would be materially advanced by going down a dark, dodgy and probably entirely futile hole in the ground.

'Okay,' said Osiris. 'Because it's there. How does that grab you?'

'Not much.'

'Ah.' Osiris smiled. 'That's because you lack insight, initiative and the holistic viewpoint. Last one down the tunnel's a cissy.'

He grabbed the wheels of his chair, shoved off and vanished into the darkness. Sandra and Carl immediately followed, Sandra expressing the view that she doubted there was anything to eat down there but she supposed it was worth a try. For want of other company, Pan turned to his sworn enemy and smiled pleasantly.

'Well,' he said, 'it takes all sorts, doesn't it. Now, what's the quickest way back up to the—?'

'About my money,' said Mithras. 'Oh, and by the way, the interest is of course compound, at let's say a flat rate of fifteen per cent, so that makes, let's see, ten to the power of nine hundred and four times sixteen point three seven eight, divide by three hundred and sixty-five and multiply—'

'Ciao,' said Pan quickly, and darted up the tunnel.

What with falling over his feet and not having a torch, not to mention ominous scuttling sounds and the smell of bonemeal, Pan found it slow and hard going. It was pitch dark and he couldn't see a thing; but, bearing in mind the scuttling sounds, that wasn't necessarily a bad thing. Don't panic, he said to himself. Well, no, I wouldn't would I? On the other hand, I could be rationally and reasonably terrified, no trouble at all. Let's give that a try and see what happens.

HALT.

Pan halted. He had no idea where the voice had come from, if in fact it had been a voice at all.

STAY EXACTLY WHERE YOU ARE.

Pan did as he was told, and as the seconds turned into minutes, the white heat of his terror began to cool ever so slightly. There was something about the voice that reminded him very faintly of something else.

DO NOT MOVE OR IT WILL BE THE WORSE FOR YOU.

'Okay. Point taken. What next?'

YOU ARE IN MY WHIRR CLUNK POWER. SURREN-DER OR DIE.

'I'll take surrender, please, chief. So what's next on the agenda?'

A full minute passed; a very long time, in context, and an even longer time down a dark, scuttling tunnel. Pan began to clap his hands together slowly.

DO NOT MOVE OR IT WILL BE THE—

Pan clicked his tongue. 'I think we've covered that bit already, thanks. Can we please get on with it?'

SORRY. I SHOULD WHEEENG PINK I SHOULD HAVE SAID ABANDON HOPE ALL YE WHO ENTER HERE.

Slowly, a grin spread across Pan's face. 'You're a recording, aren't you?'

DO NOT MOVE OR IT WILL—

'Who said anything about moving? Look, can't we just fast-forward a bit and get on to the main feature?'

YOU ARE IN MY—

'—Power, surrender or die. Yes, fine.' He tapped his fingers noisily against the wall. 'I know you've got your stuff to do and all that, but it's really not a bundle of fun standing around in a dank tunnel, probably with nightmarish insects and giant rats and snakes and things loafing around the place, so if we could just—'

RATS?

'Bound to be. There's always rats in these claustrophobia sequences. So if we could—'

I *HATE* RATS.

Pan blinked twice. 'Is that so?'

YES.

'Funny,' Pan said. 'I thought you were just a recording.'

Pause.

DO NOT MOVE OR IT WILL BE THE WORSE—

'Oh no you don't. Come on, tell me what all this is in aid of, and then we can all go home.'

DO NOT MOVE OR—

'Squeak.'

Silence. A long, eerie silence, broken only by a faint scuffling sound. This was in fact caused by Pan running his fingernails across the rough-hewn surface of the tunnel wall, but it did sound uncommonly like the scampering of rodent paws.

CUT THAT OUT, WILL YOU?

'Cut what out? Squeak, squeak.'

THAT SCAMPERING NOISE. AND THE SQUEAK-ING.

'What squeaking?'

ALL RIGHT, ALL RIGHT, YOU WIN. I AM AEACUS, GUARDIAN OF THE PORTALS OF DEATH AND WINDER-BACK OF THE TAPE OF OBLIVION. YOU AND YOUR FRIENDS HAVE TRESPASSED INTO THE KINGDOM OF DEATH, FROM WHOSE BOURN NO TRAVELLER RETURNS, AND—

'Bourn?'

BOURN. SORT OF MILESTONE. FROM WHOSE BOURN NO TRAV—

'From whose milestone no traveller returns?'

Pause. DON'T ASK ME WHAT IT MEANS, I DIDN'T WRITE IT. AND . . . OH NUTS, I'VE LOST THE PLACE NOW, I'LL HAVE TO GO BACK TO DO NOT MOVE OR IT WILL BE THE—

'Gorblimey,' said Pan, 'that was a big 'un. Great big brown hairy brute, tried to climb right up my trouser leg. Go on, shoo!'

EEEEEK!

Pan made some more scuffling noises and then called out, 'It's all right, I've got him. Here you are, have a nice piece of cheese. Sorry, you were saying?'

AND HERE YOU MUST STAY FOREVER UNTIL THE SEAS RUN DRY AND THE SKY CRACKS ARE YOU *SURE* YOU'VE GOT THAT THING UNDER CONTROL?

'Absolutely,' Pan replied. 'No question – whoops, oh no you don't, here boy, nice cheese.'

LOOK, FOR CRYING OUT LOUD—

In the darkness, Pan grinned and made a few extra-spine-shivering squeaking noises. 'Gotcha,' he said eventually. 'Now then. Here I must stay forever, is that right? Oh well, if that's the case I might as well let this rat go . . .'

It should be explained that the voice was not so much a voice as a reverberation at the back of the head, a mote on the mind's eye, tinnitus of the inner ear, a septic memory. Hitherto, at any rate. Now it was beginning to sound – well, panicky.

HERE YOU MUST S-S-S-STAY FOREVER, it said quickly, *UNLESS* YOU HAPPEN TO GO THROUGH THE HIDDEN DOOR IMMEDIATELY TO YOUR RIGHT, TAKING YOUR SODDING RAT WITH YOU, IN WHICH CASE YOU'LL FIND YOURSELF IN THE ATTEND-ANT'S ROOM OF THE PUBLIC LAVATORY AT ROME AIRPORT. IT WAS NICE MEETING YOU, GOODBYE.

'Hang on,' said Pan, dragging his fingernails across a jagged piece of scree. 'I may be many things but I'm not the sort to walk out on my friends. If they've got to stay here for ever, I guess I have to as well. No, ratty, stop that, come *back*! Who's a naughty little tinker, then?'

ALL *RIGHT*, JUST A MINUTE, I'LL BE STRAIGHT BACK, DON'T MOVE.

'Or it'll be the worse for me?'

SOMETHING LIKE THAT.

'Fortuitous,' Osiris said.

'Yeah, well.' Pan shrugged his wide, thin shoulders – a poor choice of gesture, since Carl was standing on them, trying to reach up into the cistern. 'Fortuitous is what being a god's all about, innit? I mean,' he added, remembering something he'd heard somewhere, 'the way I look at it, we hold the Fates bound fast in iron chains, sort of thing, and with our hands turn Fortune's wheel about. As it were.'

'Do we?'

'I think so. It sort of goes with the territory.'

Osiris shook his head. 'Funny ideas you Mediterranean types have,' he said. 'Where I come from, godding is basically just making sure the crops grow and remembering to switch out the lights before going to bed. Has he found it yet?'

'No,' Carl replied. 'You sure it's here?'

'Must be somewhere,' Osiris replied. 'Everything always is.'

'Oh.'

'You were there when those three old boilers gave us the

directions,' Osiris went on, 'you know as well as I do. The Runes of Power are somewhere in the gentleman's convenience immediately adjacent to the Kingdom of Death, which is where we've just been. I still think that was one hell of a coincidence, by the way.'

'The Kingdom of Death has many doors.'

'What say?'

'The Kingdom of Death,' repeated Pan firmly, 'has many doors. Well known fact. And this is a gent's bog immediately adjacent. And,' he went on, 'according to Herschel's Law of Inverse Commodity, the bigger the public building, the fewer the number of khazis. The Kingdom of Death is probably the largest public building there is; ergo, a maximum of one bog, just enough to comply with the planning regulations.'

'Cor,' Osiris said. 'Herschel's Law and everything. Where did you learn all that stuff?'

'I've been around, you know.'

'So it would seem. All right, we'd better try the next one.'

'Excuse me,' said Sandra.

Pan winced and swore. 'Mind where you're putting your feet, you idiot,' he said. 'That was my ear.'

'Sorry.'

'Excuse me,' Sandra reiterated, 'but would these be them here?'

They turned and looked. Sandra was pointing to a small framed notice on the wall just above the electric hot-air hand dryer.

'Oh.'

'Only they do say,' Sandra went on, '*Directions for finding the Golden Teeth of El Dorado*, and I gathered that was what we wanted.'

Osiris frowned. 'They're supposed to be Runes of Power,' he muttered. 'This whole carry-on is getting way above my head.'

'They probably are Runes of Power by local standards,' Pan interrupted. 'Shall we just have a look and see what they say?'

Sandra, meanwhile, had produced a small notebook with flowers and bunnies and things on the cover and written the directions down. The two gods looked at each other and shrugged.

'That's what it says,' Pan ventured after a while.

'Well.' Osiris rubbed his chin, making a noise like clapped-out sandpaper. 'We might as well give it a go, then.'

Perversely, the traction engine started first time.

'Hey,' Thor enquired, dumbfounded, 'how the devil did you do that?'

Lundqvist shrugged. 'I just pulled this handle thing here,' he said. 'Look, let's get the hell out of here, all right?'

'Switch it off and do it again. You can't have done it right.'

'Oh, for crying out loud,' Frey muttered. A Cistercian SWAT team had just discovered the stunned sentry. 'Give it some welly and let's go, quickly. Any more of this nonsense and I shan't be responsible.'

The Vatican authorities plainly hadn't had the faintest idea what one is supposed to do with a captured supernatural traction engine deposited out of the blue in one's back courtyard. Anyone with an ounce of sense would have disconnected the main rotor arm from the forcing toggle and withdrawn the split pin from the auxiliary drive sprocket, thereby immobilising the entire subordinate transmission; but the helpless unworldly monks hadn't even unclipped the Hodgson cable or overridden the HST. In all likelihood, Thor speculated, as the engine roared into life and lifted off vertically into the air, if a lightbulb goes they pray at it till it comes back on again. Idiots.

'Where to now?' Thor shouted over the roar of the flywheel.

'Home,' Odin replied, 'sharpish. There's still an outside chance She won't have noticed we're not there.'

'Pretty thin chance.'

'Never mind. Set a course north-north-west.'

'Right you are.' Frey was at the controls; a classic example of the wrong man in the wrong place at the wrong time. 'Which one's that?'

'The lever on your left,' Odin replied, 'just above your cufflink.'

'What, this one?'

'No, that's the cigar lighter.'

Lundqvist leant back against the smoke-stack, speculating as to who the hell these imbeciles were, and how soon he'd be able to get away from them. So far, he was painfully aware, his role in the quest to frustrate the diabolical schemes of Julian and the godchildren was very similar to that of sugar in petrol. What he needed in order to get his act together was a few hours to gather his thoughts and regroup, at least three self-loading firearms and a nice strong cup of coffee; none of which were likely to come his way as long as he was stuck on this amazing contraption with these three geriatric lunatics.

'Guys,' he said, 'where is it exactly you're headed?'

'Droitwich.'

'Where?'

'Well, just outside Droitwich, to be precise,' Thor replied. 'About three miles west and two miles straight up. The postal address is Sunnyvoyde.'

Lundqvist hazarded a guess. 'The retired gods' home, right?'

'Yeah.'

This, Lundqvist felt, just wasn't good enough. Wherever Osiris was headed, it most certainly wasn't the place he'd escaped from. Instinctively, though knowing in his heart it was in vain, he frisked himself for some sort of weapon. Anything, anything at all – even a Walther Model 9 in 6.35mm loaded, if need be, with 50 grain jacketed hardball – would be better than nothing. Still. Needs must.

'Okay,' he snapped, standing up and (as the engine passed

through a patch of slight turbulence) sitting down again, 'this is a hijack. Turn this thing round and fly it to Tripoli.'

'Why?'

Lundqvist shoved his hand in his pocket. 'I have a gun,' he said.

'Is this ponce serious, do you think?'

'Where's Tripoli?'

'I think it's somewhere in Tuscany, isn't it?'

'Why should having a gun make him want to go to Tuscany?'

'I thought it was in Egypt.'

'It's not a very Egyptian sounding name, Tripoli. All the places there are called Tell something.'

'Telford?'

'I think you're thinking of Tivoli, not Tripoli. Though I'm not sure Tivoli's in Tuscany, come to that.'

'We can drop him off at Telford, no trouble at all. We'll be virtually passing the door.'

'All right.' Lundqvist was back on his feet again, and maintained himself thus with a sort of bow-legged crouch. 'Okay, so I haven't got a gun. First time in over four hundred years,' he added miserably. 'But what I have got . . .' He cast his eye around the immediate vicinity, and grabbed awkwardly. 'What I have got is this spanner . . .'

'Actually, that's a four by nine Stilson,' Odin commented. 'You use it for shimming up the interfacing on the cam nuts.'

'. . . This four by nine Stilson, and unless you all do exactly what I say, you're all dead. You got that?'

There was a pause.

'Yes,' said Frey at last, 'but where exactly is it you want to go?'

'I've found Tivoli,' Odin said, looking up from the atlas. 'It's in completely the wrong direction, of course.'

'You've got the map the wrong way up, you daft old –'

'Doesn't matter, it's still completely the wrong –'

'We could go there anyway,' Frey suggested, 'and then he could maybe get a bus.'

Odin and Thor froze in mid-bicker and stared at their junior colleague. 'Don't talk soft,' Thor said, 'Tivoli's where he wants to go, what would he want to get a bus for?'

Frey shrugged. 'I've always wanted to go on a bus,' he said, 'ever since I can remember. One of those open-topped ones with the windy staircase at the back.'

'All *right*,' Lundqvist shouted. 'Forget it, will you? Forget I ever said Tripoli. Just drop me off anywhere, and that'll be fine.'

'Just drop you anywhere?'

'That'd be just fine.'

Thor shrugged. 'No problem,' he said; and did so. There was a scream, which rapidly dopplered and died away as the speck diminished away out of sight below them.

'I think,' Frey ventured, 'we're passing over the sea.'

'That's lucky,' Thor replied. 'Hope he can swim.'

Julian sat at his desk and toyed with a paperclip. It was a quarter to three in the morning, he had a headache and he hadn't made any money for well over ten minutes. He scowled.

Somehow, he couldn't concentrate. This was a nuisance; absolute, laser-like concentration, together with a total disregard for basic human dignity, is the key to success in the legal profession, and he'd always prided himself on his ability to blot out from his mind everything except the job in hand, the blood currently in the water.

Why hadn't he heard anything from those two buffoons yet?

Dammit, he'd practically done the whole job for them – fixed things up with the Cardinal, arranged for enquiry agents to trace the old bastard to Belgium, hired the heavies, planned the second hijack, everything short of actually going there himself and doing the business with the holy water. Try as he might, he couldn't for the life of him imagine how anything could possibly go wrong. A one-legged panda could have done the job standing on its head.

Yes. Well. Maybe he should have hired a one-legged panda. As it was, he was going to have to make do with what he'd got. He picked his nose thoughtfully for a while, turning over various options in his mind.

So much, he said to himself, for brute force and violence. Too clumsy, he'd always said, too gauche. There must be another way, one more in tune with the professional man's ethos. He chewed a pencil, his mind moving in many planes simultaneously.

Ah.

There is a saying, attributed to ex-President Richard Nixon and much quoted by lawyers, to the effect that once you have them by the balls, their hearts and minds will follow.

Find the weak point, the mental scab, the little encrustation of half-healed guilt, and there insert your questing fingernail. Prod and pick around the compassion of the gods, their love for their creation, their eternal subconscious self-reproach as they consider everything that they have made: *You got them into this mess, it's up to you . . .*

Yes, thought Julian, that ought to do the trick.

He lifted the telephone.

12

Squelch, squelch, squelch. Pause. Squelch.

This is the sound of Kurt Lundqvist moving semi-noiselessly, like a black shadow on the very edge of sight, up the beach and into the cover of the trees.

Semi-noiselessly, because even if, like Kurt, you spent forty years as Kawaguchiya Integrated Circuits Professor of Stealth at the Central Ninja Academy after several lifetimes of practical experience at the cutting edge of the silent killing profession, it's pretty well impossible to move in absolute silence when your boots are full of water and your socks feel like overweight jellyfish under your toes.

Having gained the relative safety of the trees, he sat down yanked off his left boot and emptied it. Out came a pint and a half of sea, some green slime and a small golden fish.

For some reason which he could never quite account for, Lundqvist whipped off the other boot, taking care not to spill its contents, scooped up the fish just as it was on the point of coughing its gills up, and dropped it into the boot. With a flick of its shimmering tail it sought safety in the toe. Lundqvist sighed; then, in his stocking feet and with a complete absence of stealth, he plodded back across the oily black mud of the beach to the water's edge and flung the contents of the boot out as far as he could. There was a tiny *plop!* as the fish hit the water. God, said Lundqvist to himself, this is it, I've finally flipped my lid. If the guys down at Kali's Diner ever found out

I'd saved a fish from drowning in air, I'd never live it down,

There was a deafening peal of thunder, followed by lightning, fireworks and piped music. Lundqvist found himself face down in the mud. A small crab scuttled up his trouser leg.

'*G'Day. I am the Dragon King of the South-East. The fish you saved was my only son. I am forever in your debt. Name your utmost wish, and it is as good as done, no worries.*'

Lundqvist looked up. Hovering over the wavetops was a dragon, of the sort familiar from countless thousands of porcelain jars, cups, soup-bowls, painted silk screens, soapstone carvings and netsuke. Its head, bewhiskered and leonine, was supported by long, sinuous curves of scaly neck and body, which in turn rested on four taloned claws, which gripped the edges of a huge jade surfboard. Around its bejewelled waist, the marvellous beast wore a pair of long fluorescent bathing trunks, and in one talon it gripped a can of beer.

Yes, thought Lundqvist, Dragon King of the South-East. Dragon Kings come from China, and south-east from China is exactly where I'm thinking of.

'Hi,' he said. 'Look, are we talking three wishes here?'

The Dragon King nodded his enormous head. '*Fair dinkum,*' he said, and his voice was like the crashing of surf on a reef of jade. '*If it hadn't been for you playing the white man back there, the little fella'd be history by now, so I reckon I owe you one. Or rather three,*' he added. '*Fair go, after all. Have a beer?*'

Lundqvist nodded, and a foaming can of lager appeared between his fingers. Dragon King of the South-East, he muttered to himself, just my goddam luck. Of all the cardinal points of all the compasses in the world, why do I have to stray into his?

'Okay,' he said, 'Let's start with some warm clothes and dry footwear.'

The air sparkled; and when Lundqvist looked down he saw that he was now wearing the same pattern of big eye-hurting beach shorts as the dragon, together with an oversize sweat-shirt in the same unfortunate colour scheme, an oversize baseball cap, plastic slip-on sandals and white socks. Something told him that it would be a good idea to get the other two wishes over and done with as quickly as possible.

'*Suits you, mate,*' said the Dragon King, thereby placing himself in the running for the Kurt Lundqvist Pillock of the Year Award. '*Now then, what else can I do for you? Fire away.*'

Lundqvist sighed and rubbed his eyes. What he really wanted right now was six hours sleep, a .40 Glock and a mammoth pastrami sandwich, in that order. From long experience, however, he knew better than most that what gift horses generally have in their mouths is big, sharp fangs.

'I'm looking for some guys,' he said. 'Maybe you can tell me where they are.'

'*Shoot through on you, did they, the bludgers?*' replied the Dragon King sympathetically, rubbing a splash of zinc cream on to the scales of its chest. '*Tell me who these blokes are, and they're found.*'

Lundqvist told him.

'*You're serious?*'

'Yes.'

'*Fair crack of the whip?*'

'Whatever that's supposed to mean, yes.'

'*Right-oh.*' The Dragon King closed his eyes, and suddenly his whole body became almost translucent, like some weird mirage. '*Central America,*' he said. '*Mexico. Sort of Mexico. One of those little bitty countries just down and across a bit from Mexico. San something or other. Big mountains. Make any sense to you?*'

Lundqvist nodded. That left wish number three, and it was patently obvious what it was going to have to be. He braced himself.

'Now then,' he said. 'Tell me what they're doing there and why.'

*

The Aztecs (explained the Dragon King) are famous for three things: gold, the incredible savagery of their gods, and chocolate. All three are inextricably linked.

Quite obviously, chocolate was reserved as the special food of the gods. Therefore, the gods ate nothing but chocolate; all day, every day. Toothbrushes, it should be noted, were unknown in pre-Columbian Central America, and fluoride was not a concept with which they were familiar.

The result: toothache. Toothache of the kind only gods can suffer. Not just the paltry, everyday, diamond-tipped pile-drivers and psychotic gnomes in the upper jaw variety that mortal men have to put up with, but the real thing. Hence the bad temper.

And after the toothache had run its hideous course, gods with no teeth. Which in turn meant no solid food. All that the Aztec pantheon could manage to get down were liquids and a little extremely soft meat that could be mumbled into digestibility between agonisingly sensitive gums. And chocolate too, of course, taken in liquid form.

Hence the notorious human sacrifices of the Aztecs, at the culmination of which the blood and hearts of the victims were laid on the altars as a banquet for the gods. The way the gods saw things, suffering isn't something you hoard, it's something you share.

Except for one god, the Highest, the Most Supreme; Azctlanhuilptlil, God of War and Dental Hygiene, aloof and apart in his unutterable splendour (or, as his colleagues muttered to themselves, bloody selfish). When all the other Aztec deities finally gave up the unequal struggle and retired to Sunnyvoyde and meagre helpings of chicken soup, Azctlanhuilptlil remained behind, able to keep going by virtue of his unique, jealously guarded, most valued possession: a gigantic set of false teeth, wrought (for this is Mexico, land of inexhaustible mineral wealth) of the finest, purest gold.

Finally, when Cortes and his conquistadores burst into Mexico, smashed the centuries-old civilisation of the Aztecs and suppressed the worship of the old gods, Azctlanhuilptlil in turn was overthrown and reduced by a unanimous vote of his extremely resentful erstwhile devotees to mortal status. His eventual fate is shrouded in obscurity, although legend has it that he ended his days, dentureless and utterly miserable, as a quality control officer at Hershey's.

As to what became of his teeth, nobody knew; but a garbled recollection of their memory circulated among the Spaniards, leading many brave fools to their deaths in the fruitless quest for the Man of Gold. The truth of the matter (so the Dragon King asserted) is that the teeth are still there, soaking the centuries away in the bowl of an extinct volcano, guarded by a dragon or something such and preserved imperishably in sixty billion gallons of Steradent.

'Thanks,' said Lundqvist, getting up and brushing mud off his legs. 'I'll be going, then.'

The Dragon King stirred. '*What about the third wish, mate?*'

'That's all right,' Lundqvist replied, 'keep the change.'

Half past twelve. Lunchtime at Sunnyvoyde.

It was a favourite adage of Mrs Henderson that one of the greatest problems with gods is that they have no sense of time. For them, day merges seamlessly with day, year with year, century with century. The result: vagueness, leading to dementia, leading to wet beds and residents tottering about the corridors on zimmers at three in the morning demanding to see a doctor. Accordingly, there was a routine at Sunnyvoyde, and nothing interfered with it. Breakfast at seven sharp; lunch at twelve thirty, on the dot; afternoon tea at four exactly; evening meal at six thirty, come rain or shine; and finally, the Twilight of the Gods at nine fifteen, lights out and not a peep do I expect to hear out of you lot until breakfast.

By and large the system worked. It instilled a sense of order into many a hitherto purposeless and unstructured divine existence. It is, to put it mildly, embarrassing for a supreme being to find himself waking up in the middle of the night asking himself questions like 'Why am I here?' and 'Is there a reason behind it all?' In Sunnyvoyde, the gods knew that they existed for the sole purpose of being present at the ordained mealtimes. Maybe it cut down on the free will side of things; but you can't be a god for very long without realising that free will and the proverbial free lunch have a great deal in common.

'Kedgeree,' grunted Nkulunkulu, Great Sky Spirit of the Zulus. 'Why does it always have to be flaming kedgeree for Friday dinner?'

'Such a bore,' agreed Ilmater, the Finnish Queen of the Air, adding that the custom of always having fish on Fridays must be somebody's idea of a sick joke, in context. Nkulunkulu nodded, and asked her to pass the salt.

'No salt at table any more, I'm afraid,' Ilmater replied. 'It's bad for us, apparently. Too much potassium or some such, or at least that's what She said. Really, it's enough to drive one frantic, don't you think?'

'No salt?' Yama, the blue-faced Hindu god of Death, scowled horribly. 'We'll bloody well see about that. Here, you. Get the manageress. I demand to see the manageress.'

The nursing auxiliary thus addressed looked through Yama as if he wasn't there and swept past, wheeling her trolley laden with covered aluminium dishes. In theory she was perfectly within her rights in doing so; Sunnyvoyde houses no less than forty-six different Kings of Death, which is far in excess of the number permitted under the Health and Safety Regulations. In order to get round this, Mrs Henderson had long ago organised a rota, whereby each one of them had a number of days on as duty King of Death; on their off days, the various Kings were deemed not to exist (but they still had to be punctual for meals).

'Haven't seen Osiris in a long time,' Nkulunkulu remarked, surreptitiously calling a small pillar of salt into being under cover of his table napkin. 'Wonder if the poor old sod has finally pegged out.'

'Pegged out what?'

'You know, pegged out. Handed in his dinner pail. Shuffled off this mortal coil. You know,' he added with rising frustration, 'kicked the bucket.'

Ilmater looked up from her plate. She had been forking through, picking out the pieces of boiled egg and depositing them carefully on her sideplate. 'Sounds like he's been terribly busy doing all those strenuous things,' she said. 'No wonder we haven't seen him for a while.'

'Died, you dozy old bat. I wonder whether Osiris has finally died.'

Yama shook his head. 'I doubt that very much,' he said, ''cos I'd have been notified if he had. We get a circular every evening,' he explained, 'to avoid duplication and conflict of interests.'

There was a flash, as Nkulunkulu's pillar of salt turned itself into a miniature model of Lot's wife, holding in her hands an LCD display reading *I told you, no salt*. 'I don't know,' he said. 'You work your fingers to the bone creating the world, making it nice for them, stocking it up with edible plants and gullible animals, and what do you get at the end of it all? Stone cold kedgeree and no bloody salt to go on it. It's enough to turn you Methodist.'

'Maybe he's on holiday.'

'Who?'

'Osiris.'

'Excuse me, young man, but are you a doctor?'

'Last time I saw him,' said Yama, 'he was talking to that nurse, you know, the chubby one. Haven't seen her in a while either, come to think of it.'

'Pity,' Nkulunkulu replied. 'Had a bit of meat on her, that

one did. Not like so many of these nurses you seem to get nowadays.'

'I don't think you're actually supposed to eat them, Nk.'

'I was speaking figuratively.'

'Oh.' Yama shrugged. 'Maybe Osiris got fed up with kedgeree and booked out,' he went on. 'I wouldn't be all that surprised, knowing him. Always did have balls – not in the right place, I'll grant you, but ...'

Ilmater shook her head. 'I don't think so,' she said. 'I rather believe booking out is against the Rules, otherwise we'd all have done it by ... Nk, who is this strange old woman and why is she showing me her knee?'

'That's Minerva,' the sky god replied. 'Ignore her and she'll go away. Tell you what, though, I'd like to see precisely where in the Rules it says you can't book out. Worth looking into, that.'

'Maybe he and the nurse eloped,' Yama mused. 'Difficult, of course, with the wheelchair and everything, but to the gods all things are – I don't believe it, rhubarb *again*. Take it away, woman, take it away, I don't want any.'

'Custard?' asked the waitress.

'No.'

The waitress looked over his head at Ilmater. 'Would you ask him if he wants custard?' she asked. 'Only I haven't got all day.'

Ilmater smiled, what she hoped was her patronising reassuring-the-servants smile. 'I don't believe he does, thank you,' she said. 'Sorry, Nk, you were saying?'

'About getting out of here,' Nkulunkulu replied. 'There probably is a way, you know, if only we could find out what it is. I'd be game, for one.'

'Just look, will you, that stupid woman's just poured custard all over my pudding. I really must insist on seeing the manageress.'

After lunch, say the Rules, residents will enjoy the peace and quiet of the common room. Nobody knows what the penalties for not enjoying the peace and quiet of the common room are, but only because nobody has ever had enough foolhardy courage to find out. As Nkulunkulu sat and stared at the television set, however, his mind remained unwontedly clear. Something was buzzing around in it like a fly in a bottle, and he wasn't quite sure what it was. Then he noticed the empty chairs.

Three of them, over by the repulsive picture of a small child with a kitten. Frantic ransacking of his memory turned up three names: Odin, Thor, Frey.

Stone me, muttered Nkulunkulu to himself, four of them AWOL. Four of them not enjoying the peace and quiet.

How many does it take, he wondered, to make up a Precedent?

'It was somewhere around here, I seem to remember,' said Osiris, looking up from the map, 'that they had the final shoot-out.'

Pan, who was trying to stand on one hoof while extracting a stone from his shoe, quivered. 'Who did?' he asked nervously.

'Butch Cassidy,' replied Osiris, 'and the Sundance Kid.'

Gravity is an evil bastard, Pan reflected as he wobbled, staggered and put his bare hoof down hard on a jagged flint. 'that was Bolivia,' he muttered.

'Oh.' Osiris shrugged. 'That's just down the road that way, I think. We might stop and have a look on the way back, if we have time.'

Pan silently vowed that they wouldn't have time, not unless he could have a nice comfy wheelchair too. 'We'll see,' he said. 'This volcano,' he went on. 'Shouldn't we be able to see it from here?'

'Look for yourself.'

Pan took the map. 'Oh hell,' he said, 'it's one of these awful modern ones, I can't read them. If it hasn't got dragons and Jerusalem in the middle I can't make head nor tail of it.' He screwed up his eyes. Not that he needed glasses – to the gods, all things are visible – but another reason why modern maps were so useless was the minuscule nature of the print. 'I'm sure you know what you're doing,' he said, and handed it back.

Nevertheless, he continued to have reservations – not a particularly unusual state of affairs; on any given subject, Pan generally had more reservations than the entire Sioux and Blackfoot nations combined – and the complete lack of distant prospects of volcanoes did little to resolve them. Nuts, he said to himself, we're lost. Again. And it's not even my fault.

'Where exactly,' he was therefore moved to ask next time they stopped, 'did you get that map from?'

'The airport,' Osiris replied. 'And you know, I have to say I don't think very much of it. That range of mountains over there, for example. Not a sign of it in here. Must be new, I suppose,' he hazarded, narrowing his eyes. 'Still, it's a poor show selling out-of-date maps, if you ask me.'

Pan nodded. 'New mountains, I see.' He took the map, looked at the cover and handed it back. 'That,' he said, 'is a street plan of Mexico City. According to which,' he added, 'that lot over there is the headquarters of the municipal fire service. How'd it be if we went back the way we came and tried to hire a taxi?'

As he spoke, the earth shook. Gods ought to be used to such things, but Pan never quite managed it; he still felt terribly guilty when, in spring, at the time of the quickening of the soil and the reawakening of the life force, he walked across somebody's nice new carpet without thinking and left behind him a trail of newly flowering primroses.

'Look,' Osiris said, and pointed.

Three of the distant mountains appeared to be on fire. Sheets of red flame were rising hundreds of feet into the air, which was now full of soft grey ash and little hot cinders, some of which settled on the back of Pan's neck.

'Headquarters of the municipal fire service,' Osiris repeated. 'Yes, you could say that. Lads, I think we're in business.'

It was, apparently, a good day for pyrotechnic displays of all kinds; because they hadn't gone more than a few hundred yards towards the mountains when the sky was lit up by a dazzling flash, and some huge fiery object streaked across it, travelling at some bizarrely high speed, and vanished over the horizon, followed for a relatively long time after by a deafening sonic boom.

'I told you,' Thor screamed, as the controls writhed in Odin's hands. 'Those head coil gaskets, I said, they're only sealed in with beeswax, go up too close to the sun and they'll melt. And what does the stupid prawn go and do?'

'Calm down,' Odin bellowed, as the slipstream ripped off his white silk scarf and sent it fluttering away into the air. 'Panicking won't solve anything. Now, when I say the word, I want you both to lean as far as you can over to your left. Right?'

The engine wobbled, jinked and turned a complete revolution around its central axis, but with no noticeable effect on its speed or trajectory. Frey, however, lost his left glove, ripped from his hand by the wind.

'I think we'll have to try an emergency landing,' Odin shouted. 'I'm just going to look around for a suitable spot.'

'Great.' Thor tried to wriggle down further into his seat. 'We're in enough trouble as it is without you crashing this poxy thing *deliberately*. Why not just sit back and let nature take its course?'

'I . . .'

'*Oh my god!*'

A fraction of a second ago, the mountains hadn't been there; then, all of a sudden, there they were. Later, Thor swore blind that they missed the peak of the tallest and sharpest of them by no more than twelve thousandths of an inch.

'That was interesting, what you just said,' roared Frey, with his eyes shut.

'Was it?'

'You said *Oh my god*. Didn't know you were religious, Thor.'

'Just an expression.'

'Ah.' Frey's knuckles whitened on the grab handle. 'Pity. We could do with some divine assistance right now.'

Odin was still wrestling with the joystick. 'What irresponsible fool put those mountains there?' he growled. 'Some people just don't think, that's their trouble.'

He jerked the joystick again, snapping it off. He stared at it for a moment and then put it carefully away under the seat. Probably get it back together again with a spot of weld, he reflected.

Thor leant out over the side. Up to a point his former view – the back of Odin's neck – had suited him fine, since it blocked out a lot of rather disturbing things, like the ground rushing up to meet them. On the other hand, he was so sick of the sight of his colleague that right now, anything would be preferable.

'Oh shit,' he groaned. 'More mountains.'

'Volcanoes,' Odin corrected. 'Active ones, by the looks of things. That's odd, you know.'

'Odd!'

Odin nodded. 'I think we may have wandered off course a bit,' he shouted. 'I don't recall there being any active volcanoes in Staffordshire.'

All this while, of course, they had been gaining rather than dissipating speed. It should therefore have been some comfort to them to reflect that even if the joystick hadn't snapped and even if the rudder had been working, there still wouldn't have been time to avoid the huge crater they now flew into . . .

But not out of.

*

'*Si, senor.*' The old peasant nodded and pointed. With a wave, the driver of the leading armoured personnel carrier waved and let in his clutch. The column moved off.

'*Medicos Yanquis,*' the peasant explained to his wife as they glumly contemplated next season's cabbage crop, over which the column had driven.

The peasant's wife scratched her brown nose, and smiled. On the other hand, she said, there was the compensation.

Compensation?

Compensation, she confirmed. When the Yankee drug police burnt down old Miguel's tomato plot last year thinking it was drugs, they paid him twice its value. And when they napalmed Salvador's beans and shot up his turnips with the helicopter gunships, he ended up with a profit of something like three hundred per cent. This year he was seriously considering hanging paper cut-out flowers on his onion sets to make them look like opium poppies, just in case they came back this way.

The peasant shook his head. Not drug people, he explained. Doctors.

Gringo doctors, his wife corrected him.

True . . .

The Guardian of the Golden Teeth stirred in his sleep.

It had been a long time since anybody had come – even mortals learn eventually, and twenty acres scattered with wind-bleached bones help to concentrate the mind. In actual fact, the bones were a job lot from a bankrupt ossuary, but the Guardian liked them. He felt they added tone.

Under him, the ground trembled, troubling his sleep with dreams of water-beds and passing trains. His subconscious mind reassured him that it was just the volcano playing up, and the dreams returned to their previous even tenor: a green baize cloth, coloured balls, a man in a waistcoat leaning pensively on a wooden shaft. The Guardian hadn't the faintest idea what the dream was supposed to be about, but so what. After the first ten years it was strangely hypnotic.

The fact of the matter was that, many years ago, a group of cunning and unscrupulous Australian television magnates, unwilling to meet the cost of launching a satellite, had found a way of using the Guardian's slumbering brain as a relay station, with the result that his primordial sleep was populated with soap operas, American films and round-the-clock sports coverage, all rattling around in his frontal lobes and frequently seeping through into the parts that processed the dreams. At one time, when the Melbourne Olympics coincided with the birth of Linda's baby and the TV premiere of *Lethal Weapon 9*, the Guardian's dreams were probably the most bizarre mental images ever generated since the death of Hieronymus Bosch.

Mortals. He could smell mortals, not too far away. And, he realised, another smell; a strange one, this, something that he could just faintly remember from a very long time ago. A worrying smell, presaging trouble.

(*'And where's one cue ball going to end up this time? Oh dear, that's exactly where he didn't want it to go. And how's Steve going to get himself out of this one, I wonder?'*)

Not mortals, the other things. Immortals. Gods. There were gods on his mountain. Dammit, when would they learn they weren't welcome here?

'Fine,' Pan said, sitting down on a rock and sinking his chin in his hands. 'Now all we have to do is find some way of moving them. Anyone think to bring a wheelbarrow?'

Below them lay the Teeth. The clear, tranquil, still slightly effervescent pink liquid that filled the crater served to distort the outline of the huge yellow objects that lay – how deep? A few metres? Fifty? A hundred? – below the surface, but in spite of that, and despite the distance from the lip of the crater to the bottom, the sight was little short of staggering.

Interesting to compare the reactions of the members of the party. Osiris had jammed the brake on his wheelchair and was gazing with one of the wildest surmises ever seen in those parts, silent on an extinct volcano in Nezahuancoyotl. Pan, as stated above, was wretchedly speculating as to who, in accordance with his usual rotten bloody luck, was going to be called upon to do the heavy lifting. Sandra was thinking, Right now, what wouldn't I give for a whacking great big cheeseburger. As far as we can tell, Carl wasn't thinking anything at all.

'Amazing,' Osiris said at last. 'All that wealth, all that ingenuity, all that manpower, and all the silly sods needed to do was invent the toothbrush.' He sighed. The older he got,

the more firmly he was convinced that all gods w̲ ̲
pillocks.

'Excuse me,' Pan interrupted, 'but if you've got some subt̲ ̲
scheme for shifting that lot, now would be a very good time to
mention it.'

Osiris brought his mind back from its reverie with an almost
audible click. 'No problem,' he said. 'We cheat.'

'We can do that, can we?'

''Course we can. We're gods, aren't we? Where's the point
in being a god if you can't bend the rules now and again?'

'There's bending rules,' Pan muttered, 'and there's the law
of conservation of matter. And before you ask,' he added, 'yes,
if they catch you breaking it they do come down on you like
a ton of bricks. Even for a first offence I believe the minimum
penalty is four thousand years' community service.'

'Relax,' Osiris replied. 'To the gods all things are possible,
remember?'

'I was afraid you were going to say that.'

'Don't be so damned negative about everything,' Osiris said
irritably. 'That's the trouble with you. At the first little sign of
difficulty you start to panic, and—'

'Well I would, wouldn't I?'

Osiris sighed. 'We cheat,' he said decisively. 'And this is how
we do it.'

Because, after all, the laws of physics are like all other laws
everywhere: designed to make life difficult and unpleasant for
the small fry like you and me, while the rich and powerful take
no notice of them whatsoever.

The basic, back-of-an-envelope logic behind it all was as
follows:

(a) Only things that are possible may be done without
violating the fundamental laws of the universe.

(b) However, to the gods, all things are possible.

(c) Therefore, *ipso facto*, anything a god chooses to do is by definition possible, and consequently entirely legal.

Fine; but that wasn't getting an extremely heavy set of false teeth shifted from the bottom of a very big crater. In order to achieve that objective, a degree more detail was required. Thus:

(a) It is extremely difficult to move a set of dentures which is huge and made of solid gold.

(b) On the other hand, it's extremely simple to move a set of dentures which is standard size and made of the latest in lightweight hard plastics.

(c) To the gods, who are eternal and enduring, all that is temporary and corruptible is pretty well the same; the atoms and molecules remain, but from time to time they make up an infinite variety of different shapes. To a god, the myriad shapes and forms that the atoms compose themselves into for a while before decay and entropy do their ineluctable stuff seem very like the individual frames that make up a length of cine film; each individual image is so transitory that the divine eye cannot perceive it, but the general theme remains behind once the image, and tens of thousands like it, have faded away into oblivion, and each single image goes towards building up the whole picture.

(d) Therefore, to a god, everything is what he wants it to be. Including ginormous sets of gold bridgework.

'Here we are,' Osiris said. He put the teeth carefully away in a jiffy bag, and stowed the parcel in his inside pocket. He turned his head towards Pan, and grinned. 'You see what you can achieve by thinking things through,' he added. 'Saves no end of mucking about.'

'Well done,' Pan replied, while his inner thoughts added *Bloody show-off*. 'And now I think we'd better be getting along, because I have this funny feeling that . . .'

In the crater, the lake was beginning to froth.

'You're paranoid, you are.'

'Am I?'

'Believe me.'

'Maybe,' Pan answered. He was looking down into the crater, where the froth was clearing on the meniscus of the lake, which was now starting to boil. 'Have you ever asked yourself what made me paranoid in the first place?'

Osiris followed his line of sight. 'On the other hand,' he said, 'standing round here chattering isn't achieving anything, and we've got a lot to do, so maybe we should . . .'

And then the volcano shook, and from the bottom of the now empty crater a waterspout leapt up, whirling and spinning. As it spun faster it seemed to take on a shape, a form branded on to the divine subconscious and signifying hassle. A few spins later, and it was solid.

'Strewth,' Carl muttered under his breath. 'It's a bloody great big snake.'

Out of the mouths of babes and morons. It was no longer even translucent; it was depressingly material, a monstrous serpent, towering above them, making a giant Redwood look like a dwarf geranium. At the top of the metallic scaled neck perched not one but very many small, diamond-shaped heads, each with its own fangs and flickering forked tongue. For the record, the Guardian had seventy-three heads, each one capable of independent action. Through his still sleeping brain, meanwhile, weird and incomprehensible messages flashed and were gone, leaving behind a sort of glow, like the flash of floundering colour you can still see with your eyes closed after looking at the sun.

Marvellous stuff, Steradent. Not only does it preserve dentures from decay and kill the lurking germs that find their way into the recesses of even the best false teeth; when the need arises, and some deadly peril threatens the teeth placed in its charge, it can (if infused with enough magic to poison a convention of wizards) turn itself into a hundred-foot-tall mythical serpent and devour all known intruders.

'Funny the way it's still bright pink,' Sandra observed. 'I wonder if it still tastes minty.'

One of the advantages of having the god Pan in your party is that you can get all the blind, unreasoning terror you could ever possibly need, the finest quality, trade. As the hydra uncoiled its grotesquely long neck and lunged, hissing (not exactly hissing; more a sort of bubbling fizz) and darting out countless pink tongues, the denture-thieves scattered and fled, leaving Osiris stranded directly in its path.

'Pan, you sodding coward!' they heard him shout. 'What the bloody hell do you think you're . . .?'

Oh no you don't, Pan reflected as he hurled himself into a narrow crevice between two split rocks and covered his head with his arms. I *know* what I'm doing, and I prefer it this way. I may be immortal, but I'd really rather not spend the rest of eternity inside the digestive organs of a fucking great snake, thank you all the same. And being a god means never having to say . . .

Oh *balls*!

Painfully and with infinite regret, he levered himself back out of safety, banged his head on a jagged rock in doing so, and ran back towards where Osiris had been.

The Guardian shuddered.

He was, of course, still fast asleep; the unofficial tenants of his brain saw to that. If he were to wake up, even for a moment, television reception on three continents would be interrupted and millions of viewers switching on for that day's episode of *The Young Accountants* would find themselves watching a rather slow and extremely esoteric documentary about the thought-processes of a pool of denture cleaner.

Since he couldn't wake up, he dreamed strange dreams. For example, his seventy-third head, through which passed live coverage of the Melbourne Open Golf Championship, was haunted by the image of one of the contestants suddenly grabbing the ball from the ninth green and making off with it. Head 34 (*A Million Menus*, with Yvonne Wilson) buzzed with a mouth-watering recipe for intruder fried in butter with fresh parsley and new potatoes. Head 41 (the popular game show *Name Your Poison*) cut out in the middle of the pushing-innocent-civilians-down-coal-shutes-and-pouring-hot-tar-on-their-heads round and started a new game entirely from scratch, the objective of which was to capture your opponent's knight's pawn and rip his lungs out with a meathook. One thing on which all the heads were decided was that as soon as there was a commercial break, they'd be out of there and hammering on the franchiser's door in search of a refund.

Burglars, whispered the night-watchman in his subconscious. Get on and eat the fuckers. Blearily, he turned his heads from side to side, scanning the surrounding area for someone to devour.

What his seventy-three pairs of eyes saw was a little old man in a wheelchair, shaking a liver-spotted fist at him and shouting angrily in a high, reedy voice. Burglars, the heads cried in unison. Do us a favour. That old codger couldn't burgle the Dogger Bank.

The Guardian was just about to give the whole thing up as a bad job and go back to his nice muddy bed when a flurry of movement caught his eyes. He hesitated, and saw another human figure sprinting awkwardly over the jagged outcrops of rock towards the old guy in the wheelchair and yelling. Two of them; rather more like it.

And a big hand, please, for our two brave contestants, who're going to step forward tonight and play Hiding To Nothing.

The wheelchair lurched forward, and it appeared that the older man was trying to move towards the younger. That, the Guardian reckoned, was thoughtful; one cyanide gas sneeze from Head 72 would do for both of them, and there was plenty of meat on the second one, even if the first was probably a trifle stringy.

The Guardian frowned and, on the basis that if two heads are better than one, seventy-three must be pretty damn smart, he considered the position in some detail, quickly drawing up a number of alternative courses of action, each one nothing more than an alternative means to the common end of making these two clowns wish they'd never been born. By the time the heads had taken a vote and decided to go for straightforward violence and mayhem, the running burglar had grabbed the handles of the wheelchair and set off as quickly as he could towards a large heap of rocks.

The hydra yawned. Oh well, he said to himself, here we go again. Another day, another mangled bag of crushed limbs.

'I don't know, Pan, there are times when I despair of you.'

Pan paused for a moment, panting for breath. This gave Osiris further scope to develop his theme.

'Call yourself a god,' he went on, 'I've seen beermats with more divinity than you. Your trouble is,' he continued, with the air of someone who had long been minded to make the ensuing points, 'you've got no sense of altruism. Can't be a god unless you care. You'd only take away the sins of the world if you could be sure of getting money back on the empties.'

'Osiris,' Pan replied, 'shut up.'

'It's all very well you saying—' Osiris got as far as saying before Pan clamped his hand firmly over his divine colleague's mouth. With the other hand he tried to push the wheelchair.

And it's Second Burglar on the inside, Second Burglar with Old Codger making a last-minute effort, is he going to make it or has he left it too late, Second Burglar coming up hard now on the inside, maybe finding the going a bit too hard for him . . .

The Guardian swooped, his heads swaying on his neck like over-heavy buds on a broken stalk, and lunged at Pan, who made a desperate effort to jump clear without letting go of the wheelchair. If the traffic wardens of physics had been standing by, they'd have given him a ticket for a flagrant breach of gravity. As Heads 63 and 47 snapped vainly at his heels he landed awkwardly, turned his ankle and bolted, jolting Osiris so violently that he almost swallowed his teeth.

'Mmm,' shouted Osiris through Pan's tightly gripping fingers. 'Mm mmm mmm mm mmm *mmmmmmmm* mm *m*!'

'I'll pretend I didn't hear you say that,' Pan gasped in reply. 'Hell's bells, that was close!'

The situation was deteriorating somewhat. He was tiring rapidly, he could feel the hot breath of Numbers 42–67 inclusive on the back of his neck and he had a sharp pebble in his shoe. It would be nice, he couldn't help thinking, if someone did something to help. Fairly soon would be nicer still.

There was a loud bang.

When a man has been in the contract killing and supernatural pest control business as long as Kurt Lundqvist, he learns to adopt a robust attitude to false modesty.

Just getting here, Lundqvist reflected, was enough to earn him a nomination for the Golden Uzi at this year's Beirut Festival. He'd walked barefoot across scalding hot deserts, climbed snow-capped mountains, living off small birds and insects and drinking the foul juice of cacti. By sheer dead reckoning he'd found his way to the only airport in a thousand square miles, hijacked a plane with nothing more lethal about his person than five days growth of beard and a plausible manner, overpowered five members of a commando unit sent to dispose of him and armed himself for the job he now had to perform from their rather inadequate kit. He was a big man, and the commandos had been highly trained, deadly and ruthless but nonetheless a bit on the petite size when it came to footwear. The largest boots they'd had between them were two sizes too small.

His seventh sense had warned him to expect to find trouble, and so he had approached the volcano circumspectly. Now, as he lifted his head and peeked out, he could see that he had been justified.

Huge pink hydras no longer fazed him. There had been a

time, a great many years ago, when a sight like the one now confronting him would have given him pause for thought, and quite possibly permanent psychological damage; but not any more. All that passed through his mind as he ducked down back out of sight was, Pink hydra, shit, how in God's name am I supposed to take out a pink hydra with this garbage?

The plane he had commandeered, it should be noted, was the flagship and one hundred per cent of the operational fleet of Air Easter Island, the recently formed national airline of that state; and although it wasn't actually powered by a rubber band, that was about all you could say for it. The commando squad sent to eliminate him had therefore been the elite forces section of the Easter Island Defence Force, and their equipment, though perfectly adequate for their purposes, was a few points behind NATO standards in terms of propinquity to the state of the art. Surveying what he'd got, Lundqvist reckoned, he'd be prepared to go a bit further than that. The only art this lot was anything like state of was probably Surrealism.

A quick mental inventory revealed:

Item; a Daisy air rifle, circa 1952.

Item; a surface-to-air rocket.

Item; a launcher for the rocket, consisting of a stick and an empty milk bottle.

Item; a Zambian Army Knife, all blades except the corkscrew broken.

Item; a Sony Walkman, 1982 model, and a tape of the Band of the Coldstream Guards playing Souza marches.

Item; a potato gun, with three rounds of Aran Piper.

Item; an RPG-7 anti-tank missile and projector.

The last item hadn't in fact come from the Easter Islanders. He'd found it in the glove compartment of the plane, and the only conclusion he could logically draw was that it had been left behind by some absentminded member of a previous hijack squad. It wasn't what he'd have chosen, but in context it was probably going to have to do.

He shouldered the RPG-7 and glanced through the sight. What met his eye wasn't the most encouraging of scenes. There was the hydra, huge great big thing with lots of heads, and directly underneath it, dodging about like a blindfolded hedgehog in the Los Angeles rush hour, was Pan, pushing Osiris' wheelchair with one hand and making feeble shooing gestures with the other.

Quickly he considered his options. In the circumstances, a head shot (his usual choice) was out of the question. That left the heart or the point of the shoulder; and since it was anybody's guess where the heart was, he opted for the latter. A well-placed hit there ought to break the spine, provided that the projectile had sufficient oomph to achieve the desired result. Probably not, he had to concede, but there's no harm in trying.

He steadied his aim, took up the slack on the trigger, aligned the sights and slowly squeezed off the last pound and a half of the trigger pull. There was a loud bang.

The Guardian froze, and all seventy-three heads turned slowly and in perfect unison towards the source of the noise . . .

. . . Which proved to be a man sitting behind a rock, holding what was undoubtedly an anti-tank missile launcher. There was no rocket in the breach. You could use the launcher as an impromptu vase for flower arranging, if you filled it with water, but that was about it.

By reflex the Guardian raised a paw and swatted at where the missile should have hit him, had it gone off. It hadn't, or rather, it had done exactly what it had originally been designed to do; it had produced a loud noise and pushed out from the muzzle a small, tatty flag, embroidered with the word:

BANG!

Marvellous, Lundqvist muttered under his breath. Millions of these RPGs were scattered about the world, and I have to get the one converted into a joke novelty. He reflected, apropos of nothing much, on his boyhood, playing tag with his father in the orchard out back of the house. His competitive instinct had compelled him to win, and on the occasion he had in mind, his father had been in hospital for three days afterwards.

The hydra, meanwhile, was turning towards him, looking with its seventy-three heads like nothing on earth so much as a very elderly mop of the sort that is made up of lots of batch ends of frayed string. It was coming this way.

'What I need,' Lundqvist said aloud, 'is an act of goddamn God.'

Which is precisely what he got.

The act in question had been performed by Odin; and to be absolutely precise it wasn't an act so much as an omission. It had been understood that when they were putting the traction engine back together again after picking it out of the side of the mountain they'd flown into, it was Odin's turn to clear out the intake valves. If that wasn't done, Thor had reminded him, the whole bloody contraption was liable to blow up.

'Can't be expected to work miracles,' Odin replied. 'All we can do is our best, that's what I always say.'

'Your best?' Thor laughed harshly. 'Are you sure you've got one? Or is it just one of your many worsts?'

Frey stirred. 'Actually,' he murmured, 'you can.'

'I can what?'

'Work miracles. It's dead easy, actually. Turn water into wine, for instance . . .'

The traction engine stalled. For a split second it hung in the air like a large, malformed cloud; then it began to fall to earth.

'Or there's loaves and fishes,' Frey continued, his hands so firmly over his eyes that powerful hydraulic rams would have been needed to dislodge them. 'I read a book about it when I was a kid. All you need is two loaves, five fishes, some sticky-backed plastic and a couple of old washing-up liquid bottles with the ends cut off . . .'

'I'm getting sick of this,' Thor growled. 'After all, it's my bloody engine, I'm a god and I've had it up to here. I'm going to do some magic.'

Odin frowned. 'We're not allowed –' he started to say.

'Bugger that.' Thor spread his arms and knotted his brows, trying to remember how you went about it. It had been quite a while and time tends to blur the sharp edges of the brain. All he could recall offhand was that in his particular method of disrupting the chain of causality, sticky-backed plastic and decapitated squeegee-bottles were conspicuous by their absence.

It was probably, he decided, a bit like mending a broken machine. You shouted at it, and if that didn't work you belted something with a bloody great big hammer.

'Right,' he yelled. 'Airbrakes!'

Nature, that much-abused personification, grinned. You want airbrakes, she whispered, you got them.

And this time it looks like the big fella's going to be in luck, he's bringing his number 42 head into position, and it looks very much like it's the end of a very courageous fight-back by Burglar, a very sporting loser here at the . . .

BANG!

The Guardian blinked, seventy-three times, simultaneously, and then fell over.

'What,' screamed Thor, who had pushed Odin aside and was wrestling ferociously with the joystick, 'the bloody hell was that?'

The traction engine was vibrating horribly; but, in some peculiar way, the impact had steadied it – broken its fall, you might say. Also, the quite stupendous jolt had had the effect on it of being thumped, very hard indeed, with a two-hundred-pound lump hammer.

It was a machine, and as such only understood one thing. Being clobbered with big hammers was something it could relate to. The motor, which had been simpering in a smug, self-satisfied way in preparation for total shutdown, coughed a few times, spluttered, caught and roared into life. They had lift-off.

'I beg your pardon?' Frey yelled back.

'I said, what was that?'

To the gods, all obscure things are clear, all hidden things are plainly visible. A god sees what is really there, disregarding the deception of form, the meretricious tricks of morphology.

'I think,' Frey therefore replied, 'we just hit a lake.'

We apologise for the temporary interference with reception, which is due to technical problems. Normal service will be resumed shortly.

The Guardian stirred, winced, and felt the side of his head. It hurt. Vague flashbacks of memory crept back, like a film of drifting smoke played backwards. A bang, a sharp blow; the silhouette of a tiny figure against the rim of the crater, with some sort of gun in its shoulder. Some bastard had taken a shot at him.

Right. We'll see about that.

On TV screens across half the globe, the test card flickered and vanished, and was replaced by what could loosely be described as drama: a huge giant kicking the innards out of a diminutive figure with a gun wrapped round its neck. *We interrupt our scheduled programme to bring you up-to-the-minute reports from our newsdesk. The attempt on the life of the Guardian of the Teeth earlier today has led to violent clashes between the Guardian and an unidentified burglar . . .*

*

Slowly, and with a certain amount of subdued fizzing, the Guardian stood up, wobbled for a moment and looked round. Because he was looking for one individual human being in particular, he failed to notice Pan, Osiris and party making a sharp tactical withdrawal in the opposite direction (taking the Teeth with them). Eventually he found what he was looking for. After a moment's thought he stooped down, uprooted a substantial boulder, and hefted it for weight and balance. Then he advanced.

Kurt Lundqvist, meanwhile, had dumped the RPG-7 and most of the rest of his captured arsenal, and was running like hell back towards where he'd left his transport. It went without saying that he did so with panther-like stealth, gliding like a dim ghost across the rocky terrain, or at least would have done if his feet hadn't kept jumping out of the tiny shoes.

He was almost in sight of safety when the light was blotted out in front of him by, he realised, a very large shadow. No need to look round and see what was causing it. Oh *god*, he muttered as he slithered and scrambled his way over the treacherous shale. God, I wish I . . .

'*Good on yer, mate. Told you you'd need the third wish sooner or later, didn't I?*'

'Screaming Jesus,' Lundqvist gasped. Although there was nothing to see, he could feel the Dragon King's presence in the air, smell its beery breath. 'You again.'

'*G'day. Looks like you've landed yourself in a spot of grief here, mate. Want me to sort it out for you?*'

'No,' Lundqvist shouted, 'absolutely not, no way. I have the situation perfectly under—'

A giant foot thundered down a mere thirty yards away, making the ground shake. The shadow grew slightly darker, if that was possible.

'*Fair go, sport, looks to me like unless you have some help smartish, you're gonna be history. You're sure about this?*'

'Yes, positive. Bugger off.'

'*I'll be saying g'day, then.*'

The air cleared around him, which only left the problem of the Guardian and his enormous rock. The latter was presently hovering about a hundred and twenty feet above Lundqvist's head, as the Guardian took aim and allowed for ground speed and windage.

Getting out of this one, Lundqvist admitted to himself, was going to be one of the most challenging problems of his professional career; and he had about half a second to do it in.

It's a truism to say that Fortune favours the brave; but the thing to remember about truisms is that they got that way by frequently being true.

Lundqvist got out of there with a margin of perhaps a fiftieth of a second; but get out he did. When the rock finally hit the ground, smashing a crater which, if flooded, would have made a wonderful yachting marina, Lundqvist was already a fair distance away, and moving fast. A specialist in gift horse dentistry might have pointed out to him that he was gripped firmly in an enormous, apparently disembodied, hand, which had appeared out of nowhere, scooped him up and carried him off; but Lundqvist was in no mood to find fault. Better, he reflected, a Lundqvist in the hand than a mangled corpse in the bush. Or words to that effect.

'Thanks,' Lundqvist called out. 'I owe you one, whoever the hell you are. Just drop me anywhere here and that'll be fine.'

'Don't tempt me.'

Lundqvist looked down. They were still many hundreds of feet above sea level, but at least they were over dry land. An island, to be precise. What was more, it had a strangely familiar look, although Lundqvist knew for a certainty that he'd never been there before.

'It was very kind of you to rescue me,' he called out. The hand tightened its grip very slightly; just enough to allow Lundqvist's circulation to continue working.

'What makes you think you've been rescued?'

Obviously, Lundqvist assured himself, a joke. After all, whoever this hand belongs to saved me from certain death.

He looked down again, and then up. You had to say this for certain death: at least it was certain. And, Lundqvist added, drawing on wide experience obtained over many years as Death's leading sales rep, it didn't usually involve hovering high up above islands tucked in the palm of giant hands, or at least not when he was administering it. A 200-grain full metal jacket slug from a .40 Glock was more his style, and by and large he had seen nothing in this character's *modus operandi* to make him revise his views. Death Lundqvist-style might be prosaic, but it avoided the vertigo and the travel sickness, and was over rather more quickly.

'Excuse me,' he asked, 'but where the hell are we?'

The air above him quivered as the proprietor of the hand chuckled disconcertingly. 'You don't recognise it?'

'Can't say that I do.'

'Look closer.'

Lundqvist did so; and it didn't take him long to notice the long rows of large, bleak, stylised anthropomorphic statues that stood in rows all over the beach and immediately contiguous area. The land mass below was Easter Island.

Ah.

'Look,' he shouted, as soon as he was able to get his larynx up and running again. 'If it's about the hijack I can explain.'

'I see. That's another useless talent you've got, is it?'

When the hand eventually stopped and the fingers relaxed a trifle, Lundqvist was no more than twelve feet off the ground, and was able to make a perfectly competent emergency landing on his head.

'By the time I've finished with you,' said the voice, 'I'll make you wish you'd never been born.'

The air swam for a moment; and then the rest of the body to which the hand was attached materialised in front of him.

Still no clues as to who or what it was, but it made the Guardian look like something found at the bottom of a breakfast cereal packet.

'Welcome,' it said, 'to Easter Island. I am Hotduyrtdx.'

'*Gesundheit.*'

'No,' said Hotduyrtdx, 'that's my name. And this,' it went on, making a sweeping gesture around the whole island, 'is my home. Or it was, at any rate. You see the statues?'

Lundqvist nodded.

'That's your fault.'

'But I've never been here in my life before.'

'Irrelevant. You're sure you don't remember what it is you've done?'

'Positive.'

The voice sighed. 'Then I'll explain,' it said.

A long time ago (said Hotduyrtdx) there was an island.

It had a population, of sorts; but far too many for the island to be self-sufficient in food. When Hotduyrtdx arrived to take up his new post as divine observer and acting pro-consul, the first thing he did was cast about in his mind for a suitable cash crop; something that would show a high, quick return on capital with minimum risk and no tax implications, making the most of locally available raw materials.

Now then, Hotduyrtdx asked himself, what is it that we have the most of? Answer: rocks. Lots of them. A fine crop, in its way, requiring the minimum of watering and potting on; but not, unfortunately, readily marketable. Think of something else.

And so Hotduyrtdx went away and thought hard and because he was a god (to whom all things are possible) and blessed with an elementary knowledge of economic theory, it wasn't long before the solution presented itself. Forget agriculture entirely. Go for broke with light industry. Make something for which there is an insatiable demand, and you're home and dry.

Such as?

Such as toupees for gods. Do you have difficulty in finding cranial accessories in your size, given that in your natural shape you're a hundred foot high and morphologically unstable? Have over-work and the pressures of executive office resulted in hair loss and premature baldness, leading in turn to a decline in worshipper credibility? Worry no longer. Easter Island Head Cosmetics will come to your rescue. Nobody, not even your fellow gods, will ever be able to see the join.

Hence the statues. None of your cheapskate synthetic rugs in a high-class establishment like this; each hairpiece was hand-made from only the very finest materials by dedicated craftsmen bound by the most dreadful oaths not to make sarcastic comments, no matter how illustrious the customer. For reasons that will shortly be made clear, the hairpieces themselves are now all long gone; but the wigstands remain behind, relics of a once massive industrial civilisation. Hundreds of them; tall angular stylised heads carved out of huge blocks of granite and basalt, all of them bald as billiard balls. Most of them, in fact, are still there to this day.

'Hey,' Lundqvist said, backing away, 'I think maybe you're overreacting a bit here. The plane's perfectly safe, I promise you. I even stopped off on the way and filled her up with gas on my AmEx card.'

Hotduyrtdx snarled, and advanced a step further. 'I'm not talking about the aeroplane,' he said. 'In fact, how do you think the plane came to be there, all nice and conveniently waiting for you? Why do you think you were able to overpower the guard and hijack it so easily?' He grinned, revealing a mouthful of teeth like the 'Before' stage of a hard-sell orthodontics advert. 'I think *set up* is the phrase you people use,' he added.

'But what have I done, man?'

A spasm of rage briefly contorted Hotduyrtdx's face (which

hadn't exactly been cuddly-looking to start with; imagine a Hieronymus Bosch watercolour left outside in the rain, and you'll get the general idea). 'For one thing,' he growled, 'I am not a man. Thanks to you I'm not a god either, not any more. But I think you've done enough damage already without adding insult to . . .'

Lundqvist tried to back away further, but an ill-mannered tree impeded his progress. 'What did I do?' he repeated. 'And when?'

'July 17th, 1469. Don't pretend you don't remember.'

'I don't have to pretend.'

'Ah well.' Hotduyrtdx shrugged. 'Actually, they say extreme agony sharpens the memory, so don't give up hope just yet.'

He swept out a talon, which Lundqvist only just avoided, and made a sound like tearing calico.

'Hey . . .' Lundqvist was just about to protest further when the librarians of his memory emerged, dusty and with cricks in their necks, from the uttermost filing cabinet of his mind. Easter Island. Yes.

It had been a very long time ago; back in the days when business had been slow and he'd supplemented his income by doing odd jobs for the Theological Survey Department. It had all been a bit of fun – his five-year mission; to explore new worlds, seek out new life forms, that sort of thing – and on the way home they'd stopped off, yes, *here*, dammit, to mend a puncture and take on water and garlic butter for the final leg of the journey. This place had changed a lot since then, of course. He shuddered.

'Remember now?' Hotduyrtdx asked. Lundqvist nodded.

One of the responsibilities of the Survey was to make routine checks on any gods or purported gods they came across, to ensure that they were complying with the various Practice Directions issued by the Department on various matters, most of them to do with the keeping of full accounts in the prescribed form and maintaining a proper level of professional indemnity insurance. It so happened that, on inspection, Lundqvist had found discrepancies and breaches of the rules, and had reported them. That, as far as he had been concerned, was the end of the matter. Certainly he'd heard no more about it at the time.

'They struck you off?' he said.

Hotduyrtdx nodded. 'And you know what for?' he went on. 'You know what it was I'd done that was so terrible I wasn't allowed to be a god any more? Go on, guess.'

'I can't.'

'I hadn't been filling out my green sheets in duplicate, like I was supposed to. Instead I was just filling out the top copy and taking a photocopy for the file. That was it. Heinous stuff, yes?'

Lundqvist cast his mind back. Green sheets – god, yes, them. He remembered now. Back then, all gods were supposed to fill out these idiotic forms each time they did a miracle. It was something to do with input tax, and the whole scheme was abandoned a short while afterwards.

'They struck you off for that?'

'Conduct unbecoming, they said.' Hotduyrtdx smiled grimly. 'The way they saw it, it was just an administrative error, and to err is human. If it'd been something really heavy, like bringing the dead back to life or wiping out a century's worth of history, I'd have got away with a reprimand, because to forgive is divine. Marvellous system, huh?'

Lundqvist nodded. He couldn't think of very much to say.

'The business had to close down, of course,' Hotduyrtdx continued remorselessly. 'All my customers were gods, see, and so I wasn't allowed to trade with them. As a result the whole population were put out of a job, they drifted back into subsistence agriculture and died out. I've been here ever since. Thanks to you.'

'I never meant . . .'

Hotduyrtdx scowled, and wisps of strange brown vapour

drifted from his nostrils. 'I don't imagine you did. Your sort never do. Ever since, I've been holed up here, brewing up moonshine magic out of anything I could lay my hands on, ready for the day when I could get even with you, you scumbag. It's been a long time.'

He advanced another two paces, until his shadow engulfed Lundqvist completely. It was hard not to notice the claws on the end of his feet.

'Would it help,' Lundqvist said tentatively, 'if I told you I was in a position to put a good word in for you with some very high-ranking gods indeed? I mean, like really top-flight . . .'

'No.'

'Okay.' He sighed. 'In that case,' he went on, 'you leave me no alternative.'

Hotduyrtdx blinked. 'What d'you mean, *I* leave *you* no alter . . .'

Lundqvist braced himself for the desperate expenditure of energy that was to come. Good old pineal gland, always been there for me when I needed you most, come through for Daddy just one more time, we all know you've got it in you. 'I just want you to know,' he said solemnly, looking for the right spot, 'that I really hate doing this. If there was any other way at all . . .'

'Doing what, for pity's sake?'

With a violent explosion of muscular effort, possible only because of countless years of specialist training, Lundqvist jumped between Hotduyrtdx's legs, hit the ground, rolled, regained his feet and used them.

'Running away,' he shouted back over his shoulder. 'I'll get you for this, you sucker!'

'Now just a flaming minute . . .'

But Lundqvist wasn't there any more. He had always been a good runner, although in different circumstances (he had always specialised in *after* rather than *away from*) and the thought of the claws and the quite staggering size of the horrible thing somehow made him able to set a pace that would have had Carl Lewis tripping over his feet in about twelve seconds. As tactical withdrawals went, it was pretty slick.

There is only so much percentage, however, in running away from someone when you're on an island; and running, as the man said, is one thing, hiding is quite another. As he ran, Lundqvist's mind kept itself occupied with figuring out how many of Hotduyrtdx's strides it would take to traverse the island from one side to the other. Not many, he decided. Not nearly many enough.

'*Ready yet?*'

'I told you,' Lundqvist panted, 'bugger off. I've got enough problems of my own without you to contend with.'

The Dragon King of the South-East shrugged his shoulders. '*Blimey, mate,*' he said, '*you're a hard bloke to help, no worries. Just say the word and I'll have you out of there in two shakes of a possum's—*'

'Go away! Piss off! Get the hell outa here!' Lundqvist yelled. 'This is your last warning, okay?'

'*Be like that,*' said the Dragon King huffily, and vanished.

Five minutes of flat-out running later, Lundqvist was so demoralised that he was beginning to wonder whether the Dragon King mightn't have been such a bad idea after all when he came to an unscheduled and quite involuntary stop. Some idiot, it seemed, had built a damn great wall right across the road. To make matters worse, they'd painted it invisible.

'Are you hurt?' said a disembodied voice.

Kurt tried to move; but the parts of his brain responsible for motor functions told him to forget it. He groaned.

'Because if you are,' the voice went on, 'we might be able to help. We're doctors, you see.'

At which point, the two doctors stepped out from behind the invisible wall. They were carrying the inevitable black bags, together with assorted firearms, hand grenades, surface-to-air missile launchers and extremely hi-tech edged weapons; in other words, almost exactly the way the young Kurt Lundqvist had imagined Santa Claus looked, except that they didn't have red robes, long white beards and flak jackets.

'Mind you,' said one of the doctors, 'it's partly your own fault for not looking at the signs.'

Lundqvist spat out a tooth. 'Signs?' he croaked.

A doctor nodded. 'Back there,' he replied, pointing. 'Big signs saying, *Caution, invisible wall*. Of course they're invisible too, but . . .'

Numb, Lundqvist lay still while they examined him and, eventually, prescribed two aspirin and a good lie down. 'What the hell do you think you're doing?' he asked.

A doctor looked at him. 'You are Kurt Lundqvist, aren't you?' he asked.

Lundqvist nodded. 'Why?'

'Good.' The doctor took out his stethoscope, blew down one earpiece and listened to Lundqvist's chest. 'Your friends are coming to rescue you,' he said. 'That's why we're setting up these invisible road-blocks. Clever, yes?'

'How did they know I was here?'

'*I told 'em, of course,*' replied the Dragon King of the South-East, materialising in a deck chair in mid-air about four feet over Lundqvist's head. '*The way I saw it, if you're such a galah you won't ask me to help you, it's up to me to use a bit of initiative.*'

Lundqvist groaned and lay back on the ground. 'I shall count to ten,' he said. 'If you're still here. . .'

'*Cheerio for now, then. Remember, you've still got one wish.*'

'I wish you'd disappear up your own arse, you fucking stupid goldfish.'

'*I'll pretend I didn't hear that,*' said the King cheerfully, and vanished.

Kurt propped himself up, painfully on one elbow, and turned to the two doctors, who were planting invisible landmines. 'You heard that,' he said, 'you're witnesses. I made a perfectly valid wish. I asked him to vanish, he vanished. Okay?'

A doctor looked at him. 'Who vanished?' he asked.

'Concussion,' said his colleague.

'Oh yes, of course. Silly me. Here, Mr Lundqvist, you'd better make that three aspirins.'

Why bother? Lundqvist said to himself. He whimpered, got slowly to his hands and knees, and crawled away behind the wall.

Fortuitously, it turned out; because no sooner had he vanished from sight than Hotduyrtdx suddenly hove into view, making the ground shake with his footsteps.

'Oy, you,' yelled a doctor. 'Not this way, there's a minefield, you could get –'

Bang.

There was a short pause, during which large chunks of uprooted turf plopped back down to earth.

'Excuse me, but are you injured at all?'

Hotduyrtdx snarled; difficult, because his body was now in more pieces than one of those incredibly complex jigsaw puzzles you were given by aunts for Christmas in your formative years, and which went straight up into the loft first thing on Boxing Day morning.

'I got blown up,' he grunted. 'I'd leave me well alone if I were you.'

The two doctors exchanged glances.

'Ah well,' one of them said at last. 'Now at least we know they still work.'

To the gods all things are possible. Well, virtually all.

'Marvellous,' Thor growled. 'Absolutely bloody wonderful. Now what do we do?'

Frey pointed. 'There's a little sticker,' he said, 'look, there on the windshield. That probably tells you the procedure.'

He leant forward and read aloud: "This vehicle has been immobilised; do not attempt to move it . . ."'

'Yes, thank you, I can read,' Odin said. 'The question is, how do we get rid of the confounded thing?'

One of the things – the very, very few things – not possible to gods is removing wheel clamps from illegally parked traction engines, using only the rudimentary tools usually carried in the glove box. 'We could pay the fine,' Frey suggested. 'I gather that usually does the trick.'

Thor snarled. Not for nothing had he been the god of thunder for countless centuries; it started to drizzle with rain.

'Over my dead body,' he said. 'Nobody wheelclamps a god and gets away with it.'

'Fine. So you do know how to get it off, then?'

'Yes. I'll, um, remember in a minute.'

Always the way, isn't it? A quick pitstop in the suburbs of Mexico City, to buy gasket sealant and gear-box oil; Odin's cheerful assurance that they could park in the No Parking zone with impunity since they were only going to be three minutes, and there were no traffic wardens in sight of his all-seeing eye. And here they were. Stuck.

Thor pulled himself out from under the chassis, oily-faced but grinning. 'I think I see how to go about it,' he said. 'Odin, I'll need the tin of grease and a cold chisel. Frey, my hammer.'

A quarter of an hour passed noisily, at the end of which time Thor had hit everything he could reach (including, on a regular basis, his own fingers) and the clamp was still there.

'All we have to do is give them some money and they come and do it for us,' Frey insisted. 'Come on, it's easy. Mortals can do it, even.'

'Shut up, I'm thinking. Odin, go and buy a hacksaw.'

Twenty minutes later; the hacksaw blade had eventually snapped, taking a lump out of Thor's thumb as it did so. Otherwise the situation was pretty well unchanged.

'On the other hand,' Frey said, 'we could stay here for ever and ever. You know, find jobs, settle down, get married, that sort of thing.'

'I said shut up.'

'Leave Frey alone, Thor. It's not his fault.'

'Yes, but he's being aggravating, and if he carries on like that I shall knock his block off with my hammer.'

'He's always aggravating. I don't notice it any more.'

'. . . Ready-made start in the scrap iron business . . .'

'You see? How am I supposed to concentrate with him mithering on all the time?'

'You've just dropped the three-eighths spanner down that grating.'

Thor sighed. 'I seem to remember,' he said dismally, 'we had a damn sight fewer problems when we were creating the Earth.'

Odin nodded. 'Me too,' he said. 'On the other hand, it's one thing making something from scratch, but mending it once it's bust is another matter entirely. Besides,' he added wistfully, 'we had the proper tools then.'

'God, yes.' Thor sighed in nostalgic reverie. 'Remember that seven-mill Bergsen cutter with the adjustable three-way head? Went through igneous rock like a knife through butter.'

'And what about the old rotary magma plane?' Odin smiled involuntarily. 'Whatever became of that, by the way? It must still be about the place somewhere.'

Thor shook his head. 'Swopped it with the Celtic mob for a set of river-bed props and a beach grinder. Load of old tat that was, too. Worst deal I ever did.'

'Bet you they let it get all rusty.'

'Never cleaned anything in their lives.'

'Excuse me,' said Frey, 'but are we going to do something about this wheel thing or are we just going to stand here chattering on until they pull the city down and build a new one?'

His two colleagues looked at him.

'Oh, shut up,' they said.

'Whose damnfool idea was this, anyway?' Osiris demanded, scratching his ear and wriggling uncomfortably in his wheel-chair. 'It certainly wasn't mine.'

It was a hot day and the hill was steep. Pan therefore had to save up his breath, like a child with a piggy bank, in order to have enough to answer.

'Don't look at me,' he said.

Neither of the mortals said anything, mainly because neither of them had a very clear idea of where they were or what they were meant to be doing. One moment they'd been escaping from an anthropomorphic oral hygiene accessory, the next they were on a Lear jet flying south-east.

'He's your friend,' Osiris retorted. 'I naturally assumed . . .'

Pan shook his head, while his lungs went into overdraft. 'I knew the man once, many years ago, but I wouldn't say we were friends. Generally I try not to associate too closely with people who spend most of their time bloody to the elbow.'

Osiris sighed. 'Well,' he said, 'we're here now, we might as well do the job. Then I suggest we get out of here as quickly as possible. This whole thing is getting unnecessarily compli-cated, if you ask me.'

'Behind you all the way,' Pan replied, and in his mind added, Yeah, pushing. Same as usual. Why do I get all the rotten jobs?

'Excuse me.'

Osiris looked back over his shoulder. 'Well?' he asked.

'Excuse me,' said Sandra, 'but the gold teeth things. What did you do with them?'

By way of reply Osiris grinned and patted his trouser pocket. Then the grin became a frown, the patting became frantic thumping, and spread to his other pockets like plague in a sixteenth-century seaport.

'You're not going to believe this,' he said.

But Pan believed it all right. In fact, he'd been waiting for it for a long time, and in a sense he was relieved it was over.

'Where,' he asked tonelessly, 'did you have them last?'

All living things are good at something; and Osiris' innate gift was for losing things out of pockets. When he was still an active god, before his retirement, this unfortunate habit was the main thing standing between him and high office within the Federation. (To give just one example: the lost kingdom of Atlantis was a centre of Mediterranean trade and marked on all the maps until one day it was Osiris' turn to lock up and switch off all the lights after the other gods had gone home. Atlantis remained lost for over four thousand years, until it eventually turned up, dusty and covered in bits of grey fluff, down the back of Osiris' sofa.)

'They're here somewhere,' Osiris was saying, in the tone of voice that implies that everything will come right just so long as you have faith. This didn't convince Pan, who knew from long experience that faith does indeed move mountains, but always puts them down again in the wrong place and invariably loses or breaks a couple of foothills in the process. 'Just bear with me a second and I'll . . .'

'You've lost them, haven't you?' he said.

'Of course I haven't lost them. How can anyone lose a set of false teeth the size of Mount Rushmore?'

'To the gods all things are possible.'

'Ah,' Osiris said, 'here they are.'

From his inside jacket pocket he produced a shiny yellow object which, on closer inspection, proved to be the upper set. Of the lower set there was no trace.

'Brilliant,' Pan said. 'Well, there's nothing for it, we'll just have to retrace our steps. It shouldn't be too hard a job,' he added grimly. 'All we have to do is find a country we've passed through or flown over which has suddenly quadrupled its national wealth overnight. Look out for new, expensive-looking warplanes with the cellophane still on the seats, that sort of thing.'

'Excuse me,' said Carl.

'Or maybe we could try the lost property offices,' Pan continued. 'Ask if anyone's handed in any gold icebergs. There are some honest people left in the world, after all, and—'

'Excuse me.'

The two gods turned round, to see Carl balancing the missing dentures on the palm of his hand. Pan swallowd hard, and grabbed.

'I think,' he said, gently but determinedly relieving Osiris of the other set, 'I'll take charge of these little tinkers for the time being. I'd prefer it if any further outbreaks of alarm and despondency were my fault. After all, that's what I'm good at.'

Osiris nodded meekly. 'Best thing to do,' he said, 'would be to get this lot cashed in as quickly as possible.'

'Cashed in?'

'Realised. Turned into money.' He hesitated, musing. 'Mind you,' he added, 'that's easier said than done. I don't think we can just wander into a jeweller's shop and expect to be paid cash.'

'We need a specialist, you mean?'

Osiris nodded. 'And come to think of it,' he said, 'I know just the very chap. More or less down my old neck of the woods. Retired now, of course, but stayed in those parts. Don't think he had much choice.'

'Excuse me.'

'Yes, thank you, Carl, we've found them now,' Pan said irritably. 'Get on with evolving into a sentient life-form or something, there's a good—'

'It's them doctors,' Carl said. 'I thought you'd want to know, that's all.'

'Where?'

'Over there.'

'*Where?*'

'Look,' said Carl, pointing. 'Just there, behind that big grey thing.'

'Oh.'

*

'You know something,' said one of the doctors to his colleague, as they lowered the lid of the tank into place and tightened up the restraining bolts, 'when this job is over I think I might retire. Pack all this in.'

His colleague wiped sweat from his forehead with the sleeve of his white coat. 'Yeah?' he said.

The doctor nodded. 'Think so,' he replied. 'Retire, open a little clinic somewhere, make people better. You know, sick people.'

His colleague frowned. 'You reckon there's a future in that, do you?'

'Could be. I mean, it's worth a shot, isn't it?'

'Might work, I suppose. Right,' he added, lighting the blowtorch. 'We'll just seal up the interstices with molten lead, and then that's that job done.'

It had been a remarkably efficient operation; basically a larger-scale version of catching rabbits with the aid of a ferret, except that the net had been a three-foot-thick sheet of invisible glass dumped across the road, and the ferret had been the two doctors plus a large group of stage extras hired for the day, equipped with uniforms, collecting tins, leaflets and Gideon Bibles.

'How was I to know,' said Pan, inside the tank, bitterly. 'They looked just like real Jehovah's Witnesses to me.'

'We should have stood our ground, in any case,' Osiris replied. 'You don't just turn tail and run as soon as you see a lot of God-botherers walking up the path.'

'I do. And so, I seem to remember, did you.'

'True.' Osiris nodded sadly. 'Basic inbuilt reflex action.' He scratched his head sadly. 'And another thing,' he went on. 'They call themselves witnesses, but they can't be. They're all too young, for a start.'

The tank was a masterpiece of applied theology. Specially

built in Germany, where they still know a thing or two about craftsmanship, to exquisitely precise specifications, it was proofed to withstand internal pressures which would make the Big Bang seem like a car backfiring, while the lining of pulped copies of standard nineteenth-century Nihilist philosophical texts was capable of damping out supernatural manifestations equivalent to 7.9 miracles. Anyone able to get out of there would have to have been capable not only of parting the Red Sea but folding it up like a newly ironed tea towel.

'Well,' Sandra said, 'you'd better hurry up and get us out of here. I really am starving, you know?'

'I'm doing my best,' Osiris replied. 'Who do you think I am?'

'Well . . .'

'Yes, point taken. Any suggestions?'

Sandra considered. Her mythological knowledge was limited to stray particles of legendary matter that had adhered to the fly-paper of her imagination. 'How about turning yourself into a shower of gold?' she suggested.

Pan and Osiris looked at each other, and simultaneously sighed.

'Listen, love,' said Pan. 'Two thousand years ago, no problem. These days, with the best will in the world, I think that at our age, between us, the best we could manage would be a small wad of Italian lire. It's a case,' he explained, 'of the spirit being willing but the currency being weak.'

Sandra wrinkled her nose. 'I see,' she said. 'All right, what about a burning bush? You could cut your way out, like one of those oxy-acetylene torch things.'

'Nah,' Osiris replied, 'that's not us, that's more your Judaeo-Christian touch. Different cultural heritage entirely.'

'Not solar-based,' Pan agreed. 'Completely different technology. Besides, we'd need goggles. We've just got to face facts, we're stuck in this bloody thing until somebody lets us out.'

'Oh yes?' Sandra enquired. 'Who, for instance?'

'Gawd only knows.'

14

Lundqvist woke up.

He found himself in a dark, gloomy cave, rank with the smell of stale air and rotting vegetation. His arms and legs were securely bound with thick electric cable, he was gagged with what tasted like a very old and lonely sock, and there was a guard with an Armalite rifle sitting about five yards away, reading a pornographic magazine.

Ah, he said to himself, back to normal. I was beginning to worry back there.

It had been, he reflected, a pretty bad run so far, by his standards. He'd divided his time on this project so far between standing about like a bottle of brown sauce at a state banquet, getting under people's feet and being in the way (which was bad enough) and being chased, scared out of his wits, abducted and made to run away (which was *awful*). He was confused, unarmed and thoroughly depressed, and he hadn't killed anything except time for as long as he could remember. The way he'd been feeling, if a spider had run up his leg he'd probably have tried to trap it in a matchbox and put it outside the door.

Now, however, things were looking up.

It was the work of a moment to fray through the cable against the rock behind him; a mere bagatelle to chew the sock in half; a trifling inconvenience to roll over, break free from his bonds and stun the guard with one blow. In fact, if he hadn't slipped on (of all things) a banana skin and nutted himself on a low shelf of rock, he'd have been out of there in less than six minutes, thereby shattering for ever the record set by Clignancourt and O'Reilly at the Grande Convention Mondiale des Assassins et Espions Professionels in 1967. As it was, he merely equalled it.

Once outside, with a rifle in his hands and (presumably) people to rescue against overwhelming odds in the face of certain death, he felt much better. His manner as he worked a steady and decidedly businesslike way through the various heavily armed men he found here and there about the place was positively jovial. He smiled as he dodged the hail of bullets from the Browning .50 calibre machine gun mounted on the back of the half-track beside the big grey rectangular box, and grinned as he kicked open the rear cargo doors and beat the occupants into insensibility with the butt of his rifle. Somwhere nearby, he felt sure, he could hear nightingales singing.

Then he caught sight of the two doctors.

Yum, he thought.

Please, he said to himself, please let them open up with a couple of Uzis, so that I can take cover, return fire, lob in a couple of these beautiful stun-grenades I found lying about over by the jeep and then go in with the cold steel. And please let them be wearing Kevlar body armour. And please let them have reinforcements standing by to try and keep me pinned down while I dynamite the lid off that big box thing.

A few helicopters wouldn't come amiss, either.

And so the day went on. The sun shone, bullets flew, plastic explosive detonated, and for once someone somewhere in the world was, for a while at least, completely well-adjusted and happy with his lot. There were, admittedly, only three helicopters; but one of them had an Oerlikon 20mm cannon, which made up for quite a lot, particularly when it crashed.

And finally, to round off a beautifully mellow afternoon, he found a tub of Semtex, blew the lid off the tank, and threw down a rope.

'*The sun has got his hat on* ... Come on, you guys, it's time to split,' he yelled. 'Grab the rope and let's get our butts outa here ... *The sun has got his hat on and he's coming out today* ... Come on, let's *move!*'

In the gloom inside the tank, Osiris stirred and looked up. Someone had just dropped a rope on his head.

'Good grief,' he exclaimed, 'it's that maniac friend of yours. The one who got us all in this mess in the first place.'

Lundqvist froze. He could feel the confidence and *joie de vivre* ebbing away. God, he hated being around gods. They did something to him.

'Took your bloody time, didn't you?' Pan said, yawning and massaging his leg, which had gone to sleep. 'Next time, a bit less of the prancing about shooting at people and more attention to the job in hand, all right?'

'Yeah, okay,' Lundqvist mumbled. 'Look, could you kinda get it moving, because they outnumber us fifteen to one and—'

'Is that all? I thought you did this sort of thing for a living.'

'I do.' Lundqvist ducked as a bullet skimmed off the side of the tank a mere inch from his head. 'I'm doing pretty damn good, if you must know. Now can we—?'

'The shooting bothering you, is it?' asked Osiris ironically. 'Well, we'll see what we can do, shall we? Just a moment. There.'

The shooting stopped.

'Hey,' Lundqvist demanded, 'what happened?'

Osiris smiled. 'I turned them all into frogs,' he replied. 'Now, will somebody please give me a hand with this rope thing?'

'You turned them all into frogs.'

'That's right.'

'Just like that?'

'Piece of cake.'

Lundqvist bit his lip. 'I see,' he said. 'Fine.'

'I mean,' Osiris went on, 'if I'd had to wait for you to finish fiddling about we'd be here all night.'

'Yeah. Right. Thanks.'

'And another thing,' Osiris added, pushing the rope aside and levitating smoothly out of the tank. 'Next time you need rescuing, get somebody else. Take out insurance or something. We're busy people, you know.'

Lundqvist looked down at his rifle, sighed, and threw it away. Never wanted to see another silly old rifle as long as he lived.

'Sorry,' he said.

In the introductory booklet that accompanies his bestselling video, *Kurt Lundqvist's Paranormal Assassination Techniques Workout*, Lundqvist was later to write that 'in ninety-nine cases out of a hundred, actually doing the job on some vampire or ghoul is the piss-easy part; getting there is where the real hassle comes in'. He wrote, obviously, from bitter experience; and some of his biographers pinpoint the journey from Easter Island to the Sinai desert as the crucial catalyst that led him to formulate this justly famous aphorism.

Hijacking a passing destroyer and hitching a forced lift as far as the Solomon Islands was, comparatively speaking, a walk-over; it was the scheduled flight to Tel Aviv, followed by the train journey, followed by the taxi ride that nearly brought him to his knees. The combination of Pan's extreme fear of air travel ('If we'd intended ourselves to fly we'd have given ourselves wings.') and Osiris' undisguised contempt for all forms of technology not directly based on magic and superstition, plus such minor details as their complete lack of either money or passports, made for a trip that was memorable in the same way that death is a unique, once-in-a-lifetime experience.

'Well,' Pan remarked, as they paid off the taxi and lifted out their luggage, 'here we are. Changed a bit since I was last—'

'Follows,' Osiris replied. 'Changed a hell of a lot since *I* was last here. It's fallen down, for a start. Now, who's got the rams' horns?'

There are few more evocative place names in the world than Jericho, and it's hard to know what to expect. The modern town, snuggled under the mountains, is just a town – 'the sort of place,' as Sandra observed, 'where you could probably get a bath and something to eat'. A few miles beyond, you come to the remains of the massive stone walls of the ancient city which, so archaeology tells us, were shaken down by an earthquake some time around 1200 BC.

'It's around here somewhere,' Osiris said, shielding his eyes against the glare of the sand. 'Exactly where, though, escapes me for the moment. I always used to get my bearings from Ameneshke's kebab stall, and I think he went bust about three thousand—'

'Me too,' Pan replied. 'Dunno why, because the old sod did a mean camel kebab. Besides,' he added, 'the old place does seem to have fallen down rather, which I find has a somewhat disorientating effect.' He prodded a pile of fallen masonry with one toe. 'Hence the expression "Jerry-built", I guess,' he said. 'Well, you have a poke about, I'm just going to see if I can't get forty winks under this bit of shade here.'

He selected a pile of millennia-old rubble, brushed away some of the dust, and lay down, his head leaning against a fragment of pillar. It moved.

The scene changed. The landscape changed. For a start, Pan was now lying on a broken column forty foot up in the air.

'Ah,' Osiris said, 'you've found it. Good lad.'

The city of Jericho, as observed above, was destroyed by an earthquake.

This snippet of misinformation emanates from the same source as the reassurance that flying saucer sightings are all hoaxes, crop circles are caused by modern fertilizers or unscheduled helicopter landings, ghosts are all done with mirrors by unscrupulous mediums and the crew of the *Marie Celeste* abandoned ship as they did because of a surprise visit from the excise men.

The city of Jericho is still, of course, there; and the piles of untidy rubble shown to visiting coach parties are mere camouflage, surreptitiously inserted by a League of Nations task force under pretence of excavating the site, shortly after the First World War.

Despite this universal conspiracy of silence (unmasked in all its Machiavellian deviousness by the late Danny Bennett in his seminal but hitherto unpublished masterpiece, *The Holy Grail and the Holy Graft*), getting into Jericho is in fact child's play. All you have to do is . . .

'When you've quite finished,' Osiris called out, 'you can come down here and do something useful for once.'

Pan, suffering from quasi-terminal agrophobia on a narrow chunk of rock which would have done St Simeon Stylites very nicely as a shooting-stick, racked his brain for an appropriately scintillating jewel of repartee.

'Help!' he said.

Lundqvist eventually got him down with the help of a long piece of rope and a few rocks; and the fun began.

To get into Jericho . . . The phrase is misleading. It's more a case of getting Jericho back.

'Because,' Osiris explained to Sandra, as he gave his ram's horn an experimental puff, 'the old place wasn't so much destroyed – how you're supposed to play one of these things I have absolutely no idea – as put away in a safe place so that it wouldn't get lost.'

Sandra squinted. 'How can you lose a city?' she replied.

Osiris grinned. 'Well, the best way is to put it in a safe place and then forget where. In fact, it's about the only way.'

'Ah.'

At the next attempt the ram's horn did indeed make a noise. It was very faint and extremely vulgar, and it made Osiris realise that there was more to this than met the eye. He wondered whether a saxophone would do instead, at a pinch.

'Now I bet you're wondering,' he went on, jabbing about

inside the horn with a piece of wire to see if there was anything inside, 'why anyone should want to lose a city. Yes?'

'Well . . .'

'Easy. It's a sort of prison.'

'Right.'

Osiris frowned. 'Well, when I say prison, more a sort of remand centre. For gods.'

Sandra looked up. 'Gods?' she repeated.

Osiris nodded. 'It's all rather sad, actually,' he said. 'Long time ago now, this area was absolutely crawling with gods. Elamite gods, Hittite gods, Phoenician gods, Philistine gods, Moabite gods, Edomite gods—'

'I thought Edom was a sort of cheese.'

'—Jebusite gods, Hivite gods, Amorite gods, Canaanite gods . . .' Osiris paused, having run out of fingers. '. . . hundreds of the little tinkers, all squabbling and bickering over who could have what and whose drains went under whose driveway and whose hedge was eighteen inches too far to the left, all that sort of thing. Well, it had to stop.'

Sandra, who had learnt a thing or two about gods during her time at Sunnyvoyde, raised an eyebrow. 'Why?' she asked. 'Sounds perfectly normal behaviour for gods, if you ask me.'

'It was letting the side down,' Osiris replied stiffly. 'Mortals were getting involved. Anyway, all the other gods got together and give them an ultimatum: pack it in, or else.'

'And?'

'Else,' Osiris replied grimly. 'They refused to take a blind bit of notice, and so we had to take steps. We locked 'em up.'

Sandra stared at him. 'Put them in jail, you mean?'

Osiris nodded. 'We had no choice, really. They were making a laughing stock—'

'Your own kind? You locked them away, just like that?'

'If there had been any other way . . .'

'Huh!'

Osiris frowned and fidgeted with his ram's horn, in which

he had just discovered a mouse nest. 'Anyway,' he said, 'here's where we put them, in Jericho. Then we sort of vanished it.'

'Sort of vanished it.'

'That's right.' Osiris rubbed his eyes. Put this way, it did seem a bit extreme. At the time, though . . . 'Jericho lies on this huge geological fault, you see,' he continued, 'and we just opened it up, dropped the city in and closed it up again. It was only a temporary measure,' he added, catching Sandra's eye, 'just to give the ringleaders, Ashtoreth and Melkart and Mammon and the rest of them, time to patch up their differences and learn to get along with each other like civilised adults.'

'Really.'

'After which,' Osiris continued, red in the face, 'they'd be sort of parolled . . .'

'Let out on Ba'al,' Pan interrupted, strolling up and rubbing germoline into the rope burns on his hands. 'Never got around to it, though, did you?'

'The time never seemed exactly right, somehow.'

Pan nodded. 'Exactly,' he said. 'The fact that you lot divided up their territories between you was neither here nor there. And neither, of course, were they.'

'I see,' Sandra said. 'And now you're going to let them out again.'

'Strictly on a trial basis.'

Pan grinned. 'He needs a favour,' he explained.

'Does he?' Sandra looked puzzled. 'From a load of gods who've been locked up in a cave for thousands of years? What on earth—?'

'Money.' Pan shrugged. 'What else?'

'They're going to pay him money?' Sandra hazarded. Pan shook his head.

'Not pay money,' he replied, grinning. 'Launder it.'

Once again, Sandra looked surprised; shocked, even. 'Launder it?' she said. 'But isn't that what criminals do? Thieves, and so on?'

'And gods, too,' Pan replied. 'Perfectly ordinary, reputable, divine behaviour. Hence such well-known phrases as "Honour among gods" and "Gods' kitchen" and "Like a god in the night". So—'

'What Pan is trying to say,' Osiris interrupted, 'is that this is an opportunity for these hitherto troublesome and disruptive members of the divine community to redeem their previous antisocial behaviour by . . .'

Like most superstitions, the concept of widdershins has its origins in very pertinent fact.

As witness . . .

Two gods, one contract killer, one lorry driver and one state registered nurse, all clutching ram's horns, all clumping very self-consciously round and round (widdershins, of course) a frost-damaged basalt pillar in the middle of the desert.

'When I say blow,' Osiris called out, 'blow your horns.'

Pan scowled. 'Who dos he think he is?' he muttered, 'Count Basie?'

'Is something going to happen?'

'Wait and see, Carl my old mate,' Pan replied, lifting his horn to his lips and making a noise rather like prrrrp

Tramp, tramp, tramp they went, seven times round the pillar; and to mark the end of each circuit, a fanfare on the horns. There have been louder fanfares, it's true, and more melodious and impressive ones too. But a crummy fanfare is still a fanfare.

'We must be complete idiots, letting ourselves get talked into—'

'Shut up, Pan. Now then,' Osiris said, quickly checking the tally he'd made on his fingers, 'that's seven, so all we have to do now is shout.'

Pan raised an eyebrow.' Shout what, pray?' he asked.

'I don't know, do I? Anything so long as it's loud.'

'*Sorry*, for instance?'

'If you must, yes.'

'Thanks,' Pan replied. 'Sort of two birds with one stone, really.'

And so the party halted and, feeling right clowns, shouted. Nothing happened. The echo died away in the desert.

And then the ground shook, and cracks began to form in the sand, giving one the impression that this was a bit of the Earth's crust the creation of which God subcontracted out to a couple of lads He'd met in a pub somewhere. There was dust, and noise and . . . movement.

And the walls of Jericho came tumbling up.

There are gods of every conceivable sort and description in the universe, all of them created, in some way or another, by Mankind in his own image. Most nations subconsciously customise their pantheon to suit their world view and basic needs, and it's largely true that humanity generally gets the gods it deserves.

Thus the Greeks created their gods in order to give names, faces and addresses to various oversize notions banging away inside their brains. The Hindus shaped their gods in order to ensure that in times of trouble there'd always be Someone standing by to lend a helping hand (or, indeed, hands; in extreme cases arms, in large quantities) whereas the various Middle Eastern ethnic groups responsible for the gaggle of divine beings locked up in Jericho (if the theory is correct) fleshed out their immortal beliefs purely and simply to tie in with some urgent need of the tribe; quite likely the need to believe, with good reason, that however daft they may look, however nastily they behave, they're still a bunch of choirboys compared with the everlasting gods.

This is probably the most useful thing a god can do for his people; but, job satisfaction aside, it doesn't have very much to recommend it. Not if you have to live, for ever and ever, with the consequences.

*

'And that,' said Osiris, 'is Jericho.'

'Um,' Sandra replied. She wasn't sure that she liked the look of it much. Certainly it wasn't anything like the picture in the *Illustrated Children's Bible* she'd doodled all over in Sunday school; for one thing the version depicted by the artist hadn't had so many searchlights, barbed wire entanglements and machine-gun emplacements. Nor had there been a big signpost with a skull and crossbones on it reading MINEFIELD – DO NOT ENTER right in front of the main gate.

'I gather,' Pan remarked in a conversational tone, 'that they've been digging an escape tunnel for the last three thousand years. Hasn't got very far, though.'

'No?'

Pan shook his head. 'Dimensions inside a geological fault get a bit muddled,' he explained. 'Damn thing kept on coming out slap bang in the middle of the same tunnel a week after they started digging. The diggers from the future were able to tell the diggers from the past not to bother after all. This,' he added with a grin, 'led to all sorts of problems, as you can imagine.'

Sandra preferred not to. 'Sorry if I've missed something,' she said, 'but aren't they going to be a bit – well, fed up after all this time? I mean, when we open the gates and go in and . . .'

Pan shuddered. 'Not bloody likely,' he said. 'No way we're going to let any of them out until . . . Oh for crying out loud, what's the stupid old fool think he's doing now?'

Osiris, pushed by Carl, was speeding towards the main gate, weaving an apparently perfectly remembered course through the minefield. In his hand he held a big bronze key.

'Can't you stop him?' Sandra hissed.

Pan smiled. 'No,' he said. 'What a pity.'

Knock. Knock. Knock. Knock.

'Who's there?'

'Osiris.'

'Osiris who?'

'Stop pissing about, you pea-brain, and let me in.'

A panel in the gate shot back and a hideous face was glimpsable for about half a second. Half a second would be approximately four hundred and ninety-six milliseconds too long.

'No, that's not it,' said a voice from the face. 'That doesn't sound right at all.'

'I said open this door, you—'

'I think,' continued the voice, 'you mean Osiris walkin' down the lane, All in the month of May—'

'Sabre-toothed ponce, or I'll make you wish . . .'

'Or maybe it was Osiris eyes are smiling,' continued the voice. 'It was something like that. Not a very good one, anyway.'

Osiris closed his eyes and counted up to ten. This wasn't to help him calm down and keep his temper. Quite the opposite.

'Hang on,' said the voice, 'isn't it, A kiss is just a kiss, Osiris just a sigh, The fundamental thi—?'

'*Right!*'

There was a flash of lightning, a peal of thunder, and a very loud crash; and the door came away from its hinges and fell. A second later, a small, weary voice was audible from somewhere underneath where it had landed.

'Okay,' it said. 'Anybody spot my deliberate mistake?'

'Ah.' The doorfiend, now visible in all his biological improbability through the vacant doorway, scratched his head. 'It was deliberate, was it? Because I thought to myself, when the hinges melted and then the door started to fall *outwards*, I thought—'

'Shut up and get me out of here.'

The doorfiend swiftly obliged, lifting Osiris out of a god-sized hole he'd been hammered into by the sudden descent of several hundred tons of wrought bronze gate.

'What was the name again?' asked the fiend.

Osiris told him.

'Cool!' said the fiend, grinning. 'I wouldn't go letting them in here find out, 'cos that's the same name as the little shit who's responsible for all this, and they might just think you were him.'

'Might they?'

The fiend nodded. 'And that'd be bad news,' he went on, ''cos really the only thing they do to help them pass the time is planning what they're gonna do to him, the real Osiris, I mean, when they get out.'

'Let me guess. Buy him dinner?'

'No.'

'Flowers?'

'Not unless you count sharpened bamboo poles as flowers, no.'

Osiris shrugged. 'Never mind, he said. 'Now then, which way to the Governor's office?'

Knock. Knock. Knock.

'Who's there?'

'It's me, Governor.'

'No, I'm the Governor, who are you?'

Osiris, having made some passing comment about crying out loud, blew open the door (this time not repeating the deliberate mistake; with the result that the door fell heavily on the doorfiend, driving him fencepostlike eight inches into the ground).

'Bloody hell fire. You!'

Osiris smiled pleasantly. 'Ba'al, my old mate,' he said, extending a hand. 'Long time no see and all that. I see they made you a trusty, then.'

'You?'

'Nice office you've got here. Splendid view of the ...' Osiris craned his neck. 'Of the exercise yard, well, that's wonderful. You always were fond of sport, I seem to remember.'

'You!'

'It's a funny thing,' Osiris went on, wheeling himself in and taking a cigar from the box on the desk. 'I was just thinking to myself the other day, I wonder how my old friend Ba'al's getting along these days. And that set me thinking, of course, about the old times. You remember the old times? Of course you do.'

'You . . .'

Osiris lit the cigar, inhaled, and coughed. 'And I thought,' he went on, 'it's never right, I thought, my dear old chum Ba'al locked up in there with a load of criminals and undesirables, there must be something I can do, see if we can't get him out on parole or whatever, I mean, what's the use of having power and influence if you can't—?'

'. . . *bastard!*'

'And so,' Osiris said, 'here I am. Got a little deal to put to you which might—'

'*CALL OUT THE GUARD!*'

'—interest you.'

'Right,' said Ba'al, rubbing his hands together. 'Any suggestions?'

The packed dining hall echoed with shouting voices. There were nine hundred and six gods jammed into a space designed to hold three hundred gods in modest discomfort. During their long imprisonment, the gods and goddesses of ancient Palestine hadn't exactly been idle.

'One at a time, now,' Ba'al shouted, waving his arms. 'Best of order, ladies and gentlemen, please. You at the back there, Mammon. I think you were first.'

Osiris, bound hand and foot in the middle of the throng, smiled serenely. This was better than he had dared hope.

'Well,' said the god at the back, 'it's got to be the oil, hasn't it. Thirty years up to his neck in boiling oil, I mean, we did discuss this in committee . . .'

'Tar.'

'I beg your pardon?'

'The chair,' yelled Ba'al forlornly, 'recognises Tanith, Queen of Darkness.'

'It was tar, you silly old fool,' said Tanith irritably. 'We put it to the vote, remember, and it was five hundred and thirteen for tar, three hundred and forty-three for oil, fifty abstaining.'

'It was not, it was oil. I distinctly remember asking where we are going to get that much oil from.'

'Pitch, you daft old cow. When we took the vote, tar hadn't even been invented.'

'Not to mention,' Mammon continued, 'fuel efficiency. To maintain tar at a constant one hundred degrees Celsius—'

'Tar, pitch, does it really matter? The point is—'

'The point is,' shouted Melkart, a short, fat god with hairy ears, 'twelve minutes in oil, the bugger'll be fried to a crisp and that'll be that, whereas with tar—'

'Thank you,' Ba'al bellowed, 'but I think we had this debate before. Will someone just look up the minutes?'

'What minutes?'

'The minutes of the—'

'I think you'll find there aren't any. I remember saying—'

'Are you telling me there aren't any minutes?'

'The chair recognises—'

'And you can shut your face and all, you daft old—'

Ba'al scowled. 'Hoy,' he growled, 'this is a democratic—'

'Since when? We're gods, aren't we?'

'Excuse me.'

Dead silence, instantaneously. It must have been, Ba'al later reflected, the way he said it.

'Thank you.' Osiris cleared his throat. 'I just wanted to say,' he went on, 'that if any of you want to get out of here – ever – then this is probably your last chance.' He paused; still silence. 'And if I were you, I'd hold the oil just for a while.'

'Not oil. Pitch.'

'Whatever.' Osiris frowned in the general direction of the heckler, and then continued. 'First,' he said, 'outside this building I have a crack team of commandos, led by someone whose name is, I feel sure, familiar to many of you . . .'

'*Lundqvist*,' someone whispered, at the back of the hall. '*He must mean Kurt Lundqvist.*' Osiris was impressed.

'Secondly,' he went on, 'the reason I'm here today is purely and simply to offer you imbeciles . . .' He paused, letting the word hang in the air. Good, he reflected, as the silence persisted, I've got 'em. '. . . imbeciles the chance of a free pardon. If you do exactly what you're told, of course. If not . . .'

The silence lingered; mellowed; ripened. And then was broken.

'I still say it was oil. I mean, boiling tar, just think of the smell . . .'

'*Sssssh!*'

It is a terrible thing to be shushed by nine hundred and five gods simultaneously. The nearest precedent is probably the piecemeal tearing of Orpheus by the Thracian Women; except that piecemeal tearing is, comparatively speaking, quick and painless. Torn piecemeal, you don't find yourself still waking up years later at three in the morning, sweating and pink to the ears with embarrassment.

'Hush, please!' Ba'al banged with his gavel for silence and smiled weakly at Osiris, who nodded affably back. 'Sorry about that,' he said politely. 'Please, do go on.'

'The way we do it,' said Ba'al, 'is this.'

Osiris nodded politely. 'Ah,' he said. 'Yes.' To the gods all things are possible, but some of them are still bloody difficult; for example, keeping your eyelids from foreclosing when someone is explaining to you how to operate a complex bond-washing deal on a five-dimensional stock exchange.

'You've heard,' Ba'al's voice was saying, 'of selling forward, like in exchange rate and commodity transactions? Well, that's basically what we do here, except we sell back. It's really pretty straightforward . . .'

Creak, creak, creak went the drawbridges of Osiris' eyes, and the strain of keeping up so much weight unsupported is pretty extreme, particularly if you're trying to stay awake at the same time. 'Good Lord,' Osiris heard himself say, 'isn't that clever.' He hoped, vaguely, that the context was right.

'. . . Whereupon the brokers *backwards* in time, who are of course selling their stocks of gold *forward* against early settlement in a bull market, buy *retrospectively* so as to get the advantage of the reverse exchange rate differential, which washes out the coupon, resulting in a very useful capital loss for tax purposes. And it's at precisely this point that we step in and buy *forward*, on a *bear* market, thereby . . .'

'Really.' If Macbeth really did murder sleep, Osiris mumbled dreamily to himself, I can quite believe that he was provoked beyond endurance. 'Now that you've explained it,' he hazarded, 'it all seems so very simple.' He smiled.

'It is,' Ba'al replied, nodding. 'And of course the effect is redoubled if you then sell back through a parallel universe, creating a Doppler effect on the commodities markets in this universe while still getting your settlement ex div *over there.*' He paused; and an allegorically minded artist, requiring a model for Smugness, need have looked no further. 'All my own idea,' he said, 'and completely legal and above board. Mind you,' he added in a whisper, 'it can have side-effects, like the San Francisco earthquake of 1906, but you can't make omelettes, can you?'

'Hmm?' Osiris woke up suddenly from a short but vivid dream involving stuffed crocodiles. 'Tricky,' he answered. 'I always find it helps stop them sticking if you whisk up the yolks in an egg-cup first.'

'Quite. Well, I'd better be making a start, hadn't I?'

'Absolutely.'

Ba'al smiled. 'Strictly speaking, of course,' he said, 'I already have. That's the joy of it, so little paperwork.' Then he laughed, indicating that that had been a funny, albeit technical, joke.

'Ha ha,' Osiris therefore said. 'Look, roughly how long will this take, because I have people waiting.'

'Ten minutes.'

'That's fine.'

'Or seventy-three years, of course, depending on temporal refraction. We'll probably get a slightly better rate if we wait for the upturn in the fiscal sinewave.'

'Oh, let's keep it short and sweet,' Osiris replied. 'Just so long as we get there in the end.'

'You're the boss.'

'Am I?'

'Yes.'

'Oh good.'

Ba'al turned to the computer console on the desk in front of him and tapped precisely four keys. 'Cup of tea while we're waiting?'

'That would be nice, thank you.'

'Milk and sugar?'

'Just milk, thanks.'

Ten minutes exactly later, the door opened and a minor demon came in with a silver tray, on which rested a small rectangular slip of paper. Ba'al picked it up, glanced at it and handed it over.

'Bearer bond,' he said. 'Best way, we always find.'

Osiris looked down at the paper. It was heavy paper, apparently composed of five per cent wood-pulp, ninety-five per cent watermarks, and the printing made his eyes hurt. In among all the squiggles, he could make out Gothic lettering, as follows:

BANK OF HELL

SEVENTY-FIVE DOLLARS

'Seventy-five dollars?'

Ba'al nodded. 'We caught the market at its absolute crest,' he said contentedly. 'I mean, in financial terms you're holding the ultimate Doomsday device, because there just isn't enough real money in the cosmos to cover it. Just wave it under a bank teller's nose and *kerbang!* there goes the economy of the solar system down the pan.'

'I see.' Osiris scratched his head, making a noise like fingernails on a blackboard. 'The, um, Hell dollar's pretty strong at the moment, then?'

There was a peculiar noise; Ba'al sniggering. 'That's a good one,' he said. 'I must remember that. Anyway, as I was saying, it doesn't actually matter so long as the money never leaves the system. I mean, it can be capitalised and written off over the years, there shouldn't be a problem. Well, very nice doing business with you.'

Osiris gripped the handrails of his chair. 'Likewise,' he said. 'And no, er, hard feelings?'

'Hard feelings?' Ba'al looked at him. 'About what?'

'About you and your friends being locked up here for the last—'

'Oh that.' Ba'al shrugged. 'I should think this makes up for it, don't you? I mean, our commission on this deal's a fiftieth of a per cent, so we aren't grumbling, are we? I think we can say that leaves us quits.'

'Oh good. And now of course,' Osiris added, 'you're free to go.'

'Yes.' Ba'al hesitated. 'I suppose so, quite. Actually,' he went on, looking slightly to one side, 'we've been thinking about that.'

'So I gathered.'

'No, not like that.' Ba'al bit his lip. 'About whether we should in fact leave or alternatively, well, stay.'

'*Stay?*'

'The thought did cross our minds, yes,' Ba'al replied sheepishly. 'Because of being offshore, you see.'

'Offshore?'

'Sort of offshore. Being in a different dimension, you see, it means we can offer our clients a distinct tax advantage.'

'You can?'

'We believe so, yes. On the basis of, if we don't exist, then how can we pay tax?'

Osiris rubbed his chin. 'Well,' he said, 'there's a sort of specious logic there, I suppose. But surely –'

'It was Mammon's idea,' Ba'al continued. 'Ever since he got out of human sacrifice and into financial services there's been no holding him. No, I think we'll stay as we are, thank you all the same.'

'Fair enough.' Osiris folded the paper carefully and put it away in his top pocket. 'I'll be saying goodbye for now, then. Thanks again.'

'Don't mention it,' Ba'al said. 'Any time. Oh, and could you lower the walls again when you leave?'

'It'll be a pleasure,' Osiris replied.

In his office, Julian leant back in his chair and scowled.

Things, he felt, were getting out of hand; and that always annoyed him. In his view, a perfect universe was one where he had everything firmly in hand, preferably with his thumb jammed hard against its windpipe. At present, however, things were far from perfect.

The latest update on the Teletext showed a colossal rise in share prices, fed by rumours of a massive input of some huge but unspecified quantity of wealth from an uncertain source. Added to this he had in front of him the latest report from his medical advisers, which wasn't exactly hopeful. The clowns had lost him. Again. This time, apparently, on Easter Island, which was in itself peculiar. Until now, Julian wasn't aware that there was anything you could lose on Easter Island, no matter how hard you tried.

And what exactly was the old fool up to? That was the

question he kept coming back to, and still he couldn't fathom it. Was he just running aimlessly away? In which case he was going about it in a distinctly peculiar manner. True, he had so far succeeded amazingly well; but that could be explained away entirely in terms of the complete and utter brainlessness of his chosen contractors. Osiris was up to something. But what?

What would I do if I was in his position?

Well, said Julian to himself as he absent-mindedly flicked through the franchise agreement on the desk in front of him, here adding a few noughts, there crossing out a paragraph, if I were in his shoes I'd find myself a bloody good lawyer, ha ha.

A bloody good lawyer . . .

But . . .

Surely not.

Suddenly, with the depressing inevitability of a car approaching at ninety miles an hour when you've just got your heel stuck in a grating as you cross the road, Julian could feel the pieces clicking smartly into place. The running about. The ducking and diving. The sudden pressing need for fabulously vast sums of money. All entirely consistent with going to consult a lawyer.

But who?

Not just a good lawyer, he mused, but the best. And there is only ever one best at a time; not that the post falls vacant very often. Ever since the legal profession began, there had only ever been one best. So far as he was aware – and if the situation had changed he'd have heard, just as the news of the end of the world would have filtered through to him somehow – the best was still the best; reclusive, all but retired from practice, but still occasionally coming out of retirement to kick the spines of young pretenders up through their ears. When it came to putting on the writs, there was only one master.

And if Osiris has gone to see him, Julian reflected, then it's time for a drastic change of approach. Like now.

He picked up the phone.

'Get me those two idiots,' he said.

15

'And what,' said Teutates, the warrior god of the ancient Celts, 'the hell is this supposed to be?'

'Rice pudding.'

Bearing in mind their unlimited power and total lack of accountability, gods are generally extremely tolerant. You can burn their temples, rape their priestesses, massacre their suppliants in the sanctuary of their holy altars, with no worse consequences than a slight upward movement of the all-seeing eyebrow. But there are limits. Gods are, after all, only human.

'Go on, eat it up,' continued the waitress. 'You like rice pudding.'

Still waters run deep; the only visible reaction from Teutates was a slight crinkling of his brow. 'You reckon?' he said.

'Look, it's getting cold and I've got all the rest of the dinners to do. You don't want me to have to get Mrs Henderson.'

Like soldiers in riots, war gods are obliged to go through certain set procedures before letting rip. Procedure one: try calm, conciliatory negotiation.

'No,' Teutates snarled, 'you look, you raddled old boiler. Either you take this pigswill away and bring me a bloody great hunk of Stilton and a box of Ritz crackers, or tonight you go home in a matchbox. Kapisch?'

This, by divine standards, is calm, conciliatory negotiation verging on wimpishness. The waitress tutted.

'Don't you use that tone of voice with me,' she replied sniffily, 'or I'll tell Mrs . . .'

Procedure two: fair warning. 'Okay, prune-face, go ahead and try it. I can't turn you into a frog because by the looks of you someone's beaten me to it, but I'm sure I'll think of something else just as appropriate.'

'That does it. Mrs Henderson!'

Procedure three: there is no procedure three.

'Mrs Henderson,' said the waitress, 'Mr Teutates is being very rude to me and he won't eat up his nice keekeekeekee-keekeekee.'

It was, in all fairness, pretty slickly done and Mrs Henderson, who had seen many such phenomena over the years, couldn't quite manage to keep the overtones of grudging admiration out of her voice.

'Thank you, Mr Teutates,' she nevertheless said, 'that'll be quite enough of that, thank you very much. Now, would you please turn Mrs Hill back into her proper shape before you put the other residents off their food.'

Teutates grinned. 'That is her proper shape,' he replied. 'Stands to reason. I've said it a hundred times, Mrs Hill's really a polecat turned into a human and it's high time someone turned her back. Ask anybody.'

'Mr Teutates . . .'

'I'm not blaming you. Must be really difficult getting staff on the wages you pay. Still, like they say, if you pay peanuts you must expect to employ monkeys. That,' he added darkly, 'can also be arranged.'

'That will do.' Mrs Henderson drew her eyebrows together, creating a formation fully as intimidating as an advancing battalion of the Imperial Guard. 'Now I've warned you about this before, and . . .'

She stopped, struggling to regain her balance. The force of the attack, the sheer malevolence, had taken her by surprise.

'Mr *Teutates*!'

It had been a long time – oh, over forty years – since one of her residents had tried to turn her into something, and never in all her experience in the residential care business had anyone ever tried to metamorphose her into one of *those*. Quite obviously there was something going on here.

Something that had to be sorted out. Just for now, though, best to play it cool.

'Really, Mr Teutates, you know better than that.' She folded her arms and gave Teutates the Number One cold stare. 'Honestly, I'd have thought you'd have more sense, at your age.'

Teutates nodded curtly, admitting that she had a point. Quite understandably given the nature of her position, Mrs Henderson was hexed about with enough protective charms, amulets, written undertakings and runes of power to withstand a direct hit from an atomic bomb. Low voltage transmigration spells bounced off her like tennis balls off a dreadnought.

'I do not,' Teutates said slowly, 'like rice pudding. Understood?'

'Now, then,' said Mrs Henderson, shaken but firm, 'of course you like rice pudding. It's good for you.'

Teutates glowered at her. 'Listen, missus,' he growled. 'In the beginning I created the Heavens and the Earth out of the curds left at the bottom of the churn of Eternity. Singlehanded I subdued the Wolves of Famine, the Three-headed Dragon of Pestilence and the Wild Dogs of Death. I can count the stars in the sky, the sands on the seashore and the days that are past. Stands to reason I can make up my own mind whether I like rice pudding or not. And I don't. You got that, or shall I write it down for you?'

'Oh.' Mrs Henderson hesitated. There was definitely something here she didn't understand; she could sense it, and it disturbed her. 'Then why didn't you say so before, you silly man?' she rallied bravely.

'I did.'

'Be that as it may,' Mrs Henderson said, 'that's no reason why poor Mrs Hill should have to be a polecat. I must insist that you turn her back at once.'

Teutates considered his options. On the one hand he was a war god, and he hadn't felt this good in nineteen centuries. On the other hand, he had to go on living here, because he had nowhere else to go; and one of the first rules you learn when you're a war god is, Don't take work home with you.

'Do a deal,' he said. 'No more rice pudding ever again and the polecat walks.'

There was a pause.

'Certainly,' said Mrs Henderson, putting a smile on her face with the same ease as one spreads butter still rock-hard from the fridge on to newly baked bread. 'You only had to ask, you know. We always bend over backwards to make life as pleasant as possible for all our residents.'

As she escorted the newly restored Mrs Hill back to the staff room for a nice lie down and a slice or two of raw liver (there's always a brief period of readjustment after a metamorphosis) Mrs Henderson came to a firm conclusion.

Something was badly wrong, and she didn't know what.

Something would have to be done about that.

The first really ominous thing that Osiris and his companions came across on what was, they fervently hoped, the last leg of the journey was a big notice nailed to a tree. It said, in big capitals:

YOU DON'T HAVE TO BE DEAD TO ENTER HERE, BUT IT HELPS

and below, in small italics:

PS All hope to be abandoned prior to entry. Please help keep eternity tidy by placing your hope in the receptacles provided.

'That's all right,' Pan commented, 'I haven't got any with me anyway. How about the rest of you?'

Nobody said anything; but nobody made an effort to abandon anything either; and into the valley of death trudged the five.

'Is where we're going hard to get to?' Sandra asked.

'To get to, no problem,' Pan replied. 'To get out of is an entirely different proposition. In theory, Ozzie and I have sort of implied return tickets – well, season tickets, really – but what I always say is, theory is fine in theory. As for you three, if I was in your shoes I'd be using them to get out of here fast. This place,' he summarised, 'gives me the creeps.'

'It does?'

'Always has.'

Sandra raised an eyebrow. 'You've been here before, then?'

'A couple of times, yes. Trade delegations, diplomatic junkets, that sort of thing.'

'You got out all right then, didn't you?'

Pan shrugged. 'It was different,' he replied. 'Those times, I was meant to be there. They gave me one of those little plastic badges you pin on your lapel that says who you are. You've no idea how comforting it is having one of them when you're down among the dead men.'

Thus far, the environment had been fairly normal, if not exactly welcoming. From Reykjavik they had caught the scheduled bus north as far as Thingvellir, and thence by a succession of progressively older and more decrepit minibuses up into Vididal. The last conveyance, which had been held together by insulating tape and force of habit, had shaken itself to bits ten miles back, since when they had dragged themselves over rocks and past the messy dribblings of volcanoes, taking it in turns to push the wheelchair, until they had arrived . . .

. . . Well, here; wherever the hell (so to speak) it was. It consisted of a cave in a cliff, which someone had rather half-heartedly tried to disguise as the result of perfectly natural seismic activity. There was a marked smell of sulphur, brimstone and stale vinegar.

Lundqvist shifted his rucksack on his back and suppressed an urge to whimper. His work had taken him to some pretty unpleasant places – the mountain lair of Mazdrhahn, King of Bats, being one example that stuck in his memory, the Los Angeles sewer network another – but while those places had been terrifying, nauseating, spine-melting et cetera, none of them had ever come anywhere close to this in sheer unmitigated dreariness. He also felt virtually nude, armed as he was with little more than a Macmillan .50BMG rifle, a .454 Casull revolver, an Ingrams sub-machine gun custom-chambered for .44 Magnum and a big sack full of hand grenades; which was the basic minimum as far as he was concerned, the sort of things he stuffed in his dressing-gown pockets if he had to get up in the night for a pee (for his motto had always been not so much *Have gun, will travel* as *Haven't gun, won't*). What he really needed in this context, he felt sure, was a squadron of main battle tanks, tactical air support, two divisions of special forces and, for choice, his mummy.

'This is it, huh?' he asked, trying to keep his voice gruffly baritone and failing.

'Sort of,' Osiris replied, aggravatingly chirpy. 'Tradesmen's entrance, really. This is the laundry chute.'

Lundqvist did a double-take. 'Laundry?'

'Oh yes,' Osiris replied airily. 'Guards' uniforms, bedlinen, tablecloths, winding-sheets, that sort of thing. They used to do it in-house but now they use a lot of outside contractors. That's why,' he added, jerking this thumb at the mysterious laundry basket thing they'd been taking it in turns to lug over the rocks and mountains, 'we need that.'

'I was wondering when you'd explain about that,' Pan said. 'What is it, exactly?'

'It's a laundry basket.'

'And what's in it?'

'Laundry.'

'I see.'

'It's our cover.'

'I thought he said it was laundry.'

'Shut up, Carl.'

'It's a freshly laundered cover,' Pan explained. 'Has to be dry-cleaned to get the bloodstains out.'

'What bloodstains?'

'Ignore him, everyone. Now,' Osiris went on, 'if you open the lid you'll find some uniforms. White coats, that sort of thing. Also, like I said, lots of pillow-cases, table-napkins, socks and the like. When you've got into the uniforms, I want you to put me in the basket and carry me through the doorway. And try and look natural, all right?'

A few minutes later, the procession found itself in total darkness, which was a blessing in fairly transparent disguise; anything you could see in a tunnel like that would probably keep you awake at nights for several years. The way the floor crunched underfoot was particularly evocative.

'It's all right him saying act natural,' Pan grumbled, 'but it's not as easy as that. I've been trying to do it all my life and I've never quite seemed to get the hang of it . . .'

The floor shook. To those of the party who had never experienced anything of the kind, it was an eerie moment; not violent, certainly not enough to shake you off your feet, but quite remarkably disorientating; rather like being told by your mother that she never really liked you anyway. And then the lights came on.

Not much to see, but what there was of it wasn't precisely reassuring. A huge wooden doorway, without a door; and nothing but shadows and a heavy smell of something unpleasant (but extremely familiar).

'Oh balls,' Pan muttered. 'I'd forgotten all about this bit. I still maintain we should have gone to the seaside again. Even Weymouth would be better than –'

'Hey,' Lundqvist interrupted. 'What goes on here, then?'

Osiris chuckled. 'You don't know?' he said. 'Read what it says over the door.'

Lundqvist did as he said, and saw the words:

BEWARE OF THE DOG

The fact that none of the three mortals turned and fled at this stage only goes to show what a disadvantage it is to try and make out in life without the inestimable benefit of a classical education.

'That's it, is it?' Lundqvist said, and relief slugged it out with disappointment for control of his voice. 'A dog. Hell, for a minute there you had me wor—'

Enter the Dog.

'Gaskets?'

'Yes.'

'Cotter pins?'

'Yes.'

'Camchains?'

'Yes.'

'Tappet return springs?'

'Yes.'

'Reciprocating mainshaft lubricator baffles?'

'Yes.'

'Mendelssohn cables?'

'Yes.'

'Cigar lighter?'

'*Yes!*'

Thor shrugged. 'Okay, then,' he said. 'Fire her up.'

The engine quivered, chugged, roared, raced and died. Thor and Frey looked at each other.

'I take it,' Thor said pleasantly, 'that you did remember to put some coal in the furnace.'

'Ah.' Odin frowned. 'There's always something, isn't there?'

'Not always, no. Only when you have anything to do with it.'

Odin ignored that, and shovelled some coal into the firebox. A few minutes later the engine quivered, chugged, roared, raced and then went catumple-catumple-catumple quietly under its breath.

'Right,' said Thor, 'and off we go.'

Slowly but with gathering momentum, the enormous engine rolled forward and thundered across the improvised jungle runway. It took it rather longer than anticipated; but the environmentally aware can rest assured that none of the trees flattened as it cut a swathe through the virgin forest was an endangered hardwood, and most of them were run-of-the-mill renewable resource softwoods.

'I'm sorry if this is a silly question,' Frey shouted, pulling bits of twig out of his beard, 'but this time are we sure we know where we're going?'

'Yes.'

'Why?'

'Because,' Thor called back, 'this time I'm navigating. All right?'

'Yes. I feel better now.'

'Thought you'd say that.' Thor glanced down at the map on his knees, consulted the position of the sun and nodded approvingly. 'Now then,' he said, 'those hills over there are quite definitely the Pennines, so that down there must be Leeds, and in another five minutes or so we'll see the M6 directly below us.'

Slowly, ponderously, in its own unique way magnificently, the giant traction engine flew on across the Amazon jungle.

★

'It's not,' hissed Pan, backing away, 'quite as bad as it seems.'

'No?'

'No. It's still pretty bad, but not that bad.'

'Ah.'

The Dog, also known as Cerberus and the Hound of Hell, rolled its six eyes and bared its three pairs of teeth, but stayed where it was. The massive iron chain fastened to the collar that surrounded the place just below where the three necks diverged probably had some influence on this, but probably not a decisive one. The chain hadn't been forged which could withstand a determined tug from Cerberus.

'Basically,' Pan went on, trying to back behind the laundry basket but finding it hard because all the space was already taken, 'it's just another official. A civil servant, if you like. Only doing its job, and all that.'

'Really.'

'Really. That explains why it says everything in triplicate.' Pan tried to sidle an extra few microns in the direction of relative safety and tripped over his own feet. 'Good boy,' he mumbled.

'Okay,' said Lundqvist, 'you guys just leave this to me.'

With the deftness of long practice he heeled a round into the chamber of the Macmillan. Bloody great big animals with teeth were what he was good at, and the combination of his skill and experience and six hundred and fifty grains of jacketed hollow-pointed bullet flying at three thousand feet a second ought, he reasoned with himself, to give him the slight edge that, in the final analysis, makes all the difference.

He stood up, took aim and fired. The bullet sang in the air for a fraction of a second too small to quantify on even the most modern equipment, and hit the Dog more or less where the heart should have been.

And bounced off.

The second, third and fourth bullets landed within half a minute of angle of the first, were flattened into thin lead and copper discs, and fell to the ground. The fifth went high, ricochetted off the Dog's collar, cannoned backwards and forwards down the passageway, and embedded itself in a large nugget of hard quartz sunk into the wall. The chips of stone thereby caused would, if properly cut, have made the Kohinoor look like the tip of a very cheap industrial glasscutter.

The grenades weren't much more use, either; and all the armour-piercing rocket that constituted Lundqvist's ultimate rainy-day backup managed to achieve was to cut the chain neatly in two. The Dog, deprived of the chain's support, lurched forward a pace or so, and growled.

'Don't be such a lot of babies,' remarked a voice, apparently inside the basket. 'They're far more afraid of you than you are of them.'

'In which case,' Pan replied, 'the poor thing must be absolutely fucking terrified. Doesn't look it, though.'

'Talk to it,' urged the voice. 'Firmly. Let it know who's the boss.'

By now there were flecks of foam on the Dog's jaw; exactly the same amount in precisely the same place on each of its three heads. It had its eye, or four of them at least, on Lundqvist's neck.

'There, boy. Sit.'

The Dog sat. After a breathless second, it wagged its tail, panted and held out one paw.

'I think,' said Carl, 'he wants to shake hands. Don't you, boy?'

'Excuse me.'

'Yeah?'

Pan swallowed and pointed. 'You sure this is working?' he asked.

Carl nodded. 'I'm used to dogs, see,' he explained. 'My sister in Neath, she's got a dog. Bigger'n this one, too.'

Two gods and two mortals stared at him as if he'd just pulled a blackcurrant and kirsch gateau out of his ear. The Dog, meanwhile, had produced three identical rubber bones out of nowhere and was offering them to Carl with the air of an envoy trying to interest Tamburlaine the Great in a spot of tribute.

'Here,' said Carl, 'fetch.'

He stooped down, picked up a stone and hurled it away. From the outer darkness there came an indignant cry. The Dog picked up its feet and scampered away, its tail thrashing like an amphetamine-crazed metronome.

'It's gone,' said Carl. 'We can go on now.'

Pan and Osiris looked at each other.

'So that's why we brought him,' said Pan, his voice heavy with enlightenment. 'I knew there had to be a reason, what with us being gods and all that.'

'Suppose so, yes.'

'We must have foreseen the Dog, or something.'

'Must have done.'

'Aren't we clever.'

'Very.'

Pan nodded. 'Absolutely bloody brilliant,' he said. 'Now, let's get out of here before it comes back.'

It was, they found, the sort of tunnel or corridor that grows on you less and less the further down it you go. It was still as dark as three feet up a drain, but by now their eyes were getting used to it, showing thereby a degree of zeal that was quite uncalled for in the circumstances; and the ill-defined shapes that loomed up at them through the darkness as they passed weren't the sort of thing you like to be in the same frame of reference with, let alone the same narrow, winding, slippery-floored, underground passage.

'Can you smell something?' Osiris asked.

'Kippers.'

'Which of you said that?'

'I did.'

'Yes, thank you, Carl, I'd rest on your laurels for a bit if I

were you. Look, can anyone beside me smell a sort of deserty
stable smell?'

'I can.'

'And which one of you said—?'

'Me.'

'Thanks. And who's me?'

The lights went on . . .

'Me,' repeated the camel.

'Our demands,' said Teutates, his tone of voice belying his air
of confidence, 'are as follows. One, we want . . .'

The wind howled, bringing with it small, hard bullets of rain
that bit into the back of his neck. It was also, he couldn't help
noticing, a long way to the ground, even for a god like himself.
He tried to huddle down a few millimetres further into his
dressing-gown.

'I do wish you'd all stop being such sillies and come down
from there,' replied the voice of Mrs Henderson, blared
metallically through a megaphone. 'You'll catch your deaths of
cold in this weather.'

Teutates steeled his heart. About ninety-three per cent of him
by volume (ninety-five per cent by weight) wanted to capitulate,
scramble back down the ladder and wrap itself round a big
bacon sandwich and a steaming mug of hot chocolate. The
other seven (or five) per cent of him, however, being the parts of
the brain i/c policy formation, held the casting vote.

'We stay,' Teutates shouted back. 'You want us, come and
get us.'

'Please yourselves,' Mrs Henderson megaphoned back. 'As
I always say to guests when they first arrive, so long as
accounts are settled promptly and you don't upset other
residents, this is Liberty Hall. I'll see you at dinner, I hope.'

'Our demands,' Teutates yelled, 'are, like I said, straightforward. First, we want a fast car, and a doctor, and two million
gold zlotys, and . . .'

(*'Did he say he was a doctor?'*
'I don't think so.'
*'I need a doctor for my leg. It's like a sort of cramp, just here,
whenever I bend my knee. Are you a doctor, too?'*)

The great sit-in on the roof of Sunnyvoyde had started off
with at least one bang and a wide selection of the very latest
crashes, quality bespoke sound effects you can be proud of.
Twenty-four hours later, there was just Teutates, Nkulunkulu,
the Great Sky God of the Zulus, and a small, unidentified
hairy deity of no apparent usefulness and incapable of saying
anything other than 'Uk!'. By the look of him he was probably
a vegetation spirit from the Maldives, but it was just possible
that he was a reporter or something in disguise. Most of the
time he slept.

'Our demands,' shouted Teutates hopelessly. As the wind
ate his words and the rain finally found a narrow accessway
down the back of his collar, he found himself reflecting that
rice pudding, in moderate quantities and with due notice, can
make a pleasant change and is not unpalatable. 'Are nego-
tiable,' he howled, just in case anyone was listening.

Back inside the comfort of her warm, dry sitting room, Mrs
Henderson caught a faint echo of the last two words and
smiled. Give them another three hours and then send the odd-
job man out with a ladder.

Nevertheless, it was worrying; very worrying. Mercifully,
the manifestation the dissident tendency had chosen on this
occasion had been wildly inappropriate, given that she had
confiscated the keys of the thunder from Thor when he first
moved in, and could summon up wind and rain whenever she
chose. Next time, they might use their common sense before
selecting their course of action.

It was all the fault of *naughty* Mr Osiris, she reflected. They
only dared behave like this because he was still on the loose,
making them think things and giving them a precedent, and
hope. The sooner he was dealt with, the better.

There was a spluttering noise from her desk, and she saw a fax worming its way through the rollers. When it had finally wiggled to a halt, she read it, and smiled again before scribbling an answer and sending it off. The number she dialled was unlisted and known to very few people, probably because the last thing the Judges of the Dead need is piles of junk faxes.

Oh *good*, Mrs Henderson thought.

It was a very odd-looking camel indeed. It was tall, with long spindly legs, and you didn't need to look twice to see that it had all its ribs. In fact it was so thin that it was probably the only known life-form capable of wearing a Calvin Klein original without bursting the zip.

'Hi,' it said.

Osiris drummed his fingers on the arm of his wheelchair. 'What,' he asked, 'the hell is going on here?'

'Weighbridge,' replied the camel, with its mouth full. 'Sort of weighbridge, anyway. At your service, distinguished patrons.'

Pan, who had been looking around, saw what he'd been looking for, and grinned. 'Clever,' he said. 'Strictly within the rules, helps keep the riff-raff out; yes, I like it. Your own idea?'

The camel shrugged, giving the impression of a conga of coathangers. 'Alas, no,' he said. 'I am merely a loyal, hard-working employee dedicated to the ideal of old-fashioned personal service. Three hundred thousand zlotys to go through.'

Osiris was becoming impatient. 'Somebody explain,' he demanded. 'To go through what, precisely?'

Pan pointed.

At first it looked like an ordinary archway, until you realised that archways aren't usually made of chrome-plated steel. Once your eyes grew accustomed to the bewildering perspectives involved, you realised that it was . . .

'The eye of a needle,' Pan said. 'You pay your money, the camel does his bit, you're in, free and clear. I assume there's a certificate or something to say you got to the other side?'

The camel nodded. 'Duly witnessed and legalised by a notary public,' it said. 'I am, as it happens, a notary public.' It lowered its voice. 'I took the exams and everything.'

'I'll bet you did,' Pan replied. 'Look, thanks for your time but we're all of us poor as church mice, so I guess we'll just carry on the way we were—'

'Ah,' said the camel. 'You mean via the toll road?'

'That's not quite what I meant,' Pan replied cautiously, 'but do please go on. You will note, by the way, that my friend over there is carrying a very big rifle, which I believe has strong Freudian overtones in his case but is nevertheless loaded.'

The camel shuddered slightly, reminding Pan of a xylophone yawning. 'There's no need to get boisterous,' it said, and pointed with a hoof towards a side tunnel. 'Pedestrians are requested to keep to the footpaths at all times,' it added. 'Have a nice day, now.'

About twenty yards in, the side tunnel grew narrow and low, so that everyone except Osiris had to duck their heads. Underfoot the ground was spongy and soft without being damp, and the sides had the same sort of feel to them. It was unnervingly like being inside somebody's intestines.

'Painfully unimaginative use of imagery,' Pan explained, wiping something sticky and yuk out of his eyes. 'If that back there was the jaws of death, this must be its gullet or something.'

'Talking of eating things,' said Sandra.

'I can hear water.'

Pan stopped. True, Osiris was a god, and gods can hear the turning of the earth, the graunching of the stars on their badly lubricated axles; but even gods can imagine things. Pan was a god too, and all he could hear was the rumbling of Sandra's stomach.

'Sorry,' he said, 'but all I've got left is a couple of cough sweets and an aspirin. They may have a handful of calories between them if you want to try.'

'Thanks,' Sandra replied, 'but I think I'll wait. There must be a diner or a Little Chef or something around here somewhere.'

'Over there, maybe,' said Osiris. 'By the river.'

There was indeed a river.

Tremendous efforts have been made in recent years to clean up the great waterways of the civilised world. Salmon now spawn in the Thames. The Loire sparkles through central Paris like Perrier on endless draught. The Tiber and the Ganges are now so pure that local inhabitants use it neat to top up their car batteries, and a company has been formed to bottle the Hudson and sell it in health food shops. But cast your mind back to the bad old days, when the smell of your average urban waterway was enough to bubble varnish, and a brick thrown from Waterloo Bridge would have bounced off the surface in a way that would have had Barnes Wallis dancing with joy.

'Where's this, then?' Pan asked.

'The Styx.'

'Sure, it's hardly downtown LA, but—'

Osiris spelt it for him. 'All we have to do,' he went on, 'is cross over and we're there. Home and dry. Well,' he amended, 'home. Now, somewhere around here there should be a ferry ...'

And sure enough, there was a ferry. It was, Pan realised with horror, more or less exactly how he remembered it from his last visit here, back in the days when there wasn't so much of this science nonsense about and you could have a really good blow-out, take in a show and still have change out of the burnt entrails of a ram. The auto-cauterising function of his memory had compiled a nice thick sheath of mental scar tissue over the whole business; it took just one look at the blunt, squat boat that nosed its way up to the bank to pick off that particular scab, leaving a big patch of raw reminiscence bare and unprotected.

'Hang on,' he said. 'We'll need tickets.'

Osiris raised an eyebrow. 'I thought you just paid the ferryman,' he said.

'Shows how much you know.' Pan took out his wallet and extracted a selection of major credit cards, supplied to him by various leading banks who afterwards found themselves trying hard to remember what the very good reason at the time had been. Then he reached across and abstracted Lundqvist's Sykes-Fairbairn knife from its scabbard on his hip.

''Scuse fingers,' he said.

'You're welcome,' Lundqvist replied automatically, and then added, 'Hey, that's my knife you just …'

Pan ignored him. Taking great care not to lacerate the ball of his thumb, he was cutting circles approximately three quarters of an inch out of the cards, two from each one.

'Origami?' Sandra asked. Pan shook his head.

'The trick is,' he replied, not taking his eyes off the job in hand, 'when crossing the Styx on that horrible contraption over there, not to get caught without a ticket when you're half way across; because if you are, you get thrown off the boat. Into that,' he particularised, pointing with the knife at the turgid crust of the river. 'No joke,' he added. 'So if you'll all just hold your water a moment.'

Osiris, meanwhile, had given his colleague up for nuts and commanded Carl to wheel him up the gangplank that the ferryman had laid down.

'Five, please,' he said. 'Two gods and three adults. Return.'

'You what?'

'Return tickets, please. What's so funny about …?'

The ferryman, who seemd to consist entirely of a big black hood and two unnervingly bony hands, stopped sniggering as if he'd just been switched off at the mains. 'Tickets,' he said.

'But I thought we pay you as we board,' Osiris replied, confused. 'Surely—'

'Not enough money in the world,' the ferryman said. 'You wanna know why you can't take it with you?'

'Why?'

'Because I takes it off you first. Show us yer ticket or sling yer hook.'

Before Osiris could remonstrate further, Pan finished sectioning the last card, gave Lundqvist his knife back and hurried up to the river bank. 'Here we are,' he said, handing out the little celluloid discs. 'Tickets.'

'Pan,' Osiris said, 'they're just little round bits cut out of credit cards. What are we supposed to …?'

He tailed off. Pan was now lying on his back, screwing the plastic circles into his eyes like oversize contact lenses. The ferryman leant over him, like the devil's optician making a house call.

'That'll do nicely, sir,' he grunted. 'Hold on just a mo while I write down the number.'

'It all started,' Pan explained, some time later, as they lurched nauseatingly across the river in the little boat, 'with the first big dose of inflation they had back along, just after the first sack of Rome. Apparently, Chummy here …' He indicated the ferryman with a jerk of his thumb. 'Chummy here got so sick of being paid in devalued Roman currency that he started to get funny about it. Started off demanding Swiss francs, even though they don't fit properly and the milled edges cut your eyelids; then it was Deutschmarks, then US dollars for a while, and then it was yen, just for a short time. Now it's plastic or nothing. And if your credit rating doesn't match up, then it's just hard luck.'

Osiris shook his head sadly, adding slightly to the already disturbing oscillation of the boat. Ever since – well, ever since he'd left Sunnyvoyde, he'd had this feeling that things were wrong. Not, of course, that they'd ever been right, not ever (as far as he could remember; and he could remember the universe when it had been in the interstellar equivalent of its very first Babygro); but never, surely, as wrong as this. True, the system had been unjust and unfair and stacked against the poor bloody mortal from the outset; but at least it had been efficient, and it had worked. Now, of course, it was all different. Gone were the days of arbitrary authority and the Divine Whim, and as a result it looked as if you needed private health insurance just to be allowed to die.

I leave them to their own devices for just five minutes, and look what they've done to it all.

He turned to the ferryman and tapped him on the shoulder. It was a bit like playing a very short piece by Stravinski on the xylophone.

'Excuse me,' he said, 'but do you own this boat?'

'What, me?'

'Yes, you.'

The cowl wobbled sardonically. 'Get real, chum,' said the ferryman. 'I just work here, all right? You got anything to say, you say it to the bloody management.'

Osiris nodded. 'I will,' he replied, 'you can count on that. Who would that be, incidentally? The management, I mean.'

'Bloke called Julian something owns this boat,' the ferryman replied. 'Least, it's a group of companies, whatever that's supposed to be, but really it's the same thing.'

'One of the godchildren, is he?'

The ferryman shrugged. 'Dunno,' he replied. 'Like I said, I only work here.'

'Thank you so much for all your help.'

'Piss off.'

It was, inevitably, Sandra who noticed it first.

'Hey,' she said, 'over there, look.'

Osiris followed her pointing finger. His eyesight was not quite so good as it might have been, what with the advancing years and the fact that the Lady Isis had, on the last occasion on which she had reassembled him, put the right eyeball in back to front; but you'd have had to be stone blind not to see the big neon sign, glaring out of the inky darkness.

THE LAST SUPPER

Best Diner in Hell

TRY OUR FABULOUS SELECTION OF BAKED MEATS

'All right,' he sighed. 'Maybe just ten minutes for a cup of coffee and a doughnut or something. We can ask the way.'

The diner was empty except for a waitress, two animated skeletons quietly eating Danish pastries in a corner, and a tall, thin man sitting on his own over an empty cup of coffee, apparently talking to himself. On closer inspection he turned out to be dictating into a pocket dictaphone. As Osiris' party passed by he put the machine away sheepishly.

'Just filing my report,' he said. 'Got to try and make the final edition.'

Pan looked at him. 'The final edition of what?' he asked. 'Are you a journalist or something?'

The man nodded. 'Danny Bennett,' he said proudly, 'special correspondent. I'm on an assignment to . . .' He looked around furtively, and whispered, 'to find out the truth. You know, what's really going on around here. At least,' he added uncertainly, 'I assume I am. Otherwise, why the bloody hell am I here?'

Pan stroked his chin, trying to remember how you did tact. 'Maybe,' he said carefully, 'it's because you're dead.'

There was a moment of profound silence; the sort of silence you get at the bottom of very deep wells, or the back of long-unopened airing cupboards. 'Nah,' the man replied at last, 'not me. I've got so much to live for – you know, my career, my public, this really incredibly big scoop I'm working on right now.'

Pan nodded. 'Been here long?' he asked.

The man rubbed his eyes. 'Now it's funny you should ask me that,' he said. 'I don't think so, but it's a weird thing, trying to keep track of time in this place really isn't easy. I may have been here weeks for all I know.'

As nonchalantly as he could, Pan looked away. 'Well,' he said, 'keep up the good work.' He drew a little nearer, and added conspiratorially, 'if you want a hot tip, check out the ferryman back there. It's all completely unconfirmed, of course, and don't quote me, but . . .'

The man nodded. 'Strictly on a sources-close-to basis,' he whispered. 'You have my word as a journalist.'

'What I've heard,' Pan went on, 'is that he's running the biggest illegal immigrant scam in the universe, right under our very noses.'

The man's eyes widened. 'Boat people?'

Pan nodded. 'Thousands of 'em,' he said. 'I mean,' he added, 'you're not going to tell me all the guys out there were born here, are you?'

The man nodded excitedly, his hand reaching for a napkin and his three-colour pen. 'It all adds up,' he said. 'God, I wish I could find out who's behind it.'

Pan looked round. 'Who do you think?' he said. 'The Mob.'

'You mean the Mafia?'

'Nah.' Pan shook his head. 'Not that bunch of choirboys. *The* Mob. The Organisation. *Them!*'

Frantically the man grabbed at Pan's sleeve. 'The Masons?' he demanded. 'The Klan? The Bruderbond? MI5? The CIA? The International Standing Commission on Food Additives? Come on, for Christ's sake, you've got to tell me. The public have a right to . . .'

Pan looked him in the eye. 'You mean to say,' he hissed, 'you don't know who *They* are?'

'No,' the man said, half hissing and half screaming. 'All my life I've been trying to find out and I don't fucking know!'

'And you call yourself a journalist?'

'Yes. I *am* a bloody journalist. Look, you have a duty to tell me, I'm Press.'

Pan looked round once more, lifted the sugar jar and shook it, and put his hand over the spout. 'I suggest, he said, 'you look them up in the phone book. Under T.'

'Right.' The man jumped up, scrabbled up his notebooks, pens and scraps of paper, and ran for the door. Pan shook his head sadly.

'I don't mind there being one born every minute,' he said. 'It's one dying every minute that lowers the tone of this place so much. Here, Sandra, mine's a cappuccino, three sugars.'

'Well,' Pan said, 'here we are.'

It was a door. Just a door, painted white, with a round doorknob and a brass plate, set in an entirely conventional doorframe in a perfectly nondescript wall. The two gods looked at each other.

'I think,' Pan went on, 'we'll just wait for you, um, out here. Don't want to intrude, after all.'

'Oh.'

'I mean to say, if you've got private family matters to discuss, last thing you'll want is us lot standing around gawping.'

'That's very ...' Osiris paused, trying to find the appropriate words. 'Nice of you,' he continued, failing. 'I don't, er, expect I'll be long.'

'You take your time,' Pan replied, turning up the collar of his coat and trying to hide behind it. 'All the time in the world. We'll just hang about here and, well, admire the scenery.'

No god has ever really mastered the knack of lying – not for want of trying, but simply because it's alien to their intrinsic natures, in the same way that water finds it hard to be thirsty. There was no scenery, none whatsoever. Apart from the building they were standing in front of, there was nothing to be seen in any direction.

'Be seeing you, then,' Osiris said.

'Bye.'

With his free hand, Osiris turned the doorknob, opened the door and wheeled himself through. He found himself in a marble-floored hallway, and in front of him were the doors of an impressive looking lift. Over the doorway, in neon letters, was the word:

QUICK

while the ornate oak-banistered staircase in the corner of the hallway was marked:

DEAD

Osiris pressed the call button, and almost instantaneously the lift doors opened. He wheeled himself in and closed the doors, noticing as he did so that they were made of seasoned, exquisitely polished pine, fitted with elegant brass handles. The inside of the lift was lined with red satin.

A moment later the doors opened again, and Osiris found himself facing a broad, impressive-looking desk, with four telephones on top of it and a middle-aged lady with a pleasant smile behind it. He rolled forward and said, 'Excuse me.'

The lady looked up. 'Mr. Osiris?' she asked brightly. 'We've been expecting you.'

Osiris nodded. 'Good,' he said. 'Is he ready for me now?'

The woman looked down at a display board with coloured lights on it. 'He won't be a moment,' she said, 'he's just on the telephone. If you'd care to wait.'

'That's fine.'

'And.' The lady smiled. She looked for all the world like the better class of aunt; the sort that doesn't expect thank-you letters and doesn't mind a bit if you forget her birthday. 'The payment, please.'

Osiris blinked. 'In advance, is it?' he said. The lady nodded, and Osiris handed over the bearer bond. It went in a drawer and was gone.

Twenty minutes later, a buzzer went on the nice lady's desk. She looked up and smiled.

'You can go in now, Mr Osiris,' she said.

The god sighed, put down the August 1974 edition of *Practical Fishkeeping* and grasped the handrails of his chair firmly.

'Right,' he said. 'Thanks.'

'My pleasure.'

As the door closed behind him, the nice lady made a note in the visitors book and scratched her ear with the end of her pencil; then she vanished, and was replaced by a thirty-foot coiled serpent with five heads and fangs like pickaxe blades. She still looked like someone's aunt, because even serpents have families, but not quite so reassuring and friendly.

'Mr Osiris. Please sit down. May I offer you a cup of tea?'

The lawyer turned round in his swivel chair, picked up a handful of something white and fluffy, and dropped it into a big, chrome-plated shredder that stood beside his desk. There was a chomping sound, and the very faint echo of distant screams.

'No thank you,' Osiris replied. 'Can we get straight down to business, please?'

'Of course.' The lawyer was fat, even by the standards of his profession, bald-headed and dressed in a rather shiny blue suit with a faint white pinstripe. It suddenly occurred to Osiris that the fluffy things were souls.

'Quite right,' the lawyer said,' nodding. 'When people say that I'm in a soul-destroying line of work, they don't know how right they are. Now then, what seems to be the problem?'

'It's like this,' Osiris replied; and as he went through the facts of the matter, he couldn't help noticing that the lawyer's eyes were very round and green, and not in the least human. Par for the course, he rationalised, and nothing to worry about; but nevertheless. There was, he calculated, more humanity in a nest of soldier ants.

'I see.' The lawyer put the tips of his fingers together, and sniffed. 'We seem to have reached an impasse,' he said. 'And you want my advice as to what you should do next.'

'That's right.' Any minute now, Osiris said to himself, that tongue'll come darting out, wrap round somebody and dart back in again. 'So what do you . . .?'

The lawyer leant forwards, giving Osiris a splendid opportunity to confirm his earlier observation that there were no lids to those bright green eyes.

'If I were you,' he said, 'I'd settle.'

There was a moment's silence.

That is a very dull, banal way of putting it; try again. There was a short interval of the sort of silence usually associated with the fraction of a second between the referee dropping the handkerchief and the faster of the two duellists pulling the trigger of his pistol. Or: there was a pause, with sound effects reminiscent of that small, sharp splinter of time that separates the mighty upward swing of the bat and the crunch of broken glass, during which time all the persons present stand rooted to the spot, watching the ball follow its inevitable parabola greenhouse-bound across the sky.

'Oh,' Osiris said. 'You would, would you?'

The lawyer nodded. 'I don't want to be overly downside-orientated,' he said, 'but I can't help but feel that the term *hiding to nothing* has a definite relevance in the context in which we presently find ourselves. Obviously,' he went on, leaning back slightly and patting the sides of his gut with the palms of his hands, 'you're right up close to the problem, so objectivity might be a little bit on the problematic side, but for me as an outsider looking in, *not* looking at the situation through rage-tinted spectacles, so to speak, I think you really ought to seriously consider the potential negative fallout of defending this action, both finances-wise and in general terms, viewing the position as a whole and from a holistic viewpoint.'

'You mean,' said Osiris slowly, 'you think I'd lose?'

The lawyer spread his hands, as if waiting for mustard-and-cress seed to fall from heaven. 'We have a saying in litigation,' he said, 'along the lines of, Going to law is a bit like picking a fight with a fifteen-stone, six-foot-nine policeman made entirely out of horseshit; even if you win, you may very well end up wishing you'd never got involved in the first place. Your best bet is to try and get the best terms you can and bow out gracefully, and I say that on the basis of five thousand years in the Law. I'm sure that, given time, I could negotiate for you a very worthwhile financial settlement, very worthwhile indeed.'

Osiris scowled. 'I'm not interested in money,' he said.

The lawyer's eyes grew rounder and rounder, making him look even more like a locust than he had done previously. 'I beg your pardon?'

'I said I'm not interested in money,' Osiris replied. 'I'm a god, remember. Money means nothing to me.'

'Really?' The lawyer scratched his ear, perplexed. 'We are talking about the same thing here, aren't we? Crinkly paper stuff with someone's head on one side and –'

'Yes. Money. The hell with it, as far as I'm concerned.'

'No, but really, I think you must be getting confused here, I'm talking about *money*, the stuff that goes in banks, makes the world go ...' The lawyer fell silent, sat still for a while and then shook his head until his chins danced. 'My word,' he said, 'maybe it is time you ret ... I'm sorry, I'm digressing. Very well,' he continued, smiling a smile not entirely unlike the grin of a peckish hyaena, 'now you're about to say that this is a matter of principle and you're damned if you're going to let the proposed plaintiff push you around, and all the rest of it. Well, that's all very fine and splendid and I want you to know that I respect principles very much, in a general sense. On a more particular level, looking towards a more balanced position of principle tempered with healthy pragmatism, I'd say forget it. I mean, what on earth do you stand to gain?

You've retired anyway. Why not let Julian take some of the load off your shoulders? I mean, you can trust him implicitly, after all, he's a lawyer, for God's sake. No, I really must urge you to consider matters very carefully, taking account of all the circumstances of the case and not allowing your judgement to be clouded by extraneous factors in any shape or form.'

Osiris bit his lower lip thoughtfully. 'You ever met my godson Julian?' he asked.

The lawyer shrugged. 'I am,' he said, with a flicker of pride, 'the spirit of Litigation, I embody the Law. All lawyers are, in a sense, my children. In that respect I've known him, and his kind, ever since the first caveman filed suit against his neighbour for violating his patent on the wheel. A dispute,' he added smugly, 'which is still dragging on in some higher court or other, so I believe.'

'I see.' Osiris nodded. 'Figures. You remind me a bit of Julian, oddly enough.'

'You must be very proud.'

Osiris shifted a little in his seat, which was the archetypal lawyers' office client's-side-of-the-desk chair. Legend has it that the prototype was designed, five millennia ago, for a three-foot dwarf with granite buttocks who had lost both legs in a mining accident. 'Let's just go over this one more time, shall we?' he said. 'You're advising that I should hand over control of the Universe to my godson, who's a lawyer, because trying to resist his attempts to have me declared officially senile would be a lot of hassle and expense. Is that it?'

'Broadly speaking,' replied the lawyer, polishing his spectacles, 'yes. I must, however, qualify that statement by urging you to consider the precise definition of hassle in this context, bearing in mind the complexity of the grey areas of the Law in this particular arena, not to mention the consideration that the Court is likely to take a poor view of your purportedly wasting its time, speaking entirely prima facie and playing devil's advocate here for a moment, in resisting an application that really does make good practical sense from the feasibility and administrative viewpoints and is probably the best outcome for all parties when push comes to shove. I take it we're basically in agreement on that score.'

Osiris stood up. 'That's your advice, is it?' he said quietly.

'In broad brush terms, taking a simplistic overview, yes, to a certain extent it is.'

'Right.' Osiris smiled. 'Then fuck you.'

'I beg your pardon?'

With a certain amount of surprise, Osiris noticed that he was standing up, which wasn't bad going for someone who'd been confined to a wheelchair since Charlemagne was in nappies. 'I said,' he said, 'fuck you. I can spell that if you like.'

The lawyer raised one eyebrow. 'You're provisionally pigeonholing my advice for mature consideration at a later date?' he hazarded.

'I'm telling you where you can stick your advice,' Osiris replied, wiggling his toes. 'If your basic anatomy's a bit rusty, it's the part of your body you seem to talk through. Goodbye.'

'But I'm your *lawyer*,' the lawyer said, and Osiris noticed that he'd gone bright red in the face, giving him the appearance of a giant strawberry. 'You really ought to give very serious consideration –'

The door slammed.

For about fifteen seconds (or, to look at it another way, eighty-six thousand dollars exclusive of taxes) the lawyer sat motionless, staring at the closed door and wondering what on earth was going on. Then he leant forwards and pressed a buzzer on his desk.

'Has Mr Osiris left the building, Miss Fortescue?'

'Yes, sir.'

'Did he pay in advance?'

'Yes, sir. Bearer bond.'

'Ah.' The lawyer relaxed, and smiled. 'That's all right, then,' he said.

*

In the corridor Osiris stopped and collected his thoughts. For the first time in centuries he found that he had nearly the complete set, including most of the first day covers.

Marvellous, he said to himself, money well spent. Now I know what to do.

Avoid going to law, because it doesn't do any good.

The Law is my shepherd, wherefore shall I have nothing. He maketh me to lie down in green pastures, shamming dead.

If Julian inherits the earth, that's what God will look like for ever and ever.

I can stand up.

We created the world, they screwed it up. We created atoms, they split them. We gave them a garden, and now all that's left is a few nibbled-off stumps, some patches of oil and the silver trails of lawyers. We gave them everything, and they have made it into nothing. We gave them Justice, and they invented the Law. And on the ninth day, they tried to have us locked up.

Cautiously, trying not to notice himself doing it in case his brain suddenly remembered about the paralysis business, he glanced down at his feet, then his shins, then his knees. Been a long time, he thought. Still, it's like riding a bicycle. Well, hopefully not at all like riding a bicycle, which is all about wobbling precariously along for two or three yards and then falling over. He raised one foot and put it down, and then repeated the experiment with the other foot. And again. And again.

Gee whiz, World, my feet work! Isn't that amazing?

I can use them for standing.

I can use them for walking.

I can use them for running.

I can use them for standing on tiptoe to reach things on high shelves.

I can use them for dancing.

And, (said the god to himself and thereby parenthetically to the cosmos at large) best of all, I can use them for giving Julian a bloody good kick up the backside.

The science of surgery has come a long way since the days when a doctor was a sawbones and the contents of his little black bag looked horribly like a collation of a carpenter's tool-roll and a torturer's equipment chest. The modern surgeon tends to use such precision implements as the fine scalpel, the forceps, the roll of suture, the miniature laser . . .

The 105mm recoilless rifle . . .

'There he is,' hissed the first doctor. He slammed in the high explosive shell and closed the breech. 'Remember, squeeze the trigger, don't pull.'

Even in his semi-trance of private meditation, Osiris heard the click of the breech-block falling into place. He turned and stared . . .

'Ah,' said the first doctor, grinning in the shadows. 'Now then, hold still, this isn't going to hurt one little bit.'

Before Osiris could move or speak, the second doctor squeezed (not pulled) the trigger, and the ground shook with the thump of the artillery piece going off. The muzzle blast knocked the first doctor to the ground.

'Hoy,' said his colleague, scrambling to his feet, 'did I get him?'

The first doctor nodded. 'You could say that,' he replied. 'All the king's horses job, by the look of it.' He removed a finger – not his own – from his ear and discarded it. 'Put another way,' he went on, 'all his insides are now outsides. Let's get out of here, quick. I never did like the sight of blood.'

The second doctor sneered. 'Huh,' he said, 'you're just like him, aren't you?'

'Am I?'

'Absolutely,' replied the second doctor. 'At the first sign of trouble you go all to pieces.'

16

'As a slogan,' said Ahura Mazda, sun god of the ancient Persians, 'it lacks a certain something, don't you feel?'

Baldur, Norse god of fertility, looked up irritably, aerosol in hand. 'You reckon?' he said.

'Well . . .' Ahura Mazda took a step back and scrutinised the wall further. 'You do want me to be honest, don't you?' he said.

'Not neces . . .'

Great oaks from little acorns; very prudently, the Sunny-voyde Residents Direct Action Committee had decided to try out its blitzkrieg graffiti campaign on the back wall of the coal bunker, down at the far end of the garden, behind the compost heap. That way, if it turned out not to be the stunningly effective medium of protest they confidently anticipated, nobody would ever know.

'I mean,' Ahura Mazda drawled on, 'banality is all right in its way, but if we were going all out for the trite approach, we can still do better than that.'

'Such as?'

'Such as, let me see, um, "Gods united can never be defeated". Or "Rice pudding? No thanks". Or "Together we can stop the courgettes". Something like that.'

'"Gods of the cosmos unite",' suggested Nkulunkulu, the Great Sky Spirit of the Zulus. '"You have nothing to lose but your . . . your . . ." Hell,' he said, furrowing his brows into a single black hedgerow. 'Nothing to lose but what, for pity's sake?'

'I like it,' Baldur growled. 'I think it has relevance.'

On the wall he had painted:

MISIS HENDRESUNS A SILY OLD BAGE

in wobbly green letters. On the other hand, it was his aerosol.

'I still think,' muttered Vulcan, the Roman god of fire, 'you should have said something about that tapioca last Thursday. It was really horrible, I thought, and lumpy, too. I can't be doing with lumpy tapioca.'

'The tapioca was fine,' retorted Viracocha, the pre-Inca All-Father of Argentina, 'compared to that yuk we had yesterday, whatever it was supposed to be.'

'Pease pudding,' said Vulcan.

'Whatever,' Viracocha snarled. 'It was absolutely yetch, you know?'

'Absolutely,' Ahura Mazda agreed. 'They make a dessert and they call it pease. I still don't think we've quite taken the possibilities of this medium of expression to their absolute limits, do you?'

Ogun, the Nigerian god of war, shook his head. 'I'm going in,' he said, 'before I catch my death of cold. If anyone wants me, I'll be in the television room.'

'Scab,' Baldur hissed, shaking the aerosol aggressively. 'Blackleg.'

Ogun gave him a long stare. 'I'll take that as a statement of fact,' he said frostily. 'So long, losers.'

Baldur sighed. In his face was reflected the transcendent pain and sorrow of all organisers everywhere who come up against total unrelenting apathy. 'Right,' he said, 'fine. From now on you can use your own bloody aerosol. I'm going to my room.'

The other members of the committee lingered a little

longer, contemplating the despised graffiti. So nearly there, they thought, but not quite.

What we need, they realised, is a Leader.

'I think there's a spelling mistake in there,' Viracocha observed. 'Aren't there two Gs in Bage?'

'I wonder where Osiris has really got to?' somebody asked.

Ahura Mazda nodded. 'Good question,' he replied. 'Typical of him, that, making himself scarce as soon as he's needed.'

'He'd know what to do.'

'Oh come on.' Ahura Mazda yawned and polished his spectacles. 'We all know what to do. It's how to do it that's got us a bit stumped just at the moment.' He looked round. 'Any suggestions, anyone?'

'Are you a doctor?'

'I suppose we could look it up in a dictionary,' Viracocha suggested.

'Look up what?'

'Bage.'

Ahura Mazda sighed. Then, from the pocket of his raincoat, he produced his own aerosol (cobalt blue gloss, for touching up scratches on 1974 Cortinas). He shook the can, playing a merry if avant-garde tune with the little ball bearing in the neck.

'Try this,' he said, and started to spray.

What he sprayed was:

HELP

Once, in the Great Night that preceded the First Day, a woman had stooped over the mangled corpse of her husband. Red to the elbows with his blood, she had gathered the torn scraps of his body in a basket and stolen them away. Under the dim light of the newly lit stars, she had put them back together, refusing to acknowledge the existence of Death, as if it had been some unstable totalitarian regime in some little dominion far away.

In her hand, cupped against the faint breezes of the first dawn, she had shielded the guttering flame of his life. Because she did not recognise Death, because she had refused to admit the possibility of something ending, her work was successful and the body, stitched together with papyrus thread and linen bandage, eventually twitched and stirred; and the mouth opened and said, '. . . -Handed cow, you've gone and bolted my trapezus slap bang in the middle of my pectoral major. Do you realise that from now on, whenever I want to scratch my ear I'm going to have to wiggle my toes?'

But that was a long time ago; and since then, Death has opened his embassies and consulates in every corner of the cosmos. Undoing Death's work is no longer a matter of putting the bits back together and turning the starting handle. Or so they say.

'Search me,' said Pan, scratching his chin. 'Try turning it round the other way and belting it a few times with the heel of your shoe.'

Sandra looked up at him. Her clothes were soaked in blood, there was blood on her face, in her hair, everywhere. In her hand she held seven inches of warm grey tubing and a bone.

'You're not really helping, you know,' she said.

Pan shrugged. 'I was beginning to wonder,' he said glumly. 'I think I'll go and see if I can get hold of lots of hot water and some clean towels.'

With an effort, Sandra cleared her mind. On the one hand, it surely stood to reason; in the old days, he was always being dismantled and put together again, so there had to be a way of doing it, a simple way that a trained nurse like herself could work out, from first principles if necessary. On the other hand . . .

'Thigh bone,' she muttered under her breath. 'The thigh bone connecka to the hip bone, the hip bone connecka to the—'

Find my head.

She looked up. The voice had sounded just like him, except that there had been no sound and no voice. She pulled herself together and picked a few bits of fluff out of what she believed as the left kidney.

Find my head and I can tell you what to do. Please.

'Osiris?' she asked faintly. 'Osiris, is that you?'

No, it's Maurice Chevalier. Of course it's me. This is my soul speaking.

'Where are you? I mean, where is it?'

You're kneeling on it.

Sandra stood up hurriedly. 'Sorry,' she said. 'Gosh, so that's what they look—'

Find my head. I'll tell you what to do. But hurry. This really isn't the most comfortable way to have a conversation, believe me.

There is something horribly comic, under all imaginable circumstances, about a head with no body attached to it. No matter how desperate the grief, how bewildering the shock, there is always the temptation, lurking in the blackness of the mind, to stick one's fingers up the neck and try to say *Bottle of beer* without moving one's lips.

When you've quite finished.

And, when the First Day dawned, the wicked prince Set looked out from his throne and saw the sun. And he turned to his two brothers and asked them what it might be.

And his brothers turned to each other in amazement (they had perfectly good names but somehow always ended up being called Game and Match) and confessed that they did not know. Something, they suspected, had gone wrong somewhere . . .

And Osiris had risen from the dead, made whole again by the love and faith of his wife, and had thrown Set and his treacherous brothers into the Pit. Thenceforth there had been day and summer, and there was no more Death except for those who did not truly understand . . .

Or so they say. It's one thing to believe in the existence of a video recorder, and another thing entirely to build one from scratch out of a cardboard box full of knobs and bits of old wire.

Except that to the gods, all things are possible . . .

'Yes, but where does this bit go?'

Osiris' head blushed; quite some feat considering that his blood supply was some five yards away. 'Stay at home a lot in the evenings, do you?' he said.

'Yes,' Sandra replied, frowning, 'as a matter of fact I do. Why?'

The head sighed. 'I wouldn't worry about it,' he said. 'I haven't actually used that bit for so long that I'm not absolutely sure myself. Ask Pan, he'll know.'

Kurt Lundqvist, meanwhile, had wandered off, quite unnoticed by his companions, on the pretext of finding the two doctors and pulling their lungs out, but really to go and have a nice sulk in the bushes, if he could find any. All this time, he reflected, he'd been tagging along like some accredited observer, pleased and grateful if anyone asked him to pass a spanner or lift a wheelchair. True, whenever he had had centre stage to himself he hadn't exactly cut the most heroic of figures, but that wasn't his fault, he felt sure. Perhaps he should just leave them a note and slip quietly away.

'Hoy, you!'

He turned.

'Whatsyername! Thingy!'

He was being addressed, he realised, by a disembodied head; and although this wasn't in fact a novel experience for him (compare the Grendel contract of AD 792, for example; or the Medusa hit, right back when he was just starting out in the business) it was nonetheless a sufficiently rare occurrence to leave him standing there with his mouth open making a sort of *Gark!* noise.

'I've got a job for you,' said the head. In his already bewildered state it took Lundqvist several seconds to notice that the head was being supported by a column of ants, none of whom seemed to know particularly how they came to be doing this.

'Pardon me,' he eventually managed to say, 'but shouldn't you be, um, over there. With the rest of you?'

The head sighed. 'They're in conference,' the head replied. 'Trying to work out which order the toes go in, would you believe. I think they've got as far as the little piggy who had roast beef. Anyway, it'll be ages before I'm needed. So I thought I'd take this opportunity to give you your orders.'

Lundqvist took a deep breath. 'Thanks,' he said, 'but I've been thinking it over and I guess I'm not really achieving anything here, and I've got this pretty major practice of my own back home that needs my full attention, so maybe it'd be better if we just call it a day, huh? I won't be sending in an invoice, naturally, because ...'

And so on. That at least was what he intended to say, but in reality he only got as far as, 'Tha.' Academic, in any case, as to the gods all things are known and no secrets are hidden.

'Easy little job,' the head continued. 'For someone with your qualifications and experience, that is. Spot of fighting, a touch of abseiling in through windows and throwing grenades, silent elimination of sentries, all that sort of carry-on. Right up your street, I reckon.'

Lundqvist nodded eagerly. 'Sure,' he said. 'No problem, glad to be of service. What exactly did you have in—'

'Well.' The head grinned. 'What it boils down to is, I want you to liberate Sunnyvoyde.'

'I beg your ...'

The head ignored him, and a seldom-used part of his subconscious mind reflected on the humiliation of a six-foot-seven man being talked to by a severed organ positioned the height of an ant's shoulders above the ground. 'Go in there,' he said, 'take out all the guards, get the residents organised, lead them to death or glory. Well, glory anyway. You think you can manage that?'

'I guess so,'

'You're sure you don't want any backup? Helicopters, armoured personnel carriers, dog-headed fiends from the land of the Dead, that sort of thing?'

'No, that's fine,' Lundqvist replied, mentally reviewing his various pre-departure checklists. 'When do I start?'

'Now,' replied the head.

'No time to lose, huh?'

The head nodded, and in doing so squashed flat about forty members of its escort. But that sort of thing is par for the course if you're a tiny individual caught up in the ebbing and flowing of the tide of Destiny; just as you're about to overthrow the forces of Darkness and bring back the old King or whatever, along comes some bastard and treads on you. Still, there it is.

'If I were you,' the head said, 'I'd get on to it right away. Tell them,' it added, 'I sent you, okay?'

'That'll help, will it?'

The head considered. 'I expect so. Still here?'

Lundqvist nodded; and then frowned, as a thought struck him. 'Hang on,' he said. 'Which way is Sunnyvoyde from here?'

The head grinned, and rolled its eyes directly upwards.

'If you lie on your back,' it said, 'just follow your nose.'

Misha Potemkin, assistant distribution manager for the Novosibirsk Tractor Co-Operative, woke to find himself in the toilet of a standard-class carriage of the Trans-Siberia express. This was pretty much what he'd been expecting.

Painfully, he pulled himself to his feet and pulled up his trousers. Too much vodka on an empty stomach at the Jaroslavsk Tractor Industries Fair, combined with not getting all that much sleep over the last four days, had obviously caught up with him. Just his luck, he reflected bitterly, massaging his querulous temples with the palm of his hand, if he'd missed his station. If he had, it'd be another twelve hours before he'd be home again.

Cautiously, he rolled back the door, staggered out into the corridor, and looked out of the window. He observed three things which gave him cause for serious thought.

He saw no train.

He saw no track.

He saw no ground.

With a gurgling noise he collapsed back into the toilet and slammed the door, bolting it behind him. His senses told him that outside the window there was nothing at all. Not even a distant prospect of the ground, such as one might expect to see if the train had derailed on a hairpin bend in the mountains, leaving half the carriage hanging out over a ravine; or clouds, or sky.

A man who has spent twenty-seven years in the nationalised tractor business knows better than that. Obviously he was suffering from hallucinations, the result of cheap Georgian vodka (probably made from freeze-dried oven chips), and until they'd stopped he was likely to be better off where he was. The last time he'd had the DTs, immediately after the Miss All-Siberian Reaper and Binder awards ceremony the May before last, he'd hallucinated some pretty unsettling things, all of which had been far too large to fit inside a small, confined space like this. They'd be hard put to get just their heads in without banging their noses on the sink.

Half an hour later his head still felt like the contents of a turbocharged cement mixer, but he hadn't had to contend with so much as a single sabre-toothed wolfhound coming through the wall at him holding a bunch of flowers. Probably, he decided, it's better now. Just to make sure, however, he opened the door on the other side of the corridor and looked out.

Still no train.

Still no track.

But at least there was some ground; there was, in fact, a stereotypical Siberian landscape (snow, snow and more snow under an iron-grey sky that looked like a photograph taken with poor quality ASA 400 film). That, he reflected, was a material advance. He closed the window, crossed to the other door and looked out.

No train.

No track.

No ground!

The holding of high-level peace conferences in railway carriages straddling the borders of the conflicting nations is an inoffensive, even picturesque tradition, and its very lack of originality gives it a degree of innate respectability, extremely useful when organising a last-ditch attempt to reach a negotiated settlement between two implacably hostile factions.

It had been Pan's idea, of course, and a very good idea too. Since Osiris had refused to return to Earth, and Julian had declined categorically to visit the extended parallel dimension, at right angles to reality, in which Osiris had pitched his base camp, it was also pretty well the only option. It had, however, taken some setting up. Simply getting the dispensation from the Physics Board of Control had been bad enough.

But there the carriage was, half in and half out of the universe of space and time, and on board were the two teams of delegates: the hand-picked elite of the legal and accountancy professions at one end of the carriage, all briefcases and laptop computers and go-anywhere fax machines, and Pan, Carl, Sandra and an old Olivetti portable at the other. Whether by luck or by judgement, however, the divine delegation had scored one of the most telling victories of the conference before a single word was spoken; they'd got the end of the carriage with the toilet.

'All right,' said one of Julian's team, a jet-propelled intellectual property lawyer from New York, attended by no less than three Principal Minions and seven Nodders First Class, 'we're prepared to back down on the watercress *if*, and this is a very big if, you guys can see your way to accommodating us on the pastrami. How about it?'

Five hours into the conference and they were still discussing what to have in the sandwiches.

All this had come about because Kurt Lundqvist had stormed Sunnyvoyde. Scroll back and edit; not so much stormed, perhaps, because he'd gained admittance by ringing the front door bell and asking to be let in, on the pretext that he'd come to mend the ballcock. Once inside, however, he had made inflammatory speeches, distributed subversive pamphlets, done all that could be expected of a front-line professional agent provocateur and diagnosed Minerva as having tonsillitis. His appearance had at first had the effect on the residents of a small Friesian calf in a ceramic pipe factory, but eventually ... Mrs Henderson was now besieged in the linen cupboard, fifty thousand tins of tapioca pudding had been dumped in the swimming pool, and the gods had signed a hurriedly drafted Declaration that dealt in lofty terms with such concepts as life, liberty and the pursuit of Black Forest gateau.

It is one thing, however, to storm the Bastille; quite another to consolidate your position to the extent that you can start issuing your own postage stamps. The godchildren had immediately retaliated by sequestrating all divine assets invested in the World Below; and, since these consisted of about ninety-five per cent of the World Below, this constituted one of the few known cases of effective economic sanctions. The next step could only be war; and, as is well known, you can't have a proper war without a failed peace conference first. It's like having dinner in a really expensive restaurant and skipping the starter.

Pan looked round and conferred briefly with his colleagues. 'Okay,' he said, 'I think we're not as far apart on this as you imagine.' He drew a deep breath. 'We'll hold our hands up on the pastrami if you'll consent to a multilateral regulatory agreement on the mineral water.'

'Policed by UN observers?'

'If necessary, yes.'

The lawyer frowned. 'We must insist.'

'Sure.' Pan nodded gravely. 'It should be plain by now that we have nothing to hide. Can we move on now, please?'

There was a general shuffling of papers. 'We now come,' said the lawyer, 'to item number two on the agenda, and I'd like to take this opportunity to point out that your party are already in flagrant breach of the pre-conference consensus on this one.' He shook his head, like a wet dog trying to shake off the sins of the world. 'I mean, come on, guys. We specifically agreed that the five coathooks nearest the doors were going to be ours.'

Pan hesitated. True, the first rule of negotiation is, Give the bastards a hard time on absolutely everything. On the other hand, his knee itched and he was getting pins and needles in his left foot. 'Okay,' he said. 'It's no big deal. You can have 'em.'

There was stunned silence on the other side of the table. 'We can?'

'Certainly. Be my guest.'

Frenzied conferring on the other side. 'But,' the lawyer pointed out, 'your coats are already in position.'

'Move 'em.'

'Are we talking a phased withdrawal here, under the auspices of a UN watchdog force, or—'

'Sling 'em on the floor,' Pan replied, smiling. 'They're only a couple of old anoraks and a parka.'

It was, one of the godchildrens' delegation admitted later, profoundly unnerving, the way Pan just sat there for the next thirty-seven minutes, giving way on every single piece of trivia they could contrive to throw at him. You got the impression, he went on, that either the guy was an absolute pro or a complete novice. When negotiating at this level, it's hard to say which is more deadly.

'We now come on,' said the lawyer, sweating, 'to item seventy-six. Who's going to rule the universe? Well, I think we can probably just flash past this one—'

'No, we can't,' Pan said. The lawyer looked the god straight in the eyes and turned quickly away. Pan didn't just have a poker face; his was the sort of expression that would convince you that he held at least four aces even before the seal had been broken on the deck of cards.

'All right,' the lawyer said, stifling a yawn. 'We propose that it should be us. You got a problem with that?'

'Sort of.'

'Nothing we can't handle, I'm sure. What's the bottom line here?'

Pan grinned. 'It's because you're useless,' he said. 'Totally and utterly incompetent. If the very best of you was given the job of organising the Budweiser annual Christmas staff party, sooner or later someone'd have to go to the off-licence. I rest my case.'

'You call that a case?' the lawyer sneered. 'Man, that'd be hard pressed to be a handbag. Where's your evidence?'

Pan laughed, raucously and on his own, for at least seventy seconds (which is a very long time), before wiping his eyes with his sleeve. 'If you want evidence,' he said, 'look around. There's nothing in the universe that isn't evidence.'

'Except woodlice.'

Pan stopped dead in his tracks and stared at the small, plump lawyer who had just spoken. 'Beg pardon?' he said.

'Woodlice,' replied the small lawyer. 'If (as if not admitted) we've cocked anything up, we sure haven't cocked up woodlice. They're doing really well under this administration. Productivity up and everything. You just go and ask one if you don't believe me.'

'And stalagmites,' added a senior accountant. 'Under this administration, stalagmites have risen by an average of sixteen point four seven two per cent. I call that a pretty conclusive argument, don't you?'

'Look . . .' said Pan.

'And,' interrupted a bald, almost circular lawyer who had hitherto been asleep, 'rotary washing lines. What did your people ever do to help facilitate open air laundry dehydration?'

'Look . . .'

'Or time,' said an even more senior accountant, pointing at Pan with a forefinger like a bratwurst. 'No fewer than five centuries actually completed ahead of schedule. That's the sort of results you just can't argue with.'

'Look . . .'

'Mountains, now,' chirruped a thin, brittle-looking actuary from the back row. 'This administration can truthfully say that it hasn't lost a single major peak since it took office. In fact, I'd venture to say that there are more quality mountains now than at any time in the last—'

'*LOOK.*'

Thank you (said Pan).

Be still and know that we are your gods. In the beginning we created the heavens and the earth, and we were without form and void.

Don't get me wrong. That was cool. It was like slopping round in your old clothes on a Sunday morning, not having to shave or put your teeth in. That's basically the way a god ought to be. And then you came along.

I remember saying to Osiris at the time, Look, Oz, just create them in your own image, it'll be a whole lot less hassle in the long run. But no, he said, that's not good enough, I want them to have all the advantages we never had. I want them to have souls, and know right from wrong. I want them to have good and evil, otherwise what purpose will there be in their poxy little lives? I want them to be *better* than us.

So we gave you morals. We gave you sensibilities. We gave

you ethics – and it wasn't easy, believe you me. You ask the average god to explain the difference between right and wrong, he'll look puzzled and ask if wrong's a dialect word for 'left'. But we wanted you to have the best of everything, and we managed, somehow.

And that meant (Pan said) that instead of just hanging loose in the void having a good time, we had to look after you. We shaped your destinies, judged your dead, zapped your perjurors, grew your crops, all that stuff. It wasn't what we wanted to do, but we did it.

And what thanks did we get? Prayers? Sacrifices? Temples with nice cosy armchairs where a god can put his feet up with the paper and have forty thousand winks? Not a bit of it. We had to put up with your suffering, your complaining, your why-me-whatever-did-I-do whingeing, your goddamned holier-than-thou attitudes. You made us doubt ourselves in everything we did. Every time we rained, we had to ask ourselves, Do the crops need rain this time of year, are they having droughts or floods down there? We couldn't so much as sneeze without running the risk of flattening one of your rotten little cities. We tried our best, and yes, I think we did a bloody good job; but every time we made just one little mistake, you were on us like a ton of bricks, with your sickeningly smug ours-not-to-reason-whying and your agnosticism and your general air of putting up with us out of the kindness of your hearts. And you know what? We respected you for it. We admired you. You made us feel really small.

And (Pan said) in the end we thought, Why bother? They're much better than we are, they've got justice and morality and all that sort of thing, and all we do is the flies-to-wanton-boys stuff. Let's hand it all over to them and call it a day. So we did. Dammit, we *believed* in you.

And look what happened. Ye have made of my Father's house a suite of offices. You've given the world over to the charge of lawyers and accountants and politicians – men whose only function in life is to make the truth appear lies and lies appear the truth. No more gratuitous violence, you said, no more inexplicable disasters, no more meaningless suffering, no more war, no more hunger, no more hatred, no more oppression.

Yes. Well.

Which is why (Pan said, and his voice shook the carriage and the surrounding hills) we're calling a halt. We never claimed to be better than you, but at least when we destroy a city or flatten a harvest we don't mean anything by it. No god ever killed anything for a principle or ruined the lives of millions for ten per cent of the gross. We may be clumsy, but evil is something you thought up all by yourselves, along with martyrdom, litigation and financial services.

And that is all I have to say on the matter.

'Fine,' said the lawyer, 'so it'll have to be war. Unless,' he added innocuously, 'you'd rather we did it the civilised way and took it to law. Just a suggestion.'

Pan thought for a moment, and grinned. 'Law?' he said. 'You mean have a trial and may the best man win?'

'Sure.' The lawyer managed to keep a straight face, because it's something you learn over the years, but his heart was rubbing its hands. We've got them, the dozy old buggers, it was saying.

'Done with you,' said Pan. 'We elect for trial by combat. We find that it's cheaper, quicker, fairer and a damn sight less traumatic for the participants. Agreed?'

The lawyer hesitated. 'All right,' he said, 'but it'll have to be by mortal rules, and with champions. You've got to admit, we'd be on a hiding to nothing fighting to the death with one of you lot.'

'Fair enough.'

'And,' said the lawyer quickly, 'we have first choice of champions, okay?'

'I suppose so, yes.'

'In that case,' said the lawyer, 'we nominate Kurt Lundqvist.'

17

'You sure about this?' asked Pan, for the forty-third time. 'I mean, you don't have to if you don't want to.'

'He's sure,' Sandra replied.

The heat from the floodlights was enough to fry eggs in sweat, and the air was the consistency of lard. Everyone who was anybody, everybody who had been anybody, and seventy-five per cent of everyone who was going to be somebody at some indeterminate point in the future, were here, shuffling in their seats, whispering excitedly, eating popcorn. In his private box in the epicentre of the dress circle, Lin Kortright, supernatural agent, focused his opera glasses, every fibre of his being intent on spotting the fresh, raw theological talent that would set the twenty-seventh century alight. On the western side of the arena, broadly speaking, sat the mortal contingent, the godchildren, their aides, assistants and support staff, demurely charcoal-suited and poised like hawks to pounce on any technical infringement of the rules. On the eastern benches sprawled the gods, a pan-dimensional charabanc trip to Weymouth, opening paper bags, pouring from thermoses, arranging rugs, crossing legs against importunate bladders, complaining incessantly and (in the front three rows at least) setting up the chant of, 'Come on, you Reds.'

Pan shook his head. 'I want you to know,' he said, 'that I have grave reservations about this whole thing.'

Carl looked up and peered at Pan through his visor.

'Grave reservations?' he repeated.

'That's right.'

'Oh. I didn't realise you had to book. I thought you just turned up in a box and they—'

'It's going to be all right,' Sandra said firmly, looking up from buckling on a shinguard. 'Don't fluster him.'

'I see. It's going to be all right, is it?'

'Yes.'

'You know this for a fact, do you?'

Sandra nodded. 'Osiris told me so himself.'

Pan's face exhibited a smile the consistency of office canteen coffee. 'Right,' he said, 'Osiris said so, point taken. Sandra, I don't want to be a wet blanket here, but I've known him rather longer than you have, and—'

'He's a god, isn't he?'

Pan blinked. Right now, he realised, her faith was strong enough to send Mont Blanc whizzing into orbit like a marble from a catapult. 'True,' he said. 'So'm I. So are all those incontinent old duffers you can see over there. For crying out loud, Sandra, you used to have to put them to bed and remind them what day of the week it was, surely you don't imagine . . .'

Sandra shook her head. 'They're not gods,' she said, 'they're just very old people. Mr Osiris is a *real* god, you can tell.'

'Oh?' Pan scowled. 'How?'

'Because,' Sandra replied with utter conviction (and it may be worth mentioning at this juncture that her grandmother was the great-great-great-great-great-great-great-great-great-great-great-great-great-great-great-great-great-great-great-grand-daughter of Joan of Arc's second cousin), 'he's the only person I know who can put a hot cup of tea down on a french-polished table and not leave a white ring. Only a true god could do that.'

'Um . . .'

'Only a true god would be that considerate. If it was someone else's table, I mean.'

Pan shook his head and wandered away. In his considered opinion, they'd been hopelessly outflanked at the very last moment, and it was time to pack it in and call it a day. It had been a good try, they'd had some fun (although offhand it was hard to call to mind a specific instance of this) but one had to be brutally realistic. The other side had Kurt Lundqvist – despite his recent mediocre form indisputably the deadliest two-legged fighting machine in the history of combat – whereas the only mortal the gods had been able to call on to fight their corner was Sandra's boyfriend Carl, he of the big ears and vacant expression large enough to store furniture in.

Carl. He'd been along from the start, Pan reflected as he marched along looking for a bookie who'd accept any odds at all on a Lundqvist victory, ever since they'd broken out and set off on this fatuous exercise; but try as he might, he couldn't actually call to mind anything the boy had done, except stand about and help with the heavy suitcases. There were some positive things about him, sure enough. He was toilet trained, he didn't seem particularly fussy about what he ate and his shoes were always dazzlingly brightly polished. More relevantly, he stood about six feet in his socks and had shoulders like an American footballer. His brain, however, seemed to be another matter entirely; like the vestigial vein of gold-bearing quartz directly underneath Bloomingdales or the Ascension Island tourist industry, it was an understandably under-exploited resource. Face facts, the lad was only slightly more sentient than a traffic light.

We're going to lose, Pan muttered to himself. What a pity. And where the devil has Osiris got to?

Ready?
'Yes, boss.'
You know what to do?

'Yes, boss.'
Remember, when I said leave all the thinking to me, I really di
mean all the thinking, all right?
'Yes, boss.'
Got everything? The baseball bat? The bag of sand?
'Yes, boss.'
Clean underpants?
'Yes, boss.'
Splendid.

Lundqvist looked up, and whimpered.

Outside, in the arena, he was going to win; he knew it as a
depressing certainty, as hopeless and ineluctable as Monday.
At his side was the .40 Glock, his trademark, with which he
could shoot the ash off a cigarette at a hundred yards.
Strapped to his ankle, the Sykes-Fairbairn fighting knife. In his
left hand, the slide-action Remington twelve-gauge. And this,
he reflected bitterly, was the absolute minimum he'd been able
to select when offered choice of weapons without laying
himself open to a charge of throwing the match.

The other side had chosen a baseball bat and a bag of sand.
Probably thought it was funny.

It goes with the territory. He could just about refuse to fight
gods, on conscientious grounds, but there was no way he
could turn down a contract to fight a fellow human being. It
was part of the price he had to pay for being a professional,
and being the best. If he hadn't been the best, he could have
chickened out on grounds of cowardice – perfectly legitimate
for any other member of the profession except himself to do
that. And if he hadn't been a professional – but he had been,
for more years (thanks to the exemption from the rules of
chronology that came with his Federal licence) than anybody
could remember. If he wasn't a professional, one hundred per
cent impartial and doing it purely and simply for the money,
then there were one hell of a lot of dead people out there who

had grounds for some extremely trenchant criticism. The defence of only-obeying-orders only holds good so long as the orders are actually obeyed.

LAYDEES AN GENNULMENN YOUR ATTENSHUN PLEEEZ . . .

It was a very special arena – unique, the first and last of its kind. They'd had to search long and hard to find a site that was a temporal anomaly and a moral vacuum and also had adequate parking for seventy million cars. The beer tent alone had required licences from no less than sixty-four different authorities, many of them the same authority at different points in time. The floodlights were all dying stars, and the PA system had been in the Beginning, and had been with God and (according to some versions of the story) was God. Certainly it hadn't come cheap.

FOR THE HEAVYWEIGHT CHAMPIONSHIP OF THE UNIVERSE . . .

And it'll all be my fault, Lundqvist said to himself. The bastards, they've gone and made me into a lawyer, a *lawyer*, for gods' sake. I may have done some pretty filthy things in my time, but I never thought it'd come to this. I wish I'd never been born.

IN THE *BLUE* CORNER REPRESENTING HEA-VEN . . .

Too late now to make a bad day's work good. Eventually there comes a time when all that matters, or at least all you think about, is doing the job and doing it well, and it doesn't matter whether or not it's a lousy rotten job that someone has to do. At the end abide integrity, skill at arms and the money, these three, and the greatest of these is the money. Everything else is vanity, vanity of vanities.

AND IN THE *RED* CORNER REPRESENTING MARKET FORCES . . .

A very great deal of money, it went without saying.

★

'Well?' demanded Bragi, the blind Norse god of poetry. 'Have they started yet?'

There are those who'd have you believe that the post of Norse god of poetry must be, at best, a sinecure and, in all likelihood, a leg-pull (like the First Lord of the Swiss Admiralty or the Australian cultural attaché). Very few such sceptics have ever said anything of the sort to Bragi's face, however, and those foolish enough to have done so tend to be easily identified by their false teeth and crooked smiles. It's amazing how much damage a lead-weighted white stick can do at close quarters.

'I don't know,' replied Ahriman, the Parsee Prince of Darkness. 'That dozy cow in front of me's got her hat on, so I can't see a damn thing.'

'I heard that. And it's not a hat, it's the top of my head.'

'Sorry, Medusa, didn't realise it was you. Look, *have* they started yet?'

The serpent-haired Queen of Terror shook her head. 'Our chap's out there already but their bloke hasn't shown yet. With luck he'll be out of time and we can claim victory by def . . . No, here he is, dammit. Booo!'

Medusa scowled. If looks could kill – if looks could still kill despite cataracts and glaucoma . . .

'What's he got?' Bragi demanded.

'Um.' Medusa squinted. 'Guns and things, I think. To be honest with you, I'm not very well up on these modern gadgets.'

'If it's Kurt Lundqvist,' Ahriman interrupted knowledgeably, 'it'll be the .40 Glock and the Remington 870. He's done all his best jobs with them.'

Bragi raised a redundant eyebrow. 'What's a Glock?' he asked.

'It's a sort of gun. Actually it's a state-of-the-art compact polymer-framed double-action semi-automatic handgun with—'

'*Glock?*'

'That's right, Glock.'

'Oh for crying out loud,' exclaimed Bragi. 'You sure it's not a Colt or something? There's masses of rhymes for Colt.'

Ahriman pushed aside a dreadlock of vipers and peered through his binoculars. 'No,' he said, 'definitely the Glock. Adopted by law enforcement agencies worldwide, this revolutionary design—'

'Block,' muttered Bragi, 'clock, dock, hock, jock, knock. What are they doing now, by the way?'

'Shaking hands, I think. That or arm-wrestling.'

'Lock, mock, nock, rock, sock . . .'

'And now,' said Ahriman, 'the referee's talking to them. Saying he wants a good clean fight, I expect, though personally I never saw a clean fight in all my life. Dust on your trouser knees at the very least.'

'Is there such a word as yock?'

'I have a feeling,' said Medusa sadly, 'that this is going to be a very short fight. Anyone like a sugared almond?'

'Not for me, thanks. Here, did you know some of your green mambas've got split ends?'

'That's their tongues, idiot.'

'There's absolutely nothing at all that rhymes with Remington,' Bragi complained bitterly, 'except possibly Leamington, and really that should be Leamington Spa, so you'd have to have Spa as an enjambement on the next line. Why can't the bastard use a spear like everybody else?'

'Hey up,' Ahriman interrupted. 'They're going back to their corners. I don't think I want to watch this.'

'Frock, crock, broch, pill*ock* . . .'

The whistle went.

Nothing personal; Lundqvist jacked a round into the chamber of the Remington and fired. There was the usual universe-filling boom . . .

He blinked. At a target fifteen yards away, with a short-barrelled shotgun loaded with #00 Buck, it's virtually impossible to miss unless you're inadvertently standing with your back to your opponent. For a moment his brain was in free-fall; and then he picked up a voice on the short wave of his subconscious. Or rather, not a voice. A smirk.

Osiris, you bastard, you're helping him.

Certainly not. It just so happens that all of the little bullet things went wide. No violation of the laws of physics there, I promise you. After all, the shotgun is scarcely an instrument of precision.

You're cheating.

Absolutely not. It was just one of those unforseeable fluke events, like a whole bag of coins falling on the floor tails upwards. What we in the trade call an Act of God.

We'll see about that, Lundqvist growled. He slammed back the action, chambered another round and fired.

Would it be Brownian motion I'm thinking of, or is it Thingummy's principle of uncertainty? I'm rather a latecomer at physics, because in my day the sky was held up on the back of the goddess Nuth. Now you may think you know a thing or two about lumbago ...

Before his conscious mind could override, Carl was on to him. Sand exploded in his face while the baseball bat sent the shotgun spinning across the arena into the crowd ...

('Stock, shock, cock, *who* threw that? Just wait till I get my hands on whoever ...')

Oh good, said Lundqvist's subconscious mind, mortal danger; now we know where we are. Before Carl could bring the bat down, Lundqvist dropped his shoulder, sidestepped, hit the ground and rolled. By the time Carl knew where he'd got to he was on his feet, the knife in his right hand. Carl struck out hard, and if he'd connected there can be no doubt that Lundqvist's head would have ended up in the press box. As it was, the bat whistled through empty air and a fraction of a second later, Carl was on the sand, vaguely wondering in those parts of his mind still open for business exactly why his legs had suddenly folded up like a Taiwanese shooting stick, and what had happened to the lungful of air he'd invested in only moments previously.

Lundqvist straightened his back and drew his pistol. It was extremely likely that he'd broken a bone in his foot, and there were small bits of glass from his watch sticking in his ear. Apart from that, he was back on top . . .

All right. You win.

When you're around gods, time tends to have all the value and relevance of a fifty-lire note. In the short space of time between the front pad of Lundqvist's forefinger tightening on the trigger of the Glock and the hammer falling, the following subliminal dialogue took place:

Do I?

Seems like it. Go on, pull the damn trigger, get it over with.

But I don't want to.

You don't?

Apparently not.

Tough. Should have thought of that before you became the greatest assassin the world has ever seen, shouldn't you?

But hey, I'm on your side, you fucker. You want me to do this?

I want you to do what's right. That's what we created you people for, for gods' sake. If you can't do a perfectly simple thing like solving an insoluble moral dilemma . . .

The hammer quivered as the sear began to roll out of its notch. In the members' enclosure, Julian was smiling. And something deep inside Lundqvist's head grabbed the mike, and shouted.

'Dragon King of the South-East,' it shouted, 'get your great scaly ass over here.'

G'day.

'Third wish, right?'

Fair go, sport. What's it to be?

'I need,' said Lundqvist, 'an act of God. Can you manage that?'

No worries. Strikes me you don't need one the way you're set, but—

'Do something.'

Like what, mate? I'm not a flamin' mind reader, you know.

'Jam the gun. Take all the powder out of the cartridge. I don't know. Just do it, okay?'

Like a rat up a drain, mate. Here's luck.

The hammer fell.

Nothing happened.

'What's happening?'

'I can't see,' Ahriman snapped. 'Look, either keep your bloody pets under control or get a haircut, all right?'

'I'm sorry. I washed my snakes last night and now I can't do a thing with them.'

'He's just standing there,' Ahriman said. 'The gun didn't go off and he's just standing there like he's waiting for ivy to grow up him or something. He's not even trying to clear the gun, although with the unique toggle action of the Glock, clearing a first position stoppage is an extremely simple—'

'Why?' Bragi howled. 'This is ludicrous. Blow yer whistle, you great fairy!'

'Now he's looking up,' Ahriman went on. 'Blowed if I know what it is he's seen. Hang about, though, there's something . . . Looks like some kind of bird. No, it's too big, it's more like a . . . Well, if I didn't know better I'd say it was a . . .'

'Doesn't look like Old Trafford to me,' Thor objected.

'I can't help it if you can't read a map.'

'And even if it is,' Thor continued, 'somehow I don't think they'd be overjoyed if we go and park this damn great thing right in the middle of the playing area.'

'Ah,' said Odin. 'Actually, it's not as if we've got a great deal of choice in the matter.'

'I see.'

Odin braced himself in his seat and gripped the joystick firmly in his right hand. 'Hold on tight,' he said. 'I should be able to bring her in smoothly if only I could just . . .'

If I were you, I'd get out of there quick.

'Yes, boss.'

I mean really quick.

'Yes, boss. Boss?'

Well?

'How far should I go, boss?'

Oh, I think about five yards should do the trick.

'Oh,' said Bragi. 'Does that mean we've won?'

Ahriman opened his eyes. He could see Carl, slowly getting up off the ground. He could see the traction engine, or at least the part of it which wasn't embedded in the earth. He could see Thor bashing Odin over the head with a length of mangled driveshaft, while Frey made a show of dusting off his elbows. He could see Julian, standing up and walking swiftly towards the fire exit. He couldn't see Lundqvist; but, since the sight of blood always made him feel faint, that was probably just as well.

'I think so,' he said. 'Just because it was a pure fluke doesn't mean to say it doesn't count.'

'Pure fluke?'

'Act of God, you might say. Right, madam, just so much as another hiss and I'll take you down the salon myself and see to it they give you a perm you'll never forget, do I make myself clear?'

The immortal soul of Kurt Lundqvist stood up, brushed bits of body off its trouser knees, and looked down. Being an immortal soul, it had no lunch to bring up, which was probably just as well.

'Hey,' it yelled at the cosmos, 'I was using that!'

No reply.

In the back of its residual consciousness, it could remember something it had once read in a Gideon Bible about how the trumpet shall sound and the dead shall be raised incorruptible, and it thought, Just my stinking luck. Come Judgement Day, and I'll be the only one going round Eternity with a flat head, one foot at right angles to the other and carrying my left arm. Thank you very, very much.

Unless, it speculated, they patch you up first.

Yes, well, that might be something of a mixed blessing, bearing in mind the standards of celestial reconstruction work he'd seen recently. If Osiris was anything to go by (and he was a goddam *god*, remember, so presumably he merited the Grade A custom deluxe service) divine reconstitution would leave him looking like something brought home from school by a nine-year-old just starting pottery classes.

It ain't so reliable, what they say in the Bible, it ain't necessarily so. Or at least, the soul fervently hoped it wasn't. It reckoned it had done its bit for these people, one way or another, and the thought of dwelling in the House of the Lord for ever as the human equivalent of a Skoda was not pleasant.

The gods as creators; the whole cosmos a Friday afternoon job if ever there was one. The imperishable part of Kurt Lundqvist shook its head and walked away.

The first thing we'll do, we'll kill all the lawyers.

No, Osiris reflected, that's looking through the wrong end of the telescope. If we're going to do this thing, we may as well do it properly.

He rose slowly out of Carl's body and resumed his own. It was like stepping out of the water back into the air.

'All right, people,' he said, 'gather round.'

The gods went into a huddle.

*

Nobody knows what actually happened to Julian Magus and the godchildren, although there are a number of extremely imaginative myths, most of which fail to convince simply because they were concocted by people who don't actually know what brimstone is.

The truth is that Julian had made plans for this, as for all other contingencies; and, like ninety-nine point seven per cent of all Julian's plans, this one worked flawlessly. Within ninety seconds of Lundqvist's death he was clambering into a waiting helicopter clutching two suitcases full of uncut diamonds, while the in-flight plastic surgeon sterilised his instruments.

'Alpha Centauri,' he snapped to the pilot, 'and step on it.'

There are places where even the gods won't follow you; and, once you've come to terms with the fact that the beaches are blue and the ocean is yellow, and the combined power of all three suns isn't enough to convert the first taramasalata pink on the shoulders and back into true California golden brown, the good life can be successfully synthesised as well there as anywhere else. Beware, however, of ninety-nine point seven per cent success. After Julian had been in Alpha City for just under three years he was waylaid by a smooth-talking financial services consultant who persuaded him to invest his entire capital in Amalgamated Heliconium 37½% Unsecured Loan Stock, and is now earning his living as a washer-up at Z[i4kh98/98fß***sgwy's Bayside Diner at the unfashionable end of Neutron Cove.

For the record, he's never been happier; which only goes to show that where gods are concerned there's no justice, but there is, occasionally, mercy.

It began to rain.

'Be reasonable,' Pan yelled, as the water started to seep through the seams of his oilskins. 'What the hell are we going to need tarantula spiders for anyway?'

'Two of them,' Osiris replied, from the shelter of the

covered wheelhouse. 'Sharpish. And remember to get a male and a female.'

The level was rising fast. Pan growled, gripped the handles of his supermarket trolley, and squelched away.

When a god wants an ark in a hurry, he doesn't muck about waking people up in the middle of the night and giving detailed specifications in cubits; he simply ordains, and there it is, riding at anchor, ready for the statutory whack round the gunwales with seventy centilitres of Moet. It was big, comfortable and well-equipped, which was a good thing in the circumstances; because this time, nobody was going to be left behind.

Sandra looked in to report on her inventory of the ship's stores. 'We've got,' she said, 'five hundred billion rounds of egg and watercress, seventy billion small cardboard cartons of orange juice, ninety billion Mars bars, forty-six billion packets of peanuts and twenty-seven billion cubic tons of freeze-dried Red Mountain coffee. Do you think that'll be enough?'

Another good thing about being a god is that people do what they're told. No sooner had the first big raindrop splatted itself like a summer bluebottle against a windscreen than the human race, all of them fast asleep, began to form orderly queues at the designated embarkation points, whence they were collected in winged minibuses. The only small gnat in the ointment was the distinctly unethical behaviour of Mercury, god of thieves, who managed to get the fast food concession for the embarkation points by asking Osiris for it when he was busy with something else. Sad to say, not one human being got on to the ark without first buying a frankfurter in a roll, smeared with blood-red sauce.

'Sugar?'

'I knew I'd forgotten something.'

'Never mind.' To the gods all things are possible. 'Let there be sugar. It doesn't actually matter,' Osiris went on, 'because all this is all illusion anyway, but there's no point in upsetting people unnecessarily. How about biscuits?'

'The whole of C Deck is full of biscuits,' Sandra replied. 'If it's an illusion, why bother?'

Osiris looked up from his charts. They were plain, unmarked blue, apart from a tiny dot representing the peak of Mount Ararat. 'It's like building an office block,' he said. 'You put up hoardings until the work is finished, so that people only see it when it's complete. It looks better that way.'

'Ah.'

Osiris shrugged, so that his yachting cap flopped down over his left eye. 'Besides,' he added, 'the other gods won't believe in it unless we do it this way. You've got to remember that your average god is about as conservative as you can get, or otherwise how come they spent thousands of years making the crops grow on manual?'

The other gods spent the entire voyage on A deck, lounging beside the pool and throwing empty cans and bottles into the water. The New Mythology states that just before the waters subsided on the third day, all these bottles drifted together and formed the continent of Australia. One of the good things about the New Mythology is that it's usually more convincing than the truth.

On B deck mankind spent the voyage bickering, going to work and fighting a few small wars over the possession of the deck quoits area. There was no point, Osiris argued, saving the human race just to have it die of culture shock thirty-six hours into the voyage.

In the engine room, black-faced, sweaty and up to their elbows in grease, Odin, Thor and Frey argued the whole time about whose job it was to lube the main drive shaft bearing. On the blueprint of the ship, Osiris had crossed out the words *Engine Room* and written in *Valhalla*.

On the third day, the waters subsided.

The dove circled.

It was confused. It had only nipped out to gorge itself on oil seed rape, crap all over a few parked cars and sit on a telegraph wire. All the sudden blue wet stuff was distinctly unfamiliar.

Doves have pretty near three-hundred-and-sixty-degree vision, so their eyes have, properly speaking, no corners out of which to spot tiny specks of darkness in vast blue horizons.

After a few wary approaches to make sure the target area didn't in fact conceal two men in camouflage clothing with shotguns and a flask of coffee, the dove put its wings back, glided down, turned into the wind and pitched on the branch of the olive tree that was, as far as it could tell, the only bit of perch space left in the whole world. It sat for a while, smugly congratulating itself, and then stretched out its neck and nibbled a leaf.

Yuk. Salty.

Don't like it here.

With the leaf still in its beak, it spread its wings and flew away.

When the waters had all subsided, B deck awoke to find that, apart from a certain degree of residual dampness, the world was exactly as it had been; which was nice.

Except that it was clean. It had been a last-minute inspiration on Osiris' part to dump sixteen billion tons of concentrated non-biological washing-up liquid over the side on the evening of day one, and an equivalent amount of fabric conditioner twenty-four hours later. By the time the oceans had receded back into their proper confines, you could have eaten your dinner off the pavement in Trafalgar Square without the unpleasant necessity of being a pigeon.

Behold, said the god to himself, I don't make a new heaven and a new earth, because that would be wasteful and extremely traumatic for the inhabitants. I make the old heaven and the old earth, only rather less grubby.

Not that that'll last; but one does one's best, just as a mother always washes and irons regardless of a world full of mud, oil and chocolate. And this time, the god resolved, a little dirt and grime won't matter very much.

This time, we will run things, but there'll be a difference. We won't let them know we're doing it.

There were some gods, however, who had no wish to go back; and that wasn't a problem, because there were always too many of them, even from the very beginning.

Understandable. It goes without saying that running the world is the ultimate in rotten jobs. It's a god's life, running the world.

For those gods who wanted out, behold he created a new Sunnyvoyde, far above the clouds in the temperate uplands of the Glittering Plains. The post of matron he gave to Sandra, who understood about gods (who are only people with an immunity to death, when all is said and done), shortly before sealing it off from the world below for ever. No reports ever filter down any more, except in very garbled form; but observers at the University of Chicopee Falls Department of Integrated Theology report that there is a seventy-nine-point-six per cent chance that rice pudding was reintroduced within six months of start of business, at the request of the residents.

Where am I?

The cloud wobbled slightly under him, and he grabbed at it. It was nothing but cloud. It righted itself and floated.

'And what the fuck,' Lundqvist demanded, 'have you bastards done to my feet?'

Perfumed winds moved the cloud along, and there was a faint suggestion of the music of stringed instruments. Below, the world lay still and fresh, the sleep of the new-born.

'What is this?' Lundqvist wailed. 'Leprosy?'

'*They're your scales, mate,*' replied the Dragon King of the South-East, steering his cloud alongside. '*Have a beer?*'

Lundqvist shook his head. 'What scales?' he said. 'Why have I got claws on the ends of my legs? And what are . . .?'

He rose six inches or so into the air, panicked and flopped back on to the cloud.

'*Wings,*' replied the Dragon King. '*You use them for flying and gliding mainly, though if you lie sort of on your side they make a really ace surfboard.*'

'Wings?'

'*What you need, my old mate,*' said the Dragon King, '*is a mirror.*'

Let there be a mirror. Lundqvist looked in it, blinked, closed his eyes and groaned.

'*I dunno,*' sighed the Dragon King, '*bloody whingeing mortals. It's really good being a dragon, you'll see.*'

'How soon till it wears off?'

'*It doesn't.*'

'Shit.'

'*I think,*' asserted the Dragon King, '*this is your reward for, like, saving the universe and allowing the powers of darkness to be defeated. You ought to be pleased, you ungrateful bastard.*'

'Pleased.'

'*Suit yourself, pal.*' The Dragon King frowned and spurred on his cloud. Lundqvist panicked.

'Hold on,' he shouted.

'*G'day again.*'

Lundqvist allowed his eyes to open again. 'Just exactly what does this dragon thing involve?' he asked. 'I mean, what are dragons, for Chrissakes?'

The Dragon King preened himself and opened another can. '*Dragons,*' he said, as if reciting a slowly learned lesson, '*are the spirits of the blessed, endowed with the wings and the fish-arse cozzie and sent forth to supervise the smooth running of their alloted sector. I cover Australia,*' he added.

'No kidding.'

'*Among my duties,*' the Dragon King continued, '*are the*

dispensation of rain, particularly on cricket fields where the Aussies are losing, the regulation of the seasons and the protection of cattle against airborne diseases. Sort of like the Flying Doctor.

'How about zapping perjurors?' Lundqvist enquired.

'Nope.'

'Incinerating bearers of false witness? Carbonising blasphemers and worshippers of false gods?'

'Not our job, sport. The lighter fuel up the hooter is purely ceremonial.'

Lundqvist frowned, a difficult thing to do when your forehead is covered with thousands of interlapping molybdenum gold scales. 'That's all you do, is it? Water the garden and worm the dog?'

'You could put it like –'

'The hell with that, man. I'm a trained killer, not a gardener. You know, fingers not so much green as red to the elbow. If they think I'm going to piss about *growing* things for the rest of . . .

The Dragon King looked at him down a runway of glistening snout. *'Steady on, cobber,'* he said mildly. *'You've finished with all that stuff now; you've attained Enlightenment.'*

'I have?'

'Yeah, no worries.'

'Oh *shit!*'

For the first hour, Lundqvist sulked.

Then it occurred to him that since he was a dragon, he had a right to breathe fire even if only for purely peaceful ends. He tried it. Good fun.

And if he was a dragon, he ought to be able to swoop dizzyingly out of a clear blue sky. Once you'd got used to the reverse G-forces trying to scoop your brain out through your ears, it was easy.

Add a nicely balanced lashable tail, claws which (he noticed) were two feet long and sharp as surgical instruments, teeth like cavalry sabres and little round red eyes that could pick out a fieldmouse at a mile and a half and, all told, it was a pretty neat package. Something you could grow to love, given time. An F-111 would have been preferable, but never mind.

And down there, even among the brassicas and legumes and Merinos and Charolais, there were still the good guys and the bad guys. Greenfly to exterminate. Coltsfoot and deadly nightshade to bring in, dead or alive. Colorado beetles to track down and destroy. Tapeworms to hunt through the labyrinthine entrails of the lowing kine. Seen in the right light, from a sufficiently raked and refracted angle, there is true heroism in pesticide.

Pesticide. Getting rid of pests. The first thing we'll do, we'll kill all the lawyers.

No? Pity. Never mind; because while there's mildew and blackspot and blackfly and ants, let's face the music and dance.

In the warm radiance of the newly polished sun, the Dragon Without Portfolio opened his wings, hiccuped green fire and headed downwards.